The Informer

Also by Craig Nova

NOVELS

Turkey Hash

The Geek

Incandescence

The Good Son

The Congressman's Daughter

Tornado Alley

Trombone

The Book of Dreams

The Universal Donor

Wetware

Cruisers

AUTOBIOGRAPHY

Brook Trout and the Writing Life

CRAIG NOVA

The Informer

A NOVEL

Shaye Areheart Books

NEW YORK

Copyright © 2010 by Craig Nova

All rights reserved.
Published in the United States by Shaye Areheart Books, an imprint of the Crown Publishing Group, a division of Random House, Inc., New York.
www.crownpublishing.com

Shaye Areheart Books with colophon is a registered trademark of Random House, Inc.

Library of Congress Cataloging-in-Publication Data
Nova, Craig.
The informer : a novel / Craig Nova. —1st ed.
p. cm.
1. Prostitutes—Fiction. 2. People with disabilities—Fiction. 3. Serial murders—Fiction. 4. Berlin (Germany)—Fiction. 5. Germany—History—1933–1945—Fiction. 6. Historical fiction. I. Title.
PS3564.O86I54 2010
813'.54—dc22   2009023689

ISBN 978-0-307-23693-7

Printed in the United States of America

Design by Lynne Amft

10 9 8 7 6 5 4 3 2 1

First Edition

FOR WALTER BENNETT

The Informer

PART 1

BERLIN — 1930

aelle turned away from the man in the car and stepped out onto the sidewalk, the money in her hand. The instant she slammed the door, she was sure of it. They were coming for her. The black cars on the avenue seemed to be a funeral procession, their movement oddly ponderous and mysterious, too. She had sold information, and yet, at the time she had done it, the future had seemed so impossibly distant, but now, of course, it arrived like claustrophobia. Perhaps the next car would be the one she was afraid of, and if not that, then maybe the one after. She guessed they would slash her, but if she was lucky they wouldn't do that or spend any time "talking" to her. Perhaps they would send a woman to kill her, but would that be any better?

It wasn't the actual being dead, she told herself, that mattered so much as how she got that way. That's why she hated knowing that it was coming, since it exaggerated her fear, the glint of the knife, the expression of malice, the frankness of the job. Perhaps she would be able to make them pay a price, since she had a small knife in her bag, but a lot of informers had carried knives, and what good had it done them? And she had heard rumors, too, that some of the women in the park had been blinded before they had been killed.

She hugged her shoulders and stood there, trying to find a way to cheer herself up. It was only a matter of going back to the darkness of the time before she had been born, but then this left her trembling, since she knew the darkness before she was born was a matter of coming toward the light, but now, if she entered it again (no, *when* she entered it again) she would be going away from the light. Please, she thought. Please. Then she stood there and trembled. It was the knives that got to her. How long did she have, one hour, two, a night? Maybe even an extra day.

The men who had come to see her, and a couple of the women, too, had tried to impress her, even though she had been paid. They had bragged about what they had done, what they were going to do, how much money was coming from Moscow, what lies the Brownshirts were going to tell, where arms were being stored. She had traded all of it, to the left and to the right, and she hadn't done so badly, either, that is in terms of money. At least she had her funeral-society dues paid up to Immertreu, one of the Rings, or gangs, in the city.

Gaelle suspected there was a difference in military terms between being a source of information, a sort of glorified gossip, and a spy. Spies were taken out and shot. Or worse. Maybe they talked to a spy for a while first. But in the end it came down to the same thing. And each group had an army. The Socialists, who were trying to run the government, had the Reichsbanner. Then there were the Brownshirts. The Communists had the Red Front Fighters. There were other vaguely military groups, too, the Steel Helmets, Organization Consul, Organization Escherich. She had spied for all of them, or she guessed she had, since often she only knew that a bit of information had been important, but not to whom or why.

Felix smiled at her as she came away from the car, and even in this light his bad teeth were visible. He was sixteen years old, his jacket a little too large for him, but it didn't make him seem like a child in a coat, but a man who had shrunk. You could see it in his tired, cagey eyes, and in his face, too, which was like that of a feral creature who knew that the most important quality was patience. His fingers touched a button on Gaelle's blouse and then undid it to expose her underwear.

She gave him the money she had just made, and he reached into his pocket for the other bills and folded the new ones into the pile.

"It's about like last night," he said. "Maybe a little slower. But it'll pick up after midnight. That's when the gentlemen come out. Why, they may have to spend a little time drinking to get up their courage, but they're good tippers, you know?"

Gaelle glanced at him uneasily and said, "Yeah. Late. That's always the way."

He was beginning to develop some peach fuzz and a little acne, too. Six months before she had found him looking for food in a trash can and had taken him to a restaurant. When he had finished a bowl of soup, a plate of sausages, boiled potatoes, and cabbage, he had said, "Now, why would you do something like that?" He had pointed at the empty bowl. "Why would you waste money on food for someone like me?"

"You've got to eat," she had said. "Why, I've been hungry myself. After a couple of days you think about eating your shoes. You've got to eat something. Why, I may be trouble but I'm not so bad as to leave you hungry."

His eyes had widened for a moment, but his surprise, which seemed innocent, only allowed a deeper look into that wary darkness. He shook his head as though someone had hit him with a stick. "Oh, you'd buy me food? You shouldn't do that. No, you shouldn't, my cream puff." He wiped his mouth on his sleeve. "That is an unnecessary expense. We will cut down on unnecessary expenses." The bottom of the bowl had a little broth in it and he tipped it up to get that. Then he had said, "You and me. We can do some business."

"You think so?" she said.

"Yeah," he said. "You could use a little help."

He lifted his pants and showed the holder he had made for the ice pick he carried inside his sock. The handle was taped to give him a good grip, and he pulled it out to show the tip, which had been ground on the curbs and stone sidewalks of Berlin. The tip showed like a star in the night sky. Then he put it away. The ice pick made him more trustworthy, or dangerous, although Gaelle saw the two as being intimately related.

He had started right away, holding the money, negotiating a price, making sure her clothes were clean and that she ate something when she forgot. He had been living in an abandoned building with some other boys his age.

Gaelle turned back to the avenue where the cars came along with that casual searching. She hadn't thought of the information as a betrayal so much as a way of making a little extra money. And she liked the idea of having something serious on someone. It could work to protect you, or it could turn into a good reason for someone to get rid of you. She had thought it would work for protection, and now she saw that wasn't anywhere near as likely as she had supposed.

So she stood there, looking at the lights, trying to judge which were looking for excitement and which were looking for her in particular.

"You look worried," said Felix. "What's bothering you?"

Gaelle just shrugged. She thought about that glint.

"I know," said Felix. "Why, people think they can get away with things, that we're just a limping boy and a girl with a scar." He looked around. "Oh, I know how to look like I'm keeping my place. But they better be careful."

"I've got things on my mind," she said.

Well, he thought, maybe a *gravelstone* was allowed to be moody, but these women with a deformity of one kind or another had value in the nighttime market of Berlin. That's something he could depend on.

"You're not eating," he said. "And you got to keep your clothes better . . ."

She wished she could go home and get into the hot water of her bath, where she looked at herself in the mirrors around the tub. Nothing had happened to her body. That was the same, even better now: she was thin, small breasted, blond, twenty-two years old. The scar on one side of her face had changed her forever, but in the slick skin of the burn her features seemed about to emerge, and it was this suggestion of metamorphosis that people craved. People saw something trying to get out, and whatever this quality was, it made them gasp. Her scar was like seeing a movie star through filmy silk that hinted at a beauty greater than the one that might actually be seen when the silk was dropped. This possibility of emerging loveliness, at once contradictory and compelling, brought the high prices she charged in nighttime Berlin. Her face suggested everything that was beautiful and yet doomed. It was a perfect expression of the erotic, or of that tension between the impulse to live and the forces arrayed against it.

She had a wild desire to go home, too, to her parents' apartment with its solid furniture, its tables and a sofa with lion's feet, the pictures of hanging game on the wall, the scent of cologne that her father, an assistant manager in a bank, wore when he went out the door in his striped trousers, his vest, his dark coat. Her mother was always glad to see her, and wanted nothing more than to be in Gaelle's presence, as though if the two of them could be together, why then there was hope. Still, the scar, which Gaelle had gotten in an automobile accident two years before, had changed everything: as far as her parents were concerned, the scar was evidence of a curse, of a lack of hope, of how they had been deceived by what they had assumed was the progression of ordinary life. Gaelle still felt the odd swaying of the automobile before it had turned sideways and rolled over and then the colognelike coolness of gasoline on the side of her face.

A car swept up to the curb with a slow, tidal movement, its brakes perfectly silent. A driver in front and one dark figure in back. Beyond the car the trees in the Tiergarten appeared like enormous black feathers against the lights of the city. The driver reached over and stared out the passenger window, as though he wasn't sure this was the right place, but after a while he crooked one of his white fingers. *Come here.*

Gaelle wanted to ask for help, but it occurred to her that maybe it was better to say nothing. Maybe they might grab Felix first, and the less he was on his guard, the more he would operate like a canary in a basket in a coal mine. If they grabbed him, she'd try to disappear into the shadows, or run into the Tiergarten, getting rid of her shoes first.

"Go on," she said. "See what they want."

He stepped off the curb like a short, troubled man. He had a little limp, too. Maybe tuberculosis in his hip. Something like that. She knew a girl who had had such a thing. How could you get it there? Then she felt her isolation and her loneliness as a physical separation from other people, as though she were wrapped up in a clear substance that could only be penetrated by that flashing blade. So she was left with emotional distance from other people, but no protection. As she stood there, waiting, she had the wild impulse for a friend, a woman she could talk to or go shopping with, someone she could trust. The other women in the park smiled, pretended to be nice, even understanding, but every one of them would turn on her in a minute. All she had was Felix, and what was that?

If only I had a friend, she thought. Is that too much to ask?

"Hey, Felix," she said.

He was halfway over to the car, but he turned and raised an eyebrow. "What?" he said.

"Come back for a minute," she said. "I got a funny feeling tonight." She took the arm of his coat, as though she could slow things down that way.

"Well, you don't eat anything," he said. "What do you expect?"

"It's not like that," she said.

"Oh, yeah?" he said. "How about a nice *Kalbshaxe*?"

She put her hand to her lip.

"Or something sweet?" he said.

"Just keep an eye out. Nothing that seems . . . you know."

"No," he said. "I don't know. What do you mean?"

"Well, like someone who isn't right," she said.

"Who's right around here?" he said.

"I mean extra that way," she said. She tried to make a gesture, a movement of the hand that suggested something freakish or horrible.

"Well, sometimes they pay more, right?"

"Yeah," she said. "Yeah. But I'm feeling funny."

"You got nothing to worry about," he said. "Won't making some money make you feel better? Then we can get something to eat. See? Just listen to me."

"Please," she said.

"Please what? What?" he said. "Are you trying to say something?"

"No," she said. "I guess not."

"Trust me," he said.

Then she realized that when they came for her they would appear normal. If she had a chance with someone odd, she should take it, because the obviously odd would be safer than the seemingly mundane man who had a taste for a *gravelstone*. The deformity always hit the normal ones the hardest, since this was a moment when they saw just how safe and protected their ordinary life really was. This experience of the abyss, of the enormous powers of chance or malice, left them trembling. One of these men had said being with Gaelle was "like being with God."

Oh, yeah, she thought. Well, maybe not God, but his messenger. And would you like to hear what I have to say, or what the message is? Then she started trembling, sick with rage, thinking of the things she felt and knew . . . When that normal man had said this, she thought, Why, let me tell you. Let me tell you. Instead, though, she was silent. She had simply stared at the man who had said this.

"I'll take a look," said Felix. "Just a sec."

He stood there, though, his glance going from one of her eyes to the other.

"I'm just uneasy," she said. "It's nothing."

"Sure," he said. "I get it."

He walked up to the car, swaggering as he went, his overlarge jacket and his cap disappearing into the glare of the headlights from the avenue. How had this happened? Because she had needed money? She had sold what she had. She had endured insults and had people gawk at her. And now a silver flash was coming out of the dark? Her desire for a friend increased in direct proportion to her terror, but her need for someone only made her feel that much more alone.

Well, she would fight. No one was going to do something to her and walk away from it without getting hurt. The sound of the engine of the car at the curb made a sad putter. Felix stepped on the running board, and the car tilted over a little.

The man in the back had white skin, perfectly combed hair, a dark suit, and he looked at Felix with a languid interest. Felix smelled a faint odor inside the car, not perfume, not pomade, something sweet and off-putting. The man said, "Is that Gaelle?"

"You want something special?" said Felix. "We understand about gentlemen. Shy sometimes, you know? But just ask."

"Just Gaelle," said the man.

"There's no 'just' about her," said Felix.

The man shrugged.

"Of course," he said. "Anything you say."

"Do you want her, or not?" said Felix. "She's been telling me how much she is ready to go all out. She doesn't get in that mood all the time."

The driver turned his head slowly, too. Everything about the car, the dark, boxy bulk of it at the curb, the sweet smell, the perfectly dressed man in the back, left Felix with the cool scent of money.

"Yes," said the man. "We'd like her."

"Just hang on," said Felix. "I'll see what I can do."

He stepped off the car's running board, the squeak of the springs, the small, silvery sound hanging there like a note against the dark. Then he looked around, thinking, Well, it's her lookout. She can take care of her-self, can't she? He had his worries, too.

Gaelle adjusted her jacket, ran a finger through her hair. She remem-bered how her mother used to like to touch her hair, which her mother had said was like "spun gold." The people she was worried about could come out of the shadows, the dim entrances of the buildings, from the trees in the park. At night, in Berlin, the ordinary was so perfectly blended with the unusual.

"He wants you," said Felix. "I got a little extra. Maybe a tip if you treat the gentlemen right? See?"

"Yes," said Gaelle.

"Still feeling funny?"

"No," she said. She shook her head. "I'm ready."

"I feel funny, too, sometimes," he said. "I get over it. A kind of mood, but that's all it is."

"Sometimes I really need you," she said.

"Sure," he said. "We need each other. We don't have to argue. It's going to be fine."

"We'll go out for dinner," she said.

"That's the way," he said.

Gaelle looked both ways. Maybe they would come in two cars. That was a possibility, she guessed. It would look like business as usual, and when she walked up to the car she was going to get into, they would come up in another one. They would want to know some details, too, and she knew they were good at that kind of work.

She came up to the car.

"Good evening," said the man in the back.

"Good evening," she said.

"What's your name?" he said.

"Gaelle."

The car appeared in grays and blacks. The man wore a wristwatch, and he checked the time, the silver glint of it hanging there like a piece of foil. Only the driver and the man in the back, or, at least, she couldn't see any-one crouching behind the driver's seat. Still, it was possible someone was there. She wondered if there was something else that would tip her off, an impalpable sense of things about to explode: wasn't there something in that moment? Then she thought, No, there isn't. It's absolutely ordinary.

"Would you like to get in?" the man said.

Gaelle looked around.

"I don't know," she said.

"Take your time," said the man. "We've agreed on a price. That's correct, isn't it?"

"Yes, yes," she said. She still looked around. She wondered how much Felix was holding for her. But it wasn't going to be enough to leave, to start over, to go to Munich or some other place. And here, where could she go? Home? They knew where she lived, not only her apartment, but where her parents lived, too. Why hadn't she been smart enough to find someplace that no one knew about, that she could go to, an apartment that she rented under an assumed name and that she hardly ever went to? Because, she thought, it always seemed like I could keep everyone in line. *In line*. She looked around.

"Well?" said the man in the car.

"I want my friend to come with me," said Gaelle.

"You mean the boy?" said the man.

"Yes."

She turned so that he could see her face, and as she moved her head it was as though a change were sweeping over her . . . then she waited, the scarred side toward the car. The man inside was silent. The driver stared straight ahead.

"Of course, before this happened, you had a different attitude," said the man. "Didn't you?"

"Yes," said Gaelle. She looked around. Was it better to be in the car or on the street. Felix stood at the side of the building, hands in his pocket.

"Like what?" he said.

She turned and stared at the man, not wanting to give him anything beyond her physical presence. If she was going to have to talk, she was going to have to get paid, especially since she couldn't lie, not in her current mood. It took energy to lie.

"I don't know," she said. She shrugged. "I want my friend to come."

"Why don't you just get in?" said the man.

He sniffed a little, as though her perfume and her beguiling fragrance blew slowly in the open window.

"Felix," she said. "Felix!"

"It won't take long," said the man in the car.

"No?" she said. "Where do you want to go?"

"To my apartment," the man said. "We could have a glass of champagne. We could listen to opera. Do you like opera?"

"No," said Gaelle. "It's too pretty."

Felix came up to the car.

"Yes?" he said.

"I want you to come," said Gaelle.

"What's the idea?" said Felix. "I can wait here, and if someone else—"

"I want you to come," said Gaelle.

"I don't get it," said Felix. "I thought we had everything settled."

"Tell me," said the man. "Did you have any ambitions? Any desires?"

"Hey," said Felix. "That's personal. It costs."

"All right," the man said. He reached into his pocket, took out his wallet, and removed a bill. Felix took it with a wild jab, like a snake killing a rat. Felix opened the door.

"Will you come?" said Gaelle. "Please, baby. Be nice."

"You've got to get hold of yourself," said Felix. "I'm not saying I don't understand. I'm saying you're letting your nerves run away with you."

"Please, baby," she said. "I'm asking you."

"OK," he said. "Sure."

Felix always bent a little at the waist, like a man trying to run under water dripping from a roof, and now he came into the car, with that same bent-over, protective way of moving.

"I'm here to help," he said. "You know that."

"Here," said the man in the back. He flipped down the jump seat, and Felix got in and sat on it, hands together in his lap. It was as though he always sat there, and this quickness, this ability to fit in someplace new, took Gaelle's breath away.

"Well?" said the man in the back. He held out his hand, white there in the darkness of the car to Gaelle, who stood on the curb.

"Hey," said Felix. "Gaelle. Are you listening, or not?"

"Yes," she said.

"Then come on," he said. "Be sweet."

She felt herself rise on the running board, the car tilting in her direction, and then she disappeared into the passenger compartment, the door clicking shut behind her. That click. The car pulled into traffic, and then she smelled the odor of the pomade that the man in the back of the car used, and as the perfume of it swept around her she wondered if they had already contacted Felix. If they had promised him something to help out with this. She looked closely now, and Felix glanced at her once and then out the window, just as blank and ordinary as always. It was one of the things she had always liked about him, his frank, unshakeable ability to continue, no matter what.

They went up Hof Jager Allee, into the Tiergarten, where it was darker. The driver seemed to be a part of the machine. The man next to her said, "I wonder if it's going to rain."

"It ain't going to rain," said Felix. "It's too late for any of that. Take it from me."

"Oh," said the man. "I can depend on you?"

"As much as anyone," said Felix. He turned to Gaelle. "Don't you think that's right?"

"I depend on you," she said.

"That's good," said Felix. "That makes me feel better."

The man glanced at Gaelle. That was how they usually began, with a small, delicious glance. The driver went up to the middle of the Tiergarten and turned right onto Charlottenburger. The trees appeared beguiling, and Gaelle wished that she could get out and walk among them. Often, late at night, when she was finished with her work, she went into the park, needing a bath but craving the dark even more. She was happy there, or something like happy, calm and hidden.

"Where are we going?" she said.

"Neu König Strasse," he said.

"Oh?" said Felix. He shrugged. Nationalists, he guessed. He didn't really like the Communists more than the Social Democrats. Everybody had an angle, he guessed.

The man next to Gaelle put his hand on the seat, by her hip. She felt her almost gravitational effect on him as he leaned her way, just to get a lit-tle closer to . . . what was it? Possibility and beauty, tragedy and fate?

The man turned to Gaelle. "And so, tell me, what did you want to do. Before."

"Me?" said Gaelle. The car slowed down. She looked at the chrome handle of the door and moved a little closer to it. Just shifting her weight. It was almost sexy, as though she were too bothered to sit still. Felix watched her. He had never seen her work before.

"A dream," the man said. "Did you have a dream?"

"I had a boyfriend," she said.

She looked around now. Why was she telling the truth? They moved along the avenue. "He wanted to pretend nothing had happened to me, but it was impossible. He tried."

"And what happened," said the man, "when he tried?"

She thought, I'm not going to get weak. No weeping. But she wasn't able to forget her boyfriend, who had finally put his head in her lap and cried inconsolably, not knowing what to do, or how to confront this thing that had happened to her.

"I don't want to talk about it," she said. "What good does it do?"

"It's interesting to think about the past," said the man.

"It depends," said Gaelle.

The neon of Berlin went by in a blur, like a rainbow laid on its side.

"Tell me," said the man. "Do you make much money?"

"What's it to you?" said Felix.

"Just curious," said the man.

"It's not healthy to be too curious," said Felix.

The man looked Gaelle.

"Yes," he said. "That's right, isn't it?"

Felix shrugged. "Where's the apartment?" he said.

"Not too far," said the man.

The car pulled up in front of a row of flats.

"Here we are," said the man.

Felix opened the door. She got out. The man came across the seat and got out, too, and even though he was in the street and she was on the curb, he was much taller than she was. His complete calmness was worse, she thought, than if he had been nervous. He turned to the driver and said, "Wait here."

He gestured toward the front door of a building. A few marble steps, a lamp, some brass that could have been polished but now just had a dull, tarnished glow in the light from the street. The hall was marble, as though they were in a tunnel through an enormous blue cheese, the veins of mold black and green. They went up to the lift, into the cage. From up above, like some machine of utter indifference, the gears and the pulleys started drawing them up.

"It's cold," said the man.

"What's cold?" said Felix.

"The champagne," he said.

"Have you got something to eat?" said Felix.

"Of course," said the man. "Are you hungry?"

"She should eat," said Felix. "She should take care of herself. I've been trying to tell her, but she won't listen."

"Maybe later," said the man.

"I'm all right," said Gaelle.

The door of the cage swung open, and all three of them walked up to the front door. Felix went in first and looked around, as though to make a list of anything valuable. Then Gaelle. Then the man. He passed them both and went into the living room, which had a view of Berlin: the avenues, the darkness of the Tiergarten, the lights on the streets like drops of water on a web.

"Come in," said the man.

He turned on a floor lamp. She sat close to it and looked out at the city. Felix sat down like a gargoyle, or a stone figure that was so still as to be hardly breathing. He looked around. Some crystal doodads, a picture, a gold lighter, what would the entire lot bring? The man went into the kitchen.

"What do you think?" said Gaelle.

"Maybe the frame is worth more than the picture, see?" he said. He gestured.

"Maybe," said Gaelle. "But I mean about this guy?"

"Him?" said Felix. "The usual. He might take his time. Nothing to worry about."

From the kitchen she heard the sound of a cork coming out of a champagne bottle. The man came in, the tray and the champagne and the glasses on it gliding in front of the window like a tray in a cabaret magic show. Floating in the dark.

"Here," he said.

He gave her a glass. Felix refused by a shake of his head.

"I'm all right," he said.

The man took Gaelle's other hand, and like a couple in a dream they went through the apartment to his bedroom. Felix just glanced at them once and turned back to going over the things in the room, the slight, almost imperceptible movement of his eyes showing what a precise inventory he was taking.

The bedroom also had a view of the red, yellow, and blue lights of the city, at once cool and romantic. A chair stood at the side of the bed. The bubbles in the champagne rose in tiny globes, which she thought of as small worlds, all moving with a kind of rush. She sat down on the chair and faced him.

"There's so much trouble in the city these days," he said. "Have you noticed?"

"I guess," said Gaelle. "I'm not interested in trouble."

She smiled, crossed her legs.

"Of course, you can have a coffee and a sweet when there's street fighting," he said. "Is that what you do?"

"I don't know," she said.

He nodded and sipped his champagne. Then she thought, He isn't going to touch me, at least not that way. He isn't going to ask me to do that.

"Or maybe drugs," he said. "I'll bet you like them? What do you like? Maybe that's something we could help you with."

"What do you want?" she said.

He looked right at her, thinking it over.

"It's pretty straightforward," he said.

He sat on the bed next to her, the mattress giving in with his weight. He was heavier than he looked.

"You don't mind if I sit a little closer, do you?" he said.

"Fine. You're paying for it," she said.

"That's right," he said.

He sipped the champagne, the bubbles rising in those wavering chains.

"Have you ever put a piece of caramelized ginger in your champagne?" he said. "It makes more bubbles."

"No," she said.

He glanced over at her and then out the window.

"There's so much trouble in the city these days," he said. "And I guess because of that I came to see you tonight. We've been watching you."

She took a sip of the champagne and let the bubbles roll across her tongue, the slight pricking of them oddly refreshing, and as she felt the fizz of them, she thought, There isn't much time. Now is the time to think of something.

"All kinds of people come to see you," said the man.

"A lot of people come to see me," said Gaelle.

"Of course, of course," said the man.

He shrugged.

"Look," she said, "if you want to do something, let's take care of it."

"In a minute," he said. "My business is information."

"What's that to me?" she said.

"Yes, what that's to you?" he said.

She sat quietly, and the man did, too, and all she could hear was the slight rustling of his starched shirt as he breathed and as he reached out to take the class of champagne. Was it a good idea to deny that she had ever sold anything? She hadn't dealt with this man, but maybe she had done something with one of his friends. He pursed his lips, touched the glass.

"Do you want me to take off my dress?" she said.

"Not yet," he said.

He spoke with an abstract air, as though he wanted her naked not because he had desire, but because she would be more vulnerable. He sat very still, staring out at the city. She guessed that he was trying to make a decision of some kind, and as she glanced at him, and felt the silence that surrounded him like the odor of dry ice, she guessed that she could break off the champagne glass, keeping just the stem. But then, she thought, what if someone else is here in the apartment.

She began to stand up, but he took her hand with a speed that was utterly surprising. It was a kind of perfect gesture, quick, precise, gently taking her wrist.

"Don't make it harder for me," he said.

"What is hard for you?" she said.

"I'm trying to be graceful. I'm not a gangster. I want you to understand that."

"Look," she said. "I've got to go. Felix!"

"What?" said Felix.

"Hush," said the man.

"Felix!"

She pulled herself away and stood back, toward the window. It was a piece of glass that was about six feet high by five feet wide, and she felt the city behind her, the distance between here and the street below.

"You really are very smart, aren't you?" he said.

"No," she said. "You think what I do is smart?"

"That depends on what we're talking about," he said.

She stepped back, against the cool glass, which was like ice. She could remember being on the black ice when she had been a kid, stretched out after falling. What had been the promise of the black ice, indifference, danger, absolute certainty of how little she really mattered in a world that was so cold? Felix came in and stood in the doorway. Then he stepped in, coming closer.

The champagne glass was on the night table by the bed, but it was too far to reach. Just her, the window, the man, who was so tall and had such white hands. Everything seemed to have been leading up to this anyway, the night, the fear, the previous customers who had come in her and then walked away, as though they were filling her with some profound indifference. They were so intense just before they did it and so disinterested afterward.

She moved along the window, putting her hands against it. Felix watched her.

"I'm not going to hurt you," the man said.

"Take off your dress," said Felix. "I think that's the best thing. Let him see how nice you are."

Gaelle lifted the dress over her head and stood there, her skin white against the city, her nipples dark, her collarbones prominent. The glass was cold glass against her hips.

"Look," he said. "I want something from you."

"I can accommodate you," she said.

"I hope so," the man said. "We've been watching you. We know you see all kinds of people. Why, ordinary . . ."

". . . Whores," she said, adding the word he was trying to avoid.

"Yes, ordinary women like you have only one kind of client. But you see all kinds. You are something special. All kinds of people. And maybe they tell you things."

"What kinds of things?" she said.

"Oh, if you are seeing someone from the left, maybe they might mention how much money is coming into Berlin from Russia. That's something we'd like to know. And if it's from our side, well, we'd like to know who can't keep his mouth shut. Of course, if the Communists are planning a demonstration, we'd like to know that, or if they are hiding weapons." He looked at her for a moment. "If you hear something, come to see me."

He took a sip of his champagne and let the bubbles wash over his tongue.

"Will you help me?" he said.

"Sure, sure," she said. "I'll help you."

"That's good," he said. "You have no idea how smart that is. Why, have you noticed the news in the papers? People get hurt all the time. Why, they're found in the river. In the park."

She swallowed.

"Let's talk about something else," she said.

He took a number of large bills out of his pocket and passed them over.

"A gesture of good faith," he said.

Gaelle went away from the window, still afraid of being pushed through it, still considering the first spiderweb of cracks. Then she thought, no, it probably wouldn't be his style to do that. This is all the fun part, at least for him.

Gaelle put on her dress, pulled it over her small hips, straightened it. Well, she had bought some time.

"My name is Bruno Hauptmann," he said. "Say it."

"Bruno Hauptmann," she said.

He took a card from his pocket with an address on it, and he passed it over.

"If you come across something, you can find me here," he said.

She took the card.

"And no lies," he said.

Then they went downstairs and got into the car, Felix folding the money, putting it in his pocket, and showing her the gold lighter that he had picked up from the table. It glowed there in the dark. She let go a long, slow breath.

"Well," she said. "That was close."

"Naw," said Felix. "The guy was a pushover. Like all those jackasses who just want to talk."

The car pulled up to Gaelle's usual spot, and they got out. Then Gaelle looked around. Felix limped a little bit beside her as they went back to the building where she waited. Gaelle thought, I've got to pull myself together. Her stockings were a little soiled at the top where an earlier customer had dripped on them, and she wished she could find a way to change them. Had she really gotten away? She looked around, trying to think it over. Felix held the lighter, which hung in the dark like reassurance itself.

"It could be plate," said Felix. "But it looked like he had good stuff."

"Thanks for coming with me," said Gaelle.

"Sure, sure," said Felix. "We're a team."

Felix looked at the lighter.

"Just a few more and we're done for the night," said Felix. "Say, you're looking better, you know that?"

"Am I?" said Gaelle. "Well, I guess."

"Sure," said Felix. "Did that guy give you a scare?"

"Everyone has an army," said Gaelle. "The Reichsbanner, the Brown-shirts, the Red Front Fighters. They shoot spies."

"Make some money," said Felix. "Keep it simple."

"That's it?" said Gaelle. "That's what you've got to say?"

"Those guys are horny for information. Easier than sex, and pays better, too. If you don't know anything, make it up. It's like money that grows on moonlight. Why, I couldn't have dreamed up something better than what we got. Armies, schemes, and enough murder to make everything seem important. A lark, see?"

Gaelle put a hand to her hair and walked around to get her knees to stop trembling, but it lingered, and she struggled with that watery sensation, that weakness in her legs.

"You see what I'm saying?" said Felix.

"Yes," she said. "I do."

rmina Treffen worked for Inspectorate A, the serious crimes section of the Berlin Police Department. At this hour, just after dawn, the park was a combination of green and gold, the tops of the trees covered with a film of gilt as the sun rose, and along with the colors, the place had a serenity, a moist silence matched only by the ominous trilling of birds. Armina was twenty-six years old with red hair and very white and freckled skin. Her eyes were green, almost the color of trees in the first light of dawn.

She was concerned about Gustave Ritter, head of Inspectorate IA, the Political Section, who was taking more interest in her cases than before. Now, as she walked up the path of the Tiergarten with the crowns of the trees like green lace, she considered Ritter. He reminded her of a puff adder in the Berlin Zoo, and while the association was one of malice, she recognized something else that was common to both: the naturalness with which they were ready to strike. Ritter wouldn't regret causing her trouble any more than the snake. How could the moon regret pulling on the oceans, or how could lightning regret setting a tree on fire?

In the park she passed a bronze statue of a poet that was the color of blackened leather, and the poet seemed forever knowledgeable and wise, although he appeared to squint with discomfort, as though what he knew had come at an eternal price. The path had benches every fifty feet or so, and at this hour they were shiny with dew, although in the stillness of dawn the atmosphere of what happened here at night seemed to linger, the women in silky dresses, their white thighs marked by a taut garter as they lifted their skirts, the men in their dark suits, the bills offered, the snap of a clasp of a handbag. Armina passed the benches and thought that this one was just a child, maybe sixteen, dressed like a schoolgirl.

The men in uniform, the Schutzpolice, stood at the top of a gully, their blue coats crosshatched by brush and new leaves, their buttons so much like those of a train conductor, as though this were a way station on the route to the underworld. The Schutzpolice murmured and looked around: they appeared lost and searching for a familiar landmark. Down below, in the bottom of the gully, the odor was of decayed leaves, and something else, too, a scent of flowers and the promise of spring.

Hans Linz stood at the bottom of the gully, his hands in his pants pockets, his eyes on the shape on the ground. He was in his thirties with a beard so heavy that even after he had shaved, his chin looked blue. He was a Communist, although he was careful about letting on about it, and more than anything else, it made him seem like a librarian with a secret. His awkwardness about it wasn't a sign of his lack of belief, but just the opposite. He cared so much as to be embarrassed.

A week before, in the middle of a tense investigation, Armina had gone out with him, and they had ended up at her apartment. She had been tired and her guard was down, or perhaps it is better to say she wanted a little time away from her mood and from scenes like this one. She let his nicotine-stained fingers fumble at the buttons of her blouse and finally lost patience and said, "Here. Let me do it." But as she undid the first one, she looked up at him and said, "You're tired. I'm tired. This is a mistake."

Then she sat back.

"You don't have to be so tough," he said. "It might be nice."

"I'm sorry. Let's forget it," she said.

Linz picked up the glass of brandy and took a sip.

"All right," he said. "If that's the way you feel about it."

He closed his eyes and looked down at his heavy, black shoes.

"Let's go into the kitchen," she said. "Would you like a sandwich?"

"Are you angry?" he said.

"No," she said. "Why would I be angry? I'm just tired. You are, too, if you'd give it half a thought."

"I want to ask you something," he said.

"All right," she said.

"What would it take for you to love me?" he said.

"Oh, god," she said. "Let's have a snack and let it go at that."

In the kitchen she made him a bacon and egg sandwich and drank a brandy while he ate. At the door, when he had put on his coat, he had kissed her cheek and said, "Well, see you around."

Now, in the park she walked down to the swale where the girl seemed to have partially melted and collected in the bottom. The body seemed pliable, almost melded with the ground. Her blond hair was cropped short, the sheen of it remarkable in the first light, although not all of it was visible, since her coat had been thrown over the side of her face and part of her head. She was facedown, her stockings around her knees, her feet without shoes. A shockingly red bird flew from one branch to another in the trees. A cardinal, Armina thought.

Everything here was final: the disorder of the girl's clothes, the skirt pulled up, the moon-shaped buttocks, the torn stockings, and above everything else, the way in which she lay against the earth. Some of the men looked through the brush around the top of the gully and in the understory that grew on the sides of the land as it sloped to the bottom. The underwear was usually found in the brush. And, as at the other places, a number of cigarette stubs, smoked down to the end, had been ground out in the leaves. So, thought Armina, he had waited, whoever he was, thinking it over, listening to see if anyone was coming. And when was that? At two or three in the morning, she guessed, one could only hear the occasional footstep of someone going home after a night in the clubs and bars and the movement of a nocturnal animal, a raccoon, or a possum, or a rat that was looking for something that had been left behind. The wind made a susurrus in the trees, and perhaps, if one listened very closely, it would be possible to hear the condensed mist as it dripped from one of the scraggly trees to the ground. The young woman's blond hair, what was visible from under the coat, looked like gold splashed on the floor of a foundry. Her skin was marked in the usual way. That, Armina guessed, was what had been done with the cigarettes.

"They're getting younger," said Hans Linz.

"This one looks about sixteen," said Armina.

"Could be younger," said Linz. "We haven't found her handbag. It's around here someplace."

"It usually is," said Armina.

The Schutzpolice and the others stepped back. They had seen enough, and since this was Armina's case, they were glad to get away. Their curiosity had been satisfied and their convictions about Berlin at night had been validated again. They looked at the collapsed figure at the bottom of the gully, now surrounded by filaments of insects in the air, and then the men turned away, everything about them saying, Here. This is yours. They shrugged and climbed the bank.

One of the young woman's shoes lay about five feet away from her stocking feet: fashionable, black with a low heel, good for walking in the park. Armina stood there while the others left, alone with the shoe. It was the same brand and model that she wore.

Armina had been hired in the mid-1920s, when women—under the laws of the new constitution—had been brought into the Berlin Police Department, but where others had been content to work the "social crimes" section (those that dealt with women, children, and domestic problems), Armina had insisted in the face of hostility and constant objections on moving into the other Inspectorates—morals, theft, murder—although as an echo of that lingering hostility, she was given cases in which a woman had been killed. She had resisted the atmosphere of contempt and had demonstrated that she was as unflappable as the rest of the members of the Criminal Inspectorates: she had eaten her lunch in an apartment where the blood stained most of the floor, and she had examined the women, like this one, to see if a rape had taken place. She had lifted a buttock and exposed a wound and said to the others, "Look. You see that? That tear? It's unmistakable."

"Well," said Linz. "This one's yours."

He shrugged.

"When they're like this, they usually are," she said.

She knew the underwear would be found close by with the usual pearly stain, and, of course, when Armina lifted the coat she would find a wound. The gully was shaped like a bowl, and Armina had the sense of being in a place where the gravity seemed to tug on everything, as though this place were at the bottom. The girl's perfume had the scent of roses and carnations, and Armina was drawn downward, as though the perfume had a variety of gravity. Along with the perfume, the moldy leaves, and the lavender soap the girl used, the girl's skin had a scent of ammonia. Sweat. Fear.

The cigarette butts were scattered in the leaves, six altogether, already yellowed by the dew, each burned down so just a half inch was left. Small blisters were on the girl's legs.

"How long does it take to smoke a cigarette?" said Armina.

Linz shook one out of his pack, put it between his full lips, and lighted it. Armina thought of his nicotine-stained fingers as he had touched her blouse: he had been tender but desperate and unsure.

Armina considered the scene as it must have been, the girl at the bottom of the gully, the man who had done this as he smoked the cigarettes, the coal like a bit of red foil on a black sheet. Did he wait to approach the girl again? Bunching her skirt, removing her underwear? Or did he sit there and consider what he had already done? She guessed the marks on the neck came from a silk cord.

"About two minutes," said Linz.

"So he was here for almost fifteen minutes," she said.

"If he smoked one right after another," he said.

"Oh," she said. "I think he's a chain-smoker."

Armina and Linz walked around the top of the gully and then spiraled slowly down to the girl. The leaves made a snakeskin pattern, the brown and light-gray shapes like ink blots. She picked up a torn ticket, a piece of cellophane, a scrap of paper—who knew what these things were. When men came back here with a woman, all kinds of things fell out of a pocket or a handbag. Linz looked more quickly and with much less interest than she did.

She picked up a crumpled cigarette package and put it in a handkerchief. Well, maybe the man who did this would have stayed longer, but he ran out of something to smoke. She thought of him going into a tobacconist's shop—his fingers stained pink as he pushed over a bill and picked up the new package, his nails pink, too, under their shape like a new moon.

"About the other night," said Linz. "I wanted to say how much I liked being with you. How good I felt."

"I think we've got other things to worry about."

"Of course. Of course. I just didn't want you to be upset."

"How could I be upset?" she said. "It meant nothing."

When will I learn to be quiet? she thought. She had spoken honestly because the presence of the girl made it difficult to lie.

"I see," said Linz again.

"Come on," she said. "Let's forget it."

"Sure," he said. "Maybe we could try another time. Nothing is hopeless."

Armina looked down at the girl's blond hair, the youthful fingers in the leaves like snakeskin. Then she nodded, although she wondered if she had committed herself to sleeping with him just to shut him up. Maybe the time had come to take a vow of celibacy, to sleep alone and to live with it. Clean living. Read a book at night. Less to drink. Everything else was causing too much trouble.

The sun was behind two trees at the top of the gully, and with the sun behind them, they appeared like the legs of an enormous man, in black trousers, who observed what happened here. Birds flitted with a nervous intensity, their cries twittering and filled with alarm. The uniformed men at the top put their heads together and spoke in low voices. Armina worked her way toward them, eyes down, keeping a lookout for anything unusual, a piece of jewelry, a card or cosmetic case, anything that a human being might have dropped.

"You know the one about the old people's home in Berlin?" said the first Shutzpoliceman. "Mostly it is filled with women."

"Yeah," said the second. "They live longer."

"That's right," said the first, "and so this man moves into the old people's home and he puts up a sign that says 'Stud.' "

"No kidding," said the second.

"Yeah. A widow comes in and asks what his fees are. And he says, well, twenty-five marks on the floor, fifty on the chair, and a hundred on the bed. The widow takes out a hundred-mark note."

" 'Once on the bed?' said the stud."

Armina stepped closer and looked at the men.

"No," she said. "Four times on the floor."

"How did you know?" said the first Shutzpoliceman.

"I'm just thrifty," she said.

The men laughed. Armina turned down the slope and felt the tug of the girl. The girl's fingers curled against the leaves, and when Armina picked them up, there were no wounds on them. The jacket, which had been laid over the side of the girl's face and the top of her head, looked like a misshapen hat.

"Putting a coat over a head is something new," Linz said.

"Yeah," said Armina. "I think it means whoever did this isn't feeling good about this one. He's ashamed."

"Because they're getting younger?" said the man.

"Maybe," said Armina. "Maybe she said something that set him back."

"What could that be?" Linz said.

"I don't know," she said. "Something sentimental probably. These assholes are usually sentimental."

The perfume was still very strong.

"What are you going to do?" he said.

The scrim of leaves at the top of the gully looked, in the rising sun, like the lace of green lingerie. Then Armina glanced at the cigarette stubs, already stained yellow where the moisture of dawn had brought out the nicotine.

"I think it's time to go to the train station," she said.

"Yes," said Linz. "That's probably a good idea. Mostly, though, that's where the boy hookers are working."

"There's someone else there," said Armina.

"I guess that's right," said Linz. "He's still there. As far as I know."

"I think it's a good idea to see what he has to say," said Armina.

"What a guy," said Linz. "You want me to go with you?"

"No," said Armina. "I think I'll go alone. It'll make it friendlier."

Armina walked around the gully, her shoes making a slight hush in the leaves just like the one, she thought, that this young woman made when she walked down here. The birds started singing again, their voices diminutive and sweet, oddly cheerful in the green clutter of the bushes at the top of the gully. The birds probably weren't singing, she thought, at three or four in the morning. Then it was just the scavengers, the rats, the moisture dripping from the leaves like a muted elegy.

"Wait," said Linz. "Here they are."

He held up the girl's underwear.

"They were back in the bushes," he said. "Just the same."

The Schutzpolice had their hands in their pockets. Soon they'd get their coffee, their jelly buns, the paper with the news of the six-day bicycle races. Armina couldn't blame them. What else could they do after a morning like this? And yet, she was convinced that something was needed, but she hadn't a precise idea what it was. The best thing, she supposed, was to go about her business, to try to find a way to get through the hours, and to keep her face blank, but recently she had found that this wasn't anywhere near enough. But what was?

"And here's her handbag," said Linz. "Her name was Marie Rote."

"All right," said Armina.

"I'll take it back to the office," said Linz. He stood there, against the brush, holding the purse. Then he shrugged. It was the usual thing.

It was the best part of the day. The streets were damp, and in the moist sheen a verdant film appeared from the trees in the park. Horse-drawn carts brought potatoes from the farm cellars outside Berlin, the black horses shimmering in the damp streets, and their hooves made a somnolent clip clop, clip clop, as though everything were possible. The smell of the horses mixed with the exhaust of the first cars. Armina's heels made a crisp cadence on the sidewalk, and as she went she thought, Yes, how deceptive appearances are. Why, anyone would think I was perfectly happy, on my way to work, that I had made a date with a good friend for lunch. Why, what would we have? A salad Niçoise, a little sweet for dessert, maybe a glass of champagne.

THE FRIEDRICHSTRASSE TRAIN station had the aspect of an elegant factory. It was enormous, and the two sections, one for foreign travel and one for local, appeared like greenhouses. The almost infinite number of glass panels in the roof suggested order and precision, and the engineering of the place could be seen in the scale of the platforms, the thin and beautiful squares of metal that held the panes of glass, and in the bridge above the street and over the river, where the trains came and went as the locomotives trailed a gray boa of smoke.

In the street the cabs and cars left off passengers who emerged in traveling clothes, the women smart and crisp, their men taking care of porters and assuming the attitude of knowing how things were done. The air of the place was at once transient and yet somehow constant, as though what flowed through here was a timeless, well-mannered vitality. The women seemed sultry and powerful, and their orchid-scented perfume melded with the smoke of the locomotives.

The interior of the station with its high ceilings, its columns, was filled with the rush of passengers and their families, and in the mass of people, who moved like skaters over a marble floor that was so shiny as to seem like ice, flowers in green florist's paper appeared as though by magic: red, yellow, and blue flowers surrounded by asparagus ferns made arrival and departure seem romantic.

The Moth sat on one of the long benches where people waited. He had reddish, thinning hair, a florid, inflamed complexion, and green eyes. He wore baggy pants, a large sweater, and comfortable although oversize shoes. The stains on the sweater and pants and on his shirt conveyed a horrifying intimacy: his most private habits were here for anyone to see. His red face, his greenish eyes, his frumpy presence seemed to imply a familiarity with the people he spoke to, as though his appearance, in all its dowdy frankness, were a way of saying that he understood all the failings of human beings, particularly the ones people found hard to ask about. He provided a group of boys and girls, under the age of fifteen, to people who were interested in them. Why, his green eyes and impertinent smile implied, I know. I know. Maybe we can work something out. Why, here is Gretchen. What do you think?

Armina stood in front of him. The pockets of his sweater were heavy with the things he had brought with him, a watch, a pen, a pocketbook, the bars of lavender soap he used to wash his hands once an hour. He was reading the want ads of the paper, General Merchandise, a pair of riding boots, a wedding dress (never worn), a set of hand tools, a double bed, a bedroom mirror.

He looked up, his green-red glance at once greasy and impertinent. Armina guessed she hated him for all the obvious reasons and for one other, too. His glance said as clearly as if he spoke out loud, I know you have a secret desire. What made this so offensive was not his correctness, since she did have one or more, but the way in which he perceived her needs would somehow diminish them to the point of being shallow or mercenary. But she did have a secret desire, which she felt here in a pulse of shame. For all her toughness, for all her eating her lunch in rooms where murders had taken place, she still longed for someone who could remove that ache she felt at three in the morning when she woke, alone, and stared at the patterns on the ceiling of her bedroom.

"So," said the Moth as he looked up from his paper. "Inspectorate E, I guess. Morals."

"Inspectorate A," she said. "Murder."

"Oh, it's all the same," he said. "Don't you think?"

He put down the paper and reached into the pocket of his sweater, where he had a sandwich wrapped in brown waxed paper.

"Sit down," he said. "You can keep me company while I eat my lunch. Blood sausage." He unwrapped the paper. "Do you like blood sausage?"

"Not really," said Armina.

"It's an acquired taste," he said. "Like a lot of things. Sit down."

The bench next to him was polished from years of sitting and had another quality, too, a film of something that Armina might have only imagined: a slime, a greasy layer that was left by his existence. Well, she wanted his cooperation. She sat down.

"What's your pleasure?" he said with his mouth partially full. He brushed the crumbs from his sweater with an old napkin. His tie was stained with white marks, like dried milk. "Have you noticed how hard it is to keep your clothes clean? Why, there are times when I am just too busy to keep up with it. Why, look."

He reached down and took a bit of lint off her skirt, on her thigh, and then held it up for her to see before dropping it on the floor. He smiled again, as though he had proved something, some similarity between them, and went back to eating, his cheeks full. There weren't any young girls standing along the walls of the station, just the flow of passengers. Armina guessed it was still early. Men of twenty or so stood by the doorways with an impatient hunger.

"All right," he said. "Let's talk."

"Yes," said Armina.

"Have you noticed the weather in Berlin in winter? It's so gray and the sky looks like the side of a frozen fish. A frozen fish! Have you noticed?"

"Yes," said Armina.

"Of course," said the Moth. "And then, in January, that's when men come to see me more than usual. Maybe they are thinking about spring-time. What do you think?"

He brushed his shirt again.

"Is that what you want to talk about?" he said.

"We've found some young women in the park," she said.

"So I've heard," said the Moth. "That's right."

He turned his green eyes with their inflamed lids toward her: in his false concern there was that same impertinence. What did she really want?

"We're interested in men who are interested in young girls," said Armina.

"Yes," he said. "I see. And you came to me. Well, I'm flattered, as you can see. A poor man like me. I am touched that you think I am so moral. So correct." He took a bite of his sandwich and chewed, brushed at his shirt-front, and then turned his smile on her and said, with his mouth still full, "And why would I want to talk to you?"

"Excuse me?" she said.

He swallowed.

"And why would I want to talk to you?" he said.

"It's always a good thing to have a friend in Inspectorate A," said Armina.

"So," he said. "You come to me as a friend. That's sweet." He nodded to himself. "Say it."

He looked up at her. She felt the insulting nature of this, since they both knew it wasn't quite friendship that was being offered so much as the possibility of some small favor. Having her lie pleased him, and she resisted the desire to slap him.

"Yes," she said. "That's right."

"Friendship," he said. "Say it."

"Friendship," she said.

He looked around. A tall, blond man began to approach, and then, after the Moth lifted his fingers, the man went away.

"And," said Armina, "a man who is hurting girls like that might hurt one of yours."

"Mine?" said the Moth. "Whatever can you mean?"

He put the last of his sandwich in the waxed paper, folded it in his napkin, and wrapped them into a bulky package that he put into his pocket.

"But still," he said. "I can imagine what you are saying. And I could depend on you. As a friend?"

"I can be a good friend," she said.

"Umpf," he said. His reddish glance met hers again, the insult of it an accurate estimation of how lonely she really was and perceiving it in the worst possible way.

"I know a man," said the Moth. "Tall. Elegant. He wears such clothes. Why you wouldn't believe. London. Paris. Why he has ties from Hermès. You can see he is from the top drawer. A university graduate. You know, he says he is a man who only wants to do good. Good. Can you imagine in a place like this? Why, look around."

He smiled as he gestured toward the men who stood in the shadows.

"Good! Why, what a perversion of meaning! What a way of using words so you can't tell what they mean!" said the Moth. "He has a rescue service for girls who work around here. Medicine girls. But you know what I think. I think there's something rum about him. Let me help you, he says. There's something rum. In my opinion," said the Moth.

"Yes," said Armina. "That's what I mean."

"Of course," said the Moth. "I understand."

He took the bar of lavender soap out of his pocket and held it in his red hand.

"Can you give me the name?" said Armina.

"Oh, the name," said the Moth. He held the lavender soap to his nose and sniffed it as gently as a flower. He looked at Armina's legs, her shoes, her hips in her gray skirt. "You know those days in the spring we get after those hard winters? Great fluffs of clouds drag along, gray underneath. A beautiful day. And that gray, on the bottom of the clouds, on the underside, don't you think it makes it better?"

"What better?" said Armina.

"Oh, everything," he said.

"The name," said Armina.

He glanced at her, sniffed the lavender soap.

"You'll have to excuse me," he said. "I like to give myself a little brushup after lunch."

He stood up, brushed the last of the crumbs from his sweater, and looked around.

"I'll wait," she said.

"Oh, it might be a long time," he said. "Sometimes you have to wait a long time for things. Think about the springtime."

"Look," she said. She swallowed. "I meant what I said about friend-ship."

"Did you?" he said. "I thought you'd say that. Bruno Hauptmann. Bruno Hauptmann. He lives in Wilmersdorf. That's where you can find him. Tall man. Well dressed. Beautiful hands."

SHE CONTACTED OTHER informers, waiters, bartenders, men and women who were involved in the cocaine and morphine trade or pornography, all of whom had a reason to be friendly with Armina, just as she spoke to men who had been arrested in compromising circumstances, such as beating a prostitute in the park. She consulted other policemen in Inspectorate A, no matter what their political bias.

Political point of view might be a problem, as it had in other murders, and even though Ritter was taking a more thorough interest in her cases, she hoped he would leave her alone about this. The dead woman in the park was a fact that should make political visions—and the desire to make details fit political beliefs—simply vanish, or so Armina hoped. Surely, no one could use this to blame one side or another.

The Inspectorate was evenly divided among the three political divi-sions in the city: the Communists, who wanted to take over; the Socialists, who were in charge and were trying to govern; and the right wing, the col-lection of such groups as the Steel Helmets, the Nazis, and others, all of whom wanted to take over, too. Sometimes it seemed that the Communists and the Nazis were working together, or, at least, they were both attacking the government. A Communist police officer (who, of course, was discreet about his affiliation) would blame a member of the right wing for a crime, and the opposite was true, too: the Nazis or the Steel Helmets blamed a Communist for a crime that was obviously done by someone else. The courts were the most biased: a Communist was far more likely to be convicted and to do time than a member of a right-wing group. Armina thought that these specious lies, told for political advantage, would have to confront the marks on the woman's legs, the torn underwear, the cigarette butts, the stained underwear. These were her arguments against the errors of perception, whether cynical or so biased as to be unable to see facts clearly.

She looked for other possibilities, although many men in Berlin had secret lives and weren't obvious in what they were up to after dark. Even so, Armina had a list of those known to informers and the police. A banker, who waited in the park at night on a bench, staring into the dark, counting the women who passed him, as though his keeping track of money left him incapable of any other appreciation but a summation. Sometimes, though, he approached a woman and said that he needed to smell a woman's hair, her clothes, her perfume, and, as he did this, he swore in a constant, increasingly violent way. His name was Weber.

Armina added his name to the list, along with the man and woman, Alda and Michael Bauer, who worked as a team. They hired a woman to come to a cheap hotel room, and then Alda held her down while the man had his way—the women from the park had said these two were odd, not in what they wanted (which was pretty common) but in their attitude in how they did it. Alda Bauer had three tattoos, one on each breast and one in the middle, the two words, just below each nipple, bound to a word between them: *Liebe* and *Hass* linked to *Wunsch. Love* and *Hate* make *Desire.* Armina added Alda and her husband, Michael, to the list.

A fireman by the name of Mueller liked to go to the park, and yet he never spoke to the women there but only communicated by hand signals, as though deaf, pointing at what he wanted and tugging a woman's hair.

And then there were men, Arnwolf, Kortig, Hahn, and others, who paid the women, dump girls, who hired themselves out to be beaten. These creatures stood in the light, as though their bruises were a kind of shingle they hung out, like a shoe above a cobbler.

Armina added the names of these men, too, along with men who had been known to push their wives around, or the ones who were so intense in this that members of the Inspectorate thought that it was only a matter of time before one of them killed a wife or someone else for that matter. Armina looked over the list and broke the names down by violence and then by geographical location. They didn't live, as she had suspected, in the worst parts of town and not the best, either, but in neighborhoods that were distinguished by how ordinary they were, all the buildings squat, relatively well maintained with flowers planted where there was a bare piece of ground.

She went to see the first one.

aelle got out of the taxi in front of her parents' building, checked to make sure she had her rhinestone handbag, took a step toward the building door, but then turned back to the cab. It was gone. She waved at it as it went down the street, trailing a long plume of exhaust, but the driver didn't see her. She'd have to go in.

The metal gate of the elevator slid aside with a creak that reminded her of a stiff joint, and when she was inside, the cage moved with a whining ascent. She took out her compact and looked at her face. Her mother had given her the compact, but before she had handed it over, she had used the flesh-colored pad and the powder to touch up Gaelle's icy cheek. "There. That's not so bad," she had said.

"Oh," said Gaelle's mother. "Oh. Come in. Come in. I was afraid you'd never come back."

"I wanted to see you," said Gaelle.

"Is something wrong?" said her mother.

"No," said Gaelle. "Can I come in?"

"Yes," said her mother. "Your father isn't here. He's at the bank."

Her mother only looked at the unmarked side of Gaelle's face, and this insistence on only one half left Gaelle with the sensation of her face being divided.

"It's so nice to see you," said her mother.

"Is it?" said Gaelle.

"Yes," said her mother. "You don't know what it's like. You can't understand what it's like to be a mother."

"What's it like?" said Gaelle.

"Oh," said her mother. "It's not like that. You can't just say that." She took Gaelle by the hand. "You know, I hear the silence here now that you're gone."

"My life is pretty noisy," said Gaelle.

"Is it?" said her mother. "Well, that's nice."

"I've missed you," said Gaelle.

"Well, I've missed you," said her mother. "It's a good thing your father isn't here."

The living room had a blue-gray sofa with a high, curved back and lion's claws for legs and a marble-topped table stood in front of it. The same pictures of hanging game, pheasants and rabbits, were still in their gilt frames. A faded Persian carpet was on the floor. A clock ticked in the hall, and for a while they both listened to the tick, tick, tick like something dripping.

"I'll get some tea," her mother said. "You remember how I brought it to you when you were sick. A surprise tea, remember? That's what I called it."

Gaelle sat on the sofa and faced the pictures of dead pheasants and rabbits, the feathers bright, the fur painted with a million fine strokes. Then she touched her face. Her fingers came away with powder, just a dry, pinkish oval at the end of each tip. From the kitchen came the sounds as her mother put sugar, some buns, jam, cream in a silver pitcher on a silver tray, and the small clinks and clicks were everything that Gaelle craved: order, small domestic pleasures, the presence of smooth china. What could go wrong in a world where such things existed? She touched the scar and then looked down at her rhinestone bag.

Her mother brought in the silver tray with the spout of the teapot trailing mist, like a minute locomotive. She poured tea into a cup with roses on it, added cream just the way Gaelle like it, and pushed it into Gaelle's hands. For a moment they both held the cup, and Gaelle felt the pressure from the tips of her mother's fingers, the same touch that she had used to tuck Gaelle in at night, to caress Gaelle's face when she had had a fever, to straighten her clothes before she had gone to school.

"So, what's wrong?" her mother said.

"I just thought I'd come here," said Gaelle.

"Home," said her mother. "Isn't that what you mean?"

"I wanted to see you," said Gaelle.

Gaelle got up from her chair and sat next to her mother, and without thinking, she put her head into her mother's lap.

"Oh," said her mother. "You haven't done that in a long time."

Gaelle shook her head against her mother's thighs.

· "Oh, darling," said her mother.

"Darling," said Gaelle. She closed her eyes and swallowed.

The scar was against her mother's thighs, and Gaelle pushed against them as though those legs could make the scar disappear, that the touch of them could somehow erase it, or at least stop the numb sense of it.

"I'm a little worried," said Gaelle.

"We're all worried," said her mother. "The slump. People out of work. Why, your father is lucky to have a job."

"I know," said Gaelle. "But it's not that kind of worry."

"Well, what kind is it?"

Gaelle shook her head.

"It's like a silence," said Gaelle. "Like what you said. I've been thinking of the time before I was born. That was dark, wasn't it?"

"I guess," said her mother. "But it was coming toward the light."

"That's right," said Gaelle. "Going toward the light."

"You could come here," said her mother. "We could protect you."

Gaelle listened to the clock tick and glanced at the teacups, which steamed on the table.

"I don't think so," said Gaelle.

"It would be fine," said her mother.

"And we'd sit here and you'd have to look at me," said Gaelle.

"But I don't mind looking at you," said her mother. "I love you."

"My face has changed things," said Gaelle.

"No it hasn't," said her mother. "I don't mind looking at you."

"But I mind," said Gaelle. "It's like a gas or something I bring into the room. Everyone looks away from me. If they could just look at me once."

They listened to the clock.

"Please," said her mother. "You could have your room. We've kept it for you."

"No," she said. "I don't want that."

"Don't want what?" said her mother.

"To be seen," she said.

They sat for a while, Gaelle so still it appeared she was asleep. The silence of the apartment surrounded them like the most smooth black silk.

"I shouldn't have come here," said Gaelle.

"Yes, you should," said her mother.

Gaelle shook her head.

"It's your home," said her mother.

"No," said Gaelle. "Not anymore."

"Why don't you come back?" said her mother.

"You don't understand," said Gaelle.

"You're just disappointed," said her mother.

"Disappointed," said Gaelle. *"Disappointed?"*

She trembled against her mother.

"Yes," said her mother. "That's all."

Gaelle sat up and turned her scar toward her mother. Then she slapped it once, and then again, much harder. It sounded like someone dropping a steak on a butcher's block.

"No," said her mother. "Don't do that. What are you doing?"

Gaelle said, "You don't understand."

Her mother kissed the cool and smooth scar and the red skin around it, whispered that it would be all right.

"You see what I mean?" said Gaelle.

"Put your head down," said her mother. "There. There."

Gaelle pressed against the thighs again, the slick material of the housedress giving under her face as she shook her head from side to side.

"I don't want to be seen," she said. "But if I have to be, I want to be in charge. That's how I can get some help. Bitch somebody up. Give them what they want."

"There. There," said her mother.

They listened to the clock for a while, the creaking of the apartment building, the sound of their breathing.

"I'm not going to cry," said Gaelle.

"Me neither," said her mother.

"I wish I could go back," said Gaelle. "To when I had a cold and you brought me a surprise, a snack."

"Me, too," said her mother. "You could think about it. You could try to come home."

"Sure," said Gaelle. "I'll think it over."

Gaelle sat up, thanked her mother for the tea, powdered her face with the compact, kissed her mother on the cheek, and went to the door. She thought she could hear the echo from the times when she had been ten and eleven and had run through the apartment when her father had come home and had called out for her to come along with him to get an ice cream. Then she was aware of the present quietness, as though the silence were a variety of scar.

"Don't worry," said her mother. "It'll be all right. Whatever it is."

"I'll find a way," said Gaelle.

Her mother reached into the pocket of her dress and took out some bills, the money that was supposed to go for the housekeeping. She held out the bills and said, "Here. This will help. Go on."

"No," said Gaelle. "It's not money."

"Please," said her mother. "Please take something from me."

She held it out. Gaelle took it.

"Thanks," said her mother.

Gaelle went into the hall and thought how she used to run down the stairs, but now she pushed the ivory button for the elevator and waited for the creak of the rising cage, and when it stopped, she opened the door with its series of elongated Xs and got in. She pulled it shut and stood behind the bars as the cage made a slow descent.

The darkness below the cage seemed like that appalling oblivion, that darkness before and after life, and as the elevator trembled in its descent, Gaelle had the fleeting vision, almost a hope, of someone who cared about her, who loved her enough to save her from that realm, that universe without stars, at once infinite and without light. She put out her hand, as though reaching for whoever this might be, this man she could trust. Then she dismissed this as another notion that from time to time she had, as cloying as cheap perfume. And yet, as she dismissed it and pushed it into the deepest recesses, she felt it growing, getting larger, even feeding on her desire not to have such ideas.

Mani Carlson, director of the Red Front Fighters in Berlin, had not kept a careful accounting of the money from Moscow. It had been brought by courier, delivered in a black gladstone bag, the bills new and bound in neat piles by strips of paper that were pasted together. The bag seemed essentially English, bloated like a man with too much money, and yet Mani ran his fingers over the good leather, the brass clasps, and felt the solid heft of the bag. Then he dismissed this as a lingering infatuation with luxury and comfort. He knew he shouldn't care about such things, and yet when he was in a pharmacy he picked up a badger shaving brush, the porcelain base of it as big around as a water glass. The idea of the thick, scented lather on his face left him calm, even hopeful. The real problem, he knew, was his sloppy accounting.

The bills in the bag had been counterfeit, but the work done in Moscow along these lines (passports, identity papers, currency) was so good that it would be impossible to distinguish it from the real thing. Mani wondered why it was that Moscow could produce such beautiful forgeries but yet couldn't make a good leather bag. That would come later, he guessed. He knew that it wouldn't be long before he was asked to show his ledgers, his receipts, the long, careful rows of figures, the black line at the bottom where the sums should balance: so much received, so much spent, so much remaining. Friends of his had been invited to Moscow, and many of them had never come back to Berlin, and, of course, accounting was one of the subjects that Moscow was most concerned about. He was a little seasick as he thought about the time when he would be asked for his accounting by the men from Moscow who were at once exhausted and jumpy, and who had dandruff and bad breath.

Mani was thirty-four years old, a man of medium height with tin colored hair, eyes a pale green like the tint of formaldehyde in a specimen bottle. A new scar ran along the side of his face from his hair to his jaw and disappeared into the top of his shirt. Members of the Reichsbanner, a group of Socialists who supported the Weimar government, had slashed him in a street fight. The men in Moscow hated the Socialists even more than they hated the Brownshirts.

Mani told himself that part of the reason he hadn't kept an accounting was that the money wasn't real, just counterfeit, and yet he knew this was no excuse. When they came for him, they wouldn't care about that. They wanted discipline, and if he didn't have it, they would get someone who did. So how would Mani cover up the money he had spent on French brandy and nights on the town?

Mani went to one of the print shops he used, a small place that smelled of solvent and the fishy stink of ink. The printer, who drank a beer while the press ran, looked up and saluted Mani with the glass.

"What can I do for you?" said the printer. "Have you got a rush job? Some posters? How long do you give the current government? Weeks? Months?"

Mani shrugged.

"It won't be long," he said. "Look. I need some blank receipts. I lost the ones you gave me."

The printer made an adjustment on the press, which made a steady *ker-chunk, ker-chunk.*

"Well, you've been a good customer," he said. He put down the beer and went to the drawer behind the counter and took out some receipts.

"I need more than that," said Mani. "A lot more."

"No kidding?" said the printer. "What have you been doing with the money?"

"What's it to you?" said Mani.

"Nothing," said the printer. "But what am I supposed to do if anyone comes around and asks for my copies of the receipts you make up?"

"Lie," said Mani.

The printer adjusted the press. The roller swept up the plate and left the ink there like the squirt of an octopus. The press made that constant *ker-chunk, ker-chunk.*

"And you'll bring me more business?" said the printer.

"Sure," said Mani.

The printer shrugged and pushed the blank receipts over.

"Careful," he said. "You've got to be careful with those men from Moscow."

"You can always say your records were stolen," said Mani.

"Let's hope I don't have to say anything," said the printer.

Mani went to the lumberyard where he had gotten materials for the street-theater stage and asked for receipts there, too. He got them from the grocers, used-clothes dealers, hardware stores where he had bought ball bearings to throw at his opponents in a street fight. Then he sat down and filled out the blank forms, careful to smudge the ink and to use different colors, too. He included amounts in his ledger that made it look as though he had gone hungry to pay the printers, the lumberyard, etc. The receipts, however, looked too new, and so he caught some cockroaches and put them in a box with the documents and left them there for a couple of weeks. After that the paper was spotted and looked older, but would they fool anyone from Moscow? After all, in Moscow they made the best documents in the world, and did that mean they were the best at spotting a phony? Mani didn't know. Soon, though, he would find out.

He had been in tight places before, and he told himself that he just had to sit tight, not to panic, to wear a dog face and to plead ignorance when he had to, although looking them in the eye in circumstances like this took energy, and he was getting tired. He wanted to sleep late and took comfort in the toasty warmth of his bed. He smoked more cigarettes and had trouble shaving every day. In his room, hidden under his bed, he had a collection of pirate stories, which he read when he couldn't sleep.

Now, at the street theater, he stood at the side of the stage. It wasn't the best crowd, but it wasn't too bad, although he wouldn't want to have these numbers if he was being observed by the men from Moscow. More and more he looked at his life through this lens, and when he did, he had trouble sitting still, in being confident, in trying to be optimistic. Maybe he would buy some cocaine to lift his mood, and if it worked even for a few hours, it would be worth it. Onstage a man in stripped trousers and a top hat was loading up a big bag with piles of stage money. The crowd booed. Mani thought about the accounting.

The young woman stood at the rear of the crowd. Early twenties, blond hair, smooth skin, a sort of sultry impatience. She wore a new gray skirt, good shoes, a blouse, and a fashionable coat. Mani guessed she was the daughter of someone who worked in an insurance office, something like that. Usually they were the easy ones: he'd charm them and get them to work for a while, sewing for the theater, working in the café, passing out leaflets, running errands. In a couple of months they'd go on to the next new thing, vegetarian cults, astrology, channeling the dead, drugs, dance crazes, new hairstyles. Then she turned and exposed her face, the mask, or half mask like one out of a Greek play.

The other members of the sparse crowd were a mixture of students with their satchels, workingmen in their blue pants and leather aprons, women who had stopped as a matter of curiosity. The usual collection. He thought that if he could just avoid looking at the girl with the scar, he could forget the shock of recognition: her presence here, the strength it took just to stand there, the odd attractiveness so bound up with what had obviously happened to her made for a charge, a kind of valence of possibility. He thought that she could understand everything.

He walked over to her. She wore a light scent, or maybe it was just the soap she used combined with her skin. Just standing next to her made him feel better, and the scar was soothing, if only because it made him feel momentarily superior. And then anything was better than his worries about the accounts, his room with the pirate books under the bed, the waiting for the knock on the door, the visit that was coming, the men from Moscow with the bad breath and black teeth.

"Hi," he said. "I haven't seen you around before."

"It's my first time here," she said.

She turned to face him, her expression one of a frank challenge. Go on, she said. Look. Do you dare?

He turned away, but he felt her presence and that challenge, and then he screwed up his courage and faced her. It was like lifting a weight. She smiled. So, he thought, she understands even this first moment.

"What do you think of the theater?" he said.

"It could be funnier," she said. "It's pretty dull."

Mani knew this was an understatement. The actors were going through the motions. The songs were sung off-key. The jokes were stale.

"Maybe it will get better," said Mani. "Come back next week. This is just a run-through, a tryout. I'm thinking of making changes."

The crowd applauded in a perfunctory way, and soon people began to wander off. At the rear of the stage, a man took off a wig, and his makeup made him look like a man who had just come up from a coal mine. Clean under his hat but dirty on his face.

"Sure," said the girl. "I thought I'd see what you are up to, you know. Look around."

"It's not only this," said Mani.

"Oh?" she said. She shifted her weight and seemed to move a little closer. "Like what? Fighting in the streets?"

"Yes," said Mani. "We fight the thugs. The Brownshirts."

"And do you stick up for your friends?" she said. "If one of your friends was having trouble with them, would you help out?"

"Of course," said Mani. "Of course."

"Hmpf," said Gaelle. "Imagine that."

"You don't sound convinced," said Mani.

"Oh," she said with a smile. "I believe you."

"Come on," said Mani. "Let's go have a sweet. We can talk things over."

"Like what?" she said.

"Maybe you can help out," he said. "We need some help."

"Really," she said. "And what's in it for me?"

"You can join us," said Mani. "Be part of something."

He noticed that something seemed to be trying to get out of the scar, and he felt this as a squirm that ran straight through him, that left him with a sudden sense of stiffening. Maybe it is just being afraid, he thought, maybe I am just desperate for a little distraction.

"My name is Gaelle," she said.

"I'm Mani," he said. "Let's have a sweet."

He thought of sitting with her while she licked chocolate off a spoon, her face so troubling, her presence having that odd gravity. For an instant, Mani had the wild desire to let himself go, to allow himself to think that her vitality, her shocking attractiveness, could save him. Then he thought, from what? From the accounting.

So, the contest began, with Mani on one side and Gaelle on the other: he wanted a demonstration of dedication, and Gaelle was willing to endure almost anything to obtain protection, to have someone to turn to when she needed help with Hauptmann. She looked at Mani with the smile of a long-distance runner who sees an amateur trying to get through a difficult course for the first time. After all, she had her experience from the park and the things she had done there. What could he do to her that she hadn't already endured?

She resisted the notion that something else was going on here, and while she made a face when she considered it, and while she pushed it further away from her usual thinking, she found that she was still interested in that hope, that cheap perfume, as she called it, that someone might care about her. It was ridiculous on the face of it, on any evidence she could find, and yet it persisted for all the arguments against it. What could love do about the fact that she had become a spy and not even a good one? That is, if you thought a good spy was one who wasn't going to end up in the river.

They began with the street theater. The stage for it was made in sections that were bolted together by members of the Red Front. Karl did most of the heavy lifting. He was six feet four inches tall and his hands were the size of baseball gloves and his face looked like a leather suitcase that had been dragged halfway around the world. His hair was thick, clipped short like a brush. His dark eyes had an expression of what seemed to be indifference but that Gaelle knew was the result of an interior life, one of hopes and desires that were fiercely denied. If a woman looked at him, he dropped his eyes, as though ashamed of his size, his hands, his roughness. He said that he didn't mind being alone, since it was like a raincoat, a way of keeping things from touching him. He said that he had gotten used to it, and once you are used to something, it doesn't matter anymore. You even grow to like it. You can make something that hurts into a kind of honor.

He moved the sections of the stage, eight-by-four rectangles of two-by-fours and plywood, from the cart that had brought them from the Red Front's storage loft to the site of the performance. He did this with an indifference to the weight of the things, as though not showing effort was part of his job, too.

Georg, who was a sheet metal worker whose hands were covered with scars that looked like fish bones, tried to lift the sections, too, but as soon as he picked one up, his arms trembled like the string of a bass instrument.

"Here," said Karl. "Get out of the way. Let me have it."

Gaelle's job was to help one of the actresses, Alice Sokoff, get dressed. Alice was Gaelle's age, and she stood with a straight posture, like classical sculpture, and her skin was as white as marble. She took it as her due that people would fuss over her, even members of the Red Front. Gaelle laid out her clothes. Polished her shoes, made sure the corset she wore was clean, checked the skirts to make sure that none was torn.

Mani came into the small tent that was used as a changing room behind the street theater. Outside, the sound of the stage being bolted together was like a house being built in a hurry.

"Alice's clothes look nice on her, don't you think?" said Mani. "But she needs help with her hair. Can you brush it?"

"Yes," said Gaelle.

"In front of the mirror," said Mani. "Stand behind her."

"Sure," said Gaelle.

She stood behind the actress and brushed the heavy blond hair, which in the dim tent still sparkled, like sand in the sunlight. Gaelle put her head next to Alice's so that they could be seen side by side, in the mirror. Mani appeared behind them, and as Gaelle worked on the hair, the brush making a hush, hush and a crackle of electricity, she looked at Mani through the mirror and kept her eyes on his and winked. "I know what you want," she seemed to say. "Can I take this? Can I compare myself to an untouched beautiful woman, can I fuss over her, as though proof that I have been so reduced? Can I do it without blinking an eye?"

"Makeup," said Mani.

Gaelle took out the kit and put down a base and eyeliner and rouge, and while she worked she still glanced up at Mani and winked, almost smiling now: it was too easy. And when the performance was over, Mani came into the dressing room again and stood there while Gaelle applied cold cream over the perfect face, rubbed it onto Alice's cheeks and then wiped it off to show the fresh skin underneath, so youthful and moist as to seem like the petal of a flower. She kept her eyes on Mani when she did this, too. Outside, the set was being struck, and the sound of it, the squeaking sigh of nails being withdrawn, the bumping of the sections of the stage being dragged by someone other than Karl, the busy gathering of tools and bolts and whatever else was left around, was like a band of gypsies trying to stay one jump ahead of someone they had cheated.

"You're pretty," said Gaelle.

"Do you think so?" said Alice.

"Oh, yes," said Gaelle. "I'm in a position to know."

"I guess that's right," said Alice.

"Here, let me help you," said Gaelle.

Gaelle took off the stage gown, undid the corset, and ran her fingers over the lines that were left under Alice's breasts, the nipples as pink as barely ripened raspberries. Gaelle used a damp cloth and washed Alice, keeping her eyes on Mani, then helped with Alice's underthings, her clothes, and passed over Alice's small, even dainty shoes.

"Alice has a future," said Gaelle, as much to Mani as to anyone else.

"Yes," said Mani. "So many people are washed up. At a young age."

Gaelle put away the makeup, folded the clothes, packed them into a small black trunk that was used for costumes, and as she did she looked at Mani, as though to say, "You can trust me. You think that I am vain? That I will flinch? Why, you poor ninny. I gave that up so long ago that I can't even remember."

Outside, as Karl lifted the sections of the stage onto the cart and tied them down with a trucker's knot, Gaelle smiled at Mani and said, "Well, is that it? Is there something else you want to do?"

"Maybe," said Mani.

"And what can you do for me?" she said.

"Oh," said Mani. "I can be around when you want me."

But even so, they continued. Mani wrote a part for a play in which a woman has been scarred by a factory owner who then neglects her. He showed the part to Gaelle, who looked at it, aware of what he was asking: would she stand on the stage, in costume, and show her face to the crowds, the men and women drinking beer and eating a sausage, or just gawking because there was nothing better to do. She put down the pages and said, "Yes."

Mani stood in the audience as she performed her part, quite convincingly, and afterward he said, "It has nothing to do with politics for you, does it?"

"Politics," said Gaelle. "You want to know what I think of politics. . . . No. I'm asking for something else."

"Sure," said Mani as he looked around uneasily. "Sure."

"I haven't got time for politics," said Gaelle. "That's a luxury."

"Sure," said Mani. "Fine."

"I haven't got time," she said. "I've done what you asked. Well?"

"All right," said Mani. "I'll stick up for you."

But the contest wasn't over, not yet. The next Saturday Mani asked Gaelle to come along with some members of the Red Front to look for a new site for the street theater, and Gaelle realized that the contest had just begun. Mani, Karl, Georg, and some others got on the train, all of them pale, their skin more the color of the scars on Georg's hand, and as they sat down together, Gaelle looked at her hands, which were pale, too, and as the train started with a slow, deep whine, like a machine from the depths of possibility, she thought that she should get some sun, but when was there time to do that? So many people in Berlin liked to sunbathe, and she imagined how it would be to have the warm caress of the sun, but all she heard was the whine of the engines.

Two stops later, the young men got on the S-Bahn and looked around the car. They had their hair combed back in a military style, and they moved as though in a squad. The first one got on the train and glanced around until he saw Gaelle, over whom he lingered with a combination of curiosity and malice. What was she doing with the Red Front? Then the next one got on and did the same thing. They weren't wearing uniforms, just brown pants, white shirts, ties that were tucked between the middle buttons of a shirt. Gaelle tried to stare at the men on the other side of the car. Clean-looking thugs. Nazis.

"You knew you were going to run into them," said Gaelle. "Right? Is that why you asked me along?"

Mani shrugged.

"I don't know," he said.

"And you're going to lie to me, too," she said.

"All right," he said. "Are you up to this or not?"

He sat with his hands in the pockets of his leather jacket, which had cracks around the cuffs.

"We're outnumbered," said Mani. "Maybe you could be a distraction. You know, tug at one of them while we let them have it."

Gaelle sat between Karl and Mani. She felt the scar on her face like a parasite, something that sucked her blood, and while it did that, it seemed to invite others to do the same, the men in the park, men like Hauptmann and Mani, too. Why, they thought they could get away with anything where she was concerned. Her vulnerability was one quality that attracted men to her in the park, and she used it when she could, but now she sat there, looking at the thugs on the other side of the train and then at Mani, who glanced back and seemed to say, Well, well? How far will you go? Can you take it? Even this? Will you let me use you in a fight like this?

No, she thought, no. Screw you.

She thought about going to work with a black eye and bruises, or worse.

"I thought you were with us," Mani said.

"I thought . . . ," she said. She bit her lip.

"What?" he said. "What did you think?"

"I was hoping you might . . . ," she said. But then she stopped. No, this is going nowhere. How could she have even considered love, or being cared about?

Karl looked one way and then another, as though the thugs on the other side of the train were of no consequence to him. If they were looking for trouble, they had come to the right man. His certainty and his serenity alarmed Gaelle, too, since how could anyone be so oblivious to danger? He didn't smile at her or sneer or anything like that at all. Instead his glance, with that same appalling certainty, seemed to hit her like a light.

Mani kept ball bearings in the pocket of his coat, and now, when he reached inside, they made a click like the kiss of a pool ball. Karl rolled his shoulder, as though trying to get loose.

Gaelle had been told that a dog could tell if someone was scared, and she wondered if the young men on the other side of the train could tell, although she realized, as she looked at them, that it wouldn't have made much difference.

Karl put his lips, as thick as sausages, next to her ear and said, "Pick one. Tug on his clothes. I'll take it from there." He nodded at a man on the other side of the train who had blond hair and very blue eyes, the color of a delphinium. "Him. I'll be waiting for you."

The S-Bahn went along the Spree, which curved through the city behind the Reichstag, the Berliner Dom, the museums, and the Lustgarten, too. A proper woman in a silk dress and furs got up and went to the door between this car and the next and pulled it open. She went through and let it slam shut behind her, without looking back.

"There's a smart one," said Georg.

Karl watched her go and said, "Yes. That's a good idea. If you don't like trouble."

The train stopped at the Zoologischer Garten station.

"This isn't like dressing a beautiful young woman. That's just vanity, you know, standing up to that kind of thing when I ask you. Or letting the crowd get a look at you."

"You'd be surprised," said Gaelle.

Mani shrugged.

"I thought I'd see how serious you were," he said.

"What I've done doesn't count for anything? You've used me and then we end up like this?"

"Just pull on one of their arms," said Mani.

"That one," said Karl.

The young men in brown pants on the other side of the car sat straight up, all watching her, or so it seemed. It was as though they were thinking

the same thing, and for all she knew, they were. The one on the end, with
the eyes as bright as a delphinium, kept staring at her. She felt the atmosphere in the car press in on her. Then she thought of the creeps she had
handled in the park. That had been all right, and she had been plenty
scared then, too. Then she thought of the parasitic aspect of the scar that
invited all the worst from those people who looked for a flaw or a weakness
to exploit.

The young men on the other side of the train stood up. Mani raised an
eyebrow, and then Karl, Georg, and the others stood up, toe to toe with the
men in brown pants. Gaelle stood up, too. Mani reached into his pocket
for a ball bearing and made a click when one of them knocked against another. Karl lifted his large hand, and held it in a fist at the side of his chest.
One of the young men looked along the line from Karl to Georg and then
to Gaelle.

"What a mug," he said. "Did you bring her along to scare us?"

"What did you say?" said Karl.

A man in a blue suit, a woman in a green dress, a boy in short pants, a
young girl with a hat that had a large glass stick pin in it moved away, and
as they went, they were careful not to look at the men in the white shirts or
the members of the Red Front.

"You heard me," said the same young man.

Mixed in with the muffled sound of someone being hit in the chest
there was another, harder crack. Gaelle had thought this kind of fighting
would be more like boxing, but instead the men shoved at one another and
hit out sloppily, like struggling through brush. Karl pushed her aside. She
stepped back. Three or four ended up on the floor of the train while the
others stood around and kicked when they had a chance. The entire mass
looked like a horse with fifteen pairs of legs that had gotten loose on the
train, although it had different shoes on its feet. That same man, the one
with the blue eyes, glanced in her direction.

The train stopped and the doors slid open. Gaelle was amazed they
worked when the men were kicking and grunting, shoving and hitting.
One of the young men in a white shirt was bleeding from the nose, and the
drops on the floor looked like red buttons that weren't the same size. This

man reached down, still dripping from the nose, and dragged a friend of his outside, onto the platform. Then Mani, Georg, Karl, and the other Red Front Fighters tumbled out the door onto the platform, too.

They formed up into two sides. Georg, Mani, and Karl and the other members of their group on one side and the young men in brown pants and white shirts on the other. Everyone hesitated, thinking things over. They swore at one another. Mani spit at the men in brown pants. Georg threw a ball bearing. Gaelle came up to the door, and as she was about to step out onto the platform, the door slid shut.

The train jerked. Karl turned from the men who were opposite him and looked at Gaelle, not seeming to judge her so much as to understand. Mani turned away from the line of men, too, and as his eyes caught hers, with the faintly greasy piece of glass of the door between them, he nodded and then, as clearly as though he were speaking out loud, he asked by his expression, the movement of his eyes, in the electric moment when he reached into his pocket for a ball bearing, just how she was going to make up for this.

Karl went on staring at her as the train began to move, and when someone hit him, he just shrugged if off and continue to stare, a little hurt now, or so it seemed, and this only made Gaelle angrier. How dare anyone accuse her? What the fuck did they know? Had they been down on their knees in front of a park bench? Had they put a face next to that of a beautiful young woman to see what fate had done just to show its power, its delight in the chaotic? Then Mani, Karl, and the others disappeared into a jumble of arms and legs as a large, brown, earth-colored thing flew over the platform. Gaelle realized that it was a potato with nails in it.

Gaelle sat there, her hands shaking. Every now and then one of the people in the car looked at her, but she didn't look back. Had someone been killed, and if that had happened, was she involved? Would she pay the price, even though she had clearly told Mani to get lost, to go screw himself, since as far as she could tell, no one else would do it. Would the police track her down in the park or at her apartment? She thought of the three-room place she had rented not too far from the Tiergarten. Her fingers trembled at her lips, and the movement reminded her of the wings of a moth she had once touched. When she looked down, she realized that the fight could have been an illusion, and if it hadn't been for the stain on the floor, she could almost convince herself of that. Underneath it all she was disappointed she had let herself consider love or affection or anything like that at all, and now she told herself she would put that into her own, most dark recesses, into a place that was going to be sealed up for good. She trembled with the effort, to get ready to do business, since that was what was so obviously required.

The train stopped. She got off and stood on the platform. Then she turned to look back along the tracks where the train had come from, and in the distance, vastly diminished, she thought she could make out the platform where Mani and Georg and the others might still be fighting. The rails were shiny and curved away into the distance. She paced back and forth, looking for an angle, a way to fix this up, to make sure she had some help. The atmosphere on the platform, which was a kind of perfume of fear, was precisely what Hauptmann had left her with: it was the scent of being alone. Then she was angry that she had found herself so neatly suspended, as she often was, between what she tried to do and what it got her.

She crossed under the tracks to the other side of the station so she could catch the next train back the way she had come. Blocks of apartments stood by the river, which made a silver path. Then she walked back and forth, wanting the train to come and dreading its arrival. What was she going to do if she got back and they were still fighting?

The train arrived and she got on. Men rustled newspapers as they shook them out and folded them, and the scent of the women's perfume hung in the air. There wasn't so much of that as there had been before the slump, but it was nice to smell. She felt the lurch of the car and wondered what would happen if the police went to her parents' apartment. At least she didn't live there anymore.

The train pulled into the station where the young men had been. She got out of the car and looked across to the other platform, but it was empty. The train pulled away with a highly geared whine, which sounded to her like a toy being wound so tightly it would finally break. She was sweating.

Finally she crossed over to the other side of the station, went downstairs and under the track and then climbed the steps, and on the platform she felt the presence of the fight, which seemed to linger like smoke. The air was warm, but she hugged herself and walked back and forth, although she stopped at some red drops about the size of a coin. The brightness of them, like new red paint, reminded her that she wasn't finished with Mani. The contest hadn't been decided, not yet.

Two uniformed officers, the Schutzpolice, stood in the street under the track. Mani had told her that in a street fight, which the police had tried to break up with men on horses, Mani had used a knife to stab a horse. He said it had been a black horse and that the blood seemed all the redder, all the more glistening, as it had run down the horse's black leg.

"So, you've come back."

The man with the blue eyes stood on the platform.

"You," he said. "I'm talking to you. Girl, come."

"Girl?" she said.

"All right. Woman. Is that better? Come," he said.

He was tall, heavy in the shoulders, tanned, with bright yellow hair. He held out his hand and beckoned to her. An approaching train made a whine, and overhead some pigeons flew into the air, their wings fluttering with an anxious sound.

"I won't hurt you," he said.

"What makes you think you could hurt me?" she said.

He smiled. Then he stepped closer, and as he did, she saw that one of his hands was swollen. He put it in his pocket and tried to look nonchalant.

"Why do you want to hang around with those people?" he said.

She stood there, thinking that she should slap him. She'd had enough. A hard, loud smack. Then she took an inventory of his features, his combed hair, which shone in the light, his rough, definite good looks, his broad shoulders, his smile.

The man glanced at her scar and watched as she turned her head a little to let him see it. He blushed.

"Come," he said. "Let's go downstairs."

"Why should I go anywhere with you?" she said.

"Because you want to," he said.

"And what are we going to do?" she said.

"We'll have a glass of beer," he said. "I want to talk to you."

"And why do you want to do that?" she said.

He looked around.

"You know what kind of trouble I could get into, just being seen with you?"

"Yes," she said. "I know."

"Have you ever taken a chance? Done something you shouldn't?"

He looked at the scar.

"Can I touch it?" he said.

She stared at him.

He looked around, too, and he wasn't smiling either. "If I'm willing to take that chance, it means I really want to talk. Doesn't that count?"

She took a step down the stairs, but he reached out and took her arm.

"No," he said. "Not that way. Can't you see the cops?"

They turned and went back to the other end of the platform, the two of them walking side by side. Then they went down the stairs and stood under the elevated tracks next to a support, which was a sort of steel pylon, four corners that were held together with metal Xs, all the way up to the tracks overhead.

He looked around.

"We shouldn't be seen together," he said. "You from your side, me from mine."

They went into a restaurant that had a long bar at the back, parallel to the windows at the front. This made the place bright, and the surface of the tables, which was a black marble, gleamed under a cloud of cigarette smoke. Some tables were arranged on the sidewalk, but Gaelle and the man went by them, inside to a table as far away from the door as possible. The man went to the bar, where people got out of his way. He brought back two glasses, which he put down just like that. Bang.

"What's your name?" she said.

"Aksel," he said. "And yours?"

"Gaelle," she said.

"Gaelle. And, Gaelle, where do you live?"

"On Fliegstrasse," she said.

"There's a park there," he said. "I know the place."

"It's a small park. Kids and their mothers."

She wanted to say something to insult him, to make this end. Why couldn't she be more in control of things like that? She had another drink.

"So," he said. "What are you doing with those guys?"

"I have my reasons," she said. "What about you?"

"In the middle of the street fights everything is clear. That's what I like."

"And are you going to be doing some fighting someplace soon?"

"You think I am that stupid," he said. "You come here with me, and then I tell you things? And you tell your pals?"

"I thought you wanted to talk," she said. "That's all."

"And what about you? Don't you want to talk to me? Isn't there something eating at you?"

"No," she said. "I have nothing to say to you."

"You're sure? You look worried," he said.

The bar was filled with cigarette smoke, and down at the end someone laughed. It all seemed so ordinary, really, just a bunch of men having some beer while outside two uniformed policeman went by.

"I tried to give you a nice time. And what do you give me? Contempt," he said. He looked right at her.

She leaned close to him and came into the slight odor of his hair and skin, and she knew that her perfume made him lean toward her. The perfume was muted and made a special scent, different on her skin than it was in the bottle. She leaned closer, and then said, "Thanks for the beer."

"That's all you have to say?" he said.

"No," she said. She looked right at him. "You're such an idiot."

"Yes," he said. "I know what you think about us on our side." He put out his hand. "Well, I won't forget you."

She almost took it, but then stopped and turned into the smoke in the bar, which was as thick as a layer of fog near the ceiling. She tried for a businesslike gait, square shouldered, passing the men at the small round tables who read newspapers, smoked, and tried to discover something in the thin lines of print. She turned and looked back when she was outside.

Aksel was still looking at her, smiling, and when she was about to turn away for good, he blew her a kiss. It was so sudden a gesture that she almost felt it, like the touch of an insect against her cheek. And while she had been infuriated, she kept thinking about it. Then she went back up to the station to go one stop to the Zoologischer Garten station and as she waited for the train, she thought, Fuck them all.

After the delicious, momentary relief from thinking this way, her sense of fear came back almost as though it were a gas that seeped up from the ground and hung around her. Like something escaped from a sewer.

She thought of the slick texture of her mother's dress, of the comfort of being there in her mother's lap, and the attractions of going home were so enormous that she momentarily forgot her isolation. But she had already tried that, and so she stood on the platform and stared into the distance. At least she took some comfort that the desire to be loved was now carefully hidden, sealed off in the most secret and darkest of recesses.

The man on the train from Moscow to Berlin was Russian, but he was traveling under the name "Gerhard Schmidt." He was over six feet tall and wore dark pants and stylish shoes made of very thin leather, which he got through the Italian embassy. His jacket was European, too, but his top-coat was Russian, long, heavy, and with a skirt that came down below his knees. He was vain about his broad-brimmed hat. He had emerged from steam on the platform of the Moscow train station as though materializing out of a dream, one hand carrying his small suitcase in which there were two shirts, two changes of underwear, his razor, a badger shaving brush, and a pistol. There was no need to worry about the pistol, since he traveled on a diplomatic passport. He had one other suitcase, too, which was filled with reichsmarks. Fresh, new, just printed. They were well made, and he doubted if someone from the German mint would be able to tell the difference between these notes made in Moscow and the ones produced in Berlin.

He turned and looked through the steam to the entrance of the platform. The streets had been almost deserted, just some hungry people who were trying to find something to eat. He thought about the days just after the revolution in Moscow when wooden houses had been pulled down for firewood. And when the peasants in the countryside had withheld food, the army had been sent to collect what was needed. The Russian peasant was going to have to be dealt with, and the question was how. Hunger. That was one way. In fact, as he smelled the machine-scented steam, he thought it was probably the best way to deal with them. Hunger was something they should be able to understand.

He thought about the Moscow River, too, and how, when it was still and reflected the city, it gave him a moment of clarity. Nothing moved then. Just the mirror of river, which showed the buildings on the other side, the bridges, the sky. It was the only memory that made him homesick when he was away, and while he had been sent to many places in Russia recently, he wasn't so comfortable leaving Moscow just now. People like him had gone to Italy or France, and then when they had come back, they had been destroyed because they had seen how people lived in Europe. Or just because they hadn't been able to keep up with developments in Moscow. And so while it was an honor to be chosen to go to Berlin, he still looked uneasily at the steam, the glistening engines, the lighted train cars. Gerhard Schmidt thought about the people the police had been pulling out of the Moscow River recently, officials of one kind or another. Then he shrugged and got on the train.

He didn't read. He sat upright, hands folded in his lap, occasionally looking out the window at the landscape. It was spring now, but he thought of fall, when the stands of popple around the fields were a haunting yellow. He liked to think about that color, as though if he could just remember it clearly enough, why then he couldn't ever really feel that he was too far away. And there was another aspect of those fields around Moscow in the fall. Some afternoons the light had a yellow, smoky quality, and while it was like a warm fog, it suggested a kind of ghost of spring, or perhaps it was just the promise of spring. Still, he liked the ghostlike association. That was probably closer to the truth.

He checked to make sure the pistol was still in his bag. He was surprised that he needed to do this, since the bag was never out of his sight, but even though he knew it was there, he still began to feel uneasy. He imagined the trouble he would have if it got out of his hands, and even though he knew this was unlikely, every hundred miles or so, maybe a little more when he tried to resist, he got up and took the suitcase down from the rack and looked inside, glancing at the sheen of black metal, touching it once and then, after he had put the suitcase away, smelling the gun oil on his hand. This was like the scent of fate. Or the scent of fate prettied up, since not only was it machinelike, but it also had a slight, sweet perfume. From time to time, when he wasn't worrying about the pistol, he thought of the man he was going to see in Berlin.

Gerhard Schmidt didn't eat much. In the pocket of his coat he had a couple of rolls and a piece of sausage, wrapped in paper stained with grease, and every three hundred miles he took out his pocketknife, cut a piece of the sausage, and tore off a piece of bread, chewing slowly, watching the countryside go by. He ate with a steady, repetitive motion, more like a man making something in a factory than actually eating. He had his orders, and he supposed he wouldn't have too much trouble. People in Berlin had to understand that changes were being made in Moscow, and that the factionalism in Russia needed to be settled, and if the other parties in other countries like Germany didn't give their support, then they would have to be informed of the dangers. No factionalism. What was good for the Soviets was good for everyone. That was his job. He had his methods.

About halfway to Berlin, a young woman sat down next to Herr Schmidt. Her hair was very dark, and her skin was so pale that he thought she was Ukrainian. He hoped that she didn't have any relatives there, since he knew what was going to happen soon, not to mention things that had already been done. No nationalism, of any group, no desire for independence was going to be tolerated. When she tried to strike up a conversation, he just looked at her. Yes, he thought, she was probably Ukrainian. Then he went back to keeping an eye on his bag or looking out the window.

He slept sitting straight up, hands in his lap. He closed his eyes, pushed his head back a little, and as he slept he could still feel the movement of the train. He dreamed of the Moscow River in the evening when the wind had died down and the surface was as smooth as a ground lens. He knew that the secret to doing what he had to do was to believe very few things. The names of people he had to see. The details of his job. If he cluttered up his head with too much theory and policy, then he would just have to forget it later when it changed. It was better to try to remember that power existed with its own beauty and clarity, like the surface of the river, and that it was his job to act on its behalf. That was all there was to it. It was difficult to see power when it wasn't being used, and so he thought of it as a shiny and beguiling surface of a river, although one that could wash over anyone who got in its way.

In Germany he looked out the window with that same green-eyed indifference, as though the landscape here were not pretty or ugly or anything at all except as a stage, a location, a site where something was going to hap-

pen. Everything else was secondary. Just when he came into Berlin, he took
the piece of paper out of his pocket, unwrapped it, and looked at the last
piece of sausage and the last piece of bread. He had made it come out perfectly, and so he ate the last part of it, watching as the train went through
the outskirts of the city, which he saw as a smear of smoke above the buildings that manufactured stopwatches. Bicycle tires. Gears. Cable. Sheets of
metal.

He stood up and took his suitcases from the rack and then walked
along the aisle between the seats. He went down the steps to the platform,
where he emerged again from the steam as though he had not taken the
train but had been transported by some new process from Moscow. Then
he started walking toward the station, where he smelled the sweet strudel,
the cinnamon, the beer from the café, and when he came up to the door, he
looked in. But that was it. He stood there, resisting it, feeling good that he
could control himself even after the days he had been on the train. Instead,
he put his bags down and brought his fingers up to his nose and smelled the
scent of gun oil. He could still smell it as he walked from the train station
to his hotel, a small, cheap place on a side street in the middle of the city.

T he living room in Armina's apartment had a sofa, a padded chair, book-
cases, pictures done in a precise, hyperrealist style, a piano and a desk.
The piano had belonged to her mother, a concert pianist who had died of a
disease of the nerves, a painful condition that had been made worse by
morphine. Her father's desk was here, too, in the corner, the top of it lined
with pigeonholes where he had kept his papers, all of the square spaces appearing as though birds could nest in them, or, at least, they looked empty.
The green blotter on the desk was still covered with ink stains. He had been
a biochemist with a specialty in pain medication, and when Armina's
mother had been sick, he had tried one compound after another, the lack of
effect making him even more exasperated, and near the end, he hardly
slept. He had sat at this desk, where he made notes, wrote formulas, consulted his notebooks, wrote letters to colleagues. What did they know
about a particular preparation of opium? Did anyone know of analgesics
found in the jungles of South America?

Armina had put flowers in the room, white and pink peonies with cen-
ters that were flecked with red. Now she sat with a glass of brandy and
looked at the piano. Then the desk. Then she had a sip.

Each night recently when she came home from work she had the impulse to write a letter. At first, she laughed at herself and thought, Grow up.
Don't be a fool. Don't act like a schoolgirl. But these interior remarks and
lack of empathy for herself only made her get up and pour herself another
drink.

The letter was to a man she didn't know and yet in whose existence she
still believed, if only by the proof of the silence of her apartment, which
seemed not just an emptiness, but also a potential that referred to a specific
human being. She imagined this as one of the varieties of silence. Well, she

thought in her own self-mockery, maybe the silence is proof of something else: that I'm filling my head with nonsense.

She resisted writing the letter on the first night, and then the second, her reports, files, crime scene descriptions on the table in front of her. At least she didn't have to hide them—there was no one to be appalled by the photographs, the descriptions of wounds, the statements of people who had found a woman in the park.

On the fourth night, she didn't open her files. She took a pen, dipped it into her black official ink, and wrote, the metal nib on the paper a sound that barely scratched the silence in the room,

"Of course it is silly for me to want to write to you, and just putting these words on paper makes me feel my embarrassment. Still, I want to do it, if only to be clear to myself about what is happening to me. Frankly, I am not sure—not really, since I seem to be in the middle of it—but I know that I crave—is this the word?—crave your understanding. I know you are here, in this city, and yet why can't I find you? And what do I have to offer you, as though what I feel could ever be part of a bargain? Loyalty. I am loyal. I am understanding. If you need something, I will try to get it. If you want something from me (a touch, a look, a gift, a surrender, a frank offer) I will give it. I am not easily frightened.

"And what do I want? Well, I will recognize it when I see it. I wonder if I pass you on the street, if you will recognize me—would we hesitate, glance at one another, shocked by the other's sudden presence. Would it be frightening? Embarrassing? Would we know what to do? Or would we just pass along, too stupid and ridiculous to take advantage of the moment?"

Then she stopped, reached the pen tip for the ink, but sat that way, arm extended: this note had explained nothing and only provided justification for her contempt, a neat trick in which she used her needs as an accusation. She ripped the paper, threw it away, the pieces of it falling like blue-gray confetti into the trash can. The record she put on was one of her mother's performances, Mozart's Piano Concerto no. 12, and as the music came into the room she had another drink. Her father's desk sat in the corner, appearing as though he would come into the room and go to work on the desk beneath the pigeonholes.

In the morning she got up and went to work as always.

Two Greek columns supported the roof of Precinct 88 and between them a bronze door led to the dim interior. Armina walked through the marble lobby and up the stairs where the brass banister was cold. On the second floor the common room for Inspectorate A was filled with desks, the papers on them square as a geometry lesson. The walls had two tones, a dark crème up to shoulder height and a lighter one above. Milk glass globes hung from the ceiling, and everything about the place was oversize and left her with the feeling of a nightmare of being a child in which everything is too large and difficult to reach. Here the doorknobs were the size of bowling balls.

The people who worked in the precinct were evenly divided, at least as far as politics were concerned, but she was irritated with politics—the Communists were either too cynical or too stupid to see the real enemy was the thugs, the Nazis, the Steel Helmets. After all, from the Communist point of view, if another war broke out in Europe, no matter who won, Europe would be exhausted and easy pickings, that is if the Russians could stay out of it. But how would they do that? Is that the way they thought? Armina assumed it was possible. She thought of a prostitute she had interviewed in a murder investigation who had said she knew the thugs were trouble because when they slept with her it was as though they were trying to fuck her to death. No tip, either.

Ritter, the head of the Political Section, considered himself a nationalist, a patriot, although this was a nostalgia, for the time before the Great War, when the Kaiser had still been in Germany. And, along with the nostalgia, he had a contempt for the current life in the city (after all, women were holding hands in the street and wearing men's tuxedos in the nightclubs, where they were hilarious with champagne and cocaine). Ritter was one of the few members of the Berlin Police Department who had been glad to move to the Political Section. Armina guessed he was a member of some pro-Kaiser organization, or something worse. The groups that existed for assassination and revenge killings, such as Organization Escherich, or Organization Consul. The Nazis. He spoke perfect French, was an excellent amateur musician, and he wrote poetry, which he had privately printed on excellent paper and bound in leather.

Armina's office had a frosted glass door and one of those large knobs.

She went in and sat down while animated shadows passed on the other side of the frosted glass like those one made on a wall to amuse a child. A note on her desk from Ritter said: "Please come up to see me, will you, when you've got a moment? Thanks, R."

She unfolded a map of the Tiergarten on which she had put crosses, in green ink, where the young women, like Marie Rote, had been murdered. Along the bottom she had written the date that the bodies had been found, and these dates had been put along a line, like a ruler. She added May 14, 1930. The newer dates were pushed closer together, and so the scale had the aspect of an accordion that was collapsed on one side. The new cross added to the pattern the others made, a semicircular array spreading from an entrance to the park, and if the lines were drawn from the entrance to each mark, it would be like an enormous shell, a scallop, say, that had been sketched on the map. Armina made an additional cross, a line over the top to make note of the fact that the faces were now being covered up. She added other marks to show what this one had in common with the others, the wound, the stained underwear left in the bushes.

Armina folded up the map. It was possible that some of these killings were the work of the Rings, the Berlin gangs, such as Immertreu, that fought over prostitution territory, which they were never able to hold for long, since they were either gaining or losing strength. Of course, the Rings did political killings, too, at a price. Beyond the door of her office men and women went by, their shadows sweeping across the icy glitter of the glass.

The city had a fascination with the sexual murders of young women, and cabarets had reenactments of some of the most notorious crimes, not to mention that some paintings were done of these assaults. Why, she wondered, were there so many more of them than before? Was there some impalpable quality in the air, some fascination with doing these things, as though the horrible violence of them served as a substitute for some otherwise lacking clarity? But, whatever the reason, she was left to clean up what was left, to go see the parents or boyfriend, to give the news no one ever wants to hear.

She had given this news on her first day at Inspectorate A, a few years before. A woman had been found in the park and the case had been given to her. The other members of the Inspectorate had other things to worry about. Of course, if she failed, which was quite possible, since these cases were almost always difficult, her job and her prospects would be diminished. But her ambition wasn't the issue here so much as the moment, which she felt as a weight, when she realized what had happened after dark in an out-of-the-way place. This sensation didn't vanish but stayed with her like an invisible mist that she could get rid of in only one way—she didn't know who would have more contempt for her if she failed, the men in the Inspectorate or herself: she'd have to admit that the things that she had seen, the evidence of such horrors, were beyond her, and a sense of incapacity was what she feared the most.

So, she began. She talked to the friends of the woman who had been found, interviewed those who had worked with her at a typewriter factory, talked to the merchants in the places where the woman had shopped, just as Armina made a catalogue of everything she had discovered. She did this for the next woman who was found and the one after that, all of them with the same marks, a welt on the neck from a cord, cigarette burns, small puncture wounds. The men in the Inspectorate came into her office, looked at her with the blank expression that detectives have perfected and said, as though through a mask, "What have you got on the cases in the park? Nothing? Hmmpf."

She went home at night to her apartment or sat in a café, always with the sensation that the evidence of her incapacity or the strength of what opposed her was getting close, reducing her to a sort of accomplice, since the man in the park did his part and then she did hers, like partners of some sort.

She found that all of the women had bought lingerie at the same store, a fashionable shop that had an antiquated elegance perfectly mixed with the erotic—young women from all over the city came to shop there. Armina talked to the saleswomen, all of whom had an elegant disdain for her, as though Armina's questions brought an air of the vulgar to a place that was calm, above the reality of what happened to women in an out-of-the-way place.

Armina's father and mother were dead, and when she was troubled, as she was now, she went to see a friend of her father's, a man in his fifties, an engineer, who had a house in a suburb outside of Berlin.

Michael Freelander was a fisherman, and whenever he had a chance to get away he was off to the Mohne, or a river in Spain or Austria to fish for trout. His living room was filled with a neat adornment of feathers and yarn, stored in a cabinet with small drawers like those in a post office, and when Armina came to talk to him, he tied flies, small ones with a cloud of hackle, upright wings, and a gray body, a tail as fine as a baby's eyelashes.

"So," he said. "You've got a woman's shop and that's it?"

"Yes," said Armina.

"And what about the dates," he said.

Armina read the dates from her notebook. Then she sat with the leather-bound thing in her lap.

"Are you worried about your job?" said Michael.

"I'm worried that I can't do it," she said. "That this is beyond me."

Michael asked her to repeat the dates. He wrote them down and asked her to go through them again before he reached to the shelf where he kept his fishing diaries. He turned the pages, looked at a map, then went back to his notebooks. The women had been found in May and June.

"He must be a fisherman," he said. "The hatches of mayflies come at regular times. Not far from here, in Spreeland, for instance, the peaks of various hatches correspond with these dates."

"So," said Armina. "This is how he gets the time? He says he is going fishing?"

"Yes," said Michael.

"He follows a woman from the shop, finds where she lives, and then when he has an excuse, he follows her and takes her into the park."

Michael looked in his fishing diaries, the blue ink of his entries in neat lines, the margins with drawings of mayflies—the next hatch, *Potamanthus distinctus,* was coming at the end of the month. It was a white mayfly, like an apple blossom.

"Week after next," said Michael. "I think you're going to find another."

Armina finished her drink and sat while Michael tied another pattern, and as he used his gray thread, on a bobbin, as he spun some fur for a body, as he set the wings upright, she kept an eye on the certainty of his movements, the precision of his work, just like an engineer making a drawing. It was as though she were watching him make a blueprint for a fly.

At the lingerie shop Armina talked her way through the disdain of the saleswomen, and when they condescended to speak to her, she found that men occasionally were customers, too. These men looked through the displays of underthings and asked about sizes by saying that a girlfriend had the shape and was the height of one of the women who worked in the shop. Armina explained again about what she had seen in the park, and after going through the details, the saleswomen agreed to say to these men that they were interested in fishing, and that they had always wanted to catch a big, cold trout. In the next week, a man who had come in and browsed through the things on display, said that he was a fisherman and he would be happy to teach a saleswoman how to catch a trout. It was all about presentation, he said, about stalking a fish, of trying not to be seen, of being absorbed by the landscape, and, above everything else, not to frighten the fish before the moment came. He left his card with the saleswoman.

Armina watched the man's apartment near the dates when *Potamanthus distinctus* was going to appear on a stream in the Spreeland. The man left his apartment with some leather cases, one of them a leather tube for a fishing rod, and a large gladstone that was just the thing to hold a fishing vest, waders, and a net. But he only went by taxi to the center of the city, where he checked into a hotel. Then he went to the bar, where he had a drink before he went out to a small park, opposite an apartment building, where he waited like a fisherman on a bank who is trying to see a fish.

Everything about his posture, his lack of movement, was mesmerizing— he hardly seemed to breathe, and he didn't flinch at the sounds of a backfire in the street or react to children who chased a ball or a woman who wheeled a baby in a perambulator. Instead, his silent immobility suggested something that coiled, that put itself in a position to gather strength for a strike. He moved his head once to follow the path of a couple, a young woman in a filmy purple dress and a man in a dark suit—the fisherman's eyes followed them with a hungry glow, a brightness that suggested a coal that had been blown into an orange intensity. Then he went back to waiting.

A woman came out of the building he watched. She was well dressed, elegant, her dark hair heavy and trimmed so it fell around her face and was touched with filaments of light. The fisherman stood up from the bench. He followed at a distance, but as the woman walked toward the park, he steadily reduced the distance, as though he were reeling her in. He had an almost perfect instinct for this: as the people on the street became more sparse, he closed in, and at the moment, a brief, almost vanishing instant, when no one else was around and when the park was close by, he took the woman's arm, whispered in her ear, and steered her, with a subdued jerk, into the park.

Armina came into the miasma of terror on the part of the woman who was almost running on the tips of her toes to keep up as the man pushed her: she seemed to think that if she just went along, if she just tried to be nice, or compliant, if she just gave in, everything would be all right. Armina arrested him and found he was carrying a package of cigarettes of the brand she usually found around a woman who had been left in the park, an ice pick (with a tapped handle to give a better grip), and a silk cord.

She was promoted, and the men in the Inspectorate took her to a bar, where they all got drunk, Armina, too. Every now and then one of the men who worked in Inspectorate A asked her for help.

The Fisherman was tried and convicted, but every detail, however horrible, came out at the trial, and given the fascination with this kind of thing, all of these details, every one, were reported in the newspapers. Everyone knew what he had done with an ice pick, the cord, how he had smoked cigarettes and left them where he had done his work. The man had used the cigarettes to make those small marks, but before that he had used the silk cord until the women were almost unconscious, and then finally he got to the ice pick. He had used the cord on himself, too, when he had had trouble keeping an erection. "To keep the hydraulics going" is the way he described it. He had told his wife, a mousy woman with a limp, who sat through the trial and bit her fingernails, that he had gone fishing. "The hatch of *Potamanthus distinctus* is close now," he'd say. "The fishing is going to be good."

Now, Armina realized that the crimes she looked at could easily be done by a man, or men, who were using the details of what they had read about the Fisherman to mask who they were. She knew that sooner or later, they would add a detail of their own, and that was what she was looking for. A new detail. Well, she had a list to begin. She'd keep an eye out for something unexpected: some correlation, like the mayflies, that suggested some actions that took place with motives disguised by the most ordinary event.

RITTER'S OFFICE WAS one flight up. She stopped in the stairwell, in the scent of soap that was used to wash the steps every night, and began to think of an excuse. Ritter had a knack, something like the Moth's: Ritter perceived her in a way that made even her best motives look like ploys, false stances, a ruse of some kind. And the only way to get away from his condescension was to appease him, to do what he wanted, so that he would give her a small, warm, almost friendly smile. Almost. She took some solace in the file that she had in her hand, where she had made a list of the names of men who interested her. And the one woman.

She went through the stairwell door to the hallway and up to Ritter's door. The sound of typing was loud here, too, slow, steady, unstoppable as it went through the details of the events that needed to be recorded in the Berlin Police Department each day. A blunt instrument. Evidence of a desperate struggle. She knocked and pushed the door open, leaning into the oak and glass door with the brass fixtures, the knob seeming bigger than ever.

"Armina," he said. "How nice to see you. Come in."

He came around and closed the door behind her.

"Well, that's better," he said. "Won't you sit down?"

She took the chair that was in front of his desk, sat back, tried to smile.

"How are you doing?"

"I'm fine," she said.

Ritter put a cigarette into his mouth, turned the wheel on a lighter, which made a spark like one from a burning fuse, and the flame looked like a yellow sequin. Armina wished he would come with her to smell the dead leaves, the lingering perfume, to look at the bunched-up skirt. . . .

"They're getting younger," she said.

"That's to be expected," he said.

"There's less time between them," she said.

Ritter flicked his cigarette against an onyx ashtray.

"Can we talk frankly?" he said.

"What other kind of talk is there?" she said.

He smiled.

"Yes, of course. What else is there? What are you doing about the women in the park?"

"I'm looking around," she said.

"That's good to hear."

"I don't think there's a political aspect to this. So, I don't think it's something for you," she said. "The best thing is to look into what is going on with an open mind."

"Yes," he said. "Of course."

The typing from the hall was insistent, as though one letter or number were being typed over and over: 9,9,9,9. She thought of the shape of a young woman at the bottom of a gully, the torn stockings, the pile of yellowing cigarette butts.

"So, who are you looking at? Have you got some names for me?"

She opened the file and took out the piece of paper with her neat handwriting on it.

"Andreas Weber, Alda and Michael Bauer," she said.

"Weber?" said Ritter. "A banker? The sniffer?"

"That's him," said Armina.

"Give him a try," he said.

"I intend to," said Armina. "Edel Arnwolf, Erich Kortig, Josef Hahn."

"Who are they?" said Ritter.

"They go to dump girls," said Armina.

"Hmmmm," said Ritter. "Scum."

"Bruno Hauptmann," said Armina.

"Where did you get that name?" said Ritter.

"I went to the train station," she said.

"The Moth," said Ritter. "He's still there? That's who you talked to?"

"Hauptmann. Bruno Hauptmann," she said, if only to get out of his office and to go about her work. "He lives in Wilmersdorf."

"I know Bruno Hauptmann," said Ritter. "I went to school with him. The *Gymnasium*. The university."

"Maybe you can help me," said Armina.

"Look. Bruno has an organization to help young women get out of the park. That's why he's being accused. Well, don't you see? The dumpy man with the red hair, the Moth, wants to get rid of anyone who would stop girls from working for him. I would have thought you were more adroit than that."

"I think we should look into it," said Armina.

"No," said Ritter. "I can vouch for Bruno. Forget it."

The typing stopped outside. They waited. A secretary ripped a piece of paper out of the carriage of a typewriter. The sound was like someone skinning a deer and pulling the hide away from the meat.

"I'm not so sure about that," she said.

"I am," he said. "Drop it."

"Look," she said.

"There's no looking," he said. "I'll vouch for Hauptmann. That's enough. Who else have you got?"

The paper trembled in her fingers, and as she looked at Ritter she was appalled he could see her anger in such a small gesture. She looked down at the sheet and then at Ritter as she made it stop.

"So?" said Ritter.

"Harvey Becker, Konrad Richter, Otto Mayer," she said.

"Who are they?" he said.

She held the paper while she kept her eyes on him. Was she going to let him push her around, just like that?

"They've hurt their wives," she said. "Put them in the hospital. They're getting worse."

"Good," said Ritter. "Stick with them. That's where you're going to find what you're looking for."

She stood up and waited, certain that if she moved toward the door she would be acquiescing. He didn't look up. She squared her shoulders, waited.

"Well, thanks for coming in. Let me know if you turn up anything else. But, be smart. Forget Hauptmann."

She stood there for a while, but finally she went to the door, certain that just by turning, by moving, some communication had taken place. Well, she would have to find a way to resist, as though it were possible to retrieve that moment in which they had both been so perfectly poised and

when anything was possible. The typing started again and the scent of cigars rose from the floor below.

In her office she opened the map of the park again, smoothing out the
paper, which made a sound like remote thunder, and when she did she
thought of a Russian toast, "To us, fuck them," but then she thought, Who
is "us"? Me and my imaginary correspondent? Stop, she thought, just stop.
You have enough to worry about.

F elix's gray skin added to the effect of his oversize coat. He looked around, from under his brows, as though he wanted to hide the fact that he was taking things in, and then he groomed Gaelle with his nicotine-stained fingers, smelled her underarms, smoothed the dress over her small hips, checked to see that the seams in her stockings were straight. "You've got to watch yourself," said Felix to Gaelle. "Why, you're an expensive item, and you want to look like it." The nicotine stains on his index and second fingers had the shape of a hemisphere.

Armina walked up the avenue and stopped behind him as his fingers touched a button on Gaelle's blouse and then undid it to expose her underwear. Then he said, with his back to Armina, somehow knowing she was there without seeing her, "Why, you must be a cop? What do you want?"

"I'd like some help," said Armina.

"You hear that, my sweet?" he said to Gaelle. "Help." He faced Armina. "You don't think much of me, do you? My skin's gray and wrinkled. So, I must be a punk, right? Isn't that what a cop thinks?"

"I don't think much of anything at all," said Armina.

"Oh," said Felix. "I know what my place is. I've been taught what it is. You won't catch me reaching for anything above my station. Why, look at my leg." He walked back and forth and hit his leg with the flat of his hand. "See? I've been taught."

"A lot of girls are frightened," said Gaelle. "What are you doing about it?"

"That's why I'm here," said Armina.

"Well, well," said Felix. "And you come down here for people like us? For a limping boy and a girl with a scar?"

Felix shook a cigarette out of a blue package with a furtive air, and lit it with a match he struck on his thumbnail. He worked on the cigarette with a quick sucking, the smoke coming out of his nostrils in two long plumes, like a horse breathing in the cold.

"You're going to stunt your growth if you keep smoking like that," said Gaelle.

"Don't make me laugh," said Felix. "That's an old wives' tale." He turned to Armina. "I take what I get. I don't ask for more. People like us, what can we expect? Mercy? Why, Gaelle, wouldn't that be nice?"

"Yes," said Gaelle. "I'd like that."

"We've got a poor man's mercy," said Felix.

"What's that?" said Armina.

"Why, you won't catch me giving an opinion on anything. Oh, no," he said. "I know what's what. And where I'm supposed to stay. I've been taught. You know what these streets are like if you haven't got any money?"

A car came along, slowed down, the driver's eyes on Gaelle. Then it speeded up again and disappeared into the clutter of automobiles.

"Do you ever go with older men?" said Armina.

"So, you want help with Marie Rote?" said Felix.

"That's right," said Armina.

"It's above me to make a comment. But there were times when I had my doubts about Marie Rote. She went with men who were nutters. Why, she'd even go with Crazy Peter."

"She was dumb," said Gaelle.

"Well, that's the way of it," said Felix. "Why, I don't think you can imagine the kinds of people who are around here after dark."

Armina looked at him.

"I think I can," she said.

Felix shrugged. The skin around his eyes was wrinkled.

"Look," said Gaelle. "Let's say a girl helps you. She starts playing around with one of these guys, you know, like the one you're looking for. What if the guy finds out she's just a tool of the cops? What is the guy going to do? How is he going to protect himself?"

"That's what I'm trying to say," said Felix. "It's just me, so you don't have to listen. But playing around with some of these guys in the park is not a smart thing."

"I'm asking for help," said Armina.

Gaelle walked back and forth, her hips sleek in her dress, her shape luminescent in the lights from the cars.

"Let me think about it," she said.

Gaelle turned her face as a challenge: was Armina a snob, a woman who was smug and condescending, who wouldn't even go shopping with someone like Gaelle? And in the gesture, in the odd vulnerability of the moment, Gaelle realized that's just what she wanted to do. They might go to the department stores, look through the lingerie, have lunch in that place where each room had a different theme, a jungle complete with rain, an American Wild West scene, a street in Paris. The fantastical quality of the decorations made Gaelle think that all things were possible, even friendship.

"Let me think about it," said Gaelle. "Do you have a card or something?"

Armina took a card from her handbag. Gaelle passed it over to Felix, who held it by the tips of his fingers, as though it were crawling with germs. He shook another cigarette from the blue package and lighted it, the smoke rising around him in a curling mass.

"So, tell me," said Armina. "What's a poor man's mercy?"

"Cunning," said Felix as he put the card in his pocket.

Gaelle woke in her small apartment and swung her feet onto the floor. Bruises, in the shape of fingertips, were on her thighs and arms, the yellowish green color like a leaf in the fall. She stood in front of the mirror and turned to the side. There were more bruises on her hips. Then she dressed in comfortable clothes that covered the marks and went downstairs and across the street to the park where women took their children to play. A child of three, with blond hair who was wearing a white shirt and brown pants with matching suspenders, came over to the bench where Gaelle sat and played a game of sticks, which turned into marking the sandy path (a river, an island, a foreign country) and then he put out his hands to her to play pat-a-cake, one hit here, on hit there, the touch of his small hands on Gaelle's having a power that was out of all proportion to the moment. He didn't notice the scar, but when she pulled up the sleeve of her shirt to play pat-a-cake, he said, "You got a boo." "Yes," she said. "I guess I do." He went back to patting her hands, first one and then another, and finally his mother came along and took him away, frowning once at Gaelle. "Don't you know better than to frighten children?" she said. Then Gaelle sat on the bench with the marks in the sandy path at her feet, the childish river, the island, the foreign country. The voices of other children who played here came and went with the cadence of birds, their laughter light and almost infectious. Gaelle touched the bruises on her arm and remembered the yellow-leaf quality of those on the inside of her thigh. She decided to go to a bar not far away, a place where she waited in the back for a man who brought opium and morphine from the East. For a moment Gaelle imagined that the boy's map, the one in the sand, was of Afghanistan.

She came out of the park and turned down the avenue.

Aksel leaned against a kiosk on which there were posters for political meetings, advertisements for a cabaret, a picture of a woman in fishnet stockings who winked over her shoulder. He shifted his weight as he kept his eye on her apartment house door, although just when she came out of the park, he turned in her direction.

He wore his white shirt, dark pants, and he had on a coat, too, a brown one that came down below his knees. He looked one way and another and then approached her.

He was taller than she remembered, and he walked next to her with a slight swagger, and as she went along, she felt the lingering buzz of the child's hand and the sting of the accusation that she had frightened him. The boy hadn't noticed her face, and it was only with children at this age that she could be herself. Now, still hearing the mother's words, she turned to this Aksel character. Who did he think he was? Someone to push her around? To accuse her? As though the scar were something she had done wrong? Did he want to make use of her? To have some fun with? Go on, she thought, make your pitch. Maybe I'll show you a trick. The touch of the child's hand lingered, and with that galling sense of accusation, she looked up at Aksel and then right up the street. She didn't know if it was worth letting him have it. Maybe it was better to go to the bar to meet her friend who went to Afghanistan.

She walked a little faster.

"Hey," he said. "Don't be like that. Wait a minute."

It was a cool afternoon, and one of her cheeks was pink, her hair filled with highlights, her lips full.

"I'm busy now," she said.

"Look," he said. "I just want to talk things over."

"What do you want to talk about?" she said.

"Well, I don't know. I just want to talk," he said.

"Sometimes I feel that way. So what?" she said.

"Do you? A young girl like you?" he said.

"I'm not so young," she said.

He looked around.

"I've been thinking about you. All the time," he said.

"You?" she said. "Aren't you interested in perfection? Girls with perfect skin, beautiful hair, long legs, pink cheeks. Classic. Isn't that the word you would use?"

"I just want to talk," he said. "I can't explain it."

"Oh," she said. "It's the forbidden part, isn't it. Well, take a look."

"Don't be like that," he said.

"Go on," she said. "Look if you dare. . . ."

They walked along Unter den Linden up to the Lustgarten, where they climbed the steps of the Altes Museum. Inside they stood in the temple of the Roman gods, the statues of which were arranged in a circle, the messengers, the gods themselves, all on columns. The place had a scent of old stone and dampness, too, as though some essence of the Nile exhibits in the next room lingered around the gods. Gaelle and Aksel sat on a stone bench at the side of the temple, their hips almost touching. Well, she thought, it's too easy with this one. She'd make him pay for the mother's accusation. No one should speak to her like that.

"So, why would you want anything to do with a damaged woman? Isn't that the way you'd think of me?" she said.

She turned the scar to him.

"It doesn't bother me," he said. "There's something in it. Something beautiful."

They looked at the gods and heard the distant and muted sound of people walking in the museum, the echoes suggesting the passage of time and the way distant events lingered.

"You can talk to me," he said. "You really can."

"Just think what your pals will do to me when they get the chance. You know, when they win. With your ideas of perfection. Hmmm. I bet they'd ship people like me to someplace far away."

"Look," he said. "You and I are more alike than you think."

"All right," she said. "Let's put it to the test. Are you ready?"

"Me?" he said. "What kind of test?"

"Make me trust you," she said. "Show me you aren't just getting a cheap thrill out of me. That's what a lot of men do."

"I'm not like that," he said.

"Oh," she said. "You're different? How many times do you think I've heard that?"

"I don't know," he said.

The stone gods put off a damp scent.

"This is a hard city to be alone in," he said.

"You think I'm worried about that?" she said. "Why I've got all kinds of friends."

She faced him and looked from one of his eyes to the other.

"How can I get you to trust me?" he said.

"Tell me something that is dangerous to talk about."

"It means so much to you?" he said.

"I want you to prove this doesn't bother you," she said. She touched her face. "To get you to prove you aren't laughing at me. Or using me. I want something from you."

"You go first," he said.

"Why should I?" she said.

"It's a two-way street," he said.

She swallowed. And yet, in the moment, she had the desire to be honest.

"I keep making mistakes." She blinked. "That's the truth."

They sat quietly in the room of the old, dead gods. He kissed her on her neck and eyes and she moved toward him, into a beam of light that came from the front door of the temple. Then she put her fingers into his hair and pulled him closer. He trembled.

"All right," he said. "I'll make you trust me. I'm not afraid."

She smiled to herself and looked at the gods.

"Something dangerous now. That's the only thing that means anything."

He leaned back, out of the light. Then he turned back to her.

"I'll tell you a secret," he said.

She nodded, her upturned, slick face in the beam of light that came into the temple.

"We have someone in the Soviet embassy, an employee. He's a German, but he works for the Soviets. He tells us everything about the Red Front. How much money they get from Moscow, what they are going to do, where they are going to demonstrate. Then we wait for them. Like shooting fish in a barrel. Why we even know where they are keeping guns."

She swallowed and looked around.

"You didn't expect a real secret, did you?"

"No," she said.

"Nothing so big, right?" he said.

"What's the name of the man who's doing this?" she said.

"Hans Breiter," he said. "I'll even give you his address. Ahnsdorf Strasse. Number fourteen."

Now, as she sat there, she knew that he had put his life in her hands, and as she realized the power of that, she felt warm, more certain, a little happier, but suddenly more afraid, as though she had something she thought she had wanted, but now that she had it, she wasn't so sure. Still, underneath it all, she remembered the way he had kissed her, the weight of the sun as it had come into the circle of gods.

He took her hand.

"Let's just sit here for a moment. I never thought people felt like this," he said.

The scent of the old stone of the gods surrounded them and the miasma of it was a damp smell that Gaelle thought must be the wake that time left behind. Then she put her head back and let the sunlight hit the scar: it was a warm, living caress that felt like hope itself. She had something to work with.

aelle sat with Mani against the wall of the main room of the Red Front's restaurant. She spoke and gestured with her hands, obviously pleading a case. She had made a mistake on the train, that was true, but this was something real, and it was proof that she was up to it, that she could be trusted. That she was needed. She hadn't given up on proving herself and she wasn't a coward, not damaged goods, whose father was a banker. It was up to Mani to see things clearly.

Mani pursed his lips, as though considering something for sale, and then went back to looking at her with that steady evaluation. Usually, he thought, they lasted a little longer than this and they didn't start hanging around with the thugs quite so fast, either. She took out a piece of paper on which she had written: "Hans Breiter. Ahnsdorf Strasse. Number 14." Then she held it, offering it as evidence of how useful she really was.

The white walls had faded to a cream color from cigarettes and the smoke that came from the fireplace at the side of the room. The ceiling fixture made a cone of light that ended in a circle on the floor. Men sat at tables in groups of two or three, all dressed in heavy pants and coats, large shoes, their thick hands holding a glass of beer or rubbing a face as they waited for the next chance, the next street fight, the next piece of action.

Karl sat at a table, and the brandy glass in front of him seemed about the size of a thimble in his fingers. He had a sip, looked at Gaelle and Mani, his doubt about both of them showing as a sour expression. He stood up, too, his size becoming more obvious as he rose from the shadows, as though emerging from the depths. His slightly humped physique seemed coiled more than deformed as he came across the room to Mani and Gaelle. He brought the last of his drink with him.

"What's going on?" said Karl.

Gaelle's pale skin was a little pink. She had washed her hair, and the shine of it looked nice.

Mani showed him the piece of paper.

"So, who's that?" said Karl. He rolled his shoulder, as though sitting still was hard and that these long periods of waiting gave him a cramp.

"This asshole is telling the Brownshirts what we are doing. He works for the Soviet embassy," said Mani.

"The Brownshirts are around a lot of times when we think we've been careful," said Karl.

"This is why," Mani. "Right here."

"We've been getting some rough knocks," said Karl.

"I'm telling you, this is it," said Mani.

Karl finished the last of his drink.

"We've got to protect ourselves," said Mani.

"I get tired of just sitting around," said Karl. "Fights on the train."

Mani turned to Gaelle, who had sat silently, her face appearing like a white flower on a black bough.

"We've got something to do tomorrow," Mani said to Karl. "In the evening."

He held out the paper.

"I know where it is," said Karl.

"Tomorrow," said Mani.

"All right," said Karl. "Fights on trains. Kid's stuff."

"We'll wait in the street," said Mani.

"That's good," said Karl. "When he comes out, I'll take it from there."

"OK," said Mani. "Tomorrow." He looked down at the paper. "You wanted to stop the kid's stuff. Well, now's our chance."

"We don't have to check with anyone?" said Karl. "With anyone in Moscow. Maybe they'd want to know about this."

Mani shook his head.

"I've made a decision," said Mani.

"Good," said Karl. "We're going to be on our own? Separate from the rest of the party?"

"Yes," said Mani. "We can't go on the way we have. We've got to make a decision. No waiting. No playing around. I'm tired of worrying about people coming in here and harassing me about accounting. . . ."

"I did it so you could trust me," Gaelle said to Mani.

"Oh," he said. "I trust you."

Then she went through the browns and grays of the restaurant where men sat at the tables under the yellow cone of light. Karl raised his glass to her in a quick, noncommittal toast. His sudden toast, after his usual patient waiting, had the quality of an insect that had been in a chrysalis and had finally broken the transparent case that had so neatly confined it. He seemed to shimmer there, for an instant, where the oily film on his coat caught the light.

till, Mani hadn't said that he would stick up for her or that she was forgiven for not fighting on the train. He had left her, as he always did,
suspended between what she wanted and what he would give. Why
couldn't she get one man, one group, someone to act in a way that she
could trust? She had dismissed the idea of love, but it still tugged on her,
and now, with a fury at the hope she shouldn't have had combined with
stark experience, she pushed the notion of love into even deeper recesses,
into the outer realm of her thoughts, at the frontier of her mind, which, she
guessed, was like the edge of a bowl, a black one that was turned upside
down. If nothing else, her sense of being betrayed, of not being loved, left
her with the frank notion that someone was going to pay the price. And the
desire for revenge was a sort of love turned upside down, and the more disappointed she was, the greater the impulse to strike back.

Surely, there wasn't anything to be gained in waiting. She showed
Hauptmann's card to Felix.

"You know where this is?" she said.

"You want to go there?" said Felix.

"Yeah," she said.

Even from a distance the banners were visible: they hung down crimson and dark over the windows that had been painted black. At Gaelle's
side Felix limped along, his head going up and down like the head of a
horse on a carousel. He looked straight ahead, his eyes on their destination,
his head pitched forward, as though no matter where he was going, it was
always downhill. Gaelle had put on a dark coat and worn dark shoes, but
somehow, even though she tried, she couldn't look as respectable as she
wanted. She put her hand to her hair, stopped and looked in her pocket
mirror, put on some lipstick. Well, maybe it was a shade too bright, but it

made her look more crisp, more desirable, and that was the most important thing.

The door to the headquarters of the National Socialist Party was halfway open, and when Gaelle pushed it open, she smelled dust. The room was like a recital hall, one where women, in black dresses that were shiny with age, gave recitals with a piano that needed to be tuned. Gaelle could almost see the yellowed sheet music as it was turned from one page to another. Chairs had been arranged in lines in front of the low stage where there was a lectern and a glass pitcher of water that was filled with small bubbles. A man, in plus fours and a white shirt, swept the floor, going between a row of chairs, where he pushed the pile of dust along, making clouds of sparkling bits, and then stopped and brushed it into a pan. Then he moved the next row of chairs into the clean path, and started back, underneath where the chairs had been. The dust, against the black cloth of curtain behind the stage, flickered in the air, where it hung with a golden sparkle.

Felix tried to walk straight up, without limping, but after a few steps he started again. Gaelle touched her hair and went up to the sweeper.

"I'd like to talk to someone," she said. She held out the card. "Is he here?"

The sweeper stopped and looked up, from her to Felix.

"About what?" he said.

"It's sort of private," she said.

"I don't think we want your kind in here," said the sweeper.

"I think someone will be interested in what I have to say," said Gaelle. She stood up straight, put her shoulders back, the bits of dust floating around her as though her perfume were visible.

"Wait a minute," the sweeper said.

He leaned his broom against the stage and went to a door at the side of the room where, if this were a musical performance, a singer and a piano player would emerge to take their places onstage. Maybe, at the end, someone would bring them a bouquet of wilted roses wrapped in florist's paper.

"Did you see the way he looked at me?" said Felix.

"Yes," said Gaelle.

"He's just sweeping out," said Felix. "A big cheese. A great big cheese. I know my place, but who is he?"

"Nobody," said Gaelle. "I don't like the waiting."

"Me neither," said Felix. "I'm going to count to fifty, and when I get there, we go. What do you say?"

Gaelle shrugged.

"All right," she said. "Start counting."

Felix did it by counting chairs, going along and touching one and then another, and after about ten chairs, the sweeper came back and said, "What are you doing there?"

"Nothing," said Felix. "Counting."

"He'll see you now," said the sweeper. "Back in there. Turn right. First door on your left."

The hallway was covered with wainscoting that had been stained dark brown, and an overhead bulb left it covered with a sheen of icy light. It was dusty back here, too, mixed with the scent of disinfectant, the sort of thing that is used in a hospital. Gaelle went along, Felix's head going up and down beside her.

"So," he whispered. "So? What are you going to do?"

Hauptmann sat at the desk, his long arms in shirtsleeves, his waistcoat trim, tight fitting, his long fingers holding a pen that had the shape of an exclamation mark. A ledger was on the desk in front of him, and he had a bottle of ink and a pen, which he held up now, with a drop of ink trembling from the nib. He tapped it against the jar of ink, tap tap, and then finished writing a number that was at the bottom of a column. Then he took a blotter and rolled it over the ink, looked at the impression on the blotter paper, and put the thing down, the entire operation having the air of a man who is grooming himself in public.

"Gaelle," he said. "The champagne girl. Well, I wondered how long it would be. Come in."

Gaelle had her small silver bag with her, and she held it in both hands. Felix looked around the room. More posters, a little yellowed, a coat hung on a hook, a desk lamp that threw a pool of light over the table.

"You asked me for help," said Gaelle.

"Yes," Hauptmann said. "That's right."

"Well, I've come to see you," she said.

"And you want some reassurance from me?" he said.

"Yes," she said.

"We never forget people," he said. "They go into a sort of file, and it's as though there's a list of the things they do. We never forget."

"It's not something that I want to get around," she said.

"Of course," said the man. "You can trust me. Look. They let me do the books. Why, isn't that proof of how I can be trusted?"

"I don't know," said Gaelle.

"So, you want to tell me something but you don't want to tell me? Is that the way of it?"

"Yes," said Gaelle

"Tell him," said Felix.

"Be quiet," said Gaelle.

"How did that happen to your face?" said Hauptmann.

"An automobile accident. Gasoline got on my face and caught on fire," said Gaelle.

"Did it hurt?" said Hauptmann.

"Not like what you'd think," said Gaelle. "Not then."

"I guess something like that would make you cautious," said Hauptmann. "That is, you wouldn't want it to happen again."

Gaelle looked around the room, her lips pursed, as though she had tasted something of uncertain quality.

"Now, now," he said. "Don't get me wrong. I'm on your side."

"Tell him and let's get out of here," said Felix.

"I know something about a man by the name of Breiter. Some people are going to hurt him. From the Red Front."

"When are they going to do that?" said Hauptmann.

"Soon," she said. "I don't know when."

"Not right away?" he said. "Not tomorrow?"

"I don't think so," she said. "He's been telling secrets. He works in the Soviet embassy. He's been telling your side some things."

"I know what he's doing," said Hauptmann.

He wrote on a slip of paper, first dipping the pen into the ink and then scribbling across a piece of scrap newsprint, where the ink bled away from the letters like blood in a bandage.

"OK," he said. "Is that it? Or is there something else?"

"No," said Gaelle. "That's enough."

"All right then," said Hauptmann. "But you're certain. Not right away?"

"I don't think so," said Gaelle. "I don't know."

Gaelle pulled her coat together at the neck, looked around at the posters on the wall, at the man with the ink-stained fingers and the ledger before him, and wished that there was something more to say. Felix looked around, too, but there was nothing but the desk, the chair, the light, and that smell of disinfectant.

"OK," she said. "Remember that I tried to help."

"Of course," said Hauptmann.

"Come on," said Felix. "Let's go."

In the hall Gaelle kept pulling her coat together at the neck, and she tried to walk with her head up, as though if she could just find some dignity, all of this would be all right. Felix tried to make loud noises with his shoes, as though he were heavier than he really was. Then they walked into the room where the man was still sweeping, the dust coming up from the head of the broom like clouds behind trucks on a dirt road.

In the evening, when Gaelle came out of her building to go to work, Karl and Mani were waiting for her. She came through the door and onto the street, and then she pulled back, as though she had forgotten something, but Mani said, "Hey, there you are."

"Hi, Karl," she said. "Mani. How are you doing?"

"We're going to need some help," said Mani. "If I go up to Breiter, he might sense something is wrong. So I was thinking we need you to go along and bump into him. That's better."

"I'll be behind him," said Karl.

"So, that's the way we're going to do it," said Mani. "Come on."

"Wait a minute," said Gaelle.

"Are you going to act like you did on the train?" said Karl.

"No," said Gaelle.

"Good," said Karl.

They took the streetcar, and through the windows the buildings slid by, brownstones with flat facades, at the tops of some of which there were neoclassical details, like a Greek temple, although here and there the buildings were marked with bullet holes from an uprising in the early 1920s. The bullet holes looked like gouges in cake. Gaelle thought about what she was supposed to do: walk up the street, bump into a man, this Breiter, and then he would turn toward her before . . . she wasn't sure what it would be, although she found that she was staring at the bullet holes. She put her hands together and thought that every time she tried to get control of things, this happened. Someone used her.

A building stood at the corner of Breiter's street and an avenue. Karl's head was almost as high as the window of the first floor, his face like a discarded leather suitcase. His eyes, though, were alert, not shiny, almost gray like a slate countertop that has been used for years.

"You don't look like you want to help us," said Mani.

"I'm sorry," she said. Of course, she thought, it is perfect that I am already apologizing.

"You know," said Mani. "We're breaking with the official line. You understand how people are going to feel about that? People in the East. The Soviet Party. So it's important that no one know about this."

"Sure, sure," said Gaelle. She licked her lips. Who were they talking about anyway? Who was in the East? She didn't understand what was going on, aside from the fact that she was trying to make a place for herself, to feel safe.

"Are we ready?" said Karl.

"Are we?" said Mani.

"Sure, Mani," she said. "I'm here, aren't I?"

He looked at her for a moment, as though considering if this was really true.

"Remember," he said to Gaelle. "No one is to know about this."

She swallowed.

"You can trust me, Mani," she said.

"All right," he said. "We've watched. We know that he comes out of his apartment and walks up this way. He has a little dog. A dachshund."

"Which apartment house?" she said.

"I'll show it to you. We'll walk by it," said Mani. "Then we'll wait at the end of the block until he comes out."

Mani and Gaelle started up the sidewalk. Here and there people strolled along, men in gray or brown suits, women in blue and red dresses, all looking forward to getting home. The building Mani pointed out had steps that went up from the street to the front door.

"This is it," said Mani.

"All right," she said.

They turned and started back for the corner. The evening was coming on now, and the sky changed from blue to dark blue, and soon the gray part would come, the stars appearing like light shining through a hole punched in black paper with an ice pick.

"Are you going to be able to do it?" said Mani.

"Sure, Mani," she said. "Sure."

"We don't need you if you are getting windy," he said.

"I'm not that way," she said. "Not really. I may look scared, but that's all it is."

Karl leaned against the building and stared down the street, his eyes swinging back and forth with the regularity of a lighthouse beacon. It was getting cool now, and Gaelle hugged herself, the touch of her own hands surprising her with their false comfort. Then she looked up the street at the people moving in such an ordered way. She wished that she could stop a man on the street to ask him what he was doing, as though a definite piece of knowledge would be useful in the face of chaos. After all, something was about to happen here, not the frank, vital moment of birth, but the thoroughly mysterious fact of death. She looked around and felt all the more frail, really, controlled by someone else, although this was balanced by an equal and panicky desire to turn and run up the street. She leaned against the building, if only to feel that there was no one behind her and that at least she had cut down the world around her by half.

"Do you want a cigarette?" said Mani.

"Sure," she said. "Maybe that will help. It's hard to wait like this."

Mani shook one out of his package. She lit it and stood there between the two of them. Then she tried to think of anything else, or at least to believe that this would all be over soon, that time was going to take care of everything here, and if she could just be patient, if she could just let things flow along, she'd be done. Then she tried to think of something pleasant, but she could only recall how she had gone with Aksel to a hotel and brazenly taken off her clothes to shock him, to take control of the circumstances, and how he had sat there on the side of the bed, reaching out for her, and saying, "Oh, you smell so good. It is like something I already know."

"There he is," said Mani.

The man they were waiting for came out of his building and stood at the landing at the top of the stairs. He wore a round hat with a brim and a brown overcoat. Then he started going down the stairs, one hand held out as though he were trying to show how tall a child was. About this high. Then Gaelle realized he was holding a leash. He was walking a dog. The man came down to the sidewalk and turned toward Mani, Karl, and Gaelle.

"Wait," said Mani. "We want to run into him about thirty yards from this corner. All right?"

"Sure," said Gaelle.

"Maybe you should ask for a light," said Karl.

"No," said Mani. "Just bump him. That's enough."

Gaelle tried to let time flow, to give in to this, but in the midst of it she felt like someone clawing up a crumbling precipice, and every time she thought she had her hand on something solid, it turned to dust. This panic was an airy feeling in her chest and stomach, as though some feathery thing were moving around inside.

The man was about forty, a little overweight. As he got to the street, the door of the house opened and a woman came out and said, "Don't forget the bread." The man looked back and nodded, not saying a word, and came along the street in a steady, thoughtful, and oddly clunky way, as though he were carrying a couple of heavy bricks in his pocket. He lumbered forward, the dog out in front, excited to be outside. It tugged on the leash and then abruptly sniffed at a spot before tugging again, although it didn't seem to bother the man. He acted as though the dog were part of his own anatomy.

Gaelle made out his face, which was not so much different from that of any man she saw on the street, or whom she had taken into the park. She thought about that part of it for a moment, amazed that she had allowed all of those things to happen, those nights when she was trying to prove she was someone other than who she was. Maybe this man had been one of her customers. Mani said, "All right. Just bump into him and move to the left."

"The left," said Karl. "Don't get confused."

"You don't look so good," said Mani.

"Maybe he'll think she's sick," said Karl.

"It'll all be over in a minute," said Mani. "Just remember that."

"I like it when it takes a little extra time," said Karl. "Like here. Look. The dog is doing his stuff."

He shook his head, as though considering the fact that the last thing this man was going to ever see was his dog taking a crap. Or, almost the last thing.

"All right," said Mani.

Gaelle started walking. The buildings were fading from the last blue color of the day to a gray, speckled quality, and here and there the lights came on in a domestic glow. How wonderful it would have been to go into one of these houses, so much like her own, and to come into a living room that smelled of dinner, of beer, of strudel, of sausage. And what, she thought, had she really wanted? She had been alone. She had wanted safety.

It was as though the entire street, the colors, the people, all had no use for her at all, and that she was somehow unwanted, despised, outside warmth or concern. She was by herself, and she knew it. She looked up at the windows, the domestic light leaving her with some wild hope that this would stop.

He wasn't that fat, really, and her collision with him was almost a relief.

"Herr Breiter?" she said.

"Yes?" he said.

The dog stopped for a moment and turned to look at her, just like its master. Gaelle stepped to the left. The man looked at her, his back to Karl.

"Do you want something?" he said.

Karl took another step. The dog started barking, not at Gaelle, but at the large man in the rough coat who appeared in silhouette against the windows. Karl seemed to be reaching for something in his pocket, and for a moment the dog lunged forward, as though it thought Karl was about to extend a treat. The man Gaelle had bumped, however, watched her. Then Gaelle took another step, hearing that sound and then feeling Mani's hand as he took her by the arm.

All three of them went by Breiter, who lay in the street as though he had a nosebleed and thought this was the best thing to do, the color of the blood in that fading light like liquid soot, or oil. The dog went on barking, lunging from side to side, but it was still confined by the leash. And when Gaelle passed the door of the apartment building that Breiter had come out of, she looked up and saw, to her horror, that the door had opened, and the woman who had appeared before stood there again, her hand to her face.

Then the woman in the doorway ran down the steps, her hair already in disarray, her heavy figure moving from side to side. She threw herself down next to the man on the sidewalk and tried to pull him up, to hug him, and then rocked back and forth, closing her eyes.

"Oh, no," she said over and over. "Oh, no. We didn't even really need the bread."

Gaelle and Mani walked up to the corner, where Karl glanced at them once and turned away, going down the avenue without saying a word. Mani said, "I'm going down this way. You keep going straight. It's better to split up."

She waited while a streetcar went by with that little *fitzing* as the machine got electricity from the overhead wires. She was mesmerized by the sound and the smell of ozone. Odd, and yet familiar. That was what she was left with now as she remembered the way the man fell, the barking dog, the look on the face of the woman who came to the door. Then she crossed the street, putting one hand to her face, and went along the next block, where the domestic light was more troubling than before, since she seemed forever excluded from it.

There was a café on the corner and she went inside and sat at a marble table and had a fruity schnapps. She had been wrong about something. Before this evening she thought that she had been lonely, just as her vanity had been injured when people used her and asked her to do things without caring about her, but these self-pitying moods were nothing compared to the way she understood things now. It was as though she had been excluded from everything, and that she was a stranger here, in this place, in this city, everywhere, and the people who could most understand her, or at least knew what she had done, were the ones she wanted to see least of all. She sat there, having a drink, until a man smiled at her. After a while he came over and asked if he could buy her a drink, and she said, "Yes. You can. Sit down."

"Nice evening," he said.

She looked at him for a moment.

"I guess it depends on your point of view," she said.

"I always like this time of night," he said. "Just when the lights come on. It's all soft and friendly."

She bit her lip.

"Not always," she said.

Armina unfolded the map of the park and began to go through it in an orderly way, from one rectangle made by the folds to another, and as she tried to think, to concentrate, to come up with some detail that while seeming mundane was actually filled with meaning, a shadow swept up the frosted glass of her door, like a vulture spreading its wings. She thought of Gaelle, who seemed to be suspended on a tightrope: maybe she would help. Maybe she wouldn't. And this uncertainty left Armina with a sense of claustrophobia: all of her effort to stop what was happening to young women in the park came down to decisions like that. It left Armina with a constant turmoil, as though something coiled in the darkness of her interior life.

Ritter stood in the doorway, a small piece of paper in his hands. Behind him, in the common room, a detective struck a match with a long scraping sound of it on his shoe and put a cigar to his mouth, which he drew on until the end made a cherry-colored button. The piece of paper in Ritter's hand trembled.

"Can you come with me?" he said. "I need some help."

They went down the stairwell, switching back and forth at the landings, and Armina felt this downward tug as something familiar, like the way water swirls around a drain. A black car was waiting at the curb, and Ritter got in, then Armina, and finally Linz. Both Ritter and Linz seemed uneasy, like men with a bomb in a suitcase. Every now and then the driver went around a cart that was pulled by a horse and piled high with furniture. Even in the car they could smell the countrified odor of the horses.

The avenue ahead of them stretched away, under the web of the wires for the streetcars, the rails of the tracks shiny, the bricks of the road covered with a filmy residue that came from the smokestacks in the city. Ritter swallowed and looked around, once at her, once at Linz, and then up the avenue.

"Where are we going?" said Armina.

"A friend was killed. Shot in the street," said Ritter.

"Oh," said Armina. "A friend."

"A good friend," said Ritter.

"It helps to know who someone was," said Armina. "That is if we're going to find out who did this. Do you want my help or don't you?"

Ritter looked down at his white hands, and in his contemplation of the manicured nails, the knuckles, the small, light hair on the back of his fingers, he obviously thought about whether it was a good idea to tell the truth.

He turned to Linz.

"Who do you think he was?" said Ritter.

"Well, he worked for the Soviet embassy," said Linz. "I knew him a little bit. Saw him from time to time. He was supposed to be with the trade section, but I doubt that."

"Yes," said Ritter. "That's right. So, who killed him?"

"Some thug," said Linz. "Someone on the right. They like doing that to anyone who works with the Soviets."

"I don't think so," said Ritter. "I think someone else did it."

Linz shrugged.

They pulled up to the sidewalk where Hans Breiter lay on his back, his nose bleeding, some silvery drool coming from his mouth. Uniformed policemen kept curious people away, although there weren't so many of these now, since the novelty of a dead man was less than it used to be.

Breiter's wife broke through the door of the house and ran down the steps, pulling at her hair as she pushed her way through the Schutzpolice who made a circle around the body.

"Oh, Jesus," said Ritter.

Through the legs of the men in uniform, Armina saw a bright rill, like a red snake that stretched from the man on his back to the gutter.

Armina got out of the car.

"Wait," said Ritter, gesturing to Breiter's wife. "You don't want any of that. Let someone else deal with her."

"Come on," said Armina. "Let's talk to her."

The street had the forlorn emptiness that a traveling circus leaves behind when it folds up its tent and moves on to the next town. Armina got out of the car and tried to take the woman's arm, but Frau Breiter pulled away from her and started running up the block. Frau Breiter scratched at her own face, and when she turned back, to take one last look at the man in the street, it appeared as though she were wearing war paint.

"Oh, no. Oh, no. I told him. How many times did I tell him? Oh, no. Oh, no. Oh, no," said Breiter's wife. The Schutzpolice walked her back up to her apartment, where she climbed the steps, her hand reaching out for the stone banister with a gentle touch as though she were saying good-bye to something. Then she started again, "Oh, no. Oh, no. Oh, no."

"I wish she'd shut up," said Linz. He looked down at the man in the street.

"Let's start by going door to door," said Armina. "Before people forget. I'll go along here, directly across the street."

Linz and Ritter looked at each other, thinking it over.

"Wait a minute," said Ritter.

Armina glanced at the buildings and guessed that there were probably thirty people, maybe more, who had seen or heard something. As she looked around, she noticed that the two men were still looking at her.

"Let's say he was up to something," said Ritter.

"Like what?" said Linz.

"Oh," said Ritter. "He might have been selling a little information. You know, like how much money the Red Front gets from Moscow. Things like that."

"The son of a bitch," said Linz.

Ritter shrugged.

"Maybe he was a patriot," said Ritter. "And, do you think the embassy would want it to get around that they had hired someone like that? Why, some heads would roll, wouldn't they?"

"Maybe," said Linz.

"I think you better check with your colleagues," said Ritter, "before we get into this."

The line of blood, like a line on a road map, turned one way and another, around the cobbles on the sidewalk until it came to the edge of the curb and there it ran straight down into the gutter, where it made a darkening pool. Linz looked at it and then turned up the street.

"Do you think that maybe someone in the Red Front found out about him?" said Ritter.

"I don't know," said Linz.

"I think it's best to keep quiet about this," said Ritter. "It's not in anyone's interest. Who knows where it could go, a thing like this? A guy in the embassy doing all kinds of things. Surely, it's in your interest to be quiet. Let me worry about mine. Leave it that I am protecting a friend's memory."

Linz kept his head down.

"So, we have a deal," said Ritter.

"I can't speak for everyone," said Linz. "But I think so. It's obvious that having this come out isn't going to help anyone in the Soviet embassy."

Ritter turned to Armina.

"We're going to let this go," said Ritter. "As a favor to Linz here. Breiter was a spy. He got what was coming."

"But I thought he was a friend of yours," said Armina.

"When you think about it," said Ritter, "that's a complicated word. At least I can protect his memory. Who has to know what he was up to? Let's just say I have reasons of my own to be circumspect."

"What reasons are those?" said Armina.

"Linz?" said Ritter. "Is it all right if I say a little something?"

"Yes," said Linz.

"The Soviets and the German army did some business. Breiter worked it out. That's all. No one wants that to be known. Not the Soviets . . ."

"No," said Linz. He shook his head. "No. We want to say nothing."

"And not us," said Ritter. "Who wants it to get around that the German army and the Soviets were partners?" He shuddered a little with some melodrama, but underneath all that, he had a genuine chill.

"Breiter could have been up to all kinds of things," said Linz. "Who knows where it could go? Children. Young women. He knew all kinds of people."

"He was that kind of guy," said Ritter. "Couldn't keep his mouth shut . . ."

The body in the street seemed to become even more still, as though life departed in a slow process, like evaporation.

"Maybe it's even a good thing," said Linz.

"So," said Armina. "You want to do nothing about this? You drag me out here and then you decide you don't really want to know."

"Calm down," said Ritter.

"Get lost," said Armina.

"What?" said Ritter.

"You heard me," said Armina.

They all turned and looked at Hans Breiter.

"There's nothing to be gained," said Ritter. "Don't you see?"

"Leave it alone," said Linz. "Sometimes it's best to do nothing."

"So, it's just us," said Ritter. "And what are we going to say?"

This was, or so it seemed to Armina, an ordinary block of gray buildings, solid, even fat stoops, cobbles in the sidewalk, bay windows, and in the distance clouds at the end of the street where the sky could be seen. Yet, to Armina, it seemed to shimmer, precisely as if it had been a hundred degrees, and in the rising heat, which gave the air a metallic, silver finish, as though it were vaporized glycerin, every brick, every window, the brass doorknobs, the cars on the street with their lines of chrome, the occasional iron fence all seemed to undulate in a way that was almost impossible to see. And along with that Armina had the sense of lightness, of being disconnected from gravity, and this hideous freedom left her almost frightened, since it was a sign of just how angry she had become. No, she thought, that's not heat. Not exactly.

She turned to face Ritter.

"Are you all right?" said Ritter.

"No," she said.

"Now look," he said. "Act like a grown-up."

"And you condescend to me, too," she said. She found that she was touching her handbag to find her pistol and then she was glad that she didn't have it.

"Leave this alone," said Ritter.

"And the woman in the park," said Armina. "That, too. Even though I think we should look at Hauptmann."

"I told you about that," said Ritter.

"So what?" she said.

"I'm warning you," said Ritter. "I have my limits. . . ."

"Your limits," she said. "Well, I suppose you do. But I want to tell you something, too. I have mine."

They stood opposite each other. They were the same height, and their noses were close together. She could smell the soap he had shaved with in the morning.

"I want to look at Hauptmann," she said. "I've got someone to help me."

"Who's that?" said Ritter.

"A girl who works in the park," said Armina. "Gaelle. She's got a scar."

"Has she agreed?" said Ritter.

"I'm working on it," said Armina.

Cars went by in the street with a sad puttering. An ambulance arrived, and the men got out with a stretcher. Ritter watched as Breiter was strapped down, covered up, then lifted into the air, and this moment of levitation, the awkward swaying of a man on a litter, seemed to be an essential part of a man's disappearance, his airy departure. And as Breiter vanished into the back of the ambulance, Ritter shrugged, as though that were the end of it. Some blood was in the street, but that would be gone soon, too, and then no sign would exist at all. Then Ritter shrugged and turned away, his shape going back to his car, where he got in, closed the door, and spoke to the driver. The car pulled away, and he didn't look back.

elix put soap into the sink, added water, held Gaelle's stockings by their tops, and slowly let them into the sink, the feet first so that the champagne-colored lingerie folded into the layer of bubbles. He took his time, since this chore had a quiet intimacy about it, especially with the scent of her soap. He was curious about the delicacy of the material, and as it got moist under his fingers, he was surprised at his sudden gentleness. He had always wondered what a man who wore armor felt like when he stepped out of it, and now he understood. Like a turtle out of his shell. He wasn't keeping his place, and he knew it. His place was the dark, where he could get those young women to trust him: that was cunning, how he used his limp, his youth, his lousy skin to seem as though he wasn't a threat at all.

He pulled the retractable clothesline from its holder, which was like a tin yo-yo, and stretched it from one tiled wall to another. Then he sat down on the side of the tub. The soap bubbles broke and reminded him of the slight tick of wet lips as they opened to give a kiss. This wet popping was like everything he didn't have but craved, a delicate touch, an understanding caress. Was it possible that one touch from another human being could make everything different? He would have been embarrassed to admit it, but he thought this was the case. He put his nose into the bubbles. It made him more certain than ever. It reminded him of the scent of Gaelle when they first started fresh in the evenings.

Ah, he thought, stop thinking like that. Do you want to get soft? There are two kinds of people in the world: those who dish it out and those who take it.

Gaelle lay on her bed on her stomach, her back bare, the dimples in her hips showing below her waist. The dimples were so deep they looked as though a small diamond could disappear in one of them. She stirred in her

sleep, vaguely restless, which was what the opiates did to her. Restless and
warm. She rolled over and opened her legs, as though offering herself. Felix
sat on the tub and watched her from the bathroom. The sun never touched
her skin, and now it looked so white as to be like the moon, powdery, pale,
and it made her seem bathed in light. Felix was attracted to that as much as
anything else, as though spending a few moments with her was a way to get
out of the darkness of the park. What he wouldn't give to be ordinary and
to have a chance to start again.

He had never slept with a woman in a normal way, and he guessed this
was because he was shy, or because he didn't know how to ask. But maybe it
wasn't a matter of asking, so much as being obviously asked by a woman,
and how did that happen? Or how did you get someone to hint that it
would be all right if you asked? How could he be so cavalier about negotiating a price for her, walking right up to the cars in the dark, sticking his
head in and judging what he could get, but now as she lay there and he
wanted to ask for himself, he felt oddly ashamed. Keep your place, he
thought. Don't ask. But how could he get out of that horror, those hours
when he appeared to be vulnerable in the park and then took his revenge?
He wanted to get down on his knees in front of Gaelle and say, Please,
please. Let me come into the light, let me touch your skin. Let me get away
from what I am.

It was possible to come up with some money to offer her, but he
didn't think that was the right thing to do. The breaking bubbles, his attempt to be close to her by washing her clothes, the tenderness with which
he touched the stockings, had nothing to do with money. Could you receive the touch that changed you forever, that made you hope for an almost
impossible connection between you and another human being, by spending money for it? And then he wondered if she would be offended. He
hoped that she wouldn't be, and yet he didn't want her to think of him as
another one of those assholes in a car with a couple of bills in hand.

This led him to wonder just how he did want her to see him. Innocent, he thought. I want her to see me as someone who hasn't been turned
into something . . . like what I am. And what's that? he thought. Someone
who knows what's what and can take care of himself. That's what. Still, for
the moment, maybe she could see him as being like the young men he had

seen who were on their way to the *Gymnasium.* Full of possibilities. Not hurt.

He let the mystery of her attraction dismiss everything else: he felt her tugging him toward her, as though she were some massive celestial object. He sat there, glancing at her open legs, and then tried to turn away, but he couldn't keep his eyes away from her for long. He wanted her to like him. He guessed it was washing the stockings that got him thinking this way, and once he started in this soft way of thinking, it was hard to stop. It felt good. Well, he wanted to be a team with Gaelle and for them to depend on each other. He wanted her not to touch him like she did those men who paid her money, but with real feeling, with consideration, and love. But this was something that was as mysterious as sex. In fact, he had to admit, he was more mystified by the possibilities of love than anything else. He knew it by its absence. There was something missing in his experience, and it was so large as to make him feel almost panicky, but it wasn't a panic that could be relieved. It just came up to the surface and made him squirm and then disappeared again. It left him like this, facing this woman, desperate to ask for something he didn't think he could ever have.

He turned back to the sink and let the water out, the stockings collecting in the bottom like some drowned thing, like a delicate creature from the bottom of the ocean. They had the texture of an oyster, particularly the lace at the top. This was as close as he ever got to being affectionate with her, and so he took his time, being careful with her stockings, as though if he rinsed them gently and hung them up with dedication, he was getting closer to her. Finally he rinsed them one last time, hung them up over the line above the tub, and then he sat there on the porcelain side of it and listened to the steady dripping. She lay there, one leg open, her body seeming muscular and trim, her ribs showing, her small breasts seeming impossibly innocent, girl-like and sad here, too, given what she did every night. He thought that maybe he would like to lie next to her, just to feel warm.

He took off his shoes. His pants, underwear, and shirt. He tried to think of her as he was supposed to, that is, as a woman who worked in the nightlife of Berlin, who came home, smelling of the twenty men she had slept with, needing to bathe, her underwear stiff with semen, her breath smelling of wine. Then he limped to the edge of the tub, sat down, and put his head in his hands. He wanted to think of her this way, but it was impossible. He sat there, cursing himself for being such a sap and so ridiculous, but she kept pulling him toward her. He sat there, on the verge of tears: how could he get across to her? It was difficult because he couldn't even say to himself what he wanted exactly, but he knew the first thing was to lie down on the bed, just to be next to her, to feel her skin against him. If she only knew how much good she could do him. Why, he could start over. He could love her. He thrilled at the words. He could emerge from his old self and drop the monstrous as though it were nothing more than a coat. He would be new.

He stepped out of the bathroom. It was cold in the room, and he was amazed that she didn't feel it. He got into bed with her. She turned and mumbled. He lay next to her, and as she turned and pushed against him, he was embarrassed that she would feel it so obviously, sticking at her, so he turned on his back. The warmth between the two of them was a substance he had only dreamed of, a sweet feeling that he had anticipated once when he had been in a church and seen a painting from Italy, with the clouds illuminated by the most benign sun. He put his lips next to her and whispered, "Gaelle."

Gaelle what? he thought.

He got up and went back into the bathroom and looked at himself in the mirror. His gray face, his lousy teeth, gray eyes and gray-blond hair, his prematurely aged expression betrayed the brutality of his needs. It was obvious even to him. He was so needy, so hungry that he was deformed by it. He didn't know which he hated the most, that he was this way or that it could be seen so clearly. He wanted her to break down that isolation and to have the bad feeling go away. God knows there was enough of that bad feeling in the park. And why was he letting go now? Didn't he have the strength to do what he had to do, to live without love or anything like it? He stood in the bathroom, feeling alone.

"What are you doing?" Gaelle said.

She stood next to him, then pushed him out of the way and sat down on the toilet. He heard the small tinkling noises and then she wiped herself and stepped to the bidet and washed herself off.

"I don't know," he said. "I'm acting funny, like I'm going to cry or something."

She looked right at him, then as she dried herself with a towel, she went back to bed, glancing at him once over her shoulder.

"Come lie down with me," she said.

He walked into the room and sat on the bed and then got under the covers. She turned him over and lay behind him.

"Let's just lie like that," she said.

"I never, you know . . . ," he said.

"What are you trying to say?" she said.

"I don't know anything about it," he said. "About doing it."

"Well, you're going to have to wait," she said.

"Why?" he said.

"I don't know," she said. "I just want to have you warm here like that. OK?"

"I washed your stockings," he said.

"Did you?" she said. "Well, that's sweet."

"I did a good job," he said.

"Thanks," she said.

He lay next to her, feeling the warmth between them.

"You know why I like you?" she said. "You can adapt to anything."

"Maybe," he said.

"Sure you can," she said.

"I want to . . . ," he said. "You know. With you."

She shook her head. Then she rolled over, and he curled up behind her. She could feel it against her, but she pushed it away.

"No you don't," she said. "Not with me."

She sat up a little and showed him her face. She looked very tired now, pale, as though she hadn't seen the sun in a long time.

"You think I'm too much of a rat," he said. "Just a convenience. I can wash your stockings and get you things, but that's it."

He stood up at the side of the bed, a thin, sixteen-year-old boy with an old face. Then he turned toward her dressing table and picked up a bottle that he threw against the wall, the thing shattering in a wet and glassy pattern.

"Stop it," she said. "What's gotten into you?"

He went on looking at her.

"It means so much?" she said. He picked up another bottle and threw it, the glass shattering. She looked at him with that speculative glance she turned on the men who paid her. "Come on."

Then he sat down at the edge of the bed and put his head in his hands. She reached out for his back and felt him sobbing. After a while she heard him say, and felt the intensity of the words in his back, "I'm sorry. I'm sorry."

Finally, he pulled away, went into the bathroom and got dressed. He got a broom and a dustpan and started to clean up the glass. She sat there, watching him, touching her face and from time to time biting her lip. Then she said, "OK. Let's forget it."

He finished cleaning up, and then she made him sit down next to her.

"You're all I've got," she said.

"I know," he said.

"I need a friend," she said. "That's all."

He nodded.

"Come on. Come over here," she said. "It only takes a minute."

He looked at her and shook his head.

"No," he said. "No. I know my place."

"I hurt your feelings," she said.

"No," he said.

Then he started crying like a boy of six who had spilled his ice cream. He sat at the edge of the bed, heaving, eyes closed, face collapsed.

"I'm sorry," he said. "I didn't mean anything."

He put his head into her naked lap, and she felt him sobbing against her.

"Oh, baby," she said. The pupils of her eyes were very small. She glanced around the room as though it were vaguely confusing. "It will be all right. We'll make the best of it. We'll be friends. I'll trust you," she said.

She felt him shaking his head against her naked thighs.

"I didn't mean anything," he said.

"I understand," she said.

"No you don't," he said. "I want you to like me."

"Sure," she said. "I like you. I really do."

He started crying all the harder. She sat there with his head in her lap and smoothed down his hair.

"Don't be like that," she said.

"OK," he said. "OK. Just give me a minute. I'm all messed up. I get all screwed up. It's hard to describe."

"Look," she said. "I can take care of you in a minute. There's nothing to it, really."

He shook his head against her thighs. No.

"Maybe some other time," she said.

"I don't think so," he said. He got up to wash his face, and in the bathroom, as he splashed himself with water, he smelled the scent of lavender. Then he stood there, looking into the mirror, watching the change in his gray expression, the constant stiffening of his features as he assumed his previous threatening look, his eyes the color of pewter under his brows. That was better, he thought. Look what happens to you if you are like a turtle without a shell. He'd stick with what he knew: looking frail and helpless but waiting for his chance to use the cord, the sharpened ice pick. Why, he stood right at the edge: he could let himself go, and the farther he fell, the bigger he became, and this attraction, this increasing scale was like a dream of perfection. No one could touch him, not in this pursuit of the darkness and the glistening depths where those shapes moved with such promise. Nothing could compare with that, and if he had a chance he would go to the museum of antiquities, where he could stand, seemingly frail and injured, but equal to everything that had been built up over thousands of years: that was the promise of the dark. Why, he was like an angel, a dark one to be sure, but he could feel the beating of those wings, which had such power and which left behind such cold wind.

Mani stared at the cracks in the wall of his room with a new interest, since every object, the lamp by his bed, the gray sheets, his writing paper and pen, his few books, had undergone a metamorphosis since the business in the street with Breiter. Before they had been neutral, or a little grubby, but now they seemed to accuse him for being impulsive. And he hadn't done it to get ready to fight the thugs in Berlin so much as he had wanted a distraction from the accounting. He stood up and looked in the box where he kept the receipts that were stained by the cockroaches, yellowed by having been left in the sun, the ink smeared by beer and wine he had applied, as though spilled, to make them look more authentic. They were poor things, he thought, and he had staked his life on them. The paint on the wall of Mani's room had faded from its original color, a froglike green, to the pastel of a new leaf, and he sat with the receipts in his hands and looked at that washed-out color, as though it were evidence of how time—that Judas—went to work to betray secrets, to reduce strength, to leave people vulnerable. The man from Moscow was in the city, and Mani knew it.

That slight rustle behind the plaster was just a rat, wasn't it? He thought that he should get a large water glass so that he could put it against the door or the walls to hear better what was happening outside. He told himself he'd have to stop biting his lip, too. It would give him away. Then he looked down at his hands and saw that his fingernails had been bitten down to almost nothing.

Then he thought, That's not a rat. That's someone coming.

A knuckle tapped against the door. At the same time, he heard another sound, which was actually a rat in the wall, and for a moment he waited, hearing the two sounds come together right where he sat at the edge of his bed. Was he going to pretend he wasn't here or go open the door? He wished he was able to make up his mind and stick with his decision, whatever it might be. The most important thing was to survive, to look for the opening, to take it.

He opened the door about an inch and saw Kathleen, the woman who ran the kitchen downstairs. She was in her late forties with a sunburned face, gray hair, and blue eyes. Her lips were close to his, almost as though she was going to give him a kiss, and then she whispered, "Someone downstairs is asking for you."

"Who?" said Mani.

"I don't know," said Kathleen. "I've never seen him before."

"OK," said Mani.

"OK what?" said Kathleen.

"OK. OK," said Mani. He swallowed. "I'll come down."

"I don't like the looks of him," said Kathleen.

She shrugged and turned back into the hall, going away with a diminishing scratching sound as she shuffled her feet along the floor and then went down the stairs. Mani closed the door and dressed, and he kept thinking, as much as he resisted it, that the rat was the sound of his lies, his fraudulent accounting being revealed for what it was.

In the restaurant Karl sat in his usual corner, enormous, humped over the table, nursing a brandy, his head bent over his hands, which were clasped together. He looked up, though, when Mani came into the room, and with the slightest gesture, the lifting of one scarred brow, the slight movement of his shaggy head, he seemed to say, Look out. I mean it.

The man from Moscow sat at a table near the rear of the room. From his vantage point he could see the door to the street and the one from upstairs. On the table in front of him he had a small cup of coffee, which his fingers touched from time to time, although he didn't drink from it. His entire attitude was one of quiet, stern caution and infinite patience. His fingers were beautiful.

"Mani?" said the man from Moscow.

"Yes," said Mani.

"Sit down," said the man from Moscow.

"Who are you?" said Mani.

"Schmidt," he said. "Gerhard."

He held out his passport, which Mani looked at for a moment. No one was better than the people in Moscow at making false documents, and this one was one of the best. He turned it over in the light, admiring the workmanship, the paper, the ink, the stamps, the signatures. The smell. Maybe it was real. Much better than the box of stained receipts upstairs.

"Well, Herr Schmidt," said Mani.

Herr Schmidt wore a dark jacket. His topcoat and hat were on the chair, and the hat looked like a brown duck that had just been shot. Next to the man's foot, on the floor, there was a small leather suitcase.

"So, how was the trip from Moscow?" said Mani.

"Oh, fine," said Herr Schmidt "You can watch the country go by. You can concentrate. You can think things over."

Mani sat down. He wanted to have some coffee, to wake up, to be right. It was almost as though the man had been waiting for him to come down here, half asleep. The way prisoners were awakened in the middle of the night. Kathleen, though, was in the kitchen. Was it worth going in there to get some coffee, or would it just show that he was vulnerable, not alert?

The features of "Schmidt" were angular, thin, and his eyebrows were prominent so that his eyes were shadowed, but not completely, since there in the dark some of the overhead light was reflected. It was like looking into a well by moonlight. Deep, with a little glow in the distance.

If Mani could just have a cup of coffee.

"Here," said the man. He pushed the cup over. "Have mine."

"That's all right," said Mani. "I'll get some in a minute."

"Are you sure?" said the man. "Oh, here she is. One coffee for Mani. Isn't that what you want?"

"Yes," said Mani.

Gerhard Schmidt had been right about the coffee, and this seemed to reassure him. He knew, or so he seemed to say, what Mani wanted. Mani looked around the room, caught Karl's eyes. Karl shrugged. That's the way it begins, he seemed to say.

Kathleen brought the coffee in a small cup and put it down.

"You take it the way I do," said Schmidt. "Bitter."

Mani had a sip, hoping the caffeine worked quickly and that he could shake off his lassitude, that feeling of gravity being stronger than usual.

"So," said Mani. "How are things in Moscow?"

"Excellent," said Herr Schmidt.

"Here, in Berlin . . . ," said Mani.

"I know where we are," said Herr Schmidt with a smile.

"Yes," said Mani. He swallowed. "We've heard about some arrests and interrogations in Moscow."

"Of course," said Herr Schmidt, but that's all he said. Then they sat together in silence.

"What do you want?" said Mani.

They drank their coffee for a while. Mani wanted to say nothing, or as little as possible, and he realized that the man opposite him was trying to get him to give away some small, exquisitely telling detail. This made Mani more reluctant, since even small talk could get him into trouble. Maybe particularly small talk, since he wasn't on guard when he indulged in it. That was the danger. Even your shield could cause you trouble. Maybe he should offer the accounting now. If he did that, maybe it wouldn't be looked at, just filed away, like a ticking bomb. No, he thought, keep your mouth shut.

"Let's not worry about Moscow," said Schmidt. "It's done. The interrogations, the arrests. That's over. It isn't our concern anyway."

"All right," said Mani.

"I wanted to tell you that we have been watching your work," said Schmidt. "Even the chairman knows your name."

The Boss, thought Mani. This should have been an honor, but Mani saw the room brighten with terror.

"Does he?" said Mani.

"Oh, yes. He said he had heard good things about Mani Carlson in Berlin. We get regular reports," said Schmidt. "He is prepared to be generous."

"And what about you?" said Mani. "Are you part of this?"

"I am just a messenger," said Schmidt. "I try to keep it simple."

Mani swallowed. If he could only find some way of slowing things down, of thinking clearly for a moment, or to understand what was happening. He tasted the bitter coffee.

"I am a practical man," said Schmidt.

Mani started sweating all the harder and then looked down at his cup. When he glanced up Schmidt was looking directly at him. What Mani wanted, right then, was to be in the street opposite one of those young men who shouted insults, who called him Red Scum. Then he would know what to do. Instead, he found himself shaking, and when he tried to be quiet, he was left with an interior noise that was so much like a nightmare.

Maybe this was an interrogation. In that instant, he thought of the advice he had heard from people who had been through it: don't hold anything back. If they arrest you and put you in a cell, don't eat the bread. Only drink the water. The bread just makes you hungry. Don't eat the salt fish. Come clean. If you hold back, they will never be satisfied, since they will think you are always holding something back. You can't throw yourself on their mercy. That is not part of it. You must make your confession as quickly as possible. That is the best you can hope for. For one instant, Mani wanted to talk and get it over with but then realized this was hysteria.

"I've come to ask for your help," said Schmidt. "I came here to see how things were going."

"Of course," said Mani. "I have my accounting upstairs."

"Yes, good," said Schmidt. "But my job has changed. I'm interested in something else now."

Mani drank the bitter coffee.

"We're concerned about a murder in Berlin."

"Well, if I can help, I'm at your service," said Mani.

"I'm glad to hear that," said Herr Schmidt. "A man was doing us a service. It doesn't matter what it was. It was important to us. It was important to the chairman."

Mani looked down at the table.

"Hans Breiter was the name of the man," said Herr Schmidt.

"What was he doing for you?" said Mani.

"For us," said Herr Schmidt. "Your interests are the same as ours in

Moscow." Herr Schmidt turned his coffee cup up to get the last, bitter dregs. "You will do what we tell you. I am giving you your orders."

"What happens if I have things to do here? Action to take that I see as being important," said Mani. "What about people who betray us?"

Herr Schmidt took a deep breath and then took a moment to stare at Mani. It was as though he had been given something shoddy, a lousy coat when he had paid for a good one.

"I'm giving you your orders," said Herr Schmidt. "You have no interests aside from the Soviet's. That's it. It doesn't matter what you think, or what you want to do. Why, you may have all kinds of crazy ideas. But you will do what we tell you to do. And that is to attack the Weimar government. That's it. If you are worried about anything else, then you aren't doing your job."

"And what about the thugs?" said Mani.

"Your job is to attack the government," said Herr Schmidt. "We'll worry about the Nazis and the others."

"From where? Moscow? What about what's happening here?"

"I'm giving you your orders," said Herr Schmidt. "Is that clear? Attack the government. Find out about Breiter."

Mani nodded.

"Say it," said Herr Schmidt.

"What was Breiter doing for you?" said Mani.

Herr Schmidt put out one hand, as though asking for an instrument used in interrogations. Then he nodded, bit a fingernail, and stared at Mani. How much to tell? Just enough to make Mani feel on the inside, but really just enough to make sure he would be eliminated soon? Was that the right summation?

"Breiter did some negotiations for us with the German army. The Boss wants a strong Germany between us and Europe. Maybe that means helping the Germans rearm. Maybe it means helping the Germans get around the limitations on arms from the Treaty of Versailles. Breiter helped. So, of course, we want to know why someone did this. That's all."

Mani swallowed and glanced at Karl. Then Mani swallowed again, but it felt like he was choking.

"Here," said Herr Schmidt. "Have a little coffee."

Mani had a sip of the cold coffee.

"Will you find out who did this?" said Herr Schmidt.

"Yes," said Mani. He took out a handkerchief and wiped the sweat off his face.

"Strangely hot in here, isn't it?" said Herr Schmidt.

"Yes," said Mani. "Maybe I've got a fever."

"Why, you should take care of yourself," said Herr Schmidt. He reached over and put his fingers on Mani's forehead. "Cool as a cucumber."

"Maybe it's an allergy," said Mani.

"Yes," said Herr Schmidt. "Of course. That's probably it." Then he laughed and said, "Mani, Mani, don't worry. I'm your friend."

Mani tried, by force of will, to stop sweating, but it didn't do any good. He couldn't swallow either.

Herr Schmidt pushed the suitcase toward Mani.

"This is a gesture from the chairman. You are going to be paid more and more regularly. You can do your work here. Keep after the government. Make trouble."

"Of course," said Mani. "I've appreciated what I had before."

"I'm very glad to hear about the accounting," said Herr Schmidt. "We will take a look at that."

"Yes," said Mani.

"So, find out about Breiter," said Schmidt. "Find out who did this thing."

He pushed the suitcase farther toward Mani. Then he finished his coffee and put it down with a harsh click.

"Count your blessings," he said. "It's hard to get good coffee in Moscow."

"How long are you going to be in Berlin?" said Mani.

"Oh," said Schmidt. "I have some things to do. I'll be around. I'll check in on you. And, if I miss you I can always ask you to come to Moscow. You'll come, won't you, if we ask? You can bring the accounting."

The coffee cup made a diminutive click, like a tumbler falling into place, when Mani put it down.

"Will you come?" said Schmidt.

"Yes," said Mani.

"Glad to hear it," said Schmidt. "Everyone will be glad to hear it." He pushed the suitcase against Mani's leg. "Don't spend it all in one place. And, of course, go on with the accounting. A revolution means keeping track of everything."

The man from Moscow stood up, like a piece of equipment being unfolded from a case, a camera tripod, for instance, and with his legs apart, he reached down and picked up his coat, which he swung around and stuck his arms through, as though he had practiced putting this coat on in a hurry. He looked around the room, as though taking inventory, and then down at Mani, who tried to appear calm, businesslike, although he was still sweating. He looked like something that had been dragged out of the river, hair pasted to the side of his face, skin white.

Mani began to stand up.

"No," said the man from Moscow. "Don't bother. I'll let myself out."

The man turned toward the door and moved with that same precision, as though counting the number of feet between the door and the table, and when he was about to disappear into the street he smiled. Everything was as it should be, right? Then he put on his hat, the brim over his eyes, and went into the street, pulling the door shut behind him.

Mani stuck his foot out and touched the heavy suitcase. Could there be that much money in it? As he pushed it this way and that with his foot, the weight of it left him more confined than before: if it was as much as he thought it might be, he was that much more obligated. It had the weight of a ball and chain.

He glanced across the room. Karl sat there, nursing his brandy, his ugly, collapsed face curious and still cautious, too, as though while he wanted to walk across the room and ask a question, he wanted to make sure that Herr Schmidt had disappeared. Kathleen came from the back, and Mani said, "Could I have a brandy?"

"I didn't like the look of him," said Kathleen.

"That's not our job," said Mani. "To make such judgments."

She raised a brow, and then brought back a glass that was filled almost to the rim. At least she could show in this way that she understood: he was scared, and that he hadn't liked the look of the man from Moscow either.

Mani hoped that the brandy would do some good, but it made him more jittery than warm, as though the alcohol brought out latent uneasiness, or enhanced what was already there rather than smoothing it over. The pendulum of the clock on the wall swung back and forth. Not even twelve-thirty. How was he ever going to get through until dawn?

Karl walked across the room and pulled out a chair so he could sit down.

"What's wrong?" said Karl. "You look dizzy. I knew a guy who looked like that and when they cut him open they found a tumor as big as a cobblestone, but sort of yellow." Karl tapped his temple. "Right here."

Mani shook his head. It was harder to swallow than ever.

"They put it in a jar so his wife could see it. She charged money to take a look."

Mani sipped the brandy, but slowly so as not to get sick.

"Of all the people," said Mani.

Karl waited. An emotional flat tire is the way Karl thought of him.

"Breiter was the wrong guy to play with," said Mani.

"Just keep quiet," said Karl.

"The people in Moscow want me to find out who did it," said Mani.

"Well, that should be easy," said Karl.

"Very funny," said Mani. "And I'll tell them you were there, too. How about that?" Mani swallowed.

"So," said Karl. "Do you want to wait for the roof to fall in?"

"No," said Mani. "Let's not wait."

"It looks like we've got something to work with, too," said Karl. He kicked the suitcase. "How much do you think is there."

"A lot," said Mani.

"All right," said Karl. "Only three people know about Breiter."

Mani had a sip of his brandy and felt the burning sensation of it on his tongue.

"Yes," said Mani. "Three of us."

"There's you and me," said Karl. "We don't have to worry about us, do we?"

"No," said Mani.

"So, that leaves Gaelle," said Karl. "She was hanging around with the other side, wasn't she? Wasn't she seeing some Brownshirt?"

Mani nodded. Yes. She was.

"Well, that puts her in the middle. They get rid of people all the time."

"I guess," said Mani.

"There's no guessing," said Karl.

"And you'd be willing . . . ," said Mani.

"What choices have we got?" said Karl. "Have you got any ideas?"

Mani shook his head.

"No," said Mani.

"Buck up then," said Karl. "Christ. What a mess. You want to do one thing and then you get windy."

"I'm not windy," said Mani.

"Hold out your fingers," said Karl.

They trembled.

"See?" said Karl. "You've got to get a grip on yourself."

"You'll take care of this?" said Mani.

"Well, who else is going to do it?" said Karl. "You?"

"If I had to," said Mani.

Karl stared at him for a while, then stood up and rolled his shoulder. The overhead light appeared like it was ready for an interrogation.

"Sure," said Karl. "You're as windy as they get."

"So, will you do it?"

"Calm down," said Karl.

"Did you see Herr Schmidt?"

"Okay," said Karl. "All right. All right. As soon as I can."

"How soon will that be?" said Mani.

"Didn't I tell you to calm down?" said Karl.

Mani swallowed.

"It's got to be soon," he said.

The setting sun covered Gaelle with a reddish and gold cast, and the figures who approached from the west looked like phantoms, shapes that vanished when they stood directly in front of the reddish globe at the end of the avenue. She'd managed to make everyone angry, that is, if they knew what she had done, and how long would it take for everyone to find out? It was all the fault of the scar, which she touched now, as though it was a toad. She had heard that informers had been killed in a particular way: often they had their lights shot out, that is, someone shot them in the eyes. Gaelle tried to stand absolutely still, as though if she were absolutely quiet, frozen in one place, she would be more safe. Or at least more invisible.

"Well, well," said Felix. "Look who's here."

Armina's hair was also bathed in the roseate light. Gaelle looked down at the cobbles, shifting her weight.

"Oh," said Gaelle. "It's you."

"I was around," said Armina. "I thought I'd see how you are doing." The cars made a sound like distant thunder where the tires went over the cobblestones.

"It's slow," said Felix. "Nothing's happening."

The trees at the edge of the park looked like lacy seaweed against the light: plants or living things from the depths of the ocean, which left Gaelle with a sense of the pressure at the bottom of the sea.

"Yeah," said Gaelle. "It's slow. What's it to you?"

"I just thought I'd drop by," said Armina. "Maybe we could talk."

"No," said Felix. "I don't think so."

Gaelle looked Armina up and down, from her dark shoes to her gray jacket. No jewelry, not much makeup. Can you trust someone like that?

Then Gaelle went back to trying to stand still, but the world seemed poised, as though ready to spring on her like a tiger.

"The stores are still open," said Armina. "We can go shopping."

"Shopping?" Gaelle said.

"There's a sale," said Armina.

"It's your funeral," said Felix.

"Stop saying that," said Gaelle. "If you say that one more time . . . All this talk about funerals. No more. I mean it."

"Sure, sure," said Felix. "It's just a way of talking. You know, a saying."

"One more time and you can look for someone else to work with."

"All right," said Felix. "I get the message."

"Let's go shopping," Gaelle said to Armina. "It's hard to breathe around here."

"I said I was sorry," said Felix.

"I'm taking a break," said Gaelle.

"You know," said Felix. "I didn't mean anything."

"Then don't say anything," said Gaelle.

"OK, OK," said Felix. "I'll line something up. Get something nice."

Gaelle and Armina walked up to the streetcar stop and Gaelle looked around, as though the solution to her trouble could be found in the passing cars, the lights of the city, the last of the blue-gold light. The most important thing was not to make any more mistakes.

On the streetcar they sat side by side, Gaelle in her slinky dress, her silver stockings and shoes, her silver handbag in her lap. What would happen if she turned to Armina and said, I've informed on everyone. They all are after me. Can you help? And I've killed someone, too? The instant Gaelle decided she couldn't say a word the turmoil seemed to rise from the darkness of her sense of herself, a sort of black rush that left her blinking and trying not to cry. How could she become so sentimental when she needed to be so tough? Because I am trapped, and when you are trapped you can't have the luxury of sentiment.

She wanted to ask if Armina had a boyfriend, and did he look at her as though she meant the world to him? Well, maybe she did, and that was one of the things that separated them. No one looked at Gaelle that way, and yet, even though she liked to think she was tough, like the cobblestones, like the sidewalk they walked on, she still wanted someone to say, "I love you, darling. You are everything." The impossibility of this happening to Gaelle seemed like a river between her and Armina, a cold one, dark, topped with dirty froth. Gaelle kicked her heels against the seat of the streetcar, the constant knocking only making her angrier. Yes, she thought, maybe I'll ask this cop about that. Maybe she has some ideas about how to get across that river. Although I doubt it: I bet she doesn't even know it's there.

Armina sat there, too, in her gray skirt and jacket, her crème-colored blouse, sensible shoes. Her red hair was short, cut along the line of her chin. No scent, although she probably used a little powder.

"Do you have a boyfriend?" said Gaelle.

"No," said Armina.

"Why not?" said Gaelle.

"I've got my work," said Armina.

"Me, too," said Gaelle. Her laugh was shallow, and then she went back to blinking and accusing herself of being sentimental. She was beyond all that.

"But you could have one?" said Gaelle. "Couldn't you?"

"I don't know," said Armina.

"I want one," said Gaelle. "Isn't that the funniest thing you have ever heard? Why, I could die laughing."

She looked down at her hands.

"I really want one," she said.

"I understand," said Armina.

"You?" said Gaelle. "What can you know about it? Why, you come to the park with me some night, and then we'll talk again."

The department store was four floors, lit in the front with a red neon sign the color of strawberry sherbet. They got off the streetcar and faced the building. Animated mannequins, a woman in a wool dress and a man in a dark suit, beckoned and waved, as though to say, "Hello, friend. Come on in!" The animated man then checked his watch.

"I just don't know what to do," said Gaelle.

"About being here? Are you scared about going in here? Because of the scar?" said Armina.

"Yeah, I'm scared," said Gaelle. "You can say that."

"There's someone here who might help," said Armina. "That's why I wanted to come. Don't you want some help?"

Gaelle swallowed, but she didn't trust herself to speak. She nodded, yes, yes, yes.

They went to the lingerie section and held up stockings, lacy garters, sheer underwear, and as they picked the things up and talked about how they would wear and if the elastic was any good, how the stockings would run and what was comfortable, everything seemed natural. Just friends talking. Looking over some clothes. Then Gaelle starting blinking, and as much as she wanted to resist it, she thought of an American song, "You are my sunshine, my only sunshine. . . ." Stop it, she thought. What's wrong with you?

"Come on," said Armina. "Let's go downstairs."

The woman at the cosmetics counter was in her fifties, and her face was perfectly made up, but the appearance was theatrical rather than beautiful, more a disguise than something enhanced. Her hair was dyed, but it was such a perfect job that the highlights in it suggested youth.

She sat behind a counter in a cloud of perfume, and her samples of lipstick, powder, pancake, pencil, and mascara were arranged like implements in an artists' supply store.

"Well, Armina," said the woman. "What can I do for you?"

"Hello, Beatrice," said Armina. "This is my friend. Gaelle."

Friend, thought Gaelle. That word again. We're on different sides of that river. And yet, as she stood there, she wanted to take Armina's hand, to be embraced, to feel that it was all right, if only for this instant. What wouldn't she give for that warmth, that touch, for the moment when she could relax.

Beatrice's gray eyes moved across Gaelle's face, and the examination of her glance was so intense that Gaelle felt it as a physical sensation, like a touch of a feather.

"Sit down," said Beatrice.

She turned the magnifying mirror on Gaelle, and in the curved glass the scar was enlarged, its sheen more metallic than ever. In the instant, Gaelle felt the mark as an alien presence, a parasite that did its work by causing trouble, that left her waiting for a man to come after her, whom she didn't know but whom she would recognize when she saw him. She'd know him by a tingling rush, like a million ants, that ran over her skin. Maybe the hair on the back of her neck would actually stand up.

"You don't want to look at it?" said Armina.

"I don't know," said Gaelle. "It's difficult to face up to things."

"Maybe they aren't so bad," said Armina.

"No," said Gaelle. "No, they're as bad as they can get. Or almost."

"Beatrice," said Armina. "Do you think that's right?"

"No," said Beatrice. "I've seen worse."

"See?" said Armina.

"The trick is going to be to work on her eyes," said Beatrice. "The eyes are the key."

"The eyes," said Gaelle. The lights. Make them more obvious, an easier target. Gaelle pulled away.

"Wait," said Armina. She put her hand on Gaelle's arm. "Wait. Give it a chance."

"Yes," said Beatrice. "That way people will look at them more than anything else."

"I'm afraid," said Gaelle to Armina.

"It won't take a minute," said Armina. "Let Beatrice try."

"It's the eyes that will do it," said Beatrice. "That's where we'll end up."

Beatrice took her mascara and started to apply it, darkening the lashes, tugging on them with the brush. It made Gaelle's eyes, which were brown and flecked with gold, seem more prominent. Gaelle felt the small brush, as though she were playing a childhood game in which a friend tugged on her lashes.

"It's the waiting that's hard," said Gaelle.

"Well, I know," said Beatrice. "When you look better, it won't be so bad."

"Maybe I'll get made up, too," said Armina.

"You don't need it," said Gaelle.

"Oh," said Armina. "I don't know."

"It will look better," said Beatrice. "Just wait a minute."

"I haven't got long," said Gaelle.

"You've got to get back to work?" said Beatrice.

"You could say that," said Gaelle.

Beatrice put on a layer of pancake makeup and then powdered both cheeks and put on some rouge, a pinkish blush that made the cheeks seem more symmetrical. Gaelle held her head so that only her eyes showed in the mirror, and for a moment it was better, but then she thought, Where am I going to go? What now? What can I do? Get on a train and leave? But where?

"What do you think I should do?" said Gaelle.

"Stick with the pancake, the powder, the blush, and the eyeliner. That's the best way, I think," said Beatrice.

Gaelle opened her handbag and took out a bill, a wrinkled one that she had taken in earlier in the evening, but Armina already reached over with some new, fresh money. It looked like it had just been ironed. Gaelle stared at it and thought, Yes, that's the difference right there. She never has ugly money, not like mine.

"My treat," said Armina.

They went upstairs, away from the scent and clouds of power, and out to the street. The crowds went by in a long stream, men and women, young people looking in the windows or going into cafés, all so ordinary and romantic.

"Call me," said Armina.

"Sure," said Gaelle.

"I can help," said Armina. "Give me a chance."

"I haven't got a chance to give," said Gaelle.

"I know you're in a tight spot," said Armina.

"Tight spot? Is that what you said?"

"I'd be afraid, too," said Armina.

"Why, you think I'm worried about what is happening to the women in the park. Why, that's not half, not a quarter. . . ." Then she stopped. Her fingers trembled.

"What else is there?" said Armina.

"Look," said Gaelle. "I didn't want to quarrel. We're just different. You're on one side, and I'm on the other. Just look how clean your money is. Just look."

"It's all right," said Armina. "Don't worry."

"Don't worry?" said Gaelle. She swallowed. "I've got to get back. Felix is waiting."

"Call me," said Armina. "Please." She took a card from her bag and held it out. "If you hear something about the women in the park."

"Sure," said Gaelle. "Thanks."

"Will you call?" said Armina. "I need help."

"Well, that's two of us," said Gaelle.

Gaelle turned and went up the avenue, her figure disappearing into the clutter of the street, the signs, the people out for a stroll, the lovers holding hands, the young people who went along in groups of ten or so, pushing and shoving, laughing, singing a popular song. There's nothing left to do but wait, thought Armina. The scar didn't look much better, either.

PART II

rmina hung up the phone and put her feet on the floor and lay back in bed, the sheets caressing her with a seductive warmth. How nice it would be to roll over and to go back to sleep again. What had she been dreaming? Climbing in the Alps, that was it, and even now she could smell the arctic scent of the ice sheets, the air tainted with a chill from higher up, and her fingers still felt the roughness of the climbing ropes and the weight of the ice axe. How nice it had been, even though a dream, to get away from her sense of failure. Why hadn't she been able to be more convincing with Gaelle? And what a bad idea to have her face made up, since it only made the scar look worse, as it was disguised. Gaelle had wanted something, and yet Armina hadn't been able to give it: a failure of spirit, of generosity, maybe even of humor. The floor was cool against her bare feet and the shadows of the room lay across the floor like a piece of gray cloth as the water dripped in the bathroom with a steady tick, tick, tick. She stood up as though she were lifting a weight.

The Inspectorate wanted her to come down to the river, to the boathouse of one of the Berlin rowing clubs where the caretaker had found something just inside the doors this morning. Right by the oar rack, is what he said when he had called the Inspectorate. By the oar rack.

There wasn't time for a bath, and so Armina washed her face, put on her clothes, and went downstairs to the street. It was just dawn, and the sky was yellow in the east. The river wasn't that far, really, and she'd probably feel better for a little fresh air. She told herself again that she was going to drink less, and that tonight she would have nothing. This couldn't go on night after night.

Up ahead schoolchildren walked in two lines, their brown and blond heads bright in the early sunshine. They were a little disorderly, not jumpy, but staggering like a line of diminutive drunks. They came two by two, their eyes a little vacuous, and some of them let their lips get wet. A girl made a soft, constant mooing. Another child rubbed his eye over and over again. The teachers with them, one in front and one at the back, seemed to be herding them. Then Armina realized they were from the special school. They came along, blinking and stumbling, not quite drooling but sniffling and breathing through their mouths, and when she was even with them, a boy with a satchel looked right at her, his glance piercing in its mystification. Then, behind her, a pigeon flew up into the first rays of sunlight, where it suddenly appeared as a bird that was covered with gilt. The boy looked at the bird, almost shaking as he saw the transformation, and then he said to Armina, his mouth wet, his eyes still insistent in their mystification, *"Ein Vogel, ein Vogel,"* a bird, a bird.

"Yes," said Armina.

"So, so pretty," said the boy.

Armina nodded. Yes. It was pretty.

The Spree was about sixty feet wide, confined by stone banks and crossed by many bridges. At this hour, when there was no wind, the river was placid and showed the pink and yellow sky.

The boathouse looked like a barn with two large doors on the side facing the river, and from the doors a ramp went down to the constant, indifferent hush of the water. The doors were open. The building was made of wood, and its upright planks had been painted a light blue, so that the side of the building appeared like the back of a theater where a play was set on a pleasant, clear day. Men in plainclothes and in uniform stood around a shape that was covered with a rubberized sheet just beyond the threshold of the open doors of the boathouse.

Armina's boss, a man by the name of Weiss, was there, too. He was heavyset, had rimless glasses, and his face was round and brooding. He wore a suit with a vest, a green tie, and dark shoes. The Nazi papers had been attacking him, and Armina new that when Weiss was gone, she'd have to go with him. Linz was there, too.

Uniformed police made all this seem ceremonial as they stood around that covered shape on the boathouse floor. It was like a formal occasion, a wedding or police reception. Linz's beard was blue and his eyes were bloodshot, as though he were in that odd zone of no longer being drunk but not yet hungover. A woman's leg stuck out from the rubberized tarp at his feet.

Weiss moved his eyes from the river to Armina. Even though he was in his neat clothes and his round glasses and his Homburg hat, he still conveyed a fatigue that was mixed with a sadness at the endless repetition of this moment. His eyes were old, like those of a man dug out of a glacier.

"So," Linz said to Armina. "Hard night?"

"I've found the best thing for a hangover is a little brandy," Weiss said. She put the back of her hand to her mouth.

"Maybe," she said. Then she reached down and pulled back the rubberized sheet. The young woman was splayed out under the boats, her skin pale verging on blue, her face against the dirt floor and her hair covered by her coat. Her presence seemed infinitely tawdry to Armina and part of an ugliness so large and originating in a stupidity so ridiculous as to defy understanding. The young woman was almost nude, aside from the coat over her head, her stockings pulled below her knees. The line on her neck was familiar, as were the red marks on her legs and buttocks and the small holes, too. For a minute, Armina was reassured by her disgust, as though, at least, she had nothing to do with this, and this distance was something she could depend on. The air, the light, the scent of the river seemed so heavy that it took effort just to stand there.

"She was here just behind the door," said Weiss. "The caretaker found her."

"Was she raped?" said Armina.

"I thought I'd let the doctor do that," said Weiss.

"I'll do it," said Armina.

She pulled back the rubberized sheet again, reached down to her buttocks, lifted one, and glanced at the wounds. At the touch of the cool skin, the sense of being separate from this vanished, and Armina was left with the conviction that this young woman was here because of Armina's failure. Her desire to stop this left her trembling, that cool touch of the woman's skin lingering on the tips of her fingers. She noticed, in the soft dirt next to the young woman, that there was a curved mark, as though someone had scored the ground with a stick, or the tip of a toe.

Then she covered the woman up again and turned to Weiss.

"Yes," she said.

Weiss shrugged.

"That's what I thought," he said. He took a clean handkerchief from his pocket and held it out, and she took it, wiping her hands slowly as she looked around.

"It's too bad she's missing so much clothing," Armina said. "It would be nice to know if someone took a souvenir. They do that, of course."

"We found her handbag, up there," said Linz. "Here's her address. She looks pretty young, doesn't she?"

Armina stepped next to the boats where the young woman's head lay, and pulled back the coat. The blond hair still smelled of shampoo, and the side of the face was oddly numb, slack, and the absence of expression was worse than horror, since the blankness suggested a thorough obliteration. Armina leaned over to look more closely, her face not that far from the young woman, and as she stood in the dimness of the boathouse, under the lines of light on the shells, she was left with the impulse to shake her head.

"Something wrong?" said Linz.

Armina stepped back from the shape under the rubberized material and down the boathouse ramp to the river. Now, as the sun rose, the river was covered with a million flecks of light, each one a sharp silver, all suggesting an enormous piece of glass that had shattered into an infinite number of bits. Armina wanted to sit down, to lean against the boathouse door, to find some way to stand here without her constant nausea, as though she were here and at the same time swinging back and forth at the end of a long piece of rope. The river went around the bend into the industrial clutter of Berlin. Her sense of responsibility, she realized, was something she had been trying to cover up, like makeup over a scar. The shock came not as a surprise, but with the sense of something being leeched out of her, as though she had been bleeding for a long time and was now getting weak. She put a hand to her face and stared at the facets of water. The points of light appeared artificial, remote as stars, and yet at the same time they conveyed the claustrophobia of the ordinary details that attended any hateful moment.

"This one's yours," said Linz.

Armina put her hand to her hair.

"Yes," she said. "I guess it is."

"Cases like this are a dime a dozen," said Linz. "Same old stuff. Someone imitating the Fisherman." He pulled his coat a little tighter. He looked around. "Who's going to tell her parents?" he said, gesturing to the body.

The others stood around, shifting from one foot to another, looking at the river. A barge went by and made a wave that washed up against the stones lining the river.

"It's the investigating officer's job," said Linz to Armina.

Armina tuned again to the luminescent chop of the river, the silver crosses of light at the top of the small waves, and as she stared a barge went by, the bow wave of it rolling toward her in a gray, green, and silver rush.

"You'll get over it," Linz said. "There's nothing to it."

"Then why don't you do it?" she said.

"I'll leave it to you."

Then he went along the river and up the stone steps that led to the avenue, his reflection like a film on the water that undulated from a passing boat. At the top of the stairs, in his dark clothes, he appeared like a man in an advertisement, at once promising something and yet not being clear about what it was. He tipped his hat to Armina and disappeared with his precise gait, as though if he walked carefully enough he could keep the hangover away for an hour more.

"Are you all right?" said Weiss.

"Yes," she said. "No. I don't know."

"That happens to all of us these days," said Weiss.

"What do you suppose they were doing, marking her like that?" said one of the uniformed officers.

"Well," said Weiss. "They were trying to get her to talk about something. That's one possibility. Maybe she owed them money."

"Are there other possibilities?" said the uniformed officer.

"They were doing it for fun," said another uniformed officer.

"No," said Weiss. "It could have been something else."

"What could that have been?" said the uniformed officer.

"Somebody who enjoyed his job," said Weiss. "You know, a collector."

The men moved around, looking one way and another. Yes, they seemed to be saying, as they looked around, that could be possible. Someone might have enjoyed his job.

"I'm going to look around," said Armina.

"Sure," said Weiss. "See you later."

Armina walked upstream. The light of the rising sun covered the east side of the buildings with a film that looked like it had been painted on. At this time even the squat, enormous buildings, like the Reichstag, looked as though they had been carved from blocks of gold. Soon the sun rose and the sky turned blue, which meant that the gray stone of the buildings revealed itself again. She went along the river with its fishy, moist odor. In some places she was able to walk under the bridges and stay by the water, but at some bridges she had to climb up to the street and cross over, going among the cars and the wagons and horses. The countrified smell of horses mixed with the fishy stink of the river, and on top of that the air had the smell of burning coal.

She kept thinking about the marks. Some of them looked like they had been done with a cigarette, but others were the work of something else, a wire perhaps. The coat thrown over the face was familiar, of course, and Armina thought that the man who had done this was ashamed. Just like in the park.

She went into the Altes Museum, behind the Lustgarten. Inside, the atmosphere was dusty and damp. The statues of Roman gods stood on pedestals, all of them contradictory in their human forms, familiar and yet strangely remote, too, since the ordinary inability to know a human being had been elevated, here at least, to the difficulty in knowing a god. So, she sat there, thinking about the signs that had been left on that young woman and that torn flesh.

Armina was left with the memory of the impulse to do the right thing, which now, or so it seemed, had led to those marks, to the shape under the rubberized sheet. And where was Armina's sense of detachment, her belief that she was remote from these things? The certainty that she was getting nowhere, just going through the motions, and that Armina had a hand in what happened settled around Armina like a fine, horrible dust, a million points of accusation, all sharp and specific. She sat there in the aroma of the stone of the old gods. Whispers came from the depths of the museum.

She started walking to the address of the girl's parents, although she stopped in front of a store that sold men's clothing. An animated mannequin stood behind in the window, a kind of machine-powered dummy. It was dressed in a brown suit and a green tie, with shiny brown shoes, and it took off the hat and beckoned to the window shopper in the street. This mechanical politeness seemed friendly, but the jerkiness of the machine made Armina feel suspicious, or it made her aware of her humanity in the face of such a creature. After all, the machine never made any mistakes. It went on tipping its hat forever.

At the river she sat on a bench by the water, which had a film of oil, separated into a dirty rainbow, at once colorful and oddly subdued, as though it had leaked up from a long-submerged and tainted source. The colors seemed leached out. Her hands trembled as she put them in her lap, and the breeze that came up left her uneasy. The light seemed to fade, or to become yellow and oddly dim.

At the next bench a man and a woman, both dressed in black, reached into a paper bag and took out small handfuls of crumbs for the cooing pigeons, some of which, in the sunlight, were marked with those same tints of a dirty rainbow. The old hands sprinkled the crumbs, and the pigeons nodded their heads and pecked. And now, she thought, I am supposed to go home, to be alone, to sit there in the dark? She sat on the bench and trembled. The old man and the old woman went on feeding the pigeons, which picked at the crumbs, their heads going back and forth.

She did her job: the parents listened with the expression of being changed forever.

On the way home, Armina stopped at the church on the side of the Lustgarten, and while she stood in front of it, she felt the attraction of the place, like a churchyard in the country. Somehow the churchyards were just as reassuring as the sound of the horses on the pavement: suggestive of the ordinary peace and tranquility that eluded her.

This is where she had come as a child on Easter with her mother and father, and Armina remembered this as the best of times, her mother's pale, translucent skin, her thick, almost black hair, her eyes that were the color of wet, gray granite. Her father had attracted this woman with his wit and his mind. He was thin and bald, a man who wore dark suits and wire-rimmed glasses.

Both parents were dead now. The best of times had been when they had all come here on Easter, when they had given in to the rustling, the shuffling of feet, the glitter of the altar. On one Easter, just before Armina's mother had died, Armina's father had said to Armina, "I love you for all the reasons a father loves a daughter. And for one other."

"What's that?" Armina said.

"You do the right thing," said her father. "You have an instinct for it."

After Armina's mother had died, Armina's father still did work on new compounds that alleviated pain, and often, when he had cut himself or fallen and turned an ankle, he said to Armina, "I hurt myself but I took a little something for it. I feel all right now." Well, those had been easier days, thought Armina, when everything had been more clear. That was the beauty of youth: even one's doubts were pretty certain. Those times when everything was muddled hadn't yet made themselves quite so obvious. Maybe her father had been right: comfort was to be had in a little warmth from one of those new drugs. What a thin hope, thought Armina. But what have I got?

The steps to the church were gray stone, and the heavy doors were open. In the gloom the gilt of the altar shone like a cat's eyes at night. Armina stood at the door. She guessed it was the memory of the best time, the closeness and the electric thrill she had gotten by holding the hand of both her mother and father at the same time: it was as though the lingering pleasure of her creation flowed from one parent to another through her. How could she resist a memory like that?

The long pews were shined by the centuries of worshippers sliding along the wood. Armina's hands gently touched the back of the long seat in front of her. Against her better judgment, she sat down, and yet what she wouldn't give for the certainty she'd had on those Easter mornings. She leaned her head against the pew back in front of her. Around her the susurrus of the church was like wind in the trees: the shuffling feet, the whispered prayers, the scent of incense. She wanted to pray and yet she didn't know what she would ask for. Or, maybe it was just that she was too despairing to pray. If only she had the energy to be furious.

Instead she listened to the hush and tried to recall the touch of her parents' fingers. How brilliant her father had been. What talent her mother had. At home Armina had a recording of her mother's, a Beethoven sonata, and when Armina was at her worst, when she was so alone that she felt she was shrinking, like a spot of water in a hot pan, she had played the record until it ended with the scratchy, repeated sound of the needle in the last grooves. She liked the idea that her father had believed in her, but she wasn't sure he was right. It would be nice, she thought, if he had been.

Her father had been killed by accident in street fighting between the Communists and the Socialists. Maybe the thugs had been there, too. They usually were.

On the way home, she stopped next to a veterinarian's office where people had lined up with their dogs to have them killed at the worst part of the inflation. It had been too difficult to feed them. Armina still didn't like to go by this place, where she had seen, as a child, the lines of people who had held their pets or stood there with the animals on leashes. It seemed to be such a poor solution, killing the animals, as though everything could be solved by death.

She pushed the door of her building open and stood in the marble foyer. The stairs were at the rear of the hall, and as she walked that way she just wanted to get upstairs, to close the door, as though that would help and that what she felt was a gas or smell that could be shut out. At the window at the back of the hall the sunlight came through in a luminescent bar, filled with dust, and as Armina watched the motes in the light, she thought, You never think you are going to doubt yourself, to think you are a failure. And when it comes it is such a surprise.

The dust went on turning as pinpricks of light, like the stars Armina had seen after she'd hit her head. She went up the stairs where her footfalls seemed final, like someone going down the hall of a prison, and in the cold vibration of the sound, which seemed to penetrate into her bones, into her skull, into the heart of the ache in her head, she remembered the hush in the church, the whiteness of her mother's skin, her father's voice when he had told her he loved her and that she did the right thing. Who was left to forgive her now, or to believe in her? She opened the door to her apartment and went into the silence.

Armina slept until dark and woke to the sound of the dripping faucet in the kitchen. The light from the window made trapezoid patterns on the ceiling, and every now and then one of these geometric shapes moved over the plaster surface, white as the moon, as a car went by in the street. She thought of the boathouse, the cigarette stubs, the pattern in the dirt of the boathouse floor that had been made by someone's impatient pacing. Armina closed her eyes and tried to fall asleep. Then, when she couldn't stand the dripping anymore, as though it were some mechanical accounting of her flaws and her errors, she threw back the covers and went into the kitchen, where she stood naked in front of the sink. She pulled on the faucet handle, but the drip only slowed, and as the cadence became more languid it seemed to be more emphatic.

Armina's apartment building was like many in Berlin, four stories, built around a small square courtyard that could be entered from the street. This meant that her kitchen looked into the apartments on the other side of the courtyard. She let the water run, touching it absently with her hand to see if it was getting cold.

Across the way, in an apartment that had been empty, she saw that a light was on. A man stood among some boxes he was about to unpack, and he obviously was thinking about what to do, looking down at the boxes and then at his shelves. She wanted to say, Put the most used things in the middle of the shelf above the sink. That's a good way to begin.

He was six feet tall, blond, although his hair was thick, like hay, and his nose was large and brows were prominent. Not much older than her. Twenty-eight? He opened a box and started to put his possessions onto the counter. Pots and pans, bottles, silver, a jar of jam that she could see was made from strawberries. From this distance she could only make out the red mass, almost like something out of a dream that suggested sweet fruit. She imagined the small blond hair on the whole berries. Then she put her mouth down to the water that came out of her tap to drink, enjoying doing something as an adult that she would have been reprimanded for as a child, and then she stood there and watched him, feeling her wet lips.

Her hands fumbled along her cabinets in the dark until they came to a bottle of French brandy, which she poured into a small glass. Like the ones in Paris cafés. She held the glass against her breasts to warm the brandy, and then had a drink. Just skin temperature. In the pale light that came in the window she looked at her skin and the freckles the color of paprika.

There was something nice about the way he moved. Now that he had arranged things on the counter he started putting them into his cabinets. He picked up the jar of jam and tossed it from one hand to another. And when he almost dropped a glass, she flinched, as though she could have caught it. When everything was put away, nice and neat, the cabinets closed, he stood there as though at a loss. What now? He reached for a bottle of brandy, and while she couldn't read the label, it looked French. He poured himself a drink and stood at the window, looking into the darkness. She had a sip when he did, and for one pleasing moment they were bound by that same hot sensation in the mouth. Then he turned out his light.

Over the next two nights, she watched in the kitchen with the light off, with the small glass of brandy. She drank it very slowly, and as she felt the warmth of it, she was uncertain as to the source of her peacefulness. Although, she had to admit, it was mixed with something else, too, the anticipation of his appearance. So, she waited, oddly peaceful and keenly alert. When he appeared, he had a reassuring posture: it was as though his movement through the room were soothing, and she supposed this happened because of his frank ease with himself, his uncomplicated ability to be a human being. And a man. She took a drink and let the liquor warm her tongue. It was possible, of course, to knock on his door and to welcome him as a new neighbor. But how could she ever be so forward, so bold? This was another item she gave herself a hard time about: in Berlin women could do just about anything, and many of them did, from using morphine and wearing a tuxedo to taking a woman as a lover, and yet she wasn't able to find anyone. Then she had a drink. For a moment, as she stood there with the warmth of the brandy in her mouth, she forgot about the hush of the water by the boathouse, the cigarette butts, the marks, the scent of ammonia on the skin of those young women. She imagined that his eyes were dark blue, the iris color of the sky in late evening. The seduction, if that is what it was, came from the fact that when she stood there she felt a little better.

She shook her head, as though to resist the spying, but she thought of being out at night when she had seen a man and a woman at a cabaret. They had been so lovely together, the woman laughing, the man pouring champagne into her glass: this delicious hilarity had left Armina with an ache. Now as she looked out the window at the man across the way that ache vanished. She didn't know what bothered her the most: that it went away under these circumstances or that it was there at all.

She told herself often that she was alone because so many men had died in the Great War, and that hers, the man who had been meant for her, had been killed. It was one reason she had gone to work for Inspectorate A. She hated what killed, what took away the possibility of ordinary life and left people just like this: looking out the window and feeling that ache. And now, after her inability to stop what was happening, she accused herself of participating in what she despised, if only by some critical omission. She should have known better. Or known what to do. Was there any way to escape who one was? Wasn't that what falling in love was: becoming someone new and better?

She looked at the light from the window across the courtyard. Her hands started shaking. She sat down at the kitchen table and wondered if you could really go mad from loneliness and self-loathing. If only someone could tell her—she didn't know what exactly—if only, she finally admitted, someone could love her, although now that was more impossible than ever. And, of course, under those circumstances, just how much of a fool could you make out of yourself? When she glanced across the way, he was there again. She wondered if he had a girlfriend, but then she thought, What business is it of mine? She shouldn't even be sitting here, like some voyeur, looking in his window.

You see, she said to herself, you are already calling yourself names. And why not? she thought.

She went to take a bath, letting the enormous tub fill with water, the ribbons of steam rising in an ominous way. She looked into the mirror and saw her red hair, pale skin, the freckles on her shoulders, her mother's cheekbones, which made her seem haughty. Another illusion.

Armina had the next day off, and she slept late. The warmth of the bed embraced her while she drifted in and out of sleep with a delicious, almost sensual caress of the sheets, and she let herself relax into the scent of the pillow, the distant sounds from the street.

She put on a robe, her slippers, and took a towel, too. On the roof there were chaise lounges, made of wood and covered with green pads. At least she'd have the place to herself and could sunbathe nude. She took off her robe and put it on a chair and took off her shoes. She was thin and her skin was white, the color of pale marble, although she had light freckles over her shoulders and across her nose. In the sunlight her hair seemed especially red, filled with highlights, and when she opened her eyes, they seemed all the more green, like a leaf in springtime. The city stretched away in a grid of blocks of apartments to the river, and here and there the tower of a church stood up. From below she heard the traffic and that sad, antiquated, and haunting sound of the horses as the hooves struck the cobblestones.

The sun lay on her skin like a film of heat, and the crimson light through her closed eyes was soporific. She breathed deeply and felt the warm air flow into her as she remembered the light in the apartment across the way. It was like the caress of the sunlight. Just breathing, slowly letting that languid part of it fill her completely. Maybe she could get away from it for a while.

She felt a shadow sweep over her.

"Hello."

The man from across the way stood with the sun at his back. It was the first time she really saw him. Not handsome, not ugly, his face symmetrical with a big, hawklike nose. Not cruel. He dropped his robe and then stretched out nude on a chaise that was close to hers.

"You don't mind, do you?" he said. "I could come back another time if you want to be alone."

"No," she said. "That's all right."

Beads of moisture formed on her upper lip and brow, on her chest. The sun had a pushing quality, which she felt as the gravity tugged her down into the chaise. It caressed her with a sense of the inevitable, as though it were the physical manifestation of her doubt, her sense of having been reduced to part of what she had always despised: those tawdry scenes in the park and along the river. She strained against it, began to sit up just to prove that she could resist it, and then lay back in a rush of embarrassment that spread across her face with heat that was just like the sun's.

The light that came through her lids was red, fuzzy, and hard to look at, and as she was suspended in that rust-colored glow, she could feel his presence, just a couple of feet away. She wanted to say something, to get control of this, to introduce herself, to make this moment seem natural and easy, but she was afraid of saying the wrong thing, of making a fool of herself. Finally, when she had to admit she was at a loss to know what to do, she stood up and put on her robe. In the distance there was a wall of clouds, like something that was sprayed on the sky, thin but broad, from one side in the west to another. It made the greens beneath it darker.

She put her hands through her hair, then tightened the belt of her robe, bit her lip.

"I wish I could stay longer," she said. "But my skin burns. I have to be careful."

She blushed, but he had kept his eyes closed, and so she just stood there, looking at him.

"So, you're new in the building?" she said.

"Yes," he said.

"Well," she said. "Welcome."

"Thanks," he said.

"I . . . ," she said. She thought for a moment of that fleeting peacefulness in the kitchen, the warmth that came from looking at him. "I'd like to invite you for dinner sometime."

"That would be nice," he said.

She blushed. He open his eyes and looked at her.

"My name is Rainer Lesser," he said.

"Armina Treffen," she said.

"Nice to meet you," he said.

She turned away. Then she went down the stairs and back into her apartment, slamming the door, and sitting on the sofa, head in her hands. Now I don't know if it was a good idea or not, she thought. Just what kind of error will this turn out to be? Am I doing the same thing here that I have done at work? Made another mistake?

Then she closed her eyes and knew that at night, when she tried to sleep, she would feel the effect of the sun when she went to bed, the heat of it caressing and maddening. She knew she'd hear that drip drip drip—the silver drop forming, swelling, and then falling away.

Armina waited in earnest now, and as she sat in her kitchen she admitted that she had abandoned all objection to looking in the window across the way. In the middle of the next week, she saw the light in Rainer's kitchen, and his shadow moved in the rear of the apartment. He had a visitor, a woman who wore a clingy silk dress that made her seem sleek and glistening when the light hit her hips and thighs. Armina sat on a stool in the dark.

The next day, when she came home, she found a note stuck under her door. It was in a gray-blue envelope and her name had been written in dark ink. She read the letter as she sat in her living room, the light there failing as the evening seeped in through the windows. The handwriting was large, basic, written with a broad-tipped pen. When she put the paper to her nose, she noticed a clean, promise-filled scent: almonds, sheets dried in the air, lavender soap. She touched her lip with an edge of the paper and wondered just what the promise of this note was, and while she knew it was there, she couldn't describe it, and the presence of something she couldn't name left her agitated, as though unable to remember the name of an old friend.

I'm sorry, the note said, that I have taken so long to write to you, but I have been busy with my sister, who has come from out of town. But now she has gone home, and I wonder if we could have that dinner after all?

Before going out for dinner, they had a drink in his apartment. It was spare and smaller than hers, a bedroom, a living room, a kitchen. The white walls, the few kitchen utensils, the furniture, some of it Bauhaus and lean, all contributed to a cool, serene quality that she thought of as monastic. He didn't seem to need anything, and in fact, when she first came in he said that the spare white walls made it easier for him to think. The place had the aspect of a mathematical diagram in a scientific paper: straight lines, cleanly intersecting on white paper, descriptive of some keen, stern beauty. The severity of the place made her uneasy.

He told her that he was a professor, but that people thought that his subject was funny.

"What's that?" she said.

"Botany," he said. "And then I have another job, too. I'm the orchid curator at the botanical garden. A lot of people think that is funny, too."

"I don't think it's funny," she said.

"Well," he said. He looked down. "I'm glad."

She thought that he had blushed. Was it possible that such a thing could happen in Berlin? Then she thought of her own confusion about the unnamed promise he suggested to her and the evenings she had spent looking out the window. She blushed, too, and then all the more so because she was blushing, and finally a third time when he noticed.

They went to a café where they were served on a white, starched tablecloth, and the waiter was formal yet warm, like the best Berlin waiters. They had champagne and a chocolate dessert, and lingered while the waiter stood a short distance away.

"Well, I've got to be up early," she said.

"I understand," he said.

"Do you?" she said.

"Well, isn't it just before dawn when things go . . . well, wrong," he said. "When you get a call to see something . . ."

"Yes," she said. "That's right. First thing, just when the sun comes up. That's when someone will notice something out of the ordinary. . . ." And when a mistake of mine is obvious, she thought.

Rainer walked her to her door and stood there, taking her hand, saying good night, smiling, thanking her for the lovely time.

Armina thought about his apartment, and how she wanted to resist it, not completely, but to make it a little more, well, she didn't want to say human, since it was surely that, but less ascetic and cold. So, she went from shop to shop, to the department stores, and then finally she came to a place not far from where she lived. It was downstairs, below the street, dark. The woman who owned it was a contradiction: her hair was gray, pulled back into a severe bun, and she wore gray sweaters and gray skirts and black shoes. No jewelry of any kind, aside from what appeared to be a stainless steel watch that hung from a chain attached to her skirt. She made quilts that were a combination of precise, small pieces of cloth, the patterns mathematically correct but mysterious, too, as though describing the way a nautilus shell grows, and at the same time the quilts were a series of the most striking colors, reds, yellows, blues, all soothing and warm. Armina had the sensation that this woman's restraint, her gray essence, her discipline, had been turned into something else, as though the woman were the chrysalis and the things she made were a butterfly.

Armina bought a quilt. Then she wrote Rainer a note and said she would like to bring him a present for his apartment, and when he called and asked her to come by, she took the quilt across the courtyard and up the stairs. The quilt was wrapped in brown paper and tied with a piece of string. She carried it up to the door, thinking that she would be upset if he didn't like it and almost praying that he would say something to hurt her so that she could forget about this. And, at the same time, she was dreading just such a comment, if only because she could imagine the silence of her apartment after such a comment had been made. She knocked on the door and stood there, holding the bundle, offering it.

He took it by the string. They went in. In the living room they sat down, the bundle between them, and then, with a look at her, he opened it, and when he took out the quilt and spread it in front of them, over his knees, he looked at her with a glance that was so pleased, so keenly delighted as to give Armina a moment's pause. The quilt, the colors, and the mathematical precision of them were absolutely right for the apartment, for his bedroom. The quilt acknowledged how he lived, the sparseness of his existence, but the colors cheered and brightened the room in just the right way, not to mention that its presence showed what had been lacking. He stood up and took it into the bedroom and put it on the bed, tucking it in, smiling, almost laughing at how she could have done that.

He thanked her and got her to sit down with him, right there, the two of them like kids, holding hands, and taking an almost youthful delight in the touch of fingers, in the faintly embarrassing sweat of hands.

He made dinner for her. They ate slowly and drank some wine and he told her the most obscene joke, which she thought was funny.

Then she waited. She had made her offer, her attempt to show how she

could fit into his life. Was that what she was really saying? Well, it was possible, she guessed, and if that's what she was saying, why then she wanted
him to respond. Or maybe she was drawn to that quality she couldn't describe. She had made a gesture, or she had tired to communicate, and now
it was his turn. She hadn't really understood that the colors and math of the
quilt would work so perfectly, or that they would suggest an understanding
that she saw now but didn't before she had given it to him. But now she
wanted some response. She wanted him to speak this same language to her,
which wasn't a matter of things so much as using things to invoke possibilities that were so complicated and delicate as to be beyond words.

So, she waited. She walked up to the building near Alexanderplatz
with the gloomy entrance, the gray stone, the stink of cigars, as though the
police were small engines that made clouds of exhaust. She came home exhausted and sometimes exasperated, too, that she was waiting for him.

One evening he showed up with a small cardboard box, which he offered as he stood at the doorway, almost as though it were a flower, an orchid for her to wear.

"I thought you might like this," he said.

So they went into her apartment and observed the ceremony as before,
or she realized that it seemed to have become a ceremony. A drink and
some talk before she opened the box. Her apartment was similar to his, although hers was more comfortable, with an overstuffed leather chair and
sofa in the living room, a painting on the wall that had been done by a
friend of her father's, which was a precise, technically exact execution of a
woman's sewing table on which bright scissors, sharp needles, and bullet-
colored thimbles were all photographically rendered.

She opened the box and removed a ship's barometer. It was as precise
as the objects in the painting but also silver and antiquated and part of a
world that had nothing to do with the miserable details she confronted
after people had made a mess. And, of course, she wanted to know what the
weather was going to be, since she often had to be outside. He had a screw-
driver and four black screws, and he put the barometer on the wall near the
door, where it gave her just the right amount of precision and beauty, but it
didn't clash with the leather furniture, the warmth of the apartment, the
flowers she liked to put on the tables in the dining room.

When she saw it as she went out the door, she realized that it had demonstrated a combination of beauty and precision that worked in her life, too, and that he had been able to do for her what she had been able to do for him, although she was still amazed at her good luck. Then she thought, with a thrill, with a delight and terror that was like looking at the stars, that maybe she was in the midst of something that was so large it worked without her even knowing it. She'd gone into the store and bought the quilt and given it to him without even having to think about it, since her knowledge of him and herself was so deep and worked so perfectly that she wasn't even aware of it, or able to name it. And, one evening, when she was thinking about this, wondering if he had gotten lucky, too, if he had stumbled on the barometer in the same way that she had found the quilt, he said, "It looks nice on the wall. I didn't really know until I gave it to you what I wanted to say. It was recognizing something when I was with you that I didn't even know about. Crazy."

"No," she said. "I don't think so."

Still, she was waiting, looking for clarification of what was happening to her. She had a superstitious notion that if she could say what attracted her or describe the precise nature of the promise she felt, she would fall in love with him—so she waited, suspended between a desire to know and a fear that she'd find out.

She continued to wait. They had dinner together, went to the cabaret, watched the Tiller girls, laughed at the jokes, and sometimes didn't laugh, and this silence, this worry was the same, too. They went by a street fight, and both looked at it with a fatigued and quiet disbelief.

He said that he wanted to go with her to Austria. She agreed, although she thought, Well, he will make a mistake here. It's going too well. When he makes a mistake, will I forgive him? Or will that be another flaw of mine: that I am so slow to forgive?

He arranged their reservations, and they took the train to Gmunden, where they stayed in an old hotel with a thatched roof. It was a quiet place where the employees went out in the morning to gather mushrooms to use in the food that was served in the evening. In the afternoon Armina and Rainer went for walks along the river, where there were benches here and there.

They hired a driver and drove into the mountains, where he went fishing in the Steyer, a stream the color of crème de menthe. She read a book on the bank while he stood in that green water, and in the evening, when it was too dark to read, she found that she was not thinking anything at all, that she was almost hovering in the warm fog that hung over the river, and then when he came up, they walked back to the car, through the pine forest close to the stream, and when they did this, the fireflies came out, some as big as her thumb, it seemed, and as they drifted along, each green pulse had about it the suggestion of something she couldn't say but still felt, as though this trip were another one of those items that revealed a matter not subject to words. As she looked around in the dark, which seemed so Old Europe, so filled with all the terrors of the night, now illuminated with these enormous glowing creatures, he reached over and took her hand, just like that, and they went up to the car and the driver in the same state of what appeared to be complete understanding.

In Gmunden, they went to a café that was on the lake. The café had a terrace and the water was about a foot away from the tables, which had white tablecloths and flowers. Mountains and a cliff were reflected in the still water. As they had an ice cream with a thin wafer, they watched as climbers worked their way up the face of the cliff, bound together by ropes. A hut sat at the top. Armina imagined that this was where the climbers were going to spend the night. A swan glided along on the lake next to the table, and the water was so mirrorlike that the swan appeared to float on its own image, or that there were two swans, one on top of another, and while Armina tasted the ice cream, which was made from wild strawberries, she thought about the almost impossible-to-discern line where the two swans were bound together. It was this membrane of silver and light that mesmerized her, since she saw it as the visual expression of how she was bound to the man in front of her. Almost impossible to describe but so obvious as to be frightening.

When they came back to Berlin, she wanted that same communication as before, as when she had given him a quilt and he had given her the barometer or taken her to Austria, where they walked in those green fireflies with the membrane of the river just behind them. Through it all, she had the oddest sensation of not being able to tell what was what: was there really something there or not?

Rainer asked her to visit him at the botanical garden. He met her at one of the hothouses, where they passed through double doors into the heat. The hothouse was onion shaped, and in silhouette it looked like a building in Arabia. It was frankly industrial, too, since the supports were riveted steel, but they weren't noticeable because they had been painted green. The glass walls rose three stories to a glass ceiling, and beneath it ferns grew in enormous fans as in a jungle. The light came down in glowing bars.

There is something in this heat, Armina thought, something that has to do with us. He must know that. Of course he does, she thought, that's why I'm here.

They went through the ferns, the tips of the fronds beaded with water. She had the same impulse to give voice to what was impossible to say, and as she watched the silver thread described by a falling drop of water, she thought, with a thrill, that the heat did just that: it made the invisible obvious. They stood in it together.

"It's hot," she said.

He pushed open the next door, where there was a sign that said THIS SECTION CLOSED. They came into another room, three stories high as well, all glass as before, but here it was more damp. The orchids hung from other plants, their petals open, some of them almost as large as her hand, the blooms white and red, lipped and wet, hanging there in the mist. Copper pipes ran along the wall of the glass, and every now and then a little spray, from a series of nipples, came into the room and turned back on itself, like smoke.

In the cascade of flowers, in the heat, she whispered, her breath against his ear. She said, "I'm so glad you brought me here."

This was his life's work, and she realized that he had brought her into it, as though he were allowing her to walk around inside him, in what he cared about and what he thought was beautiful, and in that moment of clear understanding, which again was almost impossible to articulate, she was left shaking with the realization: it was like everything else that had gone on between them. Now, though, in the scent of the flowers she was able to say what that promise was. Yes, she thought, of course . . .

"It's exciting here," he said.

"Yes," she said. "It's the heat. The dampness."

They moved farther down the line of orchids, which were white and red, the petals tumbling from some of the larger plants, and then she stopped at one the size of a hand, yellow as a daffodil. The sun came through the mist. The nipples sprayed that warm vapor.

A bench had been put back into the recesses of the hothouse, and they sat on it, the two of them watching the clouds of mist, the bright purple flowers, the pink ones, the massive bulbs of an orchid that trapped insects by emitting the most delicious fragrance. In the clouds of mist they could smell it, which was like a perfume that a woman had touched behind her ear. He makes everything seem all right, she thought. He lets me get away from those hours of doubt and the misery of being flawed.

"Are you upset?" he said.

"It's not that exactly," she said. "I'm just a little teary."

Droplets of water were released and the vapor turned white, like fog, aside from those places where the cloud of it was penetrated by the bars of sunlight.

"Everything about us seems unseen," he said. "But that doesn't mean it isn't there."

She bit her lip.

"Yes," she said. "I'm not going to ruin this by crying."

"Oh," he said. "Crying isn't going to ruin anything."

The copper tubes sprayed more water, and the droplets moved through the air with a peculiar, anxious movement, as though they were minute insects that had just hatched and instantly knew that they were about to be preyed upon. After a while he reached up and picked one of the orchids and held it out for her.

"Oh," she said. "You shouldn't do that."

"I know," he said. "But that just makes it better."

"Is that what you think of me?" she said. "Something you shouldn't do?"

"No," he said. "But there are times when I wish you were forbidden. Anything this good should be forbidden. And so it makes it better."

"Oh," she said, "you say that to all the girls."

"Jesus," said Felix. "Look at the size of that one. See him? What do you think he wants?"

"Why don't you find out?" said Gaelle. She looked at her feet when she spoke.

Down the avenue the lights were coming on and the cars made a plaintive, almost bovine mooing with their horns. Felix walked over to Karl, and when they stood side by side, Felix looked like a scale model, about one-third the size of the larger man. They both wore gray and brown clothes, had haircuts that had been done with a pair of scissors in a hurry, and both had gray skin that was scarred by acne. They walked with a plodding, subdued gait.

Gaelle guessed she had enough energy to be curious about why she wasn't running away, but not enough to do so. Maybe she didn't run because that would make all of this seem real. She stood there, trembling.

"I have to talk to you first?" said Karl to Felix. "About her?"

"Yes," said Felix. His snaggled teeth showed when he smiled. "I'm here to help. Why, if there's anything you want, you can just ask me."

"All right," said Karl. "How much?"

"Would you like to take her someplace?" said Felix.

"You could say that," said Karl.

"Where's your car? Are you going to get a taxi? We know a driver," said Felix. "I can suggest a hotel, too. Reasonable, clean as a whistle."

"We'll just go back in the park," said Karl.

"Well, my friend, she isn't so keen on that," Felix said. "It's hard on her dignity to be off in the park like that. If you don't object, that's going to be more."

"Tell me," said Karl. "Give me the price."

They agreed. Karl took the money out of his pocket and passed it over, the bills looking in his hand about the size of a theater ticket. Felix took the notes, put them in his pocket, not the one with the other money. He'd do that later when he was alone. Then he turned toward Gaelle and said, "It's OK. The gentleman and I are agreed."

"Hi," she said. "It's been a while."

"Not so long," he said. "Time goes by pretty fast."

"How's Mani?" she said.

Karl shrugged.

"The same," he said.

She guessed he wouldn't need a knife, and she was almost disappointed that the reality of the moment was so different from what she had imagined. She looked at his hands. That's how it would be done. His hands.

When she turned her head, her scar was silky and luminescent, like still water at dusk. The groove in the middle of her upper lip showed clearly in the light from the street, deep and smooth, youthful and beguiling, so much at odds with the shadows of the park. She stood in front of him, her head down as she tried to decide if she was abandoning herself or getting ready to fight: the two seemed bound together, since as she put her head down, she wanted to use her attractiveness to get control of this.

Karl wanted to get close to her, but he hesitated. He was sure, though, that if he stepped back, if he turned away, he would instantly have a sense of loss. He stared at the groove in her lip. It seemed intimate to him, as though she were naked and her beauty revealed an unexpected hope. You've seen it before, he thought. So what's different now?

She's getting ready to disappear, thought Karl.

Up until this moment he had lived in a plodding way and had sat in the Bar Restaurant until he was told what to do. At one time he had worked for the railroad, and he had done his job with a steady, machinelike precision, spreading gravel, leveling the ties with their odor of creosote. Everything had been dull, more or less. Now, he stood there and blinked.

"So what do you want?" she said.

"I don't know," he said.

He blushed. The sudden heat made him wonder if he had gotten sick, like his brother who had gone to Africa and had returned to Berlin with malaria. He stared at her scar with a shock of recognition: he had never been more certain of anything. The delicacy of her shape, the fineness of her features, the smallness of her figure and hips, the thinness of her legs, all seemed more feminine and ethereal because of the scar, which, in the most personal way possible, he understood. It bound them together. He leaned closer and smelled an orchidlike whiff of perfume and her slight, sweaty aroma. It seemed to come from her blouse, her neck and shoulders.

He had the impulse to take her hand, and for a moment he thought he had the sense not to do that, but then he reached down anyway. She put her hand out, too, and glanced up at him, and thought, That's right. His hands.

A vibrant flow ran from her hand into his and he was uncertain where he ended and where she began. He apprehended this sensation as a kind of buzzing, a soft one to be sure, although the power of it frightened him.

"You want to take a walk?" she said.

"I guess so," he said.

They went along the paths among the dark trees, and after about a hundred yards they came to a small clearing where there was a bronze statue of a man in robes, holding an open book. A bench stood at the side of the clearing, and the two of them sat down. Gaelle kept looking around, but she didn't let go of his hand, and he was beginning to think that she was holding it sincerely, too, as though even that small touch in the darkness was reassuring to her. As though she were asking him for something. She trembled there, on the bench, looking down.

He knew what he was supposed to do. The first thing was to find out if she had said anything about Breiter. Had she told anyone, and if so, who? Had Gaelle mentioned that Mani and Karl did this on their own, separate from the party?

They sat there. At the side of the clearing one of the park's decorative lamps came on. He had felt suspended but anchored by her diminutive presence, as though some invisible line ran from him to her. He was reminded of his childhood when he lived in a small town outside of Berlin and how he had flown a kite: he remembered the air, the cool breeze, the tug of the string against his hand, and as he stood at the bottom, watching the kite move this way and that way, small up there at that distance, he had experienced a small, keen, and pleasurable buoyancy in his chest. He felt that now. It had been a long time since he had felt buoyant. He wasn't cheerful now, but something very close to it: the more he gave into the touch of her hand and that lightness the more excited he became, stiff in his pants. Could she see it?

Gaelle felt a tightening that she thought was fear, although it could have been more complicated than that. How long had it been since she had felt a sense of warmth, a kind of flow? Recently she had been so fatigued and frightened that she had gone through a barrier and come out on the other side. And, as she thought it was coming, that he was going to take her back into the dark where she would be obliterated, her excitement seemed to grow. Self-loathing, she thought, such self-loathing. In the midst of this she felt that place where she had so thoroughly relegated the desire to be loved, a weight in her interior life, and now this presence, this essence opened and left her looking at this large, ugly man. Oh, no, she thought. Not now.

He had often been ashamed of his size and his battered face. People got on the S-Bahn and looked at him and glanced away, as though they had seen a dead dog in the road. He stood up to this with a blunt, distant gaze that had protected him, but as he glanced down now he realized that the same thing must have happened to her every time she got on the train. He had been able to take this isolation when he thought that he was alone in the world, that no one else had to endure this the way he did, but she had obviously had this experience, too. The shock of it left him almost disoriented. Whatever he had depended upon in the past had vanished, and he was left with the constant, reassuring buzz of her hand against his.

"So, what do you want?" she said.

"I don't know," he said.

She went through a list of what she could do, or would do, although some of these acts were more expensive than others. She spoke with a quiet whisper, almost as though she had forgotten what the words meant, or what these acts really were. Instead she seemed to concentrate on his enormous hand.

"I need a minute," he said.

"Sure," she said. "Take your time."

He looked over her head into the shadows under the trees. That was where he thought he was going to do it. It was hard to see, and the blue-gray dusk made everything appear to be part of the same substance. It was difficult to separate one thing from another, a tree, say, from someone's leg.

"I guess I want to talk," he said.

"What about?" she said. "Is there something you want to do I haven't mentioned?"

"It's not like that," he said.

"Well, what's it like?" she said.

"Do you feel it?" he said.

"Feel what?" he said.

"Like there's something running from my hand into yours," he said.

"Not really," she said.

"Try to feel it," he said. "Close your eyes."

"I don't want to close my eyes," she said.

"I'm not going to hurt you," he said.

Isn't that the sign, she thought, isn't that the beginning?

With a feeling of complete surrender, she put her head down and closed her eyes. He felt her fingers, which were half the size of his, tighten against his hand. This tightening increased that buoyant sensation, and at the same time, as a contradiction, he seemed to be more real than before. No, he thought. Not more real, more important. Their hands, where they touched, became warmer. He supposed she thought he was just another creep who held hands with women like her, and that she would start laughing, or worse, play with him in a kind of insincere, mercenary way, but instead she just sat there with her eyes closed.

Then he thought, She knows what I came for.

He put the trembling tip of his finger against the groove in her lip.

"I feel something," she said.

Then he leaned back against the bench, which like everything else was too small for him. It hit him halfway down his back, not up on the shoulders where he wanted to be supported. He watched the approach of the darkness, the trees and leaves disappearing, the cones of park lights becoming more clear, the benches, the line of the top of the foliage as it vanished.

She glanced up at him.

"You're laughing at me, aren't you?" she said.

"No," he said. He shook his head.

"You know I'm scared and you're having fun with it," she said. "That's it, isn't it?"

"Oh, no," he said.

He shook his head and tried to take her hand more completely, more gently. She began to pull away, but then stopped.

"You know what I came to do, don't you?" he said.

"Yes," she said.

He had always thought one of his strengths was the ability to say nothing. It came in handy when people pleaded and promised things and tried to get him to abandon the job he was supposed to do. Now he realized that didn't come from strength, but from the inability to speak. So, he sat there, looking at her, his silence surrounding him so completely that it was like a miasma, a stink of incapacity.

"That's what I'm supposed to do," he said. "But I don't know . . ."

"That's all you've got to say?" she said.

"I don't talk," he said.

"Really?" she said.

"I don't talk very well," he said.

"So what do you do?" she said.

He noticed that she left her hand in his. Then he tried to think of something to say. What did he do? He took orders. He waited. He did what other people wanted him to do. And as he went through these items he thought, isn't that what she did? Waited, took orders, did things that she spent a lot of effort trying to forget.

"Have you ever thought you were just going to do your job and then something happens? . . ."

"Mostly I do my job," she said.

"But you see what I mean?" he said. "You could feel funny."

"I was feeling funny earlier," she said.

"Were you?" he said. "Like what?"

"A little dizzy," she said. "You know."

They sat together for a while longer, and then, as though blurting something out in an unfamiliar fashion, almost as though speaking a language he only half knew, he said, "I've got an ugly face."

She looked up at him.

"So what?" she said.

"How can you say that?" he said.

"It doesn't matter to me," she said.

He felt so light that he was afraid to let go of her hand, since he might float away, not actually, not physically, but mentally, like madness. He started trembling.

Then she turned and looked at him.

"What are you going to do?" she said.

"First I was supposed to ask if you told anyone about Breiter."

"But that was only the first part, right?" she said.

"Yes, that was the first part," he said. "Then I was supposed to do the next thing."

It was the last part of the evening, and as the light bled away, the essence of what he was supposed to do seemed to tint the dark trees. They could almost smell it: the horror of the devastation of a human being. In the middle of it he felt the slight, tender, insistent movement of her hand as she put it back into his. The warm return of it, which was like the sensation of trust itself, left him with an increasing sense of lightness and importance, too. If nothing else, he realized what the touch of her hand meant to him: he hadn't really thought that anything was important, and now that he had a hint of this possibility, he wanted a little time to consider it.

In the instant that she realized it wasn't going to happen, the fear, the terror, the anticipation, the surrender seemed to wash through her with a tingling rush, and she was left holding his hand and leaning against him.

"Hmmmmm," she said.

Then he thought, Just do your job. This is just some doubt, some silly thing that happens to everyone. He wasn't sure about that, since he had never really talked to anyone else who had to do what he did. Mostly, it was something he had been quiet about, just as everyone else who had the same experience was quiet about it. Then he stood up.

"Come on."

"Where are we going?" she said.

"We've got to have something to eat," he said. "Will you come with me? I know a place not far from here."

She looked up at him. It almost hurt her neck, but then, in a moment of frankness in which she couldn't tell if she had really felt something in her hand, too, aside from a momentary release from terror, she said, "All right."

They walked out of the park. He was shy about taking her hand, and so they went out the way they had come, keeping a little distance, just like their business had been done. Felix was waiting with his inquisitive expression, as though trying to decide if this enormous man was going to become a regular. That was the ticket: a steady, repeating group.

"I'm hungry," said Gaelle.

"We're going to get something to eat," said Karl.

"No kidding?" said Felix. "Well, of course. Won't that be nice for a treat? Well, I'll stay around here. You know, set some things up."

Then he watched as they walked along the sidewalk, Karl's shoulders so large and broad he seemed like a door that was being moved down the street, and Gaelle next to him, seeming waiflike by comparison.

They went into a restaurant and took a table at the back. It was a medium-priced restaurant with checkered tablecloths and a waiter in a white shirt and a small black tie. The waiter gave them a quick, indeterminate glance, as though trying to decide whether to let them eat, but after Karl's keen expression of warning, the waiter bent over and waved them in, ushering them toward their table.

From the street, through the window, they ate slowly, picking at their food, although from time to time Gaelle looked up and spoke in quiet, intense bursts. She shook her head. She hadn't meant anything wrong. Maybe she had tried to make herself safe, see, that was all she wanted, and so she had gone to Hauptmann, too, but was that so bad compared to what had happened to her? Did he need proof? Look at her face. She had done her best, and look what a mess she had gotten into. Karl ate slowly, nodding, looking around. So, yes, she had told the thugs, but they had leaned on her.

When they were done, he reached across the table, took her hand and said, "What are we going to do?"

"Let's go back to my place," she said. "We can talk about it."

"Can I kiss you there?" he said. He touched her lip. "Right there."

"Yes," she said, turning her face toward him, offering it. "If you want. You can do anything you want."

He held her hand and looked at the marks in her palm, which were like the plan for a tree. He traced the lines with his finger, touched her wrist, and all the while he kept his head down, as though not wanting to be seen. Then he looked up at her and dropped her hand.

"I've been thinking it over," he said.

"And," she said. "What do you think?"

"We're in a bad spot," he said.

"Where's that?" she said. "Where's the bad spot?"

"In the middle," he said.

M ani pulled up his blanket and closed his eyes. If he could go back to sleep he could forget that the man from Moscow, Herr Schmidt, had been asking for him every afternoon. And when he forgot, he slipped into a world where the colors were bright again, but when he remembered Herr Schmidt, the reds, yellows, blues, and greens suddenly faded, like dry flowers. So he stayed in bed, suspended between the light of dawn, which came in his one small window, and the warmth under the blanket. The scent of coffee came from the café downstairs and then Mani sat up, put his feet on the floor, and rubbed his hair. It was possible that he was getting sick, but he knew this was just wishful thinking. He didn't feel this way because of a cold.

He hated lies not because he loved truth, but because lies worked so badly and required so much attention. It was like having a kid, every time he told a damn lie, since it needed to be fed and looked after. The other problem with them was that they only worked short term, and sooner or later, a new lie was required. Late at night when he heard rats in the wall, he imagined that they were lies breeding, getting ready to make trouble, to demand more attention, to betray him. How could he keep track of all the lies he had to tell and all the new lies that the previous ones required? For the first time, he saw ordinary truth as pure and clean and dependable, but impossibly out of reach.

He went to the basin, washed his face, although he didn't meet his eyes in the mirror. Then he sat at the side of the bed while he laced up his shoes. The first thing was to make sure that Gaelle went away, that there was no evidence of what Mani had done, no sign that he had indulged in factionalism. The most important thing was to keep a clear head and to work through his problems one at a time.

Mani went downstairs and sat in the corner, where Kathleen brought him a cup of coffee. His hands were shaking when he picked it up, and he looked around the room to see if anyone had noticed. Then he sat there and looked at the black circle of coffee in the cup. If he didn't know better, he would say that his silence was a variety of prayer. Well, he would have to stop this bullshit, too.

The door opened with a white light, as in a newsreel of an explosion, and for an instant Mani hoped it was Karl. The figure in the doorway stood in a hazy nimbus, and as Mani squinted into it, feeling a gritty discomfort from not having slept, all he could make out was a blurry silhouette. Then, as the door closed, a tall, thin form coalesced out of the light.

"You're a hard man to find," said Herr Schmidt.

"I've been busy," said Mani.

"Yes," said Herr Schmidt. "That's what I hear." He took off his hat and put it on a chair, his long fingers lingering over it for a moment as he put it down. Then he sat down next to his hat and coat. "Very busy. Right?"

"You could say that," said Mani.

Herr Schmidt looked from one of Mani's eyes to the other, as though they weren't showing the same thing. Kathleen came out of the kitchen like a fireplug on wheels. Herr Schmidt glanced from her, to Mani, and then back to her and said, "Coffee. Black." Then he looked at Mani. "So, tell me. What have you been doing?"

"We're making plans. We're going to have street theater. Songs. We're going to march."

"Uh-huh," said Herr Schmidt. "What do you hear about Breiter?"

"Nothing yet," said Mani. "I'm asking around. We put out feelers. We're looking into it."

"Uh-huh," said Herr Schmidt. "Where's the accounting you've been keeping?"

"Upstairs," said Mani.

Kathleen came in and put the coffee on the table. Then she turned away, as though she had just served a condemned man. Herr Schmidt took a taste.

"It's hard to get coffee like this in Moscow," he said. "But, you know, it's possible to miss home, even when things are difficult. I miss the landscape around Moscow. The river. Eel cooked in the Georgian way."

"And Ukrainian dishes?" said Mani.

He hadn't meant to ask. It had just come out.

Herr Schmidt looked at him for a long time, trying to decide if the question was anything more than a matter of asking about food. People weren't starving yet in the Ukraine, but it wouldn't be too much longer.

"I like good, Russian food. Soup with meat, *palmeni,* food you can trust," said Herr Schmidt. "The Ukrainians are interested in factionalism, in independence. That's not going to be tolerated."

They sat quietly for a while. In the kitchen Kathleen and the young man who helped her were arguing and banging pots around, and when Kathleen chopped onions and turnips, the whack, whack, whack had a staccato quality, but it was still domestic and cheerful.

"We understand that a big man was involved in the Breiter matter," said Herr Schmidt. "Broad in the shoulders. Like a barn door. Do you know anyone like that?"

"Well, I guess there are people like that around," said Mani.

"Hmpf," said Herr Schmidt. "I have a little advice for you. The first thing is to get your accounting in order. You've been given quite an honor."

"What's that?" said Mani.

"You've been invited to Moscow," said Herr Schmidt.

Mani was sweating in earnest now. He licked his lips and put his hands together, and then he took them apart and put them on the table.

"Something wrong?" said Herr Schmidt, who looked again from one of Mani's eyes to the other.

"No," said Mani. "Nothing."

"You act as though this was something to worry about. Believe me, being invited to Moscow is a sort of prize. For doing good work here."

"I see," said Mani.

"Good," said Herr Schmidt.

"I'll need a little time," said Mani.

"Of course," said Herr Schmidt. "We must make plans. I have to make reservations. We have to take care of things here. So, you'll have plenty of time."

Herr Schmidt reached over for his hat, his long fingers picking it up with an almost tender gesture, like removing a bottle from the hands of a sleeping baby, and as he put it on, he looked right into Mani's eyes.

"I will contact you when I have the date," said Herr Schmidt. "It will give you plenty of time to make sure the accounting is in order. And to finish up with the Breiter matter."

He held his hat with the tips of his fingers.

"Do you think it would be a good idea to go to Moscow with Breiter not explained?"

"No," said Mani. "But what's it to you? Or to anyone. Who cares?"

"You are supposed to be disciplined. If we care, then you care." He cleared his throat. "Well, until next time," said Herr Schmidt.

Then he got up and walked through the room, opening the door and letting that white light come in, like a flash, and then went out, into the fuzzy illumination.

"Do you want something to eat?" said Kathleen.

"No," said Mani. "I'm fine."

Mani climbed the stairs to his room like an old man whose joints hurt, but he stopped on the first landing, hand on the shiny banister, head cocked to listen to small sounds in the building. It creaked and sighed, and water hissed in the walls. Mani waited. Was anyone following him? Then he went up to his floor and into his room, where he shut the door and leaned against it. He looked at the manufactured receipts, and somehow the brownish stains seemed uniform, all of the same kind. It was an amateur job, and he flipped through one and then another, as though each were another dangerous thing to have.

Maybe a drink would help, he thought. If he could just get calm enough to think clearly. He went down the stairs, which were circular, like those in a lighthouse, and when he came to the bottom and opened the door, Karl stood in the middle of the room, head down under the overhead light. They looked at each other and then they sat down at one of the small tables, Karl's hands hard and gray, as though he had been mixing cement.

"You want coffee?" said Mani. "A drink?"

Karl shook his head.

Mani looked around the room at the rough tables, the fireplace with the smoke stains on the plaster above it, the mismatched chairs, the posters on the walls. All bland now, terrifying in the way that he felt no connection to them at all. It was as though he were falling. Get a grip on yourself, he thought, are you up to this or not?

"So," said Mani. "Where are we now? I'm mean with Gaelle?"

"I don't think it's a good idea," said Karl. "To do anything to her."

"Why not?" said Mani.

"We can just let it go," said Karl.

"What makes you think we can do that?" said Mani.

"We can agree that we'll just keep it between you and me. See? That way nothing happens."

"Oh," said Mani. "That will do it?"

"We can keep it quiet," said Karl.

Karl looked down.

"What happens when she sees a chance to make some money out of what she knows?" said Mani.

"No one should try to do anything to her," Karl said.

Mani tasted the bitter coffee.

"I want you to understand that. I mean no one," said Karl.

"You aren't safe," said Mani. "You may think you are, but that's not the way it is. You understand that?"

"I can take care of myself," said Karl.

"Don't be too sure," said Mani.

"That's the way it is going to be," said Karl. "That's it. Leave her alone."

He stood up and pulled his cap over his face so that half of his features were sliced by a shadow. He rolled a shoulder, as though he had a cramp.

"Leave her alone," said Karl. "That's what I came to say."

He turned and started walking toward the door, going around the clutter of chairs and tables, the atmosphere of smoke and stale soup, and as he went, Mani said, "You should understand. . . ."

Karl came back.

"What should I understand?" said Karl. "Are you threatening me?"

"I'm telling you there are other people involved," said Mani.

"I couldn't care less," said Karl. "About Herr Schmidt."

Karl made a brushing gesture, as though sweeping some crumbs aside.

"Let them be concerned," said Karl. "I couldn't care less. I have other things on my mind."

Karl turned in earnest now and went through the chairs and tables, and then up to the door. The light from outside came into the room like an explosion without the sound: a sudden, silent eruption of light. Mani sat there, watching the door swing slowly closed so that the room was only filled with shadows. Then he went back to his coffee.

In the evening, when it was foggy, Mani went out. He had a bundle of notes from the briefcase where he kept the money from Herr Schmidt, and it felt like a small brick in his pocket. The dampness made him keep his head down, like a man going into the wind. Every now and then a figure approached, looming up out of the fog.

Mani stopped at the door of a bar, which was the headquarters for Immertreu, one of the Rings in the city. The windows in the front of it were large, light falling out of them in a steep angle, and as Mani looked into the bar, the small beads of water on his coat appeared like jewels.

The Ring had prostitutes and pickpockets on the street, a gambling setup for boxing, and the six-day bicycle races, and they passed counterfeit bills they got from Switzerland. They fenced goods, and they knew how to break into safes. Mani had once seen their work with blowtorches and crowbars: a torn-open safe, the metal edges ragged and curled, blackened, violated. Immertreu also sold funeral insurance.

Mani went down to the end of the bar to Franz Nachtmann. On first sight Nachtmann appeared almost mild, even warm, especially in his posture, in his expression and features, which were rotund and seemingly cheerful. His cheeks were full, and he had a pug nose, which gave him the aspect of eternal youth. His lips were full, almost to the extent of looking sensual, and the feature that made him seem most harmless and even sweet, on first impression, was the groove in the middle of his upper lip.

Still, after even a short period of time Nachtmann, who ran the Ring, seemed to change, particularly if he had been considering a possibility. He

leaned his head one way and another, and his thinking, his pursed lips, his
finger picking at something in his ear all suggested a greasy malice. It was all
the more shocking, since the features that had seemed so trustworthy and
considerate appeared malignant and cruel, and it was this change that had
given him such advantage in the negotiations he carried on almost every
day of the week. I'm just a sweet guy, he seemed to say when he first shook
someone's hand. His eyes were a gray-blue, and his initial expression was
often one of charming surprise. You really want to talk to me? he seemed to
say. How nice. I'm so flattered, really. Here. Have a seat. Then he got down
to business.

"Well, Mani," said Nachtmann. "How nice to see you. It's been a
while. And what have you been up to. Staying out of trouble?"

"Not really," said Mani.

"Well, tell me about it. Sit down. Sit down. A brandy for my friend
Mani," he said to the bartender, who brought it almost instantly.

"Thanks," said Mani.

"Anything for an old friend," said Nachtmann.

Mani took a sip, licked his lips, and looked around.

"So?" said Nachtmann. He turned his eyes toward Mani now and
dropped the expression of mild surprise.

Mani reached into the pocket of his coat, took out the bundle of
money, and put it on the bar, giving it one small shove. Nachtmann looked
at it for a moment, and said, "Well, I'm sure this isn't a present."

"No," said Mani.

"All right," said Nachtmann. "What's on your mind?"

"We have some people who aren't reliable," said Mani.

"That's too bad," said Nachtmann.

"Yes," said Mani.

"So," said Nachtmann, taking the money and giving it to the bartender. "Who are they? Maybe we can work something out."

"You know Karl? He worked with me? He's got a girlfriend now,
Gaelle? The *gravelstone* with the scar," said Mani. He looked around.

"Sure," said Nachtmann.

Karl had been to Wannsee once before, and he thought that he and Gaelle could mix in with the crowd of holidaymakers, or go to the beach where the sailboats drifted by on the lake like white triangles. Perhaps they could take a tour boat, the *uuuuuunnh, uuuuuunnh* of its deep horn stirring things up. He never understood why the sound of a ship's horn, or a train whistle late at night, filled him with turmoil, but he knew that if he heard it now, while he was with Gaelle, it would be stronger than ever. Maybe she would feel it, too, that deep, vibrating reminder of impulses and hopes that are so deep and strong as to require a constant effort to deny them. Longing and regret. Or, perhaps these desires were so large that you could only feel them a little bit at a time, just for an instant at the unexpected sound of a boat horn, or a train whistle you heard as you tried to sleep.

Karl suspected they were being followed. In the beginning he looked at the men who had obviously been up all night on a party, the ones who were sick as they stood by the lake, their beards gray-blue, hungover, sour when someone tried to get them to have a good time, and while at first Karl wasn't sure why he was keeping an eye on these people, soon he knew there was a good reason for it. He guessed someone would try to kill them here.

So, he thought, who is it?

The holidaymakers on the train from Berlin to Wannsee had been dressed more formally than Karl and Gaelle. The other passengers glanced at him and then Gaelle, their disapproval sweeping over them lightly, like the touch of a feather, but leaving an impossible weight behind.

Gaelle stared straight ahead. He did, too. She whispered to him, "Don't give them a second thought."

It was the end of the season. On the train, the men told jokes and

laughed too hard. The women smiled and wanted to make the day cheerful. It was going to be the last one for a while, and that was enough to try to
make it the best day of the season. The children sat with their towels and
sand toys. The mob of holidaymakers were hilarious as the train approached Wannsee, although when the first glimpse of the water came into
view, everyone became quiet. The end of summer, the flirtations that were
coming to their only half-realized conclusions, a sense of evanescent ro-
mance, all seemed to linger in the train like the scent of suntan lotion. Karl
looked around, his eyes flitting from one man to another.

"So what are we going to do when we get there?" she said.

"Look at the water," he said. "Walk on the piers. You know."

He turned around to glance at the people behind him.

"What's the matter?" she said.

"I'm just cautious," he said. "It's a habit."

"It's been a long time since I went to the beach," she said. "Since, you
know . . ."

She touched her face.

"Well," he said. "I bet you look good in a bathing suit."

"Oh," she said. "I used to." She took his hand. "When you asked me
out here I bought a new bathing suit."

Men and women in their late teens and early twenties laughed and
shoved one another and grabbed each other's towels. Karl didn't have to
worry about them. He was looking for a solitary man who didn't quite fit.

He sat with his hands in his lap, not knowing how to tell her that he
was different from the way he used to be. He felt a little sick when he
wasn't with her. Gaelle looked out the window and watched the suburban
houses slide by, the buildings with the white plaster and timbered fronts
constantly moving into the distance behind them. Up ahead a little white
vapor hung in the air over Wannsee.

At night, in her apartment, she had touched her face against his and
made caressing, gasping movements against him. It had been like floating.
Now, if he held her hand, or kept his leg against hers, or if he could smell
her hair or her lavender perfume, or even her sweat, he was able to feel the
delicious airiness and lightness, cloudlike and mystifying.

In the distance, the lake seemed to be cut into a million blue and silver facets. People already began to reach up for the things they had brought along and had left in the overhead rack.

"What are we going to do after looking at the water and walking on the piers?" said Gaelle.

"We're going to have a good time, just like other people. See?" he said. He put his large face against her hair, close to her ear, and said, "I just like being with you, that's all."

He saw that her eyes were watering a little. She blushed, too, although the scar looked paler, more white when she did that. She slipped her hand under his arm.

The young people got up and started getting their things together, shoving one another, making jokes about one man. They called him String Bean and the Invisible Boy because he was too thin. The young man said he was just "wiry," and then he stood with his arms crooked, making muscles. One of the young women felt them and laughed. Then they all laughed, even the young man who was supposed to be too thin. When the train was empty, Karl and Gaelle got up and walked through the red seats and went out the door into the smell of the lake.

Then they went down the steps of the platform, crossed under the tracks, and climbed up on the other side to the concrete path that went along the lake. It was like a boardwalk, and couples strolled as they looked for places to eat, or for a tour boat to take. Karl heard that moan of a boat's horn. She took his arm.

"Do you hear that?" she said. "It makes me feel like when I'm waiting for you and I'm afraid you won't come."

He didn't trust himself to speak.

Then he looked around and thought, There he is.

The man was in his middle thirties, of average height, pale. His beard showed as a bluish tint, and his lips were very red. He wore gray pants, in the English style, a blue jacket, and fancy shoes, black ones with a gray weave over the toes. A member of a Ring, Karl thought. Someone who was just doing it for the money. Freierbund. Bruderbund. One of those.

"We've got some trouble," said Karl.

"I know. But let's not spoil today with things like that," said Gaelle.

"Look," said Karl. "You went to party headquarters, right? So they know you had something to do with Breiter. He was one of theirs."

"All that's above my head," said Gaelle. "I'm just trying to make a little money, have a good time. Now that I've met you."

"Yeah," said Karl. "But we've got the other side to worry about. The Soviets are interested, too. In Breiter."

"So, we're in the middle," said Gaelle. "Like you said."

"Alone is more like it," said Karl.

"But you'll be able to take care of them, won't you?" said Gaelle.

"Sure," said Karl. "Don't worry."

"I never should have gone to the party headquarters," said Gaelle.

"It's a little late for that," said Karl.

"It looked like easy money," said Gaelle. "You know, I tell them a little something. They pay me. Everything is fine. They gave me some money to listen to things."

The man was smoking a cigarette, which he finished and then flipped into the water, watching as the thing traced a smoking arc in the air and then hit the water with a *fitz*! The butt floated until a duck picked it up in its orange bill and swallowed it. The man leaned his elbows against the metal railing, made of pipe, that went along the cement walk above the lake. About a hundred yards ahead there were the piers where people bought tickets on boats to take them to more secluded beaches.

"So what do you want to do?" said Gaelle.

"I don't know, what about you?" said Karl.

"I don't know," she said.

Karl glanced at the man, who leaned against the railing.

"Do you want a sausage?" Karl said.

The man who had been leaning against the railing pushed off, with a sort of nonchalance and began to follow them.

"Two. Mustard," Karl said. The sausage vendor wore a clean white paper hat, a white shirt, and a white apron. The sign on his stand said, in red, yellow, and black letters, SAUSAGES. DRINKS. He gave them two sausages in fresh buns, wrapped in a napkin.

Gaelle took a bite of her sausage and mustard fell on her dress. She looked down at it and wiped at it with her paper napkin, but that made a yellow stain over the swell of one of her breasts. She bit her lip. Karl looked back and saw the man light another cigarette and toss the match into the water, the small piece of wood describing a smoking path, like something that was expelled by an explosion.

Karl and Gaelle came up to the Strandbad. The pool was on one side of a cement walkway, and the beach was on another, although the people were packed so closely on the beach the sand was invisible. Even the edge of the water was obscured by the number of people who were wading, splashing one another, or standing alone, staring out at the blue horizon. The shouts of bathers were indistinguishable from the cries of birds, and the line where the lake met the sky appeared like a taught wire.

"I'm so embarrassed," she said.

"Don't worry. We can fix it," he said.

"How?" she said. "I could just die."

"Up there," he said. "We can rent a changing bungalow. You can get into your bathing suit."

"You know how to rent one?" she said.

"Yes," he said.

She held the basket she had brought high up, to cover the stain. "You don't have to do that," he said.

The man with the English pants followed, a cigarette hanging from his lips, his hands in his pocket, his locomotion like someone in an American gangster movie. Karl approached the manager of the changing huts, which were arranged in a long line on the beach.

"We're all full," said the manager.

Karl stepped closer and took the man by the shirt.

"You really want to say that to me?" he said.

"I'm going to call the police," said the manager.

"Please," said Gaelle. "Please."

"What's wrong with her?" said the manager.

"We want a changing bungalow," said Karl.

"You'll have to pay something extra, since we have a lot of reservations."

Karl gave him the money, and Gaelle went into one of the bungalows.

The man in the English pants waited on the other side of the cement walk, and behind him the slight hillside was covered with the deep green leaves of late summer.

Karl walked across the concrete to the man, and some birds revolved in the air, squawking and diving for scraps that people threw in the water. Farther down the walk men fished from the rail with a somnolent patience.

"You," said Karl. "You want something?"

"Me?" he said. "I'm just having a little holiday."

Karl looked around. He couldn't do it here, not right out in the open.

"You're lucky," said Karl. "You don't know how lucky you are."

"It's funny about luck," the man said. "It's a two-way street. You could just walk out of here, just go have an ice cream. See? That would make some luck for me."

"You heard me," said Karl.

"Understand?" the man said. "Just leave her alone. Give me a chance. We're not interested in you. That's what I'm saying. Just the quim."

They're trying to separate us, thought Karl. That's how they plan on doing it. Karl put his hand around the man's arm, and for an instant it appeared like a stick in a bunch of bananas.

"I'm not a big talker," said Karl.

"Take it easy," said the man.

Karl glanced around. The boardwalk was filled with people who appeared as though they were on a conveyor belt, all moving along, women in light dresses, men in ties. Maybe Karl could just drop the man in the water, below the rail, and make it look as though he had fallen in. Then, with a little shove of dismissal, he let the man go.

The man smiled.

"I've got plenty of time," the man said. "And there's something else. There's more than one of us here today. Why don't you make it easy on yourself? Just walk off for a while and leave her alone."

Then he turned and went down the cement walk that curved between the green hillside and the lake.

Gaelle came out in her bathing suit, which made her look fresh and young. She carried her basket and her towel, and then walked toward the beach, although when they went by a restroom, she took a moment to go inside. When she came out, the dress was wet where she had scrubbed it in the sink.

"It'll dry soon," she said.

She looked up and smiled at him. The dress wasn't going to be ruined after all. The tour boat's horn sounded.

"Come on," he said. "Let's go out on the lake."

"Are you sure?" she said. "Is it going to be safe there? That's what you're worried about, isn't it?"

"How can you tell I'm worried?" he said.

"Oh, I can tell," she said.

"Maybe a little," he said. "The lake is the best place."

He paid for tickets and they found a small table on the boat, sheltered from the wind and covered with a white linen tablecloth. Gaelle put her dress over the back of an extra chair to dry and held it down with her basket. They drank white wine and watched as the boat went through the blue water, and as the ship's horn sounded, she took his hand.

"Are you glad you came?" he said.

"I've never been so happy," she said.

He felt the sweet moisture of her suntan lotion in the breeze that came over her shoulder. He wanted to explain how he had changed, but all he could do was to sit there, trying to smile, but not really knowing what to say. So, they were quiet, feeling the breeze, seeing the beaches slide by. She turned the scar toward him.

"It's been a long time since I trusted anyone," she said.

He nodded. He didn't know how to say it, not really, but he didn't think he had ever trusted anyone. He bobbed his head more intensely, up and down, hoping she understood.

The ship's horn sounded. Karl looked out at the long, receding wake.

"The scar doesn't matter to me," he said. "I wish I could say more. I mean more than that. . . ."

The horn sounded again.

"Like that," he said, gesturing to the horn. "That's what it's like."

"I know," she said.

He looked around the boat. He guessed the man had told the truth:

they were probably working in teams, and that meant the worst time would be at the end of the day, in a tunnel someplace, or after they had gotten back to the city. Maybe that's the way it would be. Toward the stern there were more tables, under a canopy, and beyond it people stood at the rail and watched the wake as it unreeled from the stern.

"I'm worried about being cut," she said. "When I think of people coming after me, I'm sure that's what they're going to do."

"Nothing like that is going to happen," he said.

He had a sip of wine and went on looking at her.

"I'd forgotten what it's like to feel young," she said.

"But you're not even twenty-five," he said.

"It's not the years," she said.

She leaned across the table and rubbed his face with her scar, as a caress of the most piercing intimacy, and said, "I don't know what I would do without you."

The horn throbbed.

"Why," she said. "You're getting teary."

"I don't know," he said.

"Why is that?" she said.

"I don't think we've got a lot of time," he said.

"I know," she said. "The afternoon goes so fast when you are having a good time."

He sipped his wine.

"See," she said. "The shadows are already coming out over the water. Sort of blue."

They had a little soup and salmon sandwiches, small ones that made Karl ashamed of the size of his fingers. The air on the lake was cool, but after a while she reached over and touched her dress and found that it was dry.

"Good," she said. "I'm going to go into the bathroom and change."

Then she stood up and went down the deck of the ship, along the bars of the rail, and as she stopped at the door to go inside, she turned and looked over her shoulder, the glint of light behind her, her hair blowing around her face, her smile genuine and inviting. She went inside and he sat there, looking over the faces in the crowd.

She came back and he said, "We're going to have to be careful going home."

"What are you worried about?" she said.

"I'm just uneasy," he said. "Maybe because I'm happy."

"We'll go with the mob of people," she said. "That's the safest thing."

"No," he said. "Let's get off at a stop before the one where we got on. We'll wait in the woods. Then we'll take a late train."

He took her hand.

"We'll hide for a while. Will that help?" she said.

"Maybe," he said. "We can hope."

"Yes," she said. "That's a nice thought, isn't it?"

rmina held the pistol in her bag on her lap as the train went to the shooting range in Wannsee, and on the way, it passed the Tudor houses in the suburbs, the beams of them dark like the wood of an old gallows. Then she considered the details of the boathouse, and the odor of dirt, the torn stockings, and the cigarette butts overwhelmed any attempt she made to excuse herself.

The brick building had stains around the window where the sooty rain had been running for years. The range officer sat in his office, although he kept the door open so he could see who came in. He ate blood sausage and bread, cabbage and potatoes, and he moved his bulk of more than three hundred pounds to reach across his desk for the tongue depressor that stuck out of a pot of mustard. Then he used his knife to plow the food toward his fork, which he gripped overhand, like a wrench, with a piece of sausage skewered on the tines. Armina watched him eat, her pistol in her handbag.

The range office gave her a box of ammunition and two targets, the first to practice on and the second to qualify. She walked out to the rear of the range where the frame for targets stood in front of a wall made of sandbags, hung the target up, walked back, and signaled to the range officer. He lifted his fork with a piece of sausage, yellow with mustard, as a sign to begin. She put two pieces of soft rubber in her ears, loaded the pistol, which was a revolver, and looked at the target. She listened to the wild throb of her heart and thought, Yes, clarity.

The target had a round, black center, arranged in concentric circles, each one numbered and separated by a small line. She had to get a score of at least seventy, which was difficult at this distance, although if she hit the line between two rings she was given the higher score. The trick was to feel her heartbeat: to hold her breath and to wait until the pistol dropped that small amount, the bead flat with the rear sight, absolutely level with it, just below that black circle.

She concentrated on those evenings when she and Rainer had been in Austria in the hotel there when she had let go, both of them looking into the other's eyes. The thrill of letting go had come over her in a rush of points along her hips and legs and even down into her heels, and the surprise of it reminded her of the cascading lights of the fireflies in the pine grove in Austria. They were related in some way: those lights in the dark grove and the tickling, lovely thrill.

The pistol went off, Bang! Bang! Bang! She listened to her heart, which came out of an interior darkness. Her sense of responsibility and the turmoil it caused reminded her of a place she had heard about in America where tar bubbled up from the depths and carried the remains of enormous creatures to the surface, toward the light, and the bones, the muck, the stink, and the atmosphere of the depths haunted her, as though they were her own terrors, her own guilt, which rose like the bubbles of gas from the depths. The monsters had been concealed, but now, with their upward movement they were coming to the surface.

She took the target over to the range officer, who looked at it and said, "Ninety-one. You don't need the practice sheet. Here. Give it back."

She handed over the second, blank target.

"What were you thinking about to shoot that way?"

His blood sausage and cabbage and potatoes with bacon and vinegar were almost gone. He had a glass of beer, too, which was the color of lemon custard.

"Food," she said.

"Yeah," he said. "That might help."

"A steak," she said. "You know, the way they have it in Paris."

"I've never been to Paris," he said.

"They make it with shallots and wine," she said.

"What's a shallot," he said.

"Sort of like a small onion, which they sauté in butter and then they put in some red wine and cook it down."

"Then what?" he said as he licked his lips.

"They put in some beef stock and cook that down," she said. "Then they cook the steak, you know, they sear it, and then put it on a plate and cover it so it cooks in its own juices. And after a while they cover it with the shallots, then serve it with fried potatoes."

"Well," he said. "I will have to go to Paris sometime."

He signed her card, which showed that she had qualified again.

"No wonder you shoot that way if you are thinking about food like that," he said. "Yes, I really will have to go to Paris."

On the way home she found a watch in the window of a jewelry store. It was large enough to fill her palm, and it had small Roman numerals on it, hands that looked almost too delicate to be anything but drawn with ink. She bought the watch and took it home, and when Rainer came in she said, "I've got something for you," and held it out.

He smiled at her and took the watch, holding it up and letting it glow there in the dim light of her living room, a sort of spun gold orb there in his palm, and as she reached to open it so he could see the fineness of the hour hand and the second hand, he put his face close to her fingers, and as he kissed them, he said, "I can smell the gunpowder on your hands."

They sat quietly, and after a while she said, "Tell me about the jungle."

"Oh," he said. "That's what you want? Ferns, the long lines of ants, like black chains, all carrying little bits of leaves, the rain. The sound."

"You could put your hand on my neck. It's stiff," she said. She turned her back to him and bent forward, exposing her neck. "Tell me about the jungle."

"It rains," he said. "It comes down in such sheets. You can't keep anything dry."

"Is that right?" she said.

"It's so hot," he said. "And everything has the odor of the jungle. It's a smell of orchids and leaves and something else, too, a kind of scent that is mysterious."

"Here. Let me pull up my shirt. Put your hand on my side. Right there. Can you undo that?"

"The wet makes everything shiny," he said. "Like silver, like sweat, sort of, like tears."

"Yes," she said. "I can imagine."

"Can you?" he said.

"Not the jungle, but the tears," she said.

"Everything drips," he said. "The trunks of the trees, the leaves, the creepers, the flowers, and you can see long silver strings. That is the basic combination, you know, silver and green, with the gray trunks of the trees. And then it comes alive. Everything that was quiet in the rain starts up again, insects, animals."

"You can take that off," she said.

"Oh, it gets so hot and so damp suddenly, since everything turns to mist. You can feel it on your skin and when you breathe," he said. "You're going to tear the buttons off my shirt if you do that."

"I like the ripping sound," she said. "Tell me about the orchids. Do they tremble? Do they become wet in that heat? And do the women in the jungle wear them in their hair? Is that how they bitch up their men?"

"That and some other ideas," he said.

"Oh," she said. "Well."

She put her fingers to her nose to smell the gunpowder as she recalled the vibrant air in the gun range, that Bang, bang, bang. The bead in the rear sight and the beating of her heart, which had the suggestion of one clear, certain thing she could depend on.

The Studio for Ballroom Dancing was on the third floor of a brownstone in a part of town that was a mixture of the genteelly run-down and the outright poor. The mechanical and almost cheerful sound of a piano came from a window where a sign said BALLROOM DANCING LESSONS, BEGINNER'S CLASS THIS AFTERNOON. PARTNERS FROM FRANCE. Mani stood in the street, hands in his pockets, looking up at the sign, but rather than going in as he wanted to, he went up to the corner where the piano was difficult to hear. Even the utilitarian piano playing had an effect on him, as though he could imagine what inspired music would sound like, and this anticipation of sincerity and beauty left Mani disoriented with forbidden ideas. He had seen one of the dance partners a few days before in her red dress as she had stood at the window, and now he imagined her small black shoes and the hush they made over the floor and how this blended with the rustle of the petticoats and the hiss of satin. How reassuring that sound must be.

The stairs went straight up, each step covered with a rubber tread as shiny as licorice, and as Mani climbed, the sound got louder until at the top of the stairs the music was so loud as to make up in volume what it had lacked in spirit. The main room of the dance studio had white walls, a hardwood floor, and the piano. The piano player wore a black dress that came up to her chin and down to her wrists, where her pale hands, almost blue, really, worked at the keys. Diagrams on the wall, with numbers and arrows and dotted lines, gave the sequence for each dance, and the outlines of the shoes in these posters looked like someone had stepped in black paint.

Three women sat on chairs by the window, all dressed in formal gowns, although the hems were worn and the cloth was musty with old perfume and powder. The one in red was in her middle twenties, trim, although her hair was messy, her lipstick a little too bright, and her petticoats showed. She looked out the window and smoked a cigarette with her nicotine-stained fingers.

Mani paid his fee, took his seat along the wall, and waited for other members of the class to arrive, and as the piano played and the other men came in, none of whom glanced at him, he tried to enjoy the anticipation of doing one small thing he had always wanted. He concentrated on the dance posters, as though learning the steps could give him a few moments of peace. Gaelle, Herr Schmidt, the invitation to Moscow, and what that meant (would they leave him in the river when they were done with him?) all seemed to be manageable in the face of those numbered steps. 1, 2, 3, forward, 1, 2, 3 to the side. A poster showed how a man was supposed to hold a woman as he danced with her, one hand at the side of her lower back, one hand held so that she could rest her fingers in it. Light, delicate, romantic. He closed his eyes when he thought about the touch of those fingers. The most important thing was to take care of himself, to do the right thing, but for a moment he wanted to get away from that.

The dancing master wore a tailcoat and striped pants with a gray waistcoat and dainty shoes. He demonstrated a few steps for the students, his shoulders gliding in a way that kept them at the same height from the floor and parallel to it. Mani wanted to be able to do that. He craved it as though he were hungry.

Ten or so students lined up along with Mani, and as the piano played, they took steps one way and then another, although none of them knew the steps as well as Mani, who had a preternatural ability to remember. The dancing master watched him for a while, nodded, and said to Mani, "Have you ever danced before?"

"No," said Mani. "Not really."

"Surprising," said the dancing master. "You seem to have a gift for it. A knack."

He gestured to the French woman in the red dress who came across the room, her skin white against the satin, her nicotine-stained fingers extended to Mani. He held out his hand to her, offering it, and she took it as he put his right hand against the side of her waist. The French woman looked over his shoulder at the wall and then out the window, and as they went around the room, with Mani making small mistakes, for which he apologized, he smelled her perfume, her powder, and the scent of her hair.

Mani wanted to dance. He had done other things, too, that were not correct. He had wanted to write a poem about a woman who lay in the sun, her skin wet with a silver film, and he wanted to show how the heat, the moisture, the wetness all revealed a wild, eternal delight: damp skin, damp underarms, damp underwear, tears of happiness or at least of pleasure so intense as to make everything clear, all silver, somehow related to the stars. Powerful and so innocent, too. He knew a poem like this was a sign of his failure, and he wondered if Herr Schmidt understood such things about him. If you were part of the machine of history did you have such impulses? Of course not.

"Are you from Paris?" said Mani.

"Lyon," she said.

"Oh," said Mani. "Is it nice there?"

"There's not so much to do," she said. "It's easy to get bored in a place like that."

"Have you been in Berlin long?" he said.

She sighed.

"No," she said.

Mani looked around the room.

"You dance beautifully," he said. "It's like . . . I don't know how to describe it. Like flying."

"It's OK," she said.

"And it makes it possible to talk, too," he said. "I'd like to talk."

"And what do you want to say?" she said.

"There are times when I feel a little funny," he said.

"Like how?" she said, perking up a little, as though she were intrigued by this.

"As though the walls are closing in," said Mani.

"Well, what do you expect when they have classes in rooms this small," she said. "I feel it all the time. Especially when I'm sitting there between lessons. We're not supposed to leave."

"Yes, yes," said Mani. "I know. When you can't get away. When you are waiting."

"It's the worst," said the woman. "Trapped."

"Yes, trapped," he said.

They went around the room, the windows sweeping by.

"Remember," she said, "One, glide, two, glide, three, glide. That's better."

She rested her hand on his shoulder, looked him in the eyes for a moment, and then watched the walls and windows.

"You can talk some more if you like," she said. "It's OK. They don't mind if we talk. He," she said, gesturing to the dancing master, "even likes it."

"I've made so many mistakes," said Mani.

"You're not doing so bad," she said. "Take it from me. There you go. Glide. Glide."

"It could have been different," he said.

"It'll get better," she said. "Practice."

The piano seemed to thump along like a machine.

"You don't dance so badly."

Mani bit his lip.

"You're doing just fine. Being scared is the worst part. If you can get over that you'll be fine." She looked around. "Don't worry about that wall feeling. They're going to get a new place. See? It will be bigger and they will have a real orchestra, not this piano. You can come back then. You'll feel better."

She swayed with a tensile resilience, muscular and slender, and he kept his hand on her waist, where he felt the movement of her hips. He closed his eyes and concentrated on the seams of the gown under his fingers and the movement of the partner from France as she responded to his slightest touch with a fluid dip and step that seemed to acquiesce, to accept and to say, Yes, glide, yes, glide, yes.

"I was scared, too, when I started," she said. "You'll get over it. You're doing just fine."

"I wish I had more time," he said.

"Well, you can take another lesson. Do you have the money?"

"Yes," he said.

"Good. Come back for another lesson. You really have a talent," she said. For an instant she looked into his face and smiled genuinely. "Really."

"I don't know what to do," he said.

"Come back for another lesson, silly," she said. "That's all there is to it. How can you dance with that woman whacking the piano?" she said. "You could think if she played it instead of beating it."

She shrugged.

"Get yourself a little book. Study the steps. We'll go dancing sometime."

Mani swallowed and concentrated on the lightness of her hand in his, the texture of the satin, the slight, raised seams along her waist. Her hips made a little dip and sway when she stepped backward and to the side. He guessed that was Chanel powder she was wearing, but he didn't know for sure, since he had never really smelled it. He thought, Please, please don't end. Just a little longer. The piano stopped.

"We could go to a bigger place. You won't feel that way," she said. "All right?"

"Yes," said Mani.

She turned and walked back to the bench, and he listened to the rustle of satin, her shoes on the floor, and felt the lingering touch of her hand in his palm. The piano began again and the dancing master gestured to Mani to get back into line, but he just turned and walked away, past the diagrams on the wall and out the door.

F elix came into the party hall and stood at the back in the shadows. He hardly moved in the flecks of dust that spun in the air. A man in plus fours arranged the chairs in front of the stage with a piece of wood that was two inches long so as to set the distance between them. They were all lined up, neat as atoms in a crystal. Felix waited, if only to decide if he would go in and see what Hauptmann wanted.

"Hey," said Felix.

The man with the chairs looked up with a sullen glance, like a watch-maker who has been distracted from a delicate repair.

"What do you want?"

"Hauptmann," said Felix. "He sent me a message."

"He's back there," said the man.

Felix walked down the aisle in the middle of the room, and he dragged his leg as he went, although he kept his head up and tried to square his narrow shoulders. He started coughing and took out his large blue handkerchief to blow his nose.

"What's wrong with your leg?" said the man.

"Nothing," said Felix.

"Oh," said the man. "Nothing." Then he went back to his chairs in their perfect rows.

The hall to the back room smelled of disinfectant, like a hospital ward for surgery patients. Felix stopped here, too, and listened. The squeak of the chairs in the outer room, the ticking of the building as it cooled, a slight rustle in the next room as someone shuffled papers and clicked the lock on a briefcase: that was it, along with Felix's own, wet breathing. What was he going to have to answer? They'd want something, but what? And could he make a little something out of it? Was it possible to do a little business? He

ran his hand down his leg, where he kept his ice pick. Then he looked
around the hall. One exit at the back. One at the front. The chairs went on
squeaking.

"Come in," said Hauptmann.

Felix emerged from the hall into the light of the room. Hauptmann's
white fingers held a pen, and his shirt, bright as laundry in the sunshine,
seemed fresh and clean. Gold fasteners on his blue suspenders. Dark tie.
The scent of his pomade filled the room and his hair was slick.

"Thank you for coming," said Hauptmann.

"It's nothing," said Felix. He dragged himself forward.

"Sit down," said Hauptmann. "Do you want to smoke?"

"Yes," said Felix.

Hauptmann pushed a glass box across the desk, the cigarettes piled as
neatly as ammunition in a case.

"I've got my own," said Felix.

He lit one and leaned forward, elbows on knees, and looked from
under his brows, his eyes shadows in the overhead light.

"I wanted to talk to you," said Hauptmann.

"Sure," said Felix. "I figured."

"We've been watching you," said Hauptmann.

"Is that right?" said Felix.

"There's not much we don't know about," said Hauptmann. "We
know what you do when you catch one of those young women alone in the
park."

"No one's seen me," said Felix. "I don't know what you're talking
about."

"Oh," said Hauptmann. "You misunderstand. We approve. You are
taking care of undesirables."

"I don't know what you are talking about."

"That's fine," said Hauptmann. "You can say that."

Hauptmann turned down to his ledger and wrote with a scratching
sound, then stopped and dipped his pen into the black ink. In the front
room there was the distant squeak of chairs as the last adjustments were
made. A vase of roses sat on the desk, the flowers dark red, the stems green
as a frog.

"That's it?" said Felix.

"No," said Hauptmann. "Not quite."

"So?" said Felix.

"We want to give you a chance," said Hauptmann. "You can take advantage of it."

"Yeah?" said Felix. "What would that be?"

"You'll like it," said Hauptmann. "I understand. I really do."

Felix ground out his cigarette and sat in his chair. The smoke hung in the air while Hauptmann sat there, looking down at his ledger, dipping his pen, scratching.

"Pick that up," said Hauptmann as he wrote.

Felix reached down for the cigarette and put it in his pocket.

"That's better," said Hauptmann.

Felix's chair squeaked. Hauptmann went on staring, eyes steady, skin pale, fingers steady. Why, thought Felix, he's enjoying himself.

"Don't do that again," said Hauptmann. "No cigarettes on the floor. Is that clear?"

"Yes," said Felix.

"All right," said Hauptmann. "Are we going to do business?"

"I guess," said Felix.

"Guess?" said Hauptmann. "I'd like something more definite than guesses. Why, I can guess all kinds of things, but what good does that do?"

"All right," said Felix. "No guessing."

"That's better," said Hauptmann. He smiled and showed his teeth, which were as white as piano keys. "I knew I could trust you."

"Sure," said Felix. "What's the deal?"

M ani took his leather bag from the closet, opened it, and then sat down on a chair and looked at the collection of objects on his bed, a cheerful net bag of lemons among them, which he had bought at considerable expense. Reports of scurvy had come from Moscow. He supposed one lemon a week would do the job. There were twenty lemons altogether, and he held them in his fingers, head down, trying to decide if he would have the time to eat them all.

Next to the lemons were two pairs of woolen pants, five cotton shirts, two sweaters, a jacket, and a tie. He hardly ever wore a tie, and while he didn't think he would be asked to wear one in Moscow, since all of that was a thing of the past, he still had seen photographs of meetings in Moscow where the men had worn ties as they stared at the camera. Mani had spent some time looking at these faces, which he knew were those of men who were about to die, but if they knew it, they were careful about showing it. In fact, they all had a similar smile, a sort of frank expression that was more poker-faced than cheerful: it gave nothing and accepted everything. He supposed that his face looked the same, although he didn't go to the mirror to see if this was true. Instead he sat down and tried to think of something that would keep him alive. Who could he betray? Could he make a case against Herr Schmidt? And wasn't this just the kind of thing that the men in those pictures from Moscow had tried to do? Their expressions so perfectly revealed failed plans, lies that backfired, small mistakes that had finally come back to haunt them. Mani needed to be ruthless, and yet while he thought this and knew this to be the right solution, it left him tired. Maybe he could just wait.

He started packing again. Some socks, underwear, a pair of boots, belt, shaving things, and a brush, a razor, which he held in his hand. Then he went back to picking up his clothing and putting it down as though this spare, stripped-down collection of items, all ruthlessly practical, contained some hint of how he had ended up this way. The sad collection of things, which revealed the paucity of his life and the barrenness of his sensibility, showed that the owner of them was the kind of man who was impulsive and stupidly self-congratulatory. He had been impulsive and had taken action, had killed Hans Breiter because he wanted to prove that he knew what was best, and look what he had gotten himself into. He hadn't listened to the people who had power, and power, he now realized, was reality. He held the lemons to his nose and closed his eyes, as though if he were in his own personal darkness he could avoid an obvious fact. No one had ever been so superficial. And yet he wanted to believe, as a variety of hope, that he could be dangerous.

He kept what was left of the money from Herr Schmidt in the suitcase that it had come in, and now he put it on the bed and looked at the bundles of bills that were still there, six altogether, not a lot, but not something to be sneered at. He usually kept it in the bottom drawer of his dresser, but he sat there and thought of the people who could come into his room when he was away. Then he pulled the chest away from the wall, pried back the baseboard with his knife, and hollowed out a place in the lathe and plaster. The rats worked in the wall, scratching and thumping around, as though they were running across the head of a tight drum. Then he put the baseboard back, cleaned up the plaster dust, which smelled like lime, and flushed it down the toilet. Finally, he put the chest back against the wall.

He began to put his clothes into the open mouth of the suitcase, as though it were a hippopotamus and he was feeding it clumps of grass. His underwear was gray and had holes in it along the waistband.

The accounting lay on the bed, too, and he hesitated when he picked it up. What could be more telling than an accounting, since it was a record of small details, money spent, bills paid, that showed just what he had been doing, and the only thing more telling than an accurate accounting was a false one. This wasn't a good job, and if anyone looked into it, they would see that he had cooked the books.

On the wall opposite him there was one of the few posters he had actually ordered and paid for: it showed a man with his arms rolled up, the muscles in his biceps large, his eyes set on the distant, vital future. A woman was with him, strong, too, with firm breasts and trim hips, dressed in pants, her hair in a bandana. He had made receipts for fifty different posters, when he had only produced fifteen.

He'd make the decision about going to Moscow at the station: it gave him a little control to say that he would make the decision in an hour, in a half hour, in fifteen minutes. Downstairs, in the café, he walked through the mismatched chairs, the walls that were the color of fog, as though the smoke had been able to cling to the walls, and in the kitchen Kathleen prepared the evening meal, her knife coming down on the block, whack, whack, whack. The domestic cadence of it left him swallowing hard, biting his lip.

He went down the avenues of the city, looking behind him from time to time and both ways whenever he crossed a street. Churches, cafés, and restaurants, an enormous department store all went by in a jittery rush, even the places where he had been in street fights: often they had been nothing more that a quick smash and bang, just a shove and a wallop and the chance to throw a rock or a ball bearing, or a potato with a razor blade in it. He stood in these places and longed for the clarity of the beginning of a fight when the moment was defined by taking action, the first sound of contact, and the relief of letting go.

He went up the steps and into the main waiting room of the train station where he was supposed to meet Herr Schmidt. The clock showed that he was still early. He stood in the middle of the station with his leather bag, with his rough clothes, and let the people move around him. He had the sensation of being in the rush of water that pushed him, like a swimmer in a riptide, toward the Moscow Express.

He went to the gates that led to a platform and watched one of the engines come in, the enormous push rods like thigh bones, although this human aspect, so melded with the machine, made the locomotive seem an emblem of a machine of the century, hostile to people, seemingly unstoppable. He stood on the platform, watching the steam as he tried to figure out how much danger he was in.

In the station the wooden benches had seats that shone like ice. The clock showed that he had two hours more. Mani didn't want the decision to go or not to be made by just waiting around until it was impossible to do anything but to get on the train to the east. He tried to imagine when the train crossed into Russia and the moment when the light would seem to be

turned down a little. He knew the tricks of an interrogation, but what good
was that? It only made him more vulnerable, since he knew what was coming. At least he wouldn't eat the salt fish; that would make him thirsty.
That's what he had to work with. No salt fish.

A man sat at the end of one of the benches, his face red, as though he had
a rash. He wore a green sweater with large pockets that bulged with the things
inside. From time to time a young man or woman came up to him, and he nodded and smiled and sometimes gave them some money from an enormous
wallet that was held shut with a green rubber band. The man's eyes were green,
red rimmed, and from time to time he looked around the station, and once he
stopped at Mani and raised a brow? Is there something you'd like?

Mani looked away. He watched the door. The clock showed an hour
and fifty-eight minutes more. Herr Schmidt might take Mani by the arm
and lead him to the platform where the porters stood in blue uniforms with
bright buttons and where the waiters for the dining car, each one dressed in
white, emerged from the steam of the engine. He imagined that the clock
was sawing through the last of his time and that the sawdust it made was a
line of black ants that started at the clock and went down the marble wall
beneath it, each one, each black creature moving this way and that, stopping and starting, like finality made visible.

He picked up his bag and walked around the interior of the station.
The decision was going to be made, he told himself, by the time he got to
the first ticket line, and then it was going to be made by the time he got to
the doors to the restaurant. He looked in at people drinking beer and talking to one another: he stood there, looking in, and when the people came
out of the door in a rush to catch a train, they bumped against him or
brushed him with a shoulder. What would happen, he wondered, if he just
missed the train? Could he brazen that out, make plans for later and hope
that everything got so muddled that he would be forgotten?

No. Herr Schmidt would stay in Berlin and track him down, or he
would go to Moscow and then have Mani brought along later.

At the baggage check he pushed his bag across the counter, and when
he received his pale blue receipt for it, he walked through the station, past
the restaurant, and when he was outside, smelling the lingering steam and
coal smoke, he thought, Well, have I done it? Have I decided not to go?

Then he put his ticket in his pocket and thought that the most important thing was to get away from the station. Surely, he didn't want to make another bad decision, and the best thing was to walk around so that he could think about it. Maybe he'd just miss the train. Things like that did happen. Maybe he'd go up to the dance studio and see the woman in the red dress. He thought of her sweaty perfume, her hair that smelled of a nutty fragrance, the way she floated over the floor.

Karl was waiting in an alley near the rear of the station.

"Hey. Mani. Are you going someplace?" said Karl.

"I've been invited to Moscow," said Mani. He said it as a threat, as though he had access to some power that was beyond Karl.

"Have you?" said Karl. "Well, don't you want to say good-bye?"

"Sure," said Mani. "I'm not sneaking away or anything. . . ."

"That's all you've got to say to me?" said Karl. "That you're not sneaking away . . ."

"Well. Good-bye," said Mani.

"Here," Karl said. "Take my hand. Let's shake on it."

Mani shook his head.

"No?" said Karl. He took Mani by the arm. "Over here. Aren't you glad to see me? I thought we were friends."

"Sure," said Mani. "Sure. We were always pretty close. I could always count on you."

Karl gave Mani's arm an impatient shake.

"Don't be that way," said Mani.

"Let's go up the street here. We've got a little business to do," said Karl.

"I don't want any trouble," said Mani.

The sidewalk was uneven, part cobblestones and part stone slabs, the combination a little disorienting at times. Four-story houses lined the streets and many of them had storefronts on the first floor. Mani and Karl walked by the spot where Hans Breiter had been killed.

"So, you're getting cold feet about going to Moscow, right?" said Karl. "You just decided, sort of suddenly, not to go."

Mani nodded.

"That's the way it is with you," said Karl. "You decide. Then you don't like it."

"It feels right in the moment," said Mani. "Don't think it doesn't."

"Oh, I know," said Karl. "What you do always feels right in the moment, but then it doesn't look so good. I'll bet that even now, just after you decided not to go, Moscow is beginning to look good again. Now that we're together."

"Let go of my arm, will you?" said Mani.

Mani's teeth rattled when Karl gave him another shake.

"Where are we going?" said Mani.

"Up to your room," said Karl. "Don't be so impatient. Let's try to relax. Let's take it easy for a while."

"All right," said Mani. "How's Gaelle? That's what this is all about, isn't it?"

"Yes," said Karl. "I said we should drop it. And then what do you do? You go around to hire someone to come after us."

He gave Mani a shake.

"Look," said Mani. "Things are different now." He looked around. "I've changed."

"Really?" said Karl.

"I've gone dancing. I've taken lessons. There was a woman from France I danced with. So light on her feet. She put her hand in mine like some creature, a bird or something that was alive," said Mani.

"Dancing," said Karl. "Well, well. Dancing."

He took Mani's arm and gave him a shake.

"Dancing," said Karl. "What kind?"

"Ballroom," said Mani.

They stopped in front of the wall with the door to the Bar Restaurant. The air smelled of the evening's soup, cooking sausage, and the bread that Kathleen made. At the back of the restaurant they went up the stairs to Mani's floor, and when they were in his room, Karl said, "The money."

"Over here," said Mani. He pulled back the chest and pried the baseboard away from the wall, then reached in and took out the last of the money, which he handed over.

"Do you have another hiding place?" said Karl.

"What a dirty mind you have," said Mani.

Karl shrugged.

"Do you have any others?"

"No," said Mani.

Karl looked at him for a while and then said, "Well, all right."

"That's it?" said Mani. "Can I go?"

"It's time to go back to the station," said Karl. "You've got a train to catch."

The rats dug in the walls and the footsteps sounded in the hall as someone came upstairs from the café. The clock on Mani's dresser made a tick tick tick, which suggested the brass gears and levers, the springs and small screws, the movement of the cheap mechanism. From time to time a car went by in the street with a sad tearing sound, like silk being ripped for a bandage.

"All right," said Karl. "Let's go. Time's short. Let's take the tram."

They went up to the corner and took the streetcar, the blue sparks appearing along the overhead wires with a snapping sound. From time to time Mani looked around and tried to find a way to run or he looked carefully at the people on the street, as though trying to decide if someone could be trusted, but Karl jerked his arm as a warning. None of that. Sit still.

The passengers still waited in the station, the floor glassy beneath their feet, all of them dressed in their best clothes, tweed coats, dark shoes, leather gloves. Everything about them, their anxious waiting, their glances at one another, suggested some final moment, as though they knew this trip was going to be a last one, and the clutter of them in the waiting room, the movement of three hundred people, left Mani dizzy. If he could just get everyone to stop so he could think.

"Get your bag," said Karl.

Mani slid his ticket across the counter and stood there, like a man waiting for a verdict. The clerk slid the suitcase across the counter, and when Mani hesitated, Karl said, "Take it."

"I don't know," said Mani.

"You can stay here with me," said Karl. "Or you can take your chances in Moscow. Which is it?"

Herr Schmidt came into the station with his small suitcase and a white paper bag, in which he had some sausage and some bread. The paper was grease stained. His legs seemed longer here than ever, like a surveyor's tripod, and his waist, marked by his leather belt, seemed to be just below his chest.

"There he is," said Karl.

"Could we let bygones be bygones?" said Mani.

"What bygones?" said Karl.

"I was your friend," said Mani.

"I don't think so," said Karl. "I asked you not to do something and what did you do?"

"And this is all over a woman?" said Mani.

"Yes," said Karl.

"I'd like to stay," said Mani. "Maybe we could work something out."

"I don't think so," said Karl. "If you go to Moscow, at least you have the time on the train. Nothing will happen until you get there."

"Yeah," said Mani. He licked his lips.

"Maybe you can think of something," said Karl.

"Do you know of anyone who came back, from a trip like this?"

"No," said Karl.

The hush of escaping steam and then its scent, a mixture of moisture and oil, came from the platforms beyond the gate. A conductor cried out one long wail of reminding. Mani closed his eyes, then nodded, bit his lip. Then he turned and walked across the station where Herr Schmidt was waiting.

They went through the gate to the tracks and into the billows of steam, which rose around the green columns that supported the roof and the infinite squares of opaque glass. Karl stood at the top of the ramp, and just before Herr Schmidt took Mani by the arm and led him into the white, roiling mist, as though both of them were going to disappear forever, Mani glanced up at Karl and lifted his hand in farewell. It was an abrupt, sharp gesture, so mechanical as to remind Karl of a guillotine. Then the two of them went into the steam of the Moscow Express.

Felix's wrists stuck out from his coat, and he slouched because he was embarrassed by how fast he was growing. He sat with Gaelle on a bench back from her usual place, and Felix unwrapped his bread and butter and a piece of sausage. Gaelle listened to the sound of the butcher paper, which was pink, almost cheerful, as it crinkled. Felix spread it over his lap and began to eat, head down, chewing steadily, looking up every now and then to make sure no one was coming. He always ate that way: out of the way, no trouble to anyone. Gaelle pinched her cheeks to do something about the paleness of her skin.

"That's good," said Felix. "Get a little color in your skin. Makes you look innocent."

"Me?" said Gaelle. "You've got to be kidding."

"It's what they want, don't you see?" said Felix.

"Not always," she said. "Let me tell you."

A black car with a passenger in the back stopped at the curb, and the engine made a slow, sad puttering. Felix folded up his paper and put it in his pocket and said, "Look. Bruno Hauptmann. I knew he'd be back. You remember him, right? He's the jackass with the ginger in the champagne. He didn't want nothing but talk."

Gaelle turned to look.

"Have we got anything good to tell him?" said Gaelle. "Some gossip. Have you heard anything juicy?"

"Nothing that he'd be interested in," said Felix. "Make something up. Start a rumor. Keep him happy. A good lie. Say you fucked a member of the government. Name a name. That always gets them."

Hauptmann was as before, sitting in the backseat in a cloud of his pomade, his collar white, his tie neatly knotted, his long, delicate, and

manicured fingers reaching from the backseat to the window on the curb
side. Then he gestured to Felix, and Felix put his head in the car so that the
two of them could talk. Hauptmann gestured. Felix nodded, yes, yes, yes.
Gaelle thought about Karl's size and his ugly face, which looked as though
he had been brought into the world with a club. She smiled when she considered his hair, which stood up like the bristles of a brush, and how much
she liked to run her hand through it. When he laughed, it sounded like
large ball bearings thumping around in a leather suitcase.

"He wants you," said Felix.

Gaelle looked around.

"Maybe I better come along, too," said Felix. "Maybe I can help."

"Really?" she said.

"Yeah," he said. "You know, he might have another lighter."

They walked to the car and Hauptmann opened the door, the black
shape of it swinging out with a creak. The driver stared ahead. The headlights on the avenue made multiple shadows of the driver move through the
backseat, and the silhouettes left the backseat cluttered with half-formed
shades. Felix held the door.

"After you," he said. "After you."

"Gaelle," said Hauptmann. "How nice to see you."

She sat down on the fuzzy material, just like that on a train, and Felix
climbed in after her, closing the door and putting down the jump seat,
where he perched with an almost complete stillness.

"Have you been well?" said Hauptmann.

"She's been OK," said Felix. "Still not eating."

"Oh," said Hauptmann. "You've got to take care of yourself."

"That's what I tell her," said Felix. "But it's like pulling teeth. She
don't listen."

"I've got things on my mind," she said.

"I guess we all do," said Hauptmann.

The car pulled away from the curb, and Gaelle felt the surge and coast
as the driver changed gears and let in the clutch. The scar was on the side
toward Hauptmann, and he spent a moment looking at it. Gaelle tried to
think of Karl and how they would spend a little time together.

I need some time to think, or to come up with a story, she thought. Why can't I lie now when I need to?

"Does the scar hurt?" said Hauptmann.

"Not in the way you'd think. It's not a physical pain but an uneasiness. Have you ever touched half-burned newspapers? It's like that sort of, dusty and dry. It puts my teeth on edge."

Up the avenue by the river the streetlights made the fog look like it was made of diamonds.

"How many young woman have been found in the park in the last couple of months?" said Hauptmann.

"A few," said Felix.

"What's the point of talking about this?" said Gaelle.

"Well, we're concerned about your safety," said Hauptmann. "You don't want to end up like one of them."

She looked around the inside of the car, where the supports of the window suddenly appeared like the bars in a cage. The odor of the pomade was stronger, and the ominous stillness of Hauptmann left her staring at the door handle. At the end of the avenue the lights bled into the fog, like watercolors on damp paper.

"Have the police talked to you?" said Hauptmann.

"Look, do you want to have a good time or not?" said Gaelle.

"Oh," Hauptmann said. "I want to have a good time."

Gaelle turned her face to Hauptmann and smiled. Then she put her hand on his leg. The lights and shadow alternated in the back of the car, and with each change, Gaelle's dizziness got worse.

"So," said Hauptmann to Gaelle. "You haven't talked to anyone about Breiter. About what happened in the street?"

"No," said Gaelle. She moved her hand along his leg, just brushing her fingers over his lap. "I'm not going to say anything."

"You said something to us," he said.

"Well, that's different," she said.

"But you wanted money," he said.

"Well, so what?" she said.

"Where are we going?" said Felix.

"I thought we'd take a drive along the river," said Hauptmann. He turned to Gaelle. "Would you like that?"

"Anything you say," she said.

"You haven't told anyone about Breiter? You haven't mentioned him to anyone?" said Hauptmann. "I just want to be sure."

"I don't know what you're talking about," said Gaelle. "It's all Greek to me. Who cares about this guy? You know?"

"We care," said Hauptmann. "We care a lot."

Gaelle felt the stop and glide of the car, the pressure of the seat in her back when it accelerated, and she listened to the clip clopping of the horses in the street as the car entered the wall of fog that boiled up from the river. The car came to a stoplight right next to the river. Gaelle looked at the door handle. Felix sat with his hands folded in his lap, still and almost serene, his eyes blank, and when she tried to get his attention, he seemed impervious, lost in his own thoughts. The signal changed.

The car moved into the fog, and Gaelle reached down and took the handle, which was cold, but very smooth, and then the door was open and she was out, at the side of the car. She went around the back, into the middle of the avenue, where she stood between two lanes.

"I'll find her. She's just moody," said Felix. He got out of the car. "I know how to handle her."

"Good," said Hauptmann. "We'll make it worth your while. As I said."

"Sure," said Felix. "But we haven't talked money."

"She's going to get away," said Hauptmann.

"I can find her," said Felix.

"All right, all right," said Hauptmann. "Name the price."

Felix gave him a figure. Hauptmann counted out the bills, flip, flip, flip. He handed them over and Felix took them.

Felix looked both ways in the fog and went through the traffic, the horns honking, the cars stopping one behind the other with Felix in the middle. He dragged himself along with a keen impatience, like a man who has been waiting for his chance and has finally seen it.

Karl, she thought. Darling. Oh, please. Please help me.

In the middle of the bridge Gaelle tasted the mist, which was a mixture of oil and exhaust and the somewhat marshy residue from the river, although it had a scent of diesel or gasoline that the barges left. She looked back the way she had come and saw a figure on the bridge, just a black outline. It could have been Hauptmann, although it was hard to tell. Hauptmann was taller than that, but the fog made it hard to judge things.

A barge sounded its foghorn and the ache of it made her feel a little closer to Karl. Then she turned and started to walk quickly, almost jogging, the clicking of her shoes on the cobblestones only audible after the horn stopped. Whoever was behind her knew she was trying to get to the river.

She crossed the bridge and went along a park that was next to the water: some trees, some benches, cobblestones, a statue, a man on a horse. Now, in her frame of mind, it seemed as though statues of men on horseback were after her, too. She went up to a tree and stood next to it. Was there a chance that the man behind her had gone the other way?

Still, as she waited, it seemed to her that this is how she had been living for years. The caress of the fog was familiar and the chill of it was similar to her realization that she was not like other people, and that, for reasons she didn't understand, she was marked. How could God have loved her so little? This question added to her mystification and her loneliness. Someone once said that the scar had spit in her soul, and as she felt the fog, she thought, yes, that is what had happened. At least until Karl came along.

The lights from the other side of the river made a wall of red, blue, and yellow, mixed together like a collapsed rainbow, as though the thing seeped down right there. A man crossed the bridge, holding a cane. She waited by the tree and noticed that its roots had pushed up the cobbles that surrounded it.

The barge horn sounded again, so plaintive and piercing that Gaelle found that she was close to tears. How could she cry here? she thought. Well, maybe I am sick of this fog, which stinks, just as I am sick of the river, so much like the wet side of a snake. If she could just find Karl, it would be all right.

She came to the small stone building where the men who worked in the park kept their brooms, shovels, a wheelbarrow, some bags of fertilizer, which they used in the spring, and when she reached up to the heavy chain that held the door shut, she found that the lock hadn't been closed. It was just hooked together. She pushed it open, and then closed the door behind her.

She sat on the overturned wheelbarrow and listened to the barge horn, which became more and more faint. She put her hand to her scar as she smelled the dirt and fertilizer. Outside, someone went back and forth in the park, and after a while she recognized this as a circuitous, but still orderly, searching. The chain rattled as whoever it was out there realized, as she had, that the door wasn't locked. She tried to imagine that darkness before she was born, and to tell herself that where she stood now, in the small shed, was like being in that darkness, especially with the smell of dirt. The door opened.

"Oh, Jesus, Felix," she said. "Is that you?"

"Yes," he said. "It's me."

The barge sounded its horn.

"Thank god. Hauptmann scared me."

"I know," he said. "What's inside here? Maybe I can find something. Step back in."

"Why?" she said.

"I'll show you."

She stepped back.

"The dirt floor here is pretty soft, isn't it?" he said. "You'd think it would be hard."

"Listen, Felix," she said. "I've got to get away."

A slash of light came in from the crack where the door wasn't closed, and in it she saw that silver flash.

"I want to think things over," said Felix. "I want to make sure."

"About what?" said Gaelle.

"Why, there are a lot of people who are interested in getting rid of you," said Felix. "That's all I need to know."

"Let's get out of here," said Gaelle.

"It's like waking up," said Felix. "When you see your chance."

"Come on, Felix," said Gaelle.

"Too many people are after you," said Felix.

"I know," said Gaelle. "It just happened. I didn't plan it."

"And if something happened to you, why, a lot of people could be blamed for it."

"Why are you saying that?" said Gaelle.

"Turn around."

"Why?" said Gaelle.

"Turn around and I'll show you," said Felix.

"Oh, Felix," she said. "What are you doing?"

The horn sounded.

"Do you hear that?" he said.

"Yes," said Gaelle. "I hear it. What a sad sound."

He rustled in the dark as he pulled up his pant leg to get the silk cord, which he kept in a pouch next to the ice pick.

"Aren't you getting enough sleep?"

"I don't ever really sleep right," said Felix.

"Felix, do you want me to make you feel nice? Is that what you want?" she said. "Just tell me."

"That's all right," he said. "Just listen to the horn."

"I'll do anything you want," said Gaelle. "I can be good at it."

"The horn," said Felix. "It runs right through you, you know?"

"Oh," said Gaelle. "It seems as though I've been hearing it all my life."

"No kidding," said Felix.

The shed was surrounded by the last of the fog, which was gray and beardlike, just shreds of mist that rose from the river. The small park was filled with the lapping of the river against the stone bank, and Armina hesitated, as though the river and the chopping sound, especially loud under the bridge, contained some hint of the mortal aspect of this moment, as though finality had a fluid essence. Then she went up to the shed, where she knew what she would find. "A woman with a scar," the Schutzpolice man had said when he called. "In a toolshed by the river."

Why did I ever mention her name? thought Armina. To impress Ritter, to show that I was doing my work? She stooped in front of the door.

Uniformed policeman stood around in clumps—their visors bright with Vaseline, their buttons shiny, all of them fatigued. The fish scent of the river was stronger that ever. Linz was there, too, his beard more blue than ever, his skin white, his knobby fingers holding a cigarette.

"The usual," he said. "In here."

"The usual?" she said.

"Yeah," he said. "What's wrong with you?"

Plenty, she thought.

The shed smelled like a root cellar, and Armina half expected a mound of potatoes in the corner, covered with gray earth as they were piled against the wall. She kneeled next to Gaelle, who's hair was still bright in the otherwise dull place. By the light that came in from the door, the scar still seemed as rigid as ever, as much a mask as though Gaelle were still alive. At least the eyes were closed. Then Armina leaned closer, into that mixture of perfume and sweat, and touched the scar. It was covered with makeup, the pancake beneath the powder that Gaelle had gotten at the department store. So, thought Armina, it had done some good after all. She must have gone back to buy some powder.

She stood up and looked around. One foot was bare, and the shoe, near the door, had a broken heel. The bunched-up skirt, pulled-down stockings, the marks. Ground out cigarettes. At Gaelle's side there was a mark, shaped like a new moon, as though someone had dragged the toe of a shoe through the soft dirt.

"Did you know her?" said Linz.

"You could say that," said Armina.

"How did she get that scar?" said Linz.

"Car accident," said Armina.

"Hmpf," sad Linz. "She must have been pretty before that."

"Yes," said Armina. "That's right."

"Too bad," said Linz. "Well, look around. This one is yours, too. The underpants are in the corner. Everything else is as always."

"All right," said Armina.

She sat down on an overturned wheelbarrow, her head in one hand. Then she looked at Gaelle. On the river, beyond the door, an enormous barge moved along, the bow wave in a silver curl, which went on forever. Then the chop hit the stone bank again.

"We've got the address of her parents," said Linz. "That's the first thing."

Armina put out her hand. Linz had written the address on a small slip of paper, like a ticket. Outside, she sat on one of the benches. The pigeons flew around in a circle and their wings made a steady pop pop pop. Everything around her, the river, the buildings, the shed, added to her claustrophobia, which was indistinguishable from anger. The slight nausea that came with it was made worse by the stink of the river.

"You're not looking too good," said Linz.

"Me?" she said. "Hard night, I guess."

"Sure," he said. "I know what you mean. But what else can you do?" He looked at the river. "Well, good luck."

"That's what you have to say?" she said. "Good luck."

"Hey," he said. "Take it easy. I'm sorry."

She nodded and stood up.

The glass door of Gaelle's building was in a heavy frame with a brass handle, and the architecture was fortresslike, although these days the suggestion of security seemed all the more frail and useless. Armina's shape was reflected in the brass banister of the stairwell. Her elongated appearance here or in the glass of an old window had been utterly insignificant, but recently these stretched or compressed images, so much like in a fun house mirror, seemed like hints as to what was really happening. She was being warped, twisted. Then she tried to imagine the sound Gaelle once made as she ran down these stairs.

Armina knocked on the door. Gaelle's mother wore a dressing gown and her hair was in disarray, partly blond, partly gray, and the skin under her eyes appeared bruised by fatigue. The woman stared at Armina. In the background Gaelle's father said, "Who the hell is it at this hour?"

Gaelle's mother didn't move.

"Well?" said Gaelle's father.

Armina held out her identification. Gaelle's mother looked at it carefully, already wanting to make sure there was no mistake and that whatever was happening here wasn't one of those things that turn out to be just a misunderstanding. Armina had the desire to lean against a wall or to sit down, to rest for a minute. Anything to stop this.

"Uli, you better come out here," said Gaelle's mother.

"Oh?" said Gaelle's father from down the hall. "Why is that?"

"The police are here," said Gaelle mother.

"It's Gaelle," he said. "Isn't it? When is it going to stop? In trouble, I'll bet. It's enough that we had to go off to some godforsaken place to see your sister yesterday. Don't you think I would like to spend a week in a sanatorium, eating cutlets. My God, how long has it been since we have had a milk-fed cutlet?"

"May I come in?" said Armina.

"Please," said Gaelle's mother.

They went into the living room with its horsehair sofa, a chair that was broad and high with carved wooden legs, bookshelves that had glass covers. Doilies were spread on the tables and on the arms of the sofa, and underneath a vase on a table filled with dried flowers and cattails. On the wall a painting was hung that showed game on a table in what appeared to be a hunting lodge: the feathers of the bird were done with such attention to detail that each fiber was as clear as a tendril of frost on a window. Gaelle's mother sat down.

"Uli," she said. "Please come in here." She turned to Armina. "Won't you sit down?"

Armina nodded, swallowed, and sat at the edge of a gray chair, her hands together in her lap.

Uli Altman appeared at the door in his brown pants, his shiny shoes, although his suspenders were hanging from his waist as he worked on his tie. The scent of soap and pomade came into the room.

"Yes?" said Uli.

"She's from the police," said Gaelle's mother.

"I knew it would come to this," said Uli. "She stays out all night. God knows where she goes. Why, she's got her own apartment. How is she paying for it, that's what I'd like to know? And you know what, she refuses to bring her friends home so we can meet them. It's always in some dance hall or cinema or in the park or something. Six-day bicycle races. Now why would anyone want to race a bicycle for six days. What can possibly be the point of that?"

Gaelle's mother began to cry.

"Look," Uli said, as though the tears settled an issue.

"I have some bad news," Armina said. In spite of herself, even when she tried to resist it, she put her face in her hands.

"How bad?" Uli said.

Gaelle's mother cried all the harder.

"Well, what has she done?" said Uli. "She has been arrested, hasn't she?"

"No," said Armina.

"Oh god, oh god," said Gaelle's mother. "I tried to warn her. I thought she was all right, you know? But she was in the park. I know it." Gaelle's mother put her hands together. "Did she drown? Did she fall downstairs? Is that what happened?"

"No," said Armina. "We don't know what happened, not yet."

Armina swallowed and looked around at the heavy furniture, the sofa with lion's feet, the hanging game in the picture. What had Gaelle's voice sounded like here?

"Oh, no," said Uli.

He sat down, too, and then Armina took a chair opposite them.

"You mean someone killed her," said Uli.

"Yes," said Armina. She closed her yes. Nodded.

Gaelle's mother reached over for Uli's hand, and he took hers with a surprising tenderness. In the innocence of their grief, the two of them appeared almost as they had been twenty-five years before: youthful, hesitant, courting. They sat together, holding hands, neither one saying a word. A horn honked outside and a horse drawing a cart made a muted sound.

"Where was she?" said Uli.

"By the river," said Armina. "By the Spree."

"She always liked the river," said Gaelle's mother. "She used to like to stand on the bridge and watch the current go by."

"That was in the old days, when she was just a girl," said Uli. "She held my hand." He swallowed. "I can't remember the last time I picked her up. There is a last time. You just never know it."

Uli shook his head. He looked around the apartment as though the things in it, the heavy curtains, the gloomy silence, were something he could hang on to but found lacking.

"I think she was going into the park," said Gaelle's mother. "With men . . ."

"No," said Uli. "We don't have to say that. What's wrong with you? Can't you leave me something?"

"You're just worried about the bank," said Gaelle's mother. "That's all. What will the bank think?"

He got up and left the room. Then they heard him moving around in the back of the apartment, opening drawers, throwing things on the floor. Gaelle's mother sat with her head in her hands. Then Uli came back with an album of pictures: Gaelle as a young girl in a white dress, eating an ice cream at a lake in the mountains. She sat at a table and put the spoon into her mouth.

"See," he said. "That is the way she was. Like that! See?"

"Please, Uli," said Gaelle's mother. "Please."

Armina felt the tug of the pictures, the innocence of them, and for a moment she just stared. Then she bit her lip.

"I'm sorry," she said.

"Of course you are," said Gaelle's mother. "It's not your fault."

"I don't know," said Uli. "I don't know."

The two of them sat side by side, looking at the photographs, turning the sepia pages, which closed with a small, sighing whoosh of air. Armina waited. Then she said that she would be calling on them again. They nodded, without looking up, and Armina went to the door. The two of them held hands, looking at the pictures of the family. Then Gaelle's mother started crying again, saying, "It was just a stage. Isn't that what we thought? Wasn't it?"

Uli concentrated on a picture, his face collapsing like an accordion.

"Yes. Yes," he said. "That's what we hoped."

Armina went down the stairs, her motion around the landings seeming to her like a mathematical illustration, a drawing of a spiral as obvious as a corkscrew, and she tried to cling to this idea, if only not to have to go on thinking, to sum up, to face that seasickness and the sense of swinging back and forth at the end of a long rope.

rmina's brother, Rolf, had been born deaf and he had grown up in a world of his deaf friends, who attended a special school with him. Often, Armina came home to find Rolf with five or six other children who spoke with their hands, although the atmosphere in her parents' house changed from the cheerful intensity of his friends when he was ten and eleven to the more sullen brooding of these get-togethers when he was eighteen and nineteen Then the movement of the fingers, the gestures, were argumentative. Rolf became increasingly sullen, and as he left a room when Armina came in, he brushed by her, even bumping her, as though this abrupt contact were a continuation of his talk with his hands. Rolf had joined a rifle club, and he was an excellent shot. In fact, he had taught Armina to shoot, and when she went to the pistol range she often thought of her brother and his advice, which he had given with his hands: feel your heart, keep the bead flat in the notch, squeeze between breaths.

He had a collection of firearms and spent hours cleaning and handling his Mannlicher-Schönauer 6.5 mm, with set triggers and a forend that ran all the way up to the muzzle. At night, he sat in his room, using an empty cartridge so he could dry fire the rifle, the click lingering in the air of the apartment like the first, innocent sound of trouble.

Rolf and his friends had a basement in an abandoned building where they met in a club they had formed called Steel Hands. It was there that Rolf had begun putting dynamite together. No one had been able to discover where he had gotten the waxy, pale yellow sticks, and when the bomb went off, with Rolf in the basement, it made a crater ten feet deep. His friends had tried to explain to Armina's parents, wiping their eyes and gesturing with wet fingers. Rolf had just liked the power of making the thing. He had never meant it to go off. He was playing.

Armina stood in front of Precinct 88 and put her fingers into her hair, then looked at herself in the windows of the café next door, ran her hand over her skirt, and stood up straight. She felt that she was somehow responsible for what had happened to her brother (if she had loved him more would he have been safer, more secure?), and now as she passed back and forth, trying to get a breath of fresh air before going in, she considered the interior silence of his life, the fact of it like a fog, like something he could never shake. She considered, too, the hush of the church when she had gone there for Easter with her parents: how reassuring it had been, and how soothing to touch two people who had so completely loved her.

The note from Ritter was in the middle of her desk, on the green blotter. He wanted to see her. Did she have a moment? He'd be in his office all afternoon. All right, she thought, why not now as any other time?

The atmosphere of the shed clung to her like the scent of smoke, made all the worse when she thought of the disorder of Gaelle's splayed legs on dirt.

She climbed the stairs, where the scent of soap was as strong as always, and in the hallway outside Ritter's office the typewriters sounded like machines of fate. She passed the doors with frosted glass and then tapped on Ritter's door.

"Armina," he said. "Come in."

He said this without looking up, although he motioned to a chair opposite his desk. She didn't think he had the authority to fire her, not on his own, but then he might try. She would have to stand up then and say, Fuck you. Was that the correct way of handling this? Or was there something else he could do, something a little more subtle, more difficult to describe but still easy to understand.

"You wanted to see me?" she said.

He looked up, his gray eyes as always, not warm, not cold, the vacuousness of their expression somehow worse than obvious viciousness and frank ill will. There was no comfort in emptiness, since it wouldn't stop anything.

She squared her shoulders and looked down at him.

"Sit down," he said.

"I'll stand," she said.

"As you please," he said.

The typing started again.

"Before we get started," he said, "I wanted to say that I am a great ad-
mirer of music. I try to get to most of the concerts in town, Brahms, Schu-
bert, Beethoven. I'm collecting recordings, too. For instance, here is one of
a Beethoven sonata. Do you recognize it?"

He reached into his desk and took out a 78, which was in a manila envelope cut so that the label, in the middle of the record, could be seen. A
red label with bright letters, like the print on a box that held the best lingerie from Paris.

"Yes," said Armina.

"Your mother was a great technical performer."

"I'd like to think it was more than that," said Armina.

Ritter raised an eyebrow.

"Well, maybe. She was precise. Lovely, really. How crisp the notes are."

A crank-up record player sat on a chest, and Ritter removed the record
from its sleeve, put it on the felt turntable, and then wound the crank as
though he were making an urgent phone call.

"Do you have to play this?" said Armina.

"Don't you want to hear your mother?" said Ritter.

"Not like this," she said.

"Do you have bad feelings about her?" said Ritter.

"No," said Armina. "I came here to talk about Gaelle."

"Gaelle?" said Ritter.

"A woman with a scar," said Armina. "She worked in the park."

"Oh, her," said Ritter. "Well, this record is part of the discussion.
Your mother was a fine musician, one of the best, but she misses a note. I
want you to hear it."

"She was sick when she made this recording," said Armina.

"Yes, I know," said Ritter.

He started the record. The music was clear and ordered, the execution
of it precise. Armina had the desire to close her eyes, as she did at home
when she listened. Sometimes, just the first note of this piece was enough to
bring tears to her eyes. Now, she stared at Ritter. The music hung in the air

like perfume. She sat down in spite of herself, as though the music weighed a hundred pounds.

"There," said Ritter. "Right there. A pity really."

Armina went on staring at him.

"I'm trying to get your attention," he said. "You seem to be ignoring my advice."

"I told you," she said. "I think they are all tied together. Hauptmann, the women in the park, Gaelle."

"Just sex, huh?" said Ritter.

"Yes," she said. "What else could there be?"

Ritter turned to the music.

"There," he said. "She's missed another note."

He raised an eyebrow.

"And what about Breiter?" said Armina. "You're skittish about that, too."

"Don't," said Ritter. He shook his head. "You want to advance here, don't you? You've worked so hard. Why make a mistake when you don't have to. You're not sick, are you?"

"No," she said.

He stood up and turned off the record player.

"I want to take a look at Hauptmann, too," she said.

"No, you don't," said Ritter. "Trust me."

He put his hand on her mother's record.

"It was such a small error," he said.

"She was ill," said Armina.

Shadows swept over the glitter of the door of his office. The typing started again. The scent of a cigar from a man lighting one in the hall came into the room.

"You've been warned," said Ritter.

"I'm not done with this," she said.

"If you're smart you are," said Ritter.

Armina stood up.

"Well," she said. "Good afternoon."

"Thanks for coming in to see me," said Ritter. "I appreciate it."

Armina put her hand on the enormous knob.

"Here," said Ritter. "Do you want this?"

He held out the recording. Footsteps went by outside. Armina stood straight up.

"It was a small flaw," he said. "But maybe it was just hiding another, larger one. Maybe it was a symptom of the flaws she carried. . . ."

"Don't," said Armina. "Don't mention my brother."

"Here," said Ritter. He held out the record. "Take it. Do the smart thing."

She didn't want the record but she didn't want him to be touching it either. He held it out. The manila sleeve was a little yellowed, and yet the passage of time had made it seem more dignified and precious, as though the aging of the paper showed how frail Armina's connection to this part of her life really was. She reached out and took it, doing so, she hoped, with a touch, a small shove.

"I told you what I'm going to do," she said.

"Well, fine," said Ritter. "That's a decision you had to make."

He turned his face down to his desk, moved some papers around, and then said with a malice so quiet that it was like a breeze, like a whiff of the first approach of winter on a wind, subtle but unmistakable, "Don't underestimate me."

"That's funny," she said. "That's just what I was going to tell you."

Armina joined the funeral for Gaelle as the members of the Ring came down the avenue, two by two, all in rented tailcoats, striped trousers, and choker collars. The men followed the four black horses whose coats were as shiny as new shoes, and behind the men came their wives and girlfriends who weren't formal members of the Ring but nevertheless still joined in. The marchers kept a two-step cadence, which ebbed and flowed and made the women's skirts sway. The procession was made of two layers, or so it seemed, a collection of white faces above a mass of black clothes. And finally, behind the mob, a man came with a shovel in case the horses made a mess in the street.

The horseshoes hit the pavement with a silvery ringing, and the sound reverberated through Armina as though a blacksmith were hitting an anvil: she didn't know why she recognized this silvery ringing, the associations of it so deeply buried as though it were a memory, but the sound left her with a sensation of some past grief combining perfectly with this one. The emptiness Gaelle left behind was like being in a room where things are obvious for the first time: how much Armina had cared, how much, in a way she found difficult to describe, she had been comforted by the scar. It had shown the possibilities of defiance, and yet, it had come to this. At least Armina could pay her respects.

Karl was a head above the rest, his hands swaying with the same motion as the woman's skirts. His shirt was buttoned up to the neck, and his rough coat was clean, but he seemed half awake as he kept up with the horses, the mourners, and the hearse with the glass sides. The crowd was a good one, and he knew Gaelle would have liked that, since she had always said to him that her funeral would be the saddest on earth: no one would come.

Karl guessed the woman with the red hair was a cop, and as she came along, swaying with the cadence of the others and flinching at the ringing of the horses hooves on the cobbles, he wanted to unburden himself, to tell her what he could to help, but to do that, he'd have to say that he was there, on the street, when Breiter was killed, that he knew that last thing Breiter saw was his dog taking a crap. So how much could he say without making trouble for himself? The horses came along with the jingling of the harness, and the glass windows of the hearse showed the blue sky, the reflection of the buildings on the street like some vision from a seance, some suggestion of a passage to the underworld. Karl walked with it and thought, I'd like to get the bastards who did this to Gaelle. I really would. So, how much can I say? I was there? I know who was after her? Although, he thought, I know only some of them. There could have been others.

Franz Nachtmann wore a black version of his usual brown suit, waistcoat included, the chain of his watch more visible. From time to time he turned to see the members of the Ring, his expression one of sweet surprise, or charmed pleasure that so many members had turned out. Then he lumbered from side to side like a man carrying a heavy trunk. At least, he thought, Gaelle had kept her funeral insurance paid up.

Armina knew Gaelle would have liked the mysterious sheen on the horses' coats, the dark tack of the harness, the steadfast expression of the coachman as the procession flowed through the cemetery gates like a snake going around a stump. And yet the marchers had an air of barely subdued hilarity, as though the open hole, the black clothes, the glass sides of the hearse, the trembling of the black feathers that stuck up from each of the four corners, even the man with the shovel were part of some ghastly joke that each one of them, at some point, was going to have to endure.

At the side of the grave, men and women looked at the hole in the ground while the black box disappeared from sight. The members of the funeral reached down for the earth that was piled near the grave, took a handful, and dropped it in.

Armina's hands trembled as she picked up some dirt, too, and let it slip out of her fingers. In the dryness of it, she still felt a mysterious tug, as though Armina were more bound to Gaelle through this moment than she was separated from her by the tawdry things Gaelle had done.

Karl's shadow swept up like someone dragging a black cape over the ground. Then he dropped some dirt into the hole, too, doing so slowly and with great delicacy. The other mourners shuffled forward, stooped to get some dirt, dropped it in, wiped their hands, and moved away. Karl's indifferent glance swept over the crowd and then stopped at Armina. Then she glanced up, too, into his face. He went right on staring at her, stepping closer, his shape blotting out the sunlight. He made a gesture to the grave and shrugged, as though this were an infinite punishment for everything he had done.

"This is it," he said.

"Why, you must be Karl," said a blond woman with lousy skin and rings under her blue eyes.

"Who are you?" he said.

"I'm Binga," she said. "Gaelle must have told you about me. I was Gaelle's pal. We worked together."

"She didn't say anything to me," he said, still looking down.

"Well, I was a friend," she said.

"She didn't have many friends," said Karl. He turned to Armina. "A cop like you must have known that."

"No, she didn't have many friends," said Armina. "Not that I ever saw."

Karl rubbed his hands together, as though washing them. He looked at Binga and then at the crowd. Then he bit his lip and put out his hand to Armina, as though offering something. He pushed some dirt with his foot and frowned: how was he going to say it? He wasn't a good liar. And yet, what he wouldn't give to explain, to get some relief by just saying what happened. So, he stood there, suspended between the desire to speak and the desire to be quiet.

"Let me think," he said.

The horses started that impatient pawing of the ground, like horses doing a counting trick in the circus. He shrugged and walked down the path between the rows of headstones, his shape disappearing among the enormous statues of angels, who didn't look upward to heaven, but downward, toward the earth, their stone wings folded along their sides. His movement through the crowd, the plodding, frank gait, made Armina think of a mule walking through the surf.

Felix came up to the mound of dirt with his furious gait, as though his leg were a dog he kept to beat, and then kneeled at the side of the grave, where he picked up a fistful of the sandy, almost orange dirt, and dropped it into the hole, letting it fall through his fingers as though it were his own life's blood that was seeping into the ground. Then he stood up and put the back of his wrist to the side of his eyes. He stepped back, dragging his leg in the dirt and leaving a new moon-shaped mark in the soil.

The mark was about a half inch deep, drawn as though with a compass, like someone making a map in the dirt to show the bend of a river. The tip of the toe of one of his shoes had made it when he pivoted on one knee while his stiff leg stood out behind him.

Binga appeared like one of the stone winged figures who stood on top of the monuments.

"Come on," said Armina to Binga. "I think we should go to the party."

"Why, I always like a party," said Binga.

Immertreu's restaurant had a long bar at the entrance, and opposite it there was a raised section where the mourners were already eating pig's feet, sausage, and potato pancakes at the fifty tables that were arranged there. They drank from glasses of beer that were a foot and a half tall as they sat at tables by the dark wainscoting of the room. The men jostled Armina as she came in, and she was pushed back, into the crush by the bar. Nachtmann sat in his usual place with a small glass of port.

A clot of mourners came in the door, shouted for drinks, and pushed against Armina. Felix was here, too, caught up in the same group of men in dark clothes, and as they pushed him farther into the restaurant, he put out his hand and pulled himself up to the bar, like a wet dog coming out of the rain. The bartender put a plate of picked pig's feet in front of him, and Felix picked up one of them, the pink jell quivering as he took a bite. He went on eating, his head to one side like a dog.

Armina worked her way out of the mob.

"I just thought I'd talk to you for a minute," said Armina to Felix.

"Not now," he said. "Leave me alone. Can't you see I'm busy?"

He turned back to the plate of pink jelly and two-toed feet, his nicotine-stained fingers picking up a morsel and bringing it up to his lips. Then he dropped the food and stared at the plate. He put his hands to the side of his face, elbows on the bar. Then he turned to Armina.

"A lot of people were after Gaelle," he said. "She got herself in the middle."

Felix picked up another pig's knuckle.

"And all I know is she went off with a guy in a black car. She saw ten guys like that every night. Silver hair, nice clothes, talked like a college professor, smelled of some kind of perfume. Cologne or something. That's it, see? A guy in a black car. Why, anyone could have gone after her."

He dropped a shiny and milk-colored piece of cartilage on his plate.

Binga came out of the stream of mourners and grabbed Armina's arm and took her two steps to the main room and then to a table close to the wall. The room was filled with the scent of new sawdust that had been put down for the party. Many of the mourners had already taken off their coats and stood with the black Xs of their suspenders in the middle of their backs.

Karl came down the bar and stood alone, his shoulders at the height of everyone's head. Armina pushed through the mourners, who were now singing an obscene song about a woman in Budapest and what she did in the evenings when the lights went out. Karl was aloof from the hilarity of the place, and he turned his head in her direction.

"Why don't you sit with us?" said Armina.

He followed her with the air of a man who was sleepwalking.

"Come on. Next to me," said Binga.

"OK," said Karl.

"So, what are you drinking, Armina?" said Binga.

"I don't know," said Armina.

"Don'cha want a little fun?" said Binga.

"A brandy," she said to the waiter who was standing next to her.

"Bring three," said Binga. "For each of us."

The waiter brought over a tray on which there were nine glasses of brandy. The noise in the room became louder, as though the voices were on a rheostat and someone had just turned it up. Like a radio program. Binga reached for her brandy, which she took in one shot, bang.

"I don't know why it is," said Binga. "But being in that graveyard, seeing those people in black, you know, why, it makes me sort of flirty. Sort of all, well, you know. Indecent. Do you feel that way, Karl?"

"No," said Karl.

"Well, maybe later," said Binga. "Have your drink. It'll help you cheer up."

Karl stared across the table, his dark eyes dry now, as though grief after a certain point were dusty and like a desert. He took up his glass, and rather than sipping it as he usually did, he took it in one quick swallow, bang.

"So," said Armina. "What do you want to say to me?"

"You're really a cop?" said Karl.

"Yes," said Armina. "Inspectorate A."

Karl turned to Binga and said, "Go to the ladies' room. Get out of here for a couple of minutes."

"Why, I'm not ready yet," said Binga.

"You heard me," said Karl. "Go on."

She stood up unsteadily, picked up her drink, and neatly took the arm of a man in his shirtsleeves who was passing by.

"Feeling lonely?" she said. "These people here don't want me around."

"Sure," said the man. "I'm always lonely."

On the far side of the room men with the X of suspenders in the middle of their backs went on with the song about the woman in Budapest. They swayed as they sung, and threw their heads back, as though braying at the heavens.

Karl picked up the next drink and took it in one quick swallow, too, and put it down, bang! The men and women in the room became quiet and turned at the same time toward the door. Outside someone yelled, as though giving a military order, which mixed in with the cadence of boots, more yelling, and then, through the window, a column of men, all in brown pants and white shirts, walked by. The men in the room pulled on their coats. The Brownshirts outside yelled, then they sang a party song.

"Everything I've done came back to give me trouble," Karl said. "You never think you can end up like this. Why, before I didn't even know what alone meant."

The men in the room began to move toward the door, and everything about their disorder, their finishing of a drink, their spoiling for a fight, left

Armina blinking, trying to be clearheaded and precise. Some glasses were left on a tray, the accumulation of them bright and somehow disordered: Armina stared at them, anxious that she was missing something, that she would come away with nothing and be left with the constant doubt and accusation that made the air seem heavy.

Karl looked up and then over the heads of the men who were going outside, where they were going to fight. He went on staring, thinking things over, glancing at Armina. The noise of the room made it difficult to think, to say the right thing, to come up with just enough, but not too much. One of the Brownshirts in the street threw a brick through the window, which collapsed into triangular shards.

"Gaelle picked up some thug, a Nazi, and he told her a secret," said Karl.

"What was the secret?" said Armina.

"That they had a spy, a guy in the Soviet embassy who was telling them what the Red Front was up to. So, she told us about it. But before we could do anything, she went to the Nazis, too. They'd been leaning on her. See? She tried to get them off her back."

"Who did she see when she went to the party?" said Armina.

"Hauptmann," said Karl. "That was the name."

More shouts came from the street.

"There was a man from Moscow in town," said Karl. "See? He wants this Breiter thing quiet, too."

"Do you know why?" she said.

"Munitions," said Karl. "The Soviets were helping the German army rearm. Breiter worked it out."

Outside, a man in uniform stood at the front of some men. He was here, he said, screaming above the crowd, to show solidarity with a woman who had been killed by the Red Front Fighters. A poor, ordinary woman, a fallen woman to be sure, but the man wasn't here to judge her but to show his solidarity with her memory. The window at the front door shattered. The men broke up the furniture in the room to make a club, or reached into a pocket for a sock filled with sand, or a knife.

Armina worked her way through the crowd, back to the bar where Felix finished a pig's foot, his fingers slick with gelatin.

"Oh," said Felix. "You again."

"Do you know a man by the name of Hauptmann?" she said.

"Hauptmann?" said Felix. "I don't know what you're talking about."

"Yes, you do," said Armina.

His dark, ash-colored eyes moved from the bar to look at her.

"You better by careful, missy," he said.

Another window broke with a tingling, almost festive sound. The mob from the dinning room went by Armina, and as she struggled against it, Karl took her by the arm. He pulled her out of the stream of men who were going to the front of the room, and said, "Come on. Out this way."

The fighting started outside on the curb in front of the restaurant. The women screamed and tried to get their coats. Outside the leg of a chair hit a man on the side of the head with a sound of bones being broken with a cleaver. A pistol went off, and the air was filled with potatoes stuck with nails, and here and there fists emerged from the mass. A few signs waved this way and that, like battle flags at the moment when all is won or lost. In the distance police whistles were frail and useless.

"But there's something else, too," said Armina. "Isn't there?"

"Yes," said Karl. He looked around. "Come on. Let's go."

"But there's something else," said Armina.

"Yes," said Karl. "I was there when Breiter got it."

"And it was politics?" said Armina. "Is that why Gaelle was killed?"

"Yes," said Karl. "But I don't know who did it. Someone on the right? The man from Moscow? I wish I knew. Oh yeah."

Karl took Armina by the arm and pulled her against the stream of men who tried to get to the front of the room. "Out this way. I'll show you." Karl pushed through the men, dragging her by her arm, and in the crush she saw Felix. He finished the last of the pig's knuckles, and as Armina went into the hallway with Karl, Felix went on staring at her. He mouthed, "Careful."

Armina saw the back door, where Karl let her go, and as she came out the door, she thought about that mark in the dirt by the grave and Felix's nicotine-stained fingers.

Armina came out of the rear of the building and walked around to the front where the voices of the men sounded like machinery in the midst of an accident: the intensity of the garbled threats, of the shouts, was like the shriek of brakes, the grinding of steel as an engineer tried to stop hundred of tons of locomotive. Here and there on the cobblestones, beneath the funeral pants of men from the Ring, bodies lay with their shoes in a V. The limbs of the unconscious were oddly loose, like rubber, and the shoes flipped back and forth as they were trampled.

Felix came out of the restaurant, looked one way and another, and pulled his head down, the gesture at once protective and familiar. Like a turtle, thought Armina. That's what it is. Felix kept his eyes on the men in the street, and when they surged one way, like surf sliding up a beach, he moved along the storefronts. Felix didn't look like much, but she guessed that was part of what made him dangerous. Just a kid, a limping boy who seemed to be stunted no matter how old he was. Forever shrunk. She put her hand in her purse and touched the pistol—sleek, heavy, and yet not giving her what she wanted, since the pistol seemed like hard chaos rather than the order she needed.

A little privacy, thought Armina. A chance to get him by himself. A chance to talk with no one around. An out-of-the-way place, quiet and private.

She stayed some distance behind as Felix dragged his leg and leaned forward, as though into a wind. He seemed harmless as he moved with that stopping and starting, and yet his awkwardness still suggested the coiled nature of a hidden danger, like a sapling trapped under a log. It was the stiff leg, she thought, that made that mark in the dirt.

Felix turned into the park, his up-and-down, stumbling gait scaring
the pigeons, which rose in a trembling, shimmering mass against the sky.
The shadows of the park at this time of year seemed blue-green, like dirty
seawater. He went along the path by the benches where lovers sat in the
evenings.

Armina went along the path, too, and she thought about that mark in
the soft dirt of the stone shed where they had found Gaelle—about two
feet long, vaguely curved like a new moon—about the depth someone
would make to plant seeds, carrots, say. Armina tried to reassure herself
with the memory of carrot tops, bushy and bright green with the texture
of lace.

The birds seemed cheerfully insistent, and she tried to remember the
names of the birds she had learned as a child. *Chettusia gregaria.* The Socia-
ble Plover. *Gregaria.* She was reassured by that. Or a Eurasian Woodcock,
Scolopax rusticola. Or the Bohemian Waxwing, *Bombycilla garrulus garrulus.* That was another one. *Garrulus.* She reached into her handbag to touch
the pistol. Time seemed to collapse ahead of her, as though the future were
so close as to deny almost any possibility she liked. She knew something
was coming and yet she was amazed that everything seemed the same: ordinary late afternoon, birds flitting from tree to tree.

Felix sat on a bench, hands in his pockets. In the afternoon light, the
trees and the grass were different shades of green, one a little more intense
than the other, and the brush was a muted color, like military fatigues.

"I've been waiting for you."

"Have you?" said Armina.

"Sure," said Felix. "I can tell when someone wants to talk. It's my job.
Why, people always get this look when they're going to ask for something,
you know, something kinky. Kind of shifty. Why, they say, will Gaelle do
this or that?"

He stopped and looked around.

"She's not going to be doing any of that," said Armina.

"No," said Felix. "At least where she's gone she's not going to have to
do that. Why, you wouldn't believe what people wanted to do to her. And
she was such a tough mutt, you know. There's nothing she couldn't take."

He stood up.

"Come on, let's walk," he said.

He stepped closer to her, almost as though he wanted to take her arm.

"Your perfume smells nice," he said. He put his nose a little closer and sniffed, the gesture so frank and intimate that Armina began to slap him, but then she stopped. Not yet, she thought. Not yet. "You know what I heard? Perfume reacts differently with different skin. Did you know that?"

"Yes," she said. "I'd heard that."

His head rose and fell as he walked next to her.

"So, where are we going?" she said.

"Just a walk," he said. "I talk better when I'm walking, don't you?"

"Sometimes," she said.

"Sure, sure," he said. "Let's get off the path. Over here."

"You seem to know the park pretty well," said Armina.

"You could say that," said Felix.

He smiled and showed his bad teeth.

"OK," she said. "How about here? What do you have to say?"

"Don't you want to walk with me? Or are you too good for that? There's a nice gully on the other side. Over there."

He raised an arm toward an open field covered with silver highlights from the moisture in the grass. A bird dipped as it flew in a looping path, like wires hung from one telegraph pole to another. The mark in the dirt had been about an inch deep, shaped like a scythe.

"It's private," he said. "We can talk."

He reached down and rubbed the side of his bad leg.

"It aches so much these days," he said. "Must be the damp, or something." He went on caressing his thin leg with a repeated touch, as though he were pushing the pain into the ground.

"You think I'm just a kid with a limp and bad teeth," he said.

"No," she said.

"I know," he said. "Nothing I can do about it. Say, how many people are working on Gaelle?"

"Oh, a lot of people are working on it," she said.

"I bet it's only you," he said. "I'd bet a lot. Come on. You need some help. Why, I'd sure like to get the guy who did it."

"Would you?" she said. "You're sure about that?"

"This thing is driving me nuts, you know that?" he said. He touched his leg. "It just won't leave me alone. It's a funny kind of pain, like slow, constant lightning. Like electricity. Come on."

They went off the path to the meadow, where they left a darker trail of footsteps in the evening's first dew. The birds flew overhead, seemingly playing with one another, one chasing another as they turned sharply at the edge of the meadow. Up ahead the green wall on the far side of the meadow faced them.

"It figures that it would only be you," said Felix. "Who cares about Gaelle? Just a woman with a funny face who still is young. Why, I was the only one to look after her. I used to wash her stockings."

"Did you?" said Armina.

"They'd get dirty and I'd wash them out and hang them up to dry. She sat around with no clothes on when I did it. Slept that way on her bed. I never bothered her."

"You don't have to walk so close to me," said Armina.

"Sure, sure," he said.

They came to the edge of the field and began to go into the green shade of the woods. A screen of undergrowth went around the top of a gully, and if she pushed her way through it, she would be able to look down below, into the depression where more brush grew. The leaves of the plants in front of her were small ones with a serrated edge, like a saw, and some of them trembled and sprinkled water on her as she pushed through them. She glanced at every detail, as though each one had some significance she could understand if she was only alert enough, or smart enough. The gully was like a dark green pool. Low plants, some grass at its edge, all dense enough to cover the ground.

Felix stopped in some brush, turned sideways into it, grabbed his leg, and lifted it over a low-growing branch. He grunted. Armina continued into the bottom of the gully. She looked from one end to the other for a bright piece of clothing, or a scarf, or any sign that something or someone was here, and as she started going over the landscape again as though to see what she missed, she realized that she had let Felix get behind her. She had thought that he was going to show her another woman here, but now she realized she had been left alone, at the bottom of a swale, the scent of the dead leaves rising slowly from the ground.

She stood still. He must have been still, too. She imagined him behind the scraggly brush that was frost burned, his acne scars perfectly blended with the brownish leaves. She waited for him to move. The birds sang, and in the distance a car tootled on the avenue and engines ran with a steady popping. A breeze came up and the leaves made a hush. A low, panting huff came from the top of the gully, and then a black dog emerged from a scrim of branches and leaves.

She started up the gully, back to the top. How could she have worn such shoes? Heels too high, soles too thin, and the soles were already wet. Her stockings had run in narrow ladders. And as she stumbled over a rotting trunk halfway up the slope, a hot spike pierced the back of her thigh, and then she turned to see that a limb had snapped back at her. For an instant, she imagined that a snake had bitten her, but could there be snakes in the middle of the city? Had one escaped from a private zoo? Then, as she twisted to see what had happened, she fell backward, as in a dream, and she landed on a hard spike, a broken stump of a piece of undergrowth, the wooden point sinking into the back of her thigh. The throb, the trickle of blood, the cold ache of the puncture left her more desperate than before. How clumsy, she thought. How could I let something like that happen now. Then she thought, that is just vanity. Get up.

At the top, behind a screen of brush, Felix waited, his gray face in an expression of extreme lassitude, as though it was difficult for him to stay awake. His eyes blinked with a slow repetition, like a lizard who sees a fly.

"So," he said. "Here we are. In the middle of the park."

The birds stopped singing, and the other sounds that she had become accustomed to, the slight movement of the leaves, which made a hush, the distant laughter of couples on a path, all ceased: the silence moved around her like the scent of a smoldering fire.

"Listen," said Felix.

"I don't hear anything," said Armina.

"That's right," said Felix. "Why, I wonder if you have ever thought of being out here alone like this, and what had happened to those women in the park. It's not safe, is it?"

She reached into her handbag.

"Oh," said Felix. "No. Don't misunderstand. You don't have to do that."

"No?" said Armina.

"I just thought it was important for you to hear that silence. It's like a warning, see?"

"About what?" said Armina.

"This city is a hard place," said Felix. "Why, all kinds of things are going on. And you can't see it."

"And you can?" said Armina. "Maybe you should tell me about it."

"You're not listening," he said. "It's all in the silence. It's not what you know, but what you don't know. That's where the trouble is. And so like a friend I am trying to help you. Why, all kinds of things can go wrong. Look at Gaelle."

"I want to talk to you about a mark in the dirt," said Armina.

He looked right at her.

"You made one by the side of the grave," said Armina.

"Why, you are going to try and take it out on my leg," he said. He slapped it. "Why, that's another thing I have against it. You won't even let me grieve for my friend." He looked around. "You're going to need a lot more than a gimpy leg."

They stood opposite each other.

"And you see out here how easy it was for me to get behind you? Why, that could happen anytime. I'm not saying me, you know, but that's what you're up against. Someone coming up behind you."

The birds went on flying, as though nothing had happened, in that same looping pattern, rising when they flapped their wings, then gliding, swooping back toward the earth.

"So, if all you've got is a gimpy leg, I'd forget about that. I'd worry about my own troubles. Like some night you hear something behind you in the dark."

He plunged up and down, pushed the leafy branches aside, and disappeared into the undergrowth. The branches throbbed back and forth, the leaves shedding the drops of water, which made a steady pattering on the ground. Armina stepped forward, looking one way and then another, and as she circled back, afraid that he had gotten behind her again, she saw the path that she had made in the leaves. Underneath them the dirt was black and rich. She pushed her toe into it, turned some of it over and saw the dark purple worms begin to move with the serpentine movement of such creatures. She thought of Gaelle and the women she had seen in the park, the weight of all of them anchoring her right here, as though they were somehow pulling her down.

She sat in the leaves, if only to think for a moment. She tapped the barrel of the pistol against her head, the hard whack of it reassuring, bracing, and she concentrated on it, as though if she could just clear her head sufficiently, she could do the right thing. The cadence of the pistol was the same as the pounding of her blood. She put her fingers along the back of her thigh and felt the cut stocking from the branch that had hit her, and when she stood up, in a moment of uneasiness, she saw a series of little flashes of light, like bits from a sparkler, that hung in the air and then popped, just like a soap bubble. She was surprised they didn't make a sound as they disappeared.

It was twilight and the sky was gray and pink. The air cooled quickly, and the grass, the frost-burned leaves were shiny in the first, sudden dew. She thought of the barometer on her wall, the little needle with the shape of a spear, the script that was as formal as that in a legal document: what did the instrument say now? Change? High pressure? She stood up and held her leg.

Felix's footsteps showed in the film of moisture on the grass of the meadow, and the pattern he left looked like a period next to a comma: one foot went directly ahead and the other swung around to keep up. She supposed that Felix might not have been alone in this. Was that right? Was she getting dizzy because she was afraid? He was just a kid, a boy with a limp, and yet he was right to invoke that silence: it was large enough and mysterious enough and so associated with the women in the park, the memory of Gaelle's face, as though the scar had been a monument to silence, to all those things that are unchangeable. It was as though Felix were an apostle of the worst silence there is: the kind that lingered around the women she had found in the park. And yet, he was just a limping boy, right? So why was Armina in such a state?

Then she tried to think of something else, and as she looked at the sky, she thought of Rainer, of sitting on top of him, of dragging a nipple across his lip, of letting him smell her, of dragging an underarm across his face.

She wished her hands would stop shaking and that she could breathe a little more slowly, but when she inhaled, she wanted to pant. And even in the cool air of the park at this hour, she was sweating.

Felix was up ahead. The brush moved, and that large black dog came back again, as though it had been hunting and was retrieving a shot bird. It panted and went by, leaving the scent of its breath.

At the entrance to the park, she saw that up-and-down locomotion, like a carousel horse. Businesslike, frank, not too hurried.

She caught him in front of the restaurant where the funeral had been. The street fight had stopped for a while, but then reinforcements had arrived on each side. The thugs had come in groups of four or five, dressed in plus fours, ties tucked into their shirts between the second and third button. Members of the Ring had scuffled with the thugs for breaking up the funeral, but then they had retreated. What, after all, they seemed to say, was the point of this? It was time for another drink.

But as the members of the Ring had retreated, the Red Front had arrived, their clothes rough, faces scarred, hands large with the jobs they had done: bricklayers, machinists, brewers, truck and train drivers. They arrived with a sullen attitude and something else, too, which was an obvious interest in finding a way to do the most damage. What would really hurt these assholes?

Now small groups mixed together, a few of the Red Front opposite a few thugs. The shoving and hitting still had a tentative quality, as though the right thing were to wait a minute to see who was here, where people were, and how to do some damage. Karl stood among them, exhausted, grief stricken, his head above the other members of the Red Front.

The Red Front had sticks and they tried to hit the kneecaps of the men in brown pants and white shirts who rushed them in squads of three and four: the street was filled with a mass of shoving men, fists raised, arms pushing—the entire group looked like a number of scrums going on at the same time.

Armina took Felix's arm.

"You," she said. She was surprised by how thin he was—his bicep was like a broomstick in a sheet.

"If you're smart," he said. "You'll leave me alone. Why, we just talked things over. Next time we might do more than talk. Nachtmann will help me. Nachtmann."

She gave him a shake.

"Leave me alone," he said.

"Tell me," she said. "What did you do?"

"I'm looking for Nachtmann," said Felix. "He runs the Ring. He knows some other friends of mine."

"Tell me," she said.

"Get lost," he said. "Go away."

She gave him a shake.

"I don't know anything," he said.

Armina pushed him toward the members of the Red Front who were hitting and pushing into the mass of men. Every now and then the sound of a direct hit, a muffled snap, came out of the scrum. A man fell here and kneeled on all fours, his nose dripping.

"I'm going to give you to the Red Front," said Armina. "Do you think they'd like to have someone who is an assassin for the thugs? That's what you are, isn't it? Isn't that why you killed Gaelle?"

He shook his head.

"Karl," yelled Armina. "Karl!"

Karl hit a man who fell to the pavement like a puppet whose strings had been cut. And as the man lay there, among the shoes and legs that moved back and forth, Karl stood over him, head down, as though grief and fury combined to make a variety of invisible but still heavy rain. The man on the ground lay perfectly still, either wise enough to hide, to play dead, or because he was protected by his unconsciousness. Finally, as though profoundly tired, Karl turned toward Armina, and then he started walking in her direction, pushing people out of the way, his large hands almost the size of the heads of the men he shoved out of the way.

"What do you want?" said Karl.

"You know Felix, don't you?" said Armina.

"Yeah," said Karl. "I had to pay him once."

"We were just talking," said Armina.

"About what?" said Karl.

"I was wondering what you would do if you could get your hands on the man who hurt Gaelle," said Armina.

"You're asking me?"

Felix pulled his arm against Armina's grip. What would it take, this small gesture implied, to break away? He glanced down at Armina's leg. Would she be able to catch him? Then he looked up at Karl, and when he did so he turned his head back, as though looking at a star overhead.

"Yes," said Armina.

"Maybe I'd take my time with him," said Karl. The men went on fighting behind him, and the sound of their scuffling, their kicking, hitting, the rough dragging sound as someone was pulled away onto the sidewalk, combined to make a sort of disturbance, a sound that was felt as much as heard. "Yeah. That's what I'd do." He looked down at Armina. "Maybe I'd take my time."

Felix tugged again. Armina tightened her grip.

"You're bleeding," said Karl.

"I fell down in the park," said Armina.

They all stood there in front of the fighting men. Felix kept his head down, looking one way and another. Little flashes of light appeared again, small burst of spectral colors, like pinpricks in the buildings, the spectacle of fighting men, the sky. The blood ticked in a long rill of moisture that ran down the back of Armina's leg, into her shoe, and then out onto the cobbles of the street.

"Where's Nachtmann?" said Felix.

"I don't know," said Karl. He turned to Armina. "Have you heard anything?"

"Have I?" said Armina to Felix.

Felix shook his head: it wasn't the gesture of refusal so much as the angry disbelief of having run out of things to do.

"Psssst," he said to Armina. "Get me out of here."

She gave him a shake so there would be no misunderstanding.

"Well?" said Karl.

"No," said Armina.

"Let me know if you do," said Karl. "I'll be around. Don't wait. Come to me if you have something. I'd consider it a favor."

"Come on," said Armina to Felix. "Over this way."

"Yeah," said Felix.

She gave Felix another shake.

"We understand one another?" said Armina.

"Yeah," said Felix.

They walked along the storefronts and over the broken glass on the sidewalk. For a moment Armina thought that the triangular pieces were related to those flashes she had seen. Then she said to Felix, "Well, well?"

He looked around, biting his lip.

"Yes," said Felix.

"Yes what?" said Armina.

"I'm ready to work something out. But don't say nothing here. See?"

n the stairwell of the Inspectorate Felix told Armina he didn't know how old he was. Maybe sixteen, he guessed, seventeen. But not twenty. He had lived for a while with his mother and sister in a basement, but his sister had asthma, and Felix couldn't stand her breathing, which took such effort. "Like she was digging a ditch with a pick," said Felix.

The stairs had the usual scent: soap and cigars. Felix sniffed it and looked around, as though this stink were a sign. Typing in the distance. They went around the landings, Armina with her hand on Felix's arm, and as they went, he pressed against her hand, as though they were on a date, as though he liked her touch. It made her want to let him go.

"Maybe we could come to an accommodation," said Felix. "Maybe I could work this off. You know, do something to make up for Gaelle."

"I don't think so," said Armina.

"I see all kinds of things," said Felix. "Why, I wouldn't even charge you much. It would be a bargain. Like some of those women in the park. Why, you'd be surprised at the things I hear."

She turned and looked at him.

"I'd like to work it off," said Felix.

They went by the second floor where the frosted glass glittered.

"Where are we going?" said Felix.

"Upstairs."

"Is that where your office is?" he said.

"No," she said.

"You didn't get hurt, did you, when you fell down?" he said.

She gave him a shake that made his teeth click.

"If I were you," she said, "I'd keep quiet about it."

"Sure, sure," he said. "That Gaelle. Just look at the trouble she got me into. And after all I did for her."

"What you did for her?" she said.

"Stop jerking me," he said.

"What about Hauptmann?" said Armina. "He's a friend of yours, isn't he?"

"He's a serious man," said Felix. "You don't want to look into this."

"Hauptmann paid you?" she said.

"I made a little something," said Felix.

"But you did more, didn't you?" she said. "You did other things. You took a cigarette . . . to Gaelle."

"I know what I did," said Felix.

"So why did you do that?" said Armina.

Felix shrugged.

"I wanted to make it look like the others. That I read about in the newspaper," said Felix. "If you're smart, you're going to let this go. I've got one word to say to you."

"What's that?" she said.

"Hauptmann," he said. "He's my friend."

"But Gaelle was your friend, too," said Armina.

"It's done," he said. "There's nothing to say."

The typing was louder on the floor of the political section. Armina and Felix came through the door from the stairwell and into the room where the typists worked: two rows of five, all women in black dresses with skin so pale it looked like desert sand at dusk. They had long hair, but each one had pulled it back into the same tight bun. They worked with a steady, frank clicking, and threw the carriage back at the end of a line—then they went back to typing until a small bell rang when they came to the end. It was a small sound, like a child's triangle. The motion of shoving the carriage back was as though they were all trying to hit something, an insect, say, and that they always did so from the left. They didn't look up as Armina and Felix walked to Ritter's office, where Armina pushed the door open without knocking.

Ritter sat at his desk, jacket off, pen in hand, a sheet of paper in front of him illuminated by his lamp. He smoked a cigarette, the tip of it newly lighted and crisp as a small red button. He drew on it and made it even brighter as he considered the spectacle in front of him, Armina in her dirty clothes, some blood on her hands, her hair in disarray, Felix next to her, stunted, face scared with acne, his eyes going around the room as though he were looking for something to steal. Ritter instinctively looked down, at Armina's leg, at her shoes, and the seeping trickle that made a shape on the floor, like a small red country on a map.

"This is Felix," she said.

He raised a brow.

"Felix?" he said.

She shook Felix's arm again. He winced and pulled away.

"Leave me alone," said Felix. "Stop pulling on me."

"So?" said Ritter. "What's this?"

"He's got something to tell you," said Armina. She shoved Felix forward. "No lies."

"Maybe I could work this off," said Felix.

Ritter drew on his cigarette and watched Felix. The two of them had the same faraway expression.

"Work it off?" said Ritter.

"He killed Gaelle," said Armina. "Didn't you?"

"I'd rather work it off," said Felix to Ritter.

Ritter sat back, flicked the ashes of his cigarette into a black onyx tray. He pushed around some of the things on his desk, a cigarette case, a small rattling box of matches, a pen. Then he inhaled again and sighed, so that the smoke came out in a pale display of uncertainty. Women typed beyond the door.

"Go on," said Armina.

"It just sort of happened," said Felix.

"But you did it, didn't you?" said Armina.

"We're going to want to know how," said Ritter. "Details. Will you give them?"

"I'd rather work this off," said Felix.

"Tell him about Hauptmann," said Armina.

"Hauptmann?" said Ritter. "Hauptmann?"

Felix looked from one of them to the other. A red crescent of blood ran from the door to the place where Armina stood on the gray linoleum. The blood had gotten into her shoes, leaked over the back of the heel, and some of it ran toward her toe, but before it got there it dripped to the floor, and when the typing stopped, the blood made an almost audible sound, a slight tick tick tick. Felix sat down in the chair in front of Ritter's desk, head forward, as though exhausted, but every so often he looked up at Ritter with an air of recognition. Then he went back to his inventory of the desk: maybe he could pick something up.

"You're hurt," said Ritter. "You need to have that looked at."

"Here he is," said Armina. "And he's going to tell us all kinds of things. He isn't going to work it off, either. He's going to tell us. Hauptmann paid him."

Armina stood there, the tickling on the back of her thigh diminished now. Ritter pushed a button on his desk. Almost instantly a member of the Schutzpolice came into the room, his buttons shiny, his visor bright with Vaseline, his expression as blank as a stone.

"Take him downstairs," said Ritter. "Hold him."

"Come on," said the Schutzpoliceman.

Felix stared at Ritter.

"It's nice to meet a gentleman," he said. "I know what a gentleman likes, see?"

"Take him downstairs," said Ritter.

The door shut, and as it closed, the sensation of the two of them being alone seeped into the room like a gas.

"You've got to get yourself looked after," said Ritter. "Do you need a ride? I'll have a car downstairs for you."

"He's going to tell us what we need to know."

"All right. All right," said Ritter. "Whatever you say. But right now you need to get yourself looked after."

"That's all you've got to say?" she said.

"Good work," said Ritter.

ksel stood on Unter den Linden with the other members of his group, each dressed in brown pants, white shirts, their hair neatly combed. They rested and looked one way and another, and then they started walking down the avenue past the Soviet embassy, where they stopped for a moment and milled around. After a while, Aksel said, "Come on. Let's get going."

The main university building had a courtyard, just behind the gate, and a wing was on each side. Students carried books through the gate and smiled and nodded at Aksel's group.

"Do you see him?" said Aksel.

"Not yet," said a tall boy with red hair.

"There's a few I'd like to talk to," said another member of the group. "Professors my ass."

Rainer thought of Armina as he came out of the main building and went across the cobblestones of the courtyard. It was a warm day, and he carried just one book, which he had been reading in his office. It had nothing to do with botany, the chemistry of orchid reproduction, the complications of breeding new species, the fragrances that had an impact on survival (drawing in insects, for instance, to orchids that fed on them). Rainer read for pleasure from time to time, and this was a book by Stefan Zweig. A clever and delicate book about a particular moment in a woman's life. Then he looked up. There were eight or ten of them.

Rainer tried to look from one face to another, as though if he could reach them one by one, he might have a chance. They stared back. Up the avenue the trees stretched away like an illustration in a book about perspective. Then he started walking.

"What are you reading?" said Aksel.

"What business of it of yours?" said Rainer. No, he thought, no. That is the wrong tone.

"There are writers who aren't worth reading anymore," said one of the young men. "From the past. Dead. They are the wrong race. With ideas we don't like. That have nothing to do with us."

"With Germany," said another.

"What would you know about Germany?" said Rainer.

"We know how it's going to be," said Aksel.

"No you don't," said Rainer.

He turned and went up the avenue, into those converging lines of perspective. It was like looking up some railroad tracks that fused into one distant spot, which, he guessed, was like the future, so far away and so confined. Then he thought, You aren't doing yourself any good, thinking that way.

The young men came with him, not too far behind, but not so close as to allow him to talk to them without having to raise his voice. There were other people on the avenue, polite-looking men and women, dressed in dark clothes, some of the women carrying parasols against the sun. The men wore dark ties and stiff collars and the women wore stockings and shoes with heels. Rainer looked back over his shoulder. The young men were still there.

Maybe they would go all the way down to the Brandenburg Gate, and if he went into the park, they would follow him, and he wished that he hadn't gone this way. Still, he had to get home, and that would take him close to the park. Was he going to let himself be pushed around, just like that?

The young men came closer, one on one side and one on the other, and as they began to surround him, just coming up next to him, he picked up his pace a little. They did, too. The other people on the street glanced at him and went on walking. No one wanted any trouble, and when he looked back, over his shoulder, he saw one of his fellow professors come out of the university gate, glance once in Rainer's direction, and then turn the other way.

He turned to face the young men. They stopped and formed a circle around him while he stood with his back against an iron fence. The beauty and precision of the world of the book that he carried seemed to exist right here, as though the object were not a thing, but alive or at least part of an imaginative world. So he stood there, looking at the young men. They looked back.

The heavy pants the young men wore, their white shirts, the buildings behind them, the cars in the street, the bright and clingy dresses that the women with parasols wore all had an extra clarity, as though everything were preserved in glass.

"What's that you're reading?" one of them said.

"What's it to you?" said Rainer.

They grabbed the book and threw it on the ground and one of them kicked it so that it fluttered along the stone gutter. Rainer was struck by how much it looked like a dead bird, wings out, animated only by the kick. Rainer stepped down and went after the book, and when they kicked it again, he continued walking. As it slid along it seemed not to be just the object that was skittering this way, not the printed paper, but the entire world of the book that was being kicked. Rainer apprehended this as a physical sensation, although it was hard to distinguish it from a fury that made him nauseated.

They let him come up to the book. And as he reached down to pick it up, one of them began to kick it again, and as he did, Rainer said, "I wouldn't do that. I really wouldn't."

The young men thought it over.

A group of young men from the Red Front Fighters crossed the street, and when they approached, the members of Aksel's group stepped back a little, their eyes turning as one toward the young men in rougher clothes, with their caps and scarred faces. They didn't retreat so much as spread out a little farther down the street, so as to be able to fight better. Before they left, Aksel said to Rainer, "Maybe some other time."

The men in brown pants moved back where they would have a little cover at their back. When the young men from the Red Front Fighters came up to Rainer, they looked at him with a quiet fury, and one of them said, "We should have let them take this one."

"It's all right," said another. "His time is coming. We have a new literature based on science. On the inevitable." He looked at Rainer. "Your time is over. We will obliterate you."

"I teach science," Rainer said stupidly.

"We have new science, too," said the young man.

Then they went in the opposite direction, as though some mutual truce had been negotiated between the two groups. They slipped away, moving up the sidewalk in a mass, and made people cross the street or step into the gutter. Rainer turned and walked away, up Unter den Linden until he came to the Hotel Aldon, where he went into the bar and asked for a brandy.

Everything here was ordinary, elegant, shiny. The chandelier was bright, and people moved with a quiet gait over the heavy carpet, the sound of their feet subdued and soothing, but when he glanced down, he saw his fingers were shaking. It was nothing, really, he thought as the brandy lifted his mood. Nothing at all. Everyone had difficulties, and this was his. So what?

He wanted to call Armina, but what could he say? He wanted the expectation of her arrival, the experience of being together, as though they touched when their eyes met. That moment, when their eyes met, was the one he craved: it was the sense of one mind touching another.

In the morning her leg was stiff and a bandage left Armina with the sensation of a lump at the back of her leg, like awkwardness itself. The cotton pad was covered with the tarlike color of iodine. She sat at the side of the bed and looked at her feet, the veins blue just beneath the skin, and after a while she stood up and waited for a moment in the gray shadows of the apartment. The silence existed like something she could almost hear, like the pitch of a whistle for a dog.

She took a taxi to the Inspectorate, and as she climbed the steps to the front door, in a burst of pigeons like a feathery explosion, Linz came out.

"Armina," he said. "Got a minute?"

"Sure, she said.

"Let's go next door," he said. "Let's have a cup of coffee."

The café had marble counters, small chairs made of heavy-gauge wire, round tables with marble tops, too, and it smelled of strudel and cinnamon, coffee and tobacco smoke, which hung like a blue cloud.

"You remember that night I came to your apartment," said Linz.

"I remember," said Armina.

"What a missed chance that night," said Linz.

The waiter arrived in his brown apron and white shirt. They asked for coffee.

"It would have been a mistake," said Armina.

"I don't know. I don't know. I wish we'd had a chance. I'm not such a bad guy. I can be nice. Considerate in bed."

"I know," said Armina.

The waiter put down the bitter coffee—just like the coffee in Vienna. Armina moved her leg one way and then another. Her thigh stopped hurting right after she moved it, but then instantly it started again, a cold sensation that ran through her leg as though the pain were a liquid that wanted to drain itself into the ground.

"It would have made it easier to talk," said Linz.

"Would it?" she said. She smiled and put a hand to her red hair. "Maybe we wouldn't be talking at all. That's the usual thing."

"I'd like to think we'd still be talking," he said. He took a sip of the coffee. "And that you'd trust me."

"I trust you," she said.

"And there's no chance for us?" he said.

She shook her head and tasted the coffee. Just like Vienna.

"Well," he said.

"Is that it?" she said.

"No," he said. "You've got to trust me."

"About what?"

"Ritter let your boy go," he said.

"Felix?" said Armina.

"Ritter thought Felix would be better as an informant."

"Did he?" said Armina. The throbbing came in the same cadence as her heart.

"Yes," said Linz.

She reached for her handbag, but Linz stopped her.

"No," he said. "Just wait a minute. Don't go up there."

"Why not?" she said.

"Don't go up there angry," said Linz.

"And how should I go up there?" she said.

"Trust me," said Linz. "Can't you trust me? He'll get rid of you. Don't you see? He's playing you like a drum. He'll get you angry and you'll make a scene. . . ."

"That's right," she said. "I'll make a scene."

The room was filled with the silver clink of the spoons, the click of a coffee cup against the marble, the sound of the cars in the street. Armina shifted her weight, but she couldn't get away from that throb that ran down to the sole of her foot.

"I just wish we'd had a chance in your apartment," said Linz. "It would have been nice."

"Oh, Christ," said Armina. "Give it a rest."

She stood up. Linz had the keen, silly expression of regret.

"I'm sorry," she said.

"Me, too," he said.

She picked up her bag.

"I'll get this," he said. "I'll pay for the coffee."

"No," she said. "No."

She took a bill from her bag and slapped it on the table: the sound was like a fish dropped on a bed of ice.

"What are you going to do?" he said.

"I don't know," she said.

"Well, think about it," he said.

She went into the street and looked down the avenue. The lines disappeared into the distant clutter, horses, cars, exhaust, clouds like an ill-meaning ghost. She tried to walk, to escape, to think, but she was left with that throb. It was cold, inescapable, like the memory of being hurt in the snow. She took a taxi home and waited for Rainer.

"WHEN YOU FEEL this way, there's only one thing to do," said Rainer. "Let's go out. Have a good time. Come on."

Rainer wore a new jacket, a white shirt, a silk tie, and his hair was brushed back. He walked with a slight swagger, which Armina understood as a variety of defiance, just a small detail that was evidence of the desire to make a decision, no matter how difficult. They went up the avenue and walked along the lights from the cars, which coalesced into a bright stream. The restaurants they passed filled the street with fragrance, and Armina and Rainer played a game: what made such a delicious aroma, pheasant in wine with morels served with buttered peas? She could imagine the green circles of peas, the sheen of butter, the texture of the morels. Or maybe it was a roast of beef with horseradish sauce, served with thin, crisp potatoes. Fresh bread with a crust as delicate as eggshell, desserts, like strudel, with apples and cinnamon. The collection of scents seemed like vitality itself.

At the corner a movie theater showed *All Quiet on the Western Front.* A mob of Brownshirts was in the street, and they waved signs that said PACI-

FIST PROPAGANDA. Their white faces, so pasty in the lights of the marquee, all turned in the same direction, like stalks of wheat in a breeze. Armina and Rainer came to the edge of the mob and then crossed the street and went along that same stream from the headlights of the cars. Then they turned into a side street to take a shortcut to the cabaret they wanted to go to, and as they turned off the avenue the shouts from the men in front of the theater diminished, like a repeating echo.

Rainer took her hand and said that, no matter what, he wanted her to know that he loved her. No one had ever understood him the way she had. And when he was with her he became someone he always wanted to be—that was why he really loved her—and this was far more than the fun they had, or his disappearing into a kind of golden haze when they got into bed. She made him think that he could live up to his own most secret hopes for what he could be. She forgave him, too, for his flaws in the way he wanted to be forgiven, and this wasn't generic, but specific, in that her understanding was precise, never condescending (or better, almost conspiratorial) and always dependable. Anyway, no matter what happened he wanted her to know that.

His hand pressed against hers, and the warmth of being loved reminded her of the swans in Austria, one welded to its reflection in the mirror of the water, or the fireflies in that stand of enormous pines. This warm pleasure imbued the details of ordinary life, the touch of his hand, the restaurants they had passed, the aroma of the food, the pheasants and morels, the scents of cinnamon and apples, the appearance of the salads of baby lettuce leaves, green and silvery as they were dressed, all of it, in his presence, became evidence of the pleasures of being alive and the possibility of enjoying it, too. She walked along, not trusting herself to speak and realizing with a thrill that she didn't have to.

The shadows in a side street hung like a black sheet. Armina and Rainer walked over the cobbles of the sidewalk and passed the darkened windows of houses where the glass seemed like ice. A sound seemed to emerge from the shades and dark planes, a steady pat, pat, pat. The blandness of it and the lack of light made it difficult for Armina to tell where the sound came from, and for an instant she thought it surrounded them, as though it were in the air. The street was almost empty and silent, too, aside

from that sound. Perhaps a roof of one of these building didn't drain prop-
erly and the sound was a steady dripping of water from a pool after the last
rain. She even imagined the drips as they fell, the drops like silver lines
through the shadows, like wire against a black cloth.

She turned, but the street was empty, just the sheen on the cobbles and
the darkened windows of the apartments—up ahead, at the next avenue, which wasn't so busy as the one they had passed, the headlights floated
away, as delicate as a dandelion in the breeze.

"Do you hear that?" she said.

"It's nothing," he said.

"How can you be so sure?"

Overhead the street was covered by an impenetrable fog, part clouds,
part smoke, although it was filled with a muted, reddish glow. The sound
came again, that steady pat, pat, pat. Leather, she guessed, on the small
cobbles of the sidewalk. She stopped and turned, but the street was so dark,
and there were so many openings under the stoops of the buildings, all
opaque as the clouds overhead, that it was impossible to see. Was someone
there or not? The silence was like that in the park when she had faced Felix
and he had gotten behind her. Listen, he had said. It's what you don't
know.

She tried to remember the times she and Rainer had danced, his chest
against hers, and the heat that rose between them, like a soft weld. And the
absence of it, too, when she had sat alone in her kitchen, brooding with a
glass of brandy.

"There's someone back there," she said.

"Well," he said. "The worst place to have an argument is in a place like
this. Let's just keep going."

She swallowed and looked around and faced the impenetrable shapes,
the geometry of darkness, those planes that were at once black and oddly
filled with menace. Was it possible that ill will actually changed the dark so
that the shadows had an almost imperceptible turmoil, like the surface of a
river at night? She thought she detected the essence, at once delicate and so
obvious, that surrounded a creature who lay in wait.

So, she thought, who is it? One of Ritter's friends? Had someone really
come from Moscow? And what would he be like, this man from Moscow?

Something else was in the shadows, too, a perfume of malice, as though all those mornings when she had stood at the bottom of a gully and looked at those torn stockings and marked skin had somehow been concentrated here.

A creature moved at the top of a building and then flew from the roof. She guessed that there were owls in the city that hunted rats after dark. Then she thought about the man from Moscow, who was just a sort of potential, but a pretty likely one. Then she thought about Ritter.

Would they come for me? she thought. As they had for Gaelle? What was to stop them? And then there was the darker layer, the one she didn't want to consider but that the geometry of shadows seemed to insist on: Ritter had let Felix go because Felix had an interest in making her disappear. And to whom could she go for help? The police?

She concentrated on the tapping and tried to think clearly about two things. Was there someone there, and if so who was it? On the avenue, which was close now, a car honked with a sad yearning. Rainer said, "Here we are."

The cabaret was on a corner of a side street at the edge of the park, and through the windows men and women, all of them hatchet-faced, pale, elegantly dressed, turned their faces toward a small stage.

"Come on," said Rainer. "We're going to miss it."

The maître d', in his evening clothes, took them to some seats at the rear of the room that had a table covered with a cloth made from a piece of the flag from the Republic. The red and yellow seemed oddly diminished here, not festive, but somehow like a dress that had been abandoned in a hotel room. They sat down and quickly ordered a salad, a lamb chop, roast potatoes, champagne. Armina fingered the tablecloth, her hands touching the edge. How long can a government last when its flag is used as a tablecloth? And what then?

On the other side of the room Ritter sat with another man. Their evening clothes made their skin seem white, as though powdered, and the other man's fingers were nested together on the tablecloth, as though he was demonstrating infinite patience. Ritter spoke and the man nodded, Yes, yes. Of course. Then he looked across the room at Armina. He nodded again.

The needling of the bubbles of champagne on Armina's tongue were keen, and yet the touch of them seemed to her like vulnerability itself, sharp, small, evanescent. They left a lingering sharpness, which she tried to make last, but soon it was gone, too.

A man stood on the stage, his hair glistening in the lights, his vest under his tuxedo made from a flowery material. The faces around Armina were at once restrained and oddly expectant: what next? The faces were pale if young, powdered if old, all distinguished by a fatigue that was kept going by a sad humor.

Armina stood up and walked across the room, and as she went Ritter and the other man followed her with their eyes, their expression blank as a stone: that was part of what made this difficult, since they gave no hint, nothing she could depend upon, nothing clear, nothing that she could use against them.

"Armina," said Ritter. "How nice to see you."

"You think so?" said Armina.

"Of course," said Ritter.

"You let Felix go," she said.

"Let's not talk shop," said Ritter. "Let's have some fun. Let's relax. Do you know my friend, Bruno Hauptmann?"

"Oh," said Armina.

Hauptmann raised an eyebrow, stood up, and extended his hand. "I've heard a lot about you." He turned to Ritter. "Haven't I?"

"Yes," said Ritter. "We were just talking about you."

The pale fingers were extended in her direction, the nails manicured, the hand absolutely steady, marblelike, as though it were from a statute, and as she stood there, his hand had the attraction of the abyss at the edge of a cliff, somehow compelling if only for its horror: Armina reached out and took it, the fingers cool and dry. She looked him in the eye and then dropped his hand.

"You let Felix go," she said to Ritter.

"He's more useful this way," he said. "We'll pick him up later when we've gotten what we want."

"How much later?" she said.

"Oh," said Ritter. He hesitated and his eyes went over her face, as though considering something he saw for the first time, as though looking at her when she was dead. "Soon. Soon."

"Maybe I'll find him first," said Armina.

"Maybe," said Hauptmann. "A very dangerous young man, don't you think?"

"The songs are about to begin," said Ritter. "Let's forget all this for now."

Hauptmann sat down. Armina still felt the buzzing in her hand where he had touched her, and as she stared at Ritter, she picked up his champagne class. Ritter stared back, raised a brow. The members of the audience shifted in expectation, murmured, turned toward the stage, and everywhere the room was filled with the glitter of glass and diamonds, of the glint of silver and the crème-colored china on the tablecloths. Armina moved the glass, as though to throw the wine in Ritter's face. He flinched. She went right on staring at him and then slowly put the glass back on the table.

"So," he said. "Cheap tricks. I wouldn't expect it of you. But listen." He looked up at her. "Listen."

He beckoned with his fingers, the gesture quick and insistent, as though he were pulling a trigger and didn't care who he hit. He beckoned again, his eyes on hers, his expression so angry that he seemed almost vibrant, like the string of an instrument.

"Come closer," he said. "Here."

She put her head next to his lips, and for a moment she almost expected that he would bite her. His breath was tinted with the sour odor of champagne.

"Listen. Are you listening?" he said.

"Yes," she said.

"I don't want there to be any misunderstanding," he said.

"I'm listening," she said.

He put his lips closer yet and said, "Breiter was helping the Soviets and the Germans make arms in Russia. To get around the Treaty of Versailles. Now, no one, not the Russians, not us, wants that known. So it isn't just the fact that he got killed. We don't care about that. We care about silence. Silence."

She pulled back, her hand touching her ear, as though she could wipe away the touch of his breath.

"And after that," she said. "What do you want?"

Ritter turned to Hauptmann and said, "What do we want?"

Hauptmann began to crack his knuckles, the snapping coming from one finger and then the other. He went about it slowly, as though using the cracks, the splitting sound to count something. Then he laced his fingers together to see if there was anything more, another sound, another crack. Then he started again, going through his fingers to find one that would make a snap, his eyes on Armina, as though that sound were the answer he wanted to make.

"Do you hear that?" said Hauptmann.

"Yes," she said.

"Don't forget it," he said.

Hauptmann turned to a woman who sat near the stage, her legs bouncing up and down with a sultry impatience in the opening where her skirt was only partially buttoned together. Then Hauptmann's eyes swung toward Armina. His eyes were dull and seemingly without interest, but nevertheless, he still seemed mesmerized by possibilities of malice. Then he went back to looking at the woman on the other side of the room.

"And now that you've been warned you can do what you want and see what it gets you," he said. "Go on. I invite you. Look into this some more. Be my guest."

He looked toward the stage.

Armina went back across the room, trying to walk straight up, shoulders square, dignified and unintimidated. Then she sat down, slumping into her chair.

"Is there something wrong?" said Rainer.

She tried to speak, but then bit her lip. The light in the room made the women's jewelry bright, sidereal in its glitter, and the silver chains, the diamonds seemed like points of light, like the tips of swords for dueling. The gold appeared almost liquid in its sheen. Rainer went on looking at her, but she shook her head, not No, I won't tell you, but No, I can't speak.

Rainer took her hand, and she pressed his fingers against it.

The singer said, "Oh, I understand what fun you've had. Oh, I know. . . ." He sang a song about Berlin where he had had too much of everything, too much to drink, too much to eat, too many lovers, too many escapes, and between each verse, he blew into a small tube connected to a gimmick, an inflatable bladder, under his flowery vest. He appeared to swell, as though the excesses were visible, right then. His chest and stomach became enormous, and the singer patted himself, as though this bloat was a matter of pride. It wasn't easy to get this way. Oh, no. But with each passing verse he swelled that much more, and as he did, he became alarmed. Why, he seemed to say, he had lost control after all, but what could he do? This is the way he lived. The audience laughed and applauded: yes, it had been wonderful. They'd never forget it. The singer laughed, his enormous belly and chest bouncing in the light.

The singer finished his song to more applause and then let the air out of the gimmick under his clothes. Yes, he seemed to say, what a relief. The air rushed out, his belly collapsed, and he stepped offstage. The audience applauded.

Ritter and Hauptmann sat on the other side of the room, where they clapped before they turned to Armina. Ritter dipped his head, as though to say, Good night, good night. Hauptmann just stared.

Armina's fingers touched the flag, and as she felt the glance from across the room, she took Rainer's hand and said, "Let's go home. I've had enough."

AT THIS HOUR the traffic had thinned out in the street, but bicycles still went along with the motorcars and carts drawn by horses. Armina took Rainer's arm as they went down the avenue.

A cart filled with watermelons, lettuce, tomatoes, and potatoes for the morning market came along, its horse driven by a man who sat on a small seat. Automobiles passed it. A car honked. The driver of the cart turned to see what was wrong, and his horse screamed and reared in the traces. The horse looked like a figure made out of black metal. In the headlights of the cars everything could be seen, each spoke of the wheels, the mountain of vegetables like a pile of cannonballs, and the driver holding the reins. The horse stood on two legs and twisted in the traces. The cart driver jumped up from his seat and swore, but his voice was lost in the screams of the animal and the impact of the car that hit it squarely in the ribs. The cart driver hung in the air, suspended in the posture of holding the reins. A second car crashed into the one that had collided with the animal, the hood collapsing like a black accordion while the headlights made an almost bell-like sound as they shattered.

The horse hit the pavement with a smack, and the water from the broken radiator made a pissing sound. The driver of the cart now fell, straight down, like a man dropped from the second story of a building into the black mess, which was part animal, part machine, hysterical where it was alive, dark and losing oil where it was inanimate. Armina and Rainer stopped at the side of the mess, which leaked steam, blood, and oil.

The horse lay on its side, its eyes rolled back. The watermelons broke on the pavement, and the sanguine pulp mixed with the horse's blood, its froth, and the ooze of oil from the car. A mist from the radiator hung over everything, machinelike in its stink but having the fragrance of the shattered fruit and the odor of manure. The horse kicked as it tried to get up, one leg waving with a floppy uselessness. The glass on the ground, so bright with spectral colors and filled with a sidereal glitter, made the street look like the heavens where a new constellation, part machine, part animal, had just appeared.

"Do you have your pistol?" said Rainer.

"Yes," said Armina.

"Do you want me to do it?" said Rainer.

"No," said Armina. "I guess not."

Armina came forward, reached into her bag, and as she stepped down from the curb, trying to get around the panting animal, she slipped in the bloody oil. Rainer took her arm and helped her up, and while she looked at the slime, the oil and blood and water on her coat, he took the pistol. The warm slime seeped down to her skin, and the touch of it, the oily caress, seemed to be everything that scared and trapped her, that confined her and left her hands shaking. That warm touch was everything she wanted to get away from, as though fear had become this liquid combination of blood, oil, and dirty water.

"Oh, no," said Armina.

"It's a mess," said Rainer.

"A mess," said Armina. She pulled the warm, sticky clothes away from her skin.

"You can get cleaned up," said Rainer.

"Oh, no," said Armina. "No."

"I'll get you some new clothes," he said.

She shook her head. The animal screamed.

"The Soviets have been helping the Germans make arms," she said. "Now what good can come of that? They want to hush it up."

"And?" he said. "What else?"

She put one hand against another, as though she were going to crack one of her knuckles to remind herself of the sound: that snap and breaking, that crack, like finality itself.

He stood with the pistol in his hand, his eyes on the lunging horse.

"What else?" he said.

"That sound," she said. "That sound. Of a cracking knuckle . . ." She made a gesture, as though to include everything around them. "We're not safe. You know that, don't you?"

Rainer moved back and forth in front of the combination of harness and engine, of tires and wooden cart, glass and leather. He put the revolver against the horse's head. Then, in the bang of the shot the horse dropped its head in an infinitely gentle way, just lying down in the street as though taking the most delicate nap, and as it rested on the pavement with a touch as soft as a sigh, Rainer kept his eyes on Armina.

"We've got to go," said Rainer.

"I can't hear," she said. "My ears are ringing."

"I said we've got to go," said Rainer.

"Gaelle knew something about Breiter, the man in the street. So, if I look into her, I will have to look into the Soviets and making arms."

She cracked one of her knuckles.

"Like that," she said. "Just like that."

The driver of the cart rose from the damp slag of the accident, one broken arm hanging straight down. Vapor rose from the horse and folded into the steam of the car as the radiator went on hissing. The driver squatted in the country man's way, just sitting on his heels, and rocked back and forth, saying to the dead animal, "Oh, my darling. Oh, my little one."

Bystanders picked up his produce, and the uniformed police, who had now arrived, tried to keep the other cars away. The cart driver reached out with his good arm and touched the horse's head. Then he went back to rocking, the tears streaming down his face. The driver of the car sat in the gutter, one hand to his bleeding nose, and watched the driver of the cart.

"We need an ambulance," said Armina.

"All right, all right," said a member of the Schutzpolice.

On the curb, on solid ground, or on ground that at least wasn't covered with blood and oil, Rainer gave her the pistol. Then the two of them stood there. The driver of the cart said, over and over, "Oh, no. Oh, no. Oh, my darling. My little one."

Every now and then someone tried to pick up an onion or tomato that had rolled away.

"Just look," said Armina. "Look."

In the gutter the water, oil, and blood ran up to a drain, the petroleum making a rainbow on the surface that bent and disappeared into the depths of the sewer. She brushed at the slime, the blood and oil on her coat, but it only rubbed it in.

"I can't get it off," she said. "Look." She put her head against Rainer and said, "If I could only stop crying. Why can't I stop?"

Steam rose from the horse and from the hot water in the gutter.

"So," she said. "Which one of us is going to leave this city first? What do we have here?"

He looked at the mass of car and horse, machine and blood.

"More of this," he said.

"Let's go by the avenue on the way home," she said. "Let's stay in the lights."

"Sure," he said. "Away from the shadows."

"I just want a bath," she said. "Then we'll pack. Tonight."

"Yes," he said. "Tonight."

"Come on," she said. "Before the stores turn their lights out."

PART III

n New York City, in the spring of 1945, Armina looked through the window at the detectives from the War Department who came down West Twelfth Street in their dark coats, heavy shoes, and with that blank expression she recognized from Berlin: suspicion hiding behind a slack, numb face. Their hats bobbed along as they approached her building. She had been reading a letter when she had pulled back the curtains, which she did often these days, and after guessing that the men were detectives, she let the curtains fall and swing back and forth. Armina went back to the letter from Rainer, who wrote from an island in the Pacific.

Armina had come to the States, after a year in England that she remembered even now as an exercise in being so cold that even the summer wasn't enough to get rid of the chill. She had found a place to live in New York, but a job had been difficult, especially when people were still out of work. She had worked as a secretary for a German company that went out of business, and then she had worked as a waitress in a German restaurant, bringing her tips home and keeping them in a jar, which she shook from time to time, as though the sound were evidence of how precarious her position was.

It had been easier for her to come to the States, because she had been a police officer, or that is what she guessed. For Rainer, it was another matter, and he applied for admission and waited and then went around to the greenhouses and botanical gardens in England, but no one wanted him. It didn't matter that he was a refugee, that he was violently opposed to what was happening in Berlin. He was suspect, a liability, someone who could be a spy for all anyone knew. He thought he might get a job on the river, and tried the docks, approached tugboat captains, but they were uneasy, too. Why did he want to be around the docks, where so much shipping came and went? He waited, wrote letters to Armina. She thought of going back to England to be with him, but that made no sense as far as he was concerned. He would wait. She would have to wait, too.

Rainer arrived a couple of years later, and they lived together on West Twelfth Street, although he had trouble, too, in finding work. He taught botany at a high school in the Bronx, and then got a job on Saturdays at the Botanical Gardens on the grounds crew. He had done translation of scientific papers, tried to publish his own work on new varieties of orchids, and finally in the late 1930s when the war began, he lied about his age and joined the army. He wasn't allowed to fight in Europe, since he was German. His letters from the Pacific were becoming rarer. It had been three months since she had last heard from him.

My dearest Armina.

Of course, I miss you, as I'm sure you know, and this is one of those times when I want to get across to you in the old style, as when we first met, that is, I am trying to suggest to you what can't be said. First, I should say that I am on an island in the Eastern Carolines, which I am sure the censor will let through, since it is no secret that we are here. The Eastern Carolines are south of Japan. It is a pretty large island, about fifty miles long and twenty wide. The jungle here starts at the coast, where there are mangrove swamps, which seen from the ocean have a dark green color, like jade, and behind them the trees begin, gray as elephants and so tall as to make it hard to see the top, that is, you have to put your head so far back to look straight up that it hurts. Creepers, as thick as a man's forearm, hang from the trees and here and there you can see ferns that are twelve feet tall, the fronds spread out like a fan.

I have found many varieties of orchids here, and some that, as nearly as I can tell, are entirely new. Let me describe one to you. It has large, broad petals that have a sheen I have never seen before, something like nylon stockings in incandescent light, and the color of them is like gray silk, and yet the center is pink and has that same sheen as the petals. They put off an odor, too, a perfume that somehow pierced me when I first came across it, something nutty, skin l ike, sweet and at odds with the muskiness of the floor of the jungle. Like that perfume you used to wear that smelled one way on the glass dauber and another way when you touched it to the skin behind your ear. So you will understand what I felt when I say that I walked into the woods and saw the cascades of blooms, not only the new ones with that sheen, like wet silk, but some that I had collected for the Berlin hothouse. I saw some purple varieties like a storm at its most intense. You know, that color in the sky that looks like a bruise. I have spent time looking at that color and have tried to describe, to myself, just how the color makes the malignant into such beauty. Do you know that in one of your eyes there is a small streak of purple? I am not sure you do, since you would have to be very close to a mirror to see it. It is just the color of these flowers. So, walking here is like being in my memories of you, and when I reached up to take a flower, I heard your voice saying, "You shouldn't do that." It is the sound of your voice that mixes with the partial silence of the jungle, which has a constant whir. I don't know if I am cheered up or miserable when I saw that color, as though we were bound together by it while having it as a reminder of how far apart we are. The color left me drawn, like a string, which vibrated when I thought of you. Of course, I didn't think people could actually tremble with missing someone, but then I have learned a lot out here.

I went into the jungle the other day with a man who lives on the island. He speaks some English, and it is funny when he can't understand my German accent. Still, we went farther into the jungle than I had been before, wading streams that got us wet, and as we went he was cautious, hesitating before coming into a clearing, but then the island had been occupied and who knows if anyone is left. We came to some ruins.

They were made of black stone that had been fashioned into long octagons, as big around as a log. These stones were piled up to make walls, just as they had been arranged on the ground to make a plaza. Everything here was covered with vines, and so it was like a green and black bower, filled with sparkles where the light hit the pyrite in the stone. The silence is difficult to describe, more complete *than in the jungle, and when I stood in it, in that shower of light, the man who took me there said, "The god who lived here flew away to Truk when the missionaries came."*

I wondered what that must have been like, when the god flew away. Such a beating of wings, a blast of dark air like the worst hurricane, although dry and cool, and I tried to imagine the sound of it, too, when this creature left on enormous, transparent wings. I think of the desolation that it left behind, which, of course, is still here, in that silence. I am sure you know that this silence, this loss, this sense of departure and dark air is how I miss you. Like the loss of one's god. I don't have to go on about this. That you understand is such a comfort to me. And then, of course, I walked down from the ruins into the jungle, where I can find those flowers with that purple color like your eyes.

The censor will stop some of the following, but I want to try to tell you. On   we had hard fighting for   and afterward we couldn't   the bodies   days, so   you had to dig through   and the smell of the island could be detected twenty miles from land

We are bathing out of a helmet, but over the reef, which goes around the island, you can see a rainbow when the sun rises in the mist from the breaking waves. . . .

There is only one other thing. I look at the stars at night and realize that you don't see the same ones, but I know that you can go to the Botanical Garden in the Bronx and see some of the same flowers, and so I hope that is what you will do on your day off. It will be like the time you used to look in the window and we both had a glass of brandy. The sensation of beauty will make us feel close.

Armina put the letter down and thought of her work, which was the best she could get now. No one trusted her to work where munitions were manufactured, and the only job she could find was in a factory that made portable organs for chaplains, and one day, when she was stapling the leather of the foot-cranked bellows of the instrument, she wondered if one that she had worked on would be used on an island where Rainer was stationed.

She kept to herself, mostly, although from time to time men from the War Department came to see her to ask about people she had known in Berlin. Still, she was careful these days, since one day a man had approached her in the diner where she had breakfast and asked if she would be willing to "help him out" by doing "some work," which involved taking pictures of ships in the harbor. She had immediately called the police.

She tried to explain the lack of letters from Rainer in every conceivable way but one. A ship that was carrying the mail could have been sunk, or an airplane that was filled with sacks of letters could have been shot down. A fire could have broken out in a jungle station where the mail had been kept. The letters could have been lost on a jungle trail, soaked with rain, dropped in the Pacific when they were being loaded onto a ship. It had come to the point where this list of possibilities was a litany she went through at night, and during the day when she had a chance (such as when she was on the train coming up from the shooting range). She wished that Rainer hadn't told her about the god who had flown away, and the rush of air, since when she went through the possibilities and still had no concrete idea of what had happened, she was left, through a process of elimination, with the one possibility she couldn't face. Then she imagined that rush of air, that enormous presence of wings so large she could only feel diminished.

She joined a pistol club downtown, where New York City detectives took target practice. And when she went into the range and loaded that pistol, holding the bead flat in the rear sight and feeling the beating of her heart, it was as though she was trying to concentrate on one thing against the dark rush, that breeze that left her so alone as to think all she had was the throb and Bang! throb and Bang!

At the bottom of her fear and despair, she considered something else. At first, she had tried to pretend that she was far enough away from Berlin to have escaped her obligations there, but with each passing month, and as the months had turned into years, she had discovered that just the opposite was true: the distance only increased her feeling of having left something undone. And when she woke at two and three in the morning, unable to

get back to sleep, and after reading the few letters that she had, opening
them carefully and handling them only by the tips of her fingers (in which
she could recall the touch of his skin, or the texture of his hair) she felt the
gravitation of Berlin. She got up in the middle of the night and looked at
herself in the mirror, and then she walked around her small apartment,
hearing the old building creak, and all of it, the sleeplessness, the sense of
living in the wake of a god that flew away, the sounds of the building, left
her with the desire she couldn't quite articulate. She wanted to do anything
that would let her sleep at night, to be at peace, to stop having the impulse
to scratch her face or pull her hair or be someone, or so she told herself,
who probably deserved to have the man she loved end up on the floor of
some jungle, in that sound of insects, and beneath the orchids that were so
wet and fragrant. Then she started the entire process again, going through
the possibilities of why she hadn't heard anything from Rainer and coming
back to that same feeling of being incomplete. She hadn't finished her work
in Berlin, and she could feel the ghost of what remained undone.

　　She closed her eyes, but she saw swirling arms of light, so much like
the Milky Way, the movement of them seeming slow but yet still upsetting,
and when she opened her eyes, as though she had been drinking, she saw
quite clearly the pulled-down stockings, the red blisters, the faces turned
toward the leaves, as though giving up, dying there against the earth with a
caress, a sigh of exhaustion after what they had endured. The pad of the fingers curled so gently into the dirt, and the posture of the young women, so
loose against the bottom of the gullies where they had been found seemed,
from Armina's bed, in the dark, an accusation and a plea. How could she
have so utterly failed them? It hadn't been for want of trying, and yet that
didn't do her any good at all. In fact, she thought that this might even be a
larger indictment, that she had tried and failed and showed herself lacking
some critical item, some aspect of personality that, if she had been able to
obtain it, would have saved those women in the park. At dawn, when the
first pale light came in through the windows, Armina wanted to shout, to
get up and break the glasses and plates in the kitchen, anything to violate
the silence of the apartment, which for her seemed to be a kind of hiss of
the obligations of the dead. The marks, the posture, the sad perfume left
over from the previous night, the pale skin, all of it lingered as a constant,

unavoidable indictment. Armina went through each one she had found and suspected she just wasn't good enough. Yes, she thought, the obligations of the dead. If I could just appease them, if I could somehow do the right thing, I'd be able to rest. I could sleep. Rainer would come home.

The men in the dark clothes had come up to the bottom of her steps, and then they stopped and looked in a notebook, checking the address before looking at the front door. Their expressions were now a little more blank, a little more masked, and she knew that this meant they wanted something. She held back the gauzy curtain as they climbed the steps, their leather shoes slapping on the brownstone. The super slammed a trash can lid like a shot. Her buzzer rang.

"Armina Treffen?" said one of the men. He had taken off his hat and showed his thinning hair. The other one just stood there.

"Yes," she said.

The man showed his ID. The War Department.

"Can we come in?" said the first one.

"Of course," she said.

Perhaps, she thought, the War Department was running short of people to notify relatives of men who had been killed in action and so people like these were left to do the job. Or maybe it was done with a telegram. That was the proper way. She put her hand to her face.

They came in. It was a Saturday afternoon. The detectives sniffed at the coffee that was on the stove, and she asked if they wanted a cup. They agreed. Yes. They would like one. Did this mean that they had come about Rainer? She poured the coffee into two cups, brought them out, and put them on the table in her small living room. Then she brought a bowl of sugar, a small pitcher of milk, a plate with a couple of cookies on it. Finally she sat down with her own cup, the gentle rattling of it in her saucer unstoppable, and so she put it down and sat there, hands together. They sipped their coffee.

"So," she said. "Is he dead?"

"Not yet," the first one said. "But soon."

"How do you know?" she said.

"We have connections there," said the other. His voice was deeper, like the base note of an organ in a church, like a croaking frog.

"Where? How do you know anything about the Pacific?" she said.

"The Pacific?" said the first. "No, we meant Berlin."

"Oh," she said.

"Hitler will be dead soon. And a lot of others . . ."

"Oh," she said. "Thank God."

She swallowed. Then she took up the coffee and drank from it.

"We don't know much about the Pacific," said the other.

"No," said the other.

But soon, they said, they were going to need people to go back to Berlin, who knew the city, who spoke German fluently, who knew the police department from the days before the war, who could help with an investigation. Would she be willing? they said.

"When would you want me to go?"

"The Soviets are almost there," one said.

"It will take a little time to stabilize," the other said. "The end of the summer."

When she arrived in Berlin, no one checked her at customs, although a British soldier said, "I wouldn't go around alone, if I were you."

"Why is that?" she said.

"I'd be careful," he said. "Particularly in the Russian sector."

Then she managed to get a ride to the building where she was going to stay, a brownstone that wasn't too far from where she had lived before. She unpacked her suitcase in the stink of what could have been dead rats, but which she was sure was something else. She sat on the edge of the single cot in her room. The light came in the window, at once luminescent and oddly gray, and she tried to reconcile the subtle effect of it (as though it were a sensation of isolation made visible) with her desire to come home.

Berlin was now a city of women. They had been hired to clean up the bricks and to salvage what they could to rebuild. Armina went by women who sat by piles of the rubble where they chipped mortar off bricks with a mason's hammer and then made a neat stack, just like in a brickyard. Others dragged I beams out of the mess, fifteen or so on one piece of steel, straining together, their hair in kerchiefs covered with dust, their fingers cement colored as they gripped the top of the I beam.

The city looked like a boneyard of itself, but here you didn't see ribs and tusks, but empty buildings without windows and roofs, just the skeleton of the city after everything else had been burned by the incendiary bombs. The houses stretched off in endless repetition, only varying in the shapes of the roofs, which suggested broken teeth. The buildings seemed to be made out of smoke that had turned into a hard substance.

The most obvious landmarks were gone, although from time to time Armina found the remains of a store, a movie theater, a shop, a restaurant that she had known, but as she walked through a city she remembered but yet only partially she was unsure as to what was here, what was real, and what was just sentimental memories and half-baked expectation. Armina began to think of herself as being like the city, somehow reduced to a variety of rubble. The women who chipped mortar from a brick with a mason's hammer were resolute in their almost furious attempt to put things back together.

A pile of bricks, like a gray slag heap, was all that was left of the Inspectorate. In fact, she wasn't even sure if this was the place, and she stood there, facing the next block over where a lattice of windows appeared in a building that had burned but not collapsed. She reached down and picked up a brick, the weight of it as familiar as old desire.

Armina had been assigned to a section of the Berlin Police Department in the American sector, and the Inspectorate was set up in a brownstone building at the end of a side street. The usual craters marked the places where buildings had been, and beyond them the walls of masonry and brick stood with that gray and black wall that had the pattern of a waffle, and the pattern, the empty windows in the half-burned walls, repeated itself wherever she could see between two buildings or look over the piles of bricks. Paths had been cleared here and there between the mounds of rubble, and a postman, with his sack, made his way, looking for people who lived in cellars.

The police precinct was in a brownstone that had a few windows, although most of the frames were filled with cardboard and wood from packing crates. It had electricity, although it came from the Russian sector and was intermittent. The odor of the street was dust, soot, and the miasma of dirty socks and rotting meat that rose like a gas from the piles of brick.

She went up the steps of the station and through the door, which opened with a creak that seemed to linger. A man sat at a desk made of three planks and two packing crates from the American army that had held mortars, the word stenciled on the wood in a sort of frank, almost innocent script. His chair was made of oak with slats at the back, and he kept it well polished. The thing glowed in the otherwise dusty room, and Armina wondered how many cigarettes the furniture polish had cost on the black market.

Armina gave him her name and the clerk said that her boss would see her in a minute. Would she like to sit down? Herr Ritter wouldn't be too long, although he was busy these days. There was a lot to do.

"Who did you say?" she said.

"Ritter," said the man without looking up.

She sat down on a bench that looked like it had come from the pew of a church, and as she waited she assumed, for a moment, that she hadn't heard correctly. It was all by association, she guessed, and she was so troubled by coming back to this place that she naturally was hearing things that weren't there, as though her feelings were so strong as to leave her in a dreamlike state, not really here, not really in Berlin before the war. She had the impulse to walk out into the ghostly street, to go back to her room, to pack her bag and to find a way to leave. Instead she sat there on the long bench, feet together, hands in her lap, shoulders square, as though by being precise in the way she sat, she could bring precision to her thoughts. The man at the desk read a report, and in the silence of the lobby she heard the sighing of the wind as a piece of cardboard dragged a little in a window frame, the papery grating starting and stopping and then beginning again.

After the Russians had arrived, the police department had been revived, although the men who worked for it had no experience as policemen and some of them had just gotten out of jail for robbery, murder, and extortion. They guessed that the best place to hide was on the police force, which gave them an air of respectability, not to mention a sort of license to do what they wanted, particularly where the black market was concerned. It needed, as far as they were concerned, a little regulation, a sort of tax, although this was becoming more dangerous as the black market was acquiring better protection from the military government. After all, how else could occupying soldiers obtain good scotch, fresh strawberries, silk sheets, and other things that made life in Berlin a little easier, not to mention the number of antiques that could be shipped back home?

It didn't take long for the military government to realize it needed people with experience to run the police department, men who understood how to run an organization, and if that meant using members of the regime, even party members, they looked the other way.

In the distance three rifles went off in an uneven salvo. Ban-ban-bang. The man at the desk said, "The Russians, I guess. They shoot any civilian caught carrying a firearm. No trial. Nothing like that. Summary. I guess that's what it was."

They went back to waiting. The cardboard in a window had stains on it, and Armina tried to see shapes in them, as though they were countries on a map. Argentina? What was the shape of Argentina?

"He'll see you," said the man at the desk. "One flight up."

Ritter sat at a desk that was polished and untouched, as shiny as a piano lid and as black. A lamp stood on the desk, the yellow circle of its light on the papers in front of Ritter. It winked out as she stood opposite him.

"That's the Russians for you," said Ritter. "It'll come back on."

The dim light came in from the window. Ritter was still thin and tall, but he didn't look elegant so much as worn down, as though he were only the pattern of what he had been before, the plan, not the realization of it. He looked like a car from before the war that is still running, still showing its lines, but that sags on its springs. His clothes were large, and the bagginess made him seem as though he had shrunk. His hair was thinner, gray as dust, combed back. His eyes were alert, but he seemed less obvious in his intent, more hidden than before.

"Armina," he said. He held out his hand. She stared at his long fingers, his pale palms, his wrists that came out of the sleeve of a coat made from an army blanket. The sound of someone chipping away on a brick came into the room with a steady tap tap tap, then the hollow click as the brick was added to a pile.

"I see," he said. He dropped his hand. "Sit down."

"What are you doing here?" she said.

"Why, I have a job," he said. "I have an organization to run."

"And what about the past?" she said.

"Oh," he said "I was never a big fish. Not really. And this is Berlin. I have papers that give me a clean bill of health. Politically speaking."

"Really?" she said.

"You must understand how things are," he said. "We have a job to do." He cleared his throat. "I am useful."

"And what about the clean bill of health?" she said.

"Everything can be arranged. Why, people are desperate. Haven't you looked around?"

"What did you pay for your bill of health?" she said.

"Ten pounds of butter," he said. "And a bargain at the price. Are you going to work with us or not?"

He picked up a list of names.

"The military government is interested in these people. Many of them were in the city before the war. You probably even know what some of them look like."

He held out the sheets. The tapping as the mortar was chipped off a brick came into the room.

"The black market meets in a lot of places, but behind the Reichstag in the morning is a good place to begin. I'll bet you could find some of these men there."

He held out the papers.

She stood up straight up, if only because her dismay left her with the impulse to slump down, to lean against the wall, and to slide to the bottom. Her arm rose, not to take the papers, but to slap him, and for an instant she imagined the satisfying sound, the smack of her open hand against his cheek, the jerking of his head, the look in his eyes. She leaned closer, over the desk, directly opposite him. He didn't blink, since he seemed too tired to do that.

"Are you going to do the right thing?" he said.

"Who are you to talk about the right thing?" she said.

"Forget about me," he said. "What about you? Are you going to run away? Nothing is clean the way you want it. Nothing. So, what are you going to do?"

She sat down, opposite him. In the street a tired woman chipped away at the mortar on a brick.

"Don't you have some unfinished business here?" said Ritter. "Why else would you come back?"

The room shimmered, as though heat were rising from the floor. She thought of those nights when she had been alone, thinking of the islands in the Pacific, and when she had craved something to make her feel that she could sleep, that allowed her to go on, to get up, to stop flinching whenever she thought of herself. And now it had come to this. She stood up and took the papers.

"All right," she said.

"Good," he said. "The light will go back on soon."

He stood up.

"It's good to see you," he said.

She went on staring at him.

"Oh," he said. "You'll get over all of that."

DOWNSTAIRS, SHE SAT on the steps of the building and looked at the names on the list. She supposed she would find what she needed in the black market, since information could be bought and sold as well as strawberries or champagne, but it wasn't just the men on the list she wanted to find, but a detail that suggested certainty. If nothing else she was left with a desire for clarity, or a way of confronting those obligations she had felt so keenly at three in the morning when she considered those women in the park, how they had been found, the delicacy of their fingers in the leaves, the brutality of those marks.

It was difficult for her to believe some of the rumors about the black market, but she guessed that the stories contained an element of truth, at least as far as the spirit of them was concerned. For instance, there was the story of a wounded veteran who stood on the street with his crutches, and when a girl came by, he asked her if she would deliver a letter for him. He seemed pale and sick and he said he was too tired and too uncomfortable to do it himself, and when she agreed, he said, "There' s a good girl." But as she walked the few blocks to the apartment where the letter was supposed to be delivered, she fingered the envelope. Even children were suspicious, particularly young women, and as she walked along, she finally got over her uneasiness about opening someone else's mail. It said, in formal script, in the kind of hand that a schoolmaster before the war might have used, "Here's the butter I owe you."

In the morning the sellers arrived with the last of their possessions, silk nightgowns, an antique chair, an umbrella, a leather briefcase, a silver picture frame (from which the photograph of a marriage had been removed), a man's suit, a pair of shoes that were sold for some potatoes. One man had a suitcase of his wife's clothes, and he took them out and displayed them, evening gowns, stockings, all of the things that his obviously dead wife had worn. He stood with a blank face, just hoping for a good price from a farmer whose wife wanted some clothes. Even fresh flowers could be had, since when they were left at a hospital by a relative who had come to visit a patient, a nurse brought them here before they had wilted. And one of the most sought-after items was powder, since women had long since been unable to bath, and instead they dusted themselves in the morning. There were rumors, too, of cannibalism, stories of the disappearance of children that contained the same truth as the story of the butter, not so much fact, although that was possible, but the suggestion of just how desperate people were.

At night, by the light of a kerosene lantern, Armina looked at a blank sheet of paper—she wanted to write to Rainer, but what could she say or how could she describe the atmosphere of desperation, the look in the eyes of the man who waited with his wife's clothes? And worse, was she beginning to have that same blank expression? Did she have it because she had agreed to go back to work? Shouldn't she have gone home, if there was a place she could call home? She put the paper aside and got into her single bed and pulled up the blanket. The shadows of her head and hands, which slid across the walls with such delicacy as she reached out to turn off the lantern, reminded her of just how alone she really was and how the sense of it entered her awareness with the same delicacy as the shadows that moved across the walls. Then she was left in the dark.

The first thing was to find water. As Felix searched for it, his gray coat acted as a camouflage as he walked between gray piles of brick that had an almost natural appearance, as though this were a desert of undulating hills that had been pushed up by some geological force. If he stood still, no one could see him. This was important, if only because he wanted not to be seen by the Russians, who were so unpredictable, sometimes friendly, sometimes angry, always looking for wristwatches. They used a toilet to wash potatoes, and when they flushed it and the potatoes disappeared, they'd shoot up everyone in the house. Sometimes, when he climbed over a mound of bricks, the Russians' brown-green uniforms were in the distance. At least he didn't want to be seen by them now, although later, when the still was running, he guessed they'd find him. He was hungry, getting thinner, more tired with each passing day.

Felix had found the pipe at the rear of a building in what had been the kitchen. He turned the tap and the water came out, a silvery ribbon that ran into what was left of the sink. He quickly turned it off, as though he was afraid that someone would hear the sound and try to take the water away. The kitchen was concealed from the plain of bricks and dust, although Felix guessed the smell might give him away. They'd have to come here, though, since he didn't want to have to carry the stuff very far, just as he thought that the best thing would be for the Russians to bring their own bottles.

He needed a cooker and a screw. In the basement of what had been a hotel he found a copper pot with a lid that had a hole in it, and he dragged it across town, not looking one way or another, as though an obvious purpose might protect him. The pot had been used to make stock, and when he had first dragged it over the piles of brick, he thought the thing looked like a tub out of a cartoon in which missionaries were cooked by cannibals. The lid would have to be soldered, and he knew that he would have to trade on the black market for that. The copper tube had come from a ball bearing factory, and before Felix had made it into a screw, it had been used to convey oil from a tank to the milling machines used to fabricate the rings that held the bearings. It had been hard to get it clean, and Felix guessed that the first couple of batches might taste a little funny because of the milling oil, but from what he had heard the Russians weren't too particular.

Felix was thirty-one years old, although he looked much younger. He still walked with a limp, and he dragged his leg behind him, but now he was less concerned about what had caused him so much grief, his gimpy leg, the hump in his back: they had been just enough to keep him out of the army until the last futile defenses had been organized. Then he had found a place to hide, although he had come out to see others who had been hung, with the signs pinned to their clothes that said I WAS A COWARD. He had experienced the bombing of the city with an intensity that was too large to be good or bad, something that left him almost relieved, as though the explosions, the fire, the endless reverberation were all evidence of some truth that Felix believed but yet couldn't really articulate. He liked the smell of an exploding bomb. It was proof that no one cared what he had done before the war.

He needed help, too, and he found Frieda as she was looking for something to eat in the Tiergarten. She was so thin as to look like the frame of an umbrella, her hair short as it grew in after being shaved to get rid of the lice. It gave her a goofy, childlike quality, which was enhanced by her thinness. She lived underground in a cellar with her grandparents, and although Felix had never been inside, he sensed them there in the darkness, blinking at the light behind him. Felix's gray coat made him appear like a vampire who had fallen on bad times, but Frieda had looked him over and thought, Well, at least he's cunning.

Felix didn't know how to run the still himself, but he had found a man who had worked as a distiller in the 1930s and during the war, too, and who said that he could keep Felix's apparatus producing something that, while rank, would still be able to do the job. Felix imagined this stuff as coming out of the copper screw one drip at a time, just like coins into his hand.

The distiller's name was Manfred. He was a man in his sixties, and hadn't served on the eastern front or any other front, since being a distiller was considered a critical job, and the breweries and the distilleries had been running right up to a few months before. Manfred looked like he had been made out of pipes, as though he were part of a species of robots constructed out of junk, related to one another. Frieda, for instance, could have been his daughter.

Felix had been able to get fermentable garbage and yeast. While the garbage, warm water, and yeast bubbled in the kitchen, and while Manfred came to keep an eye on it, Felix and Frieda went to the park to gather wood. They worked along some of the paths that Felix remembered from before the war, and from time to time he looked up to see the gentle swaying of Frieda in her dress, which was so worn as to seem almost sheer. Felix had an axe head on a stick and a pruning saw with a taped handle, and they cut and dragged wood back to the kitchen. They stacked it against the wall in neat piles, the cut ends white and clean against the bricks. The bubbles rose from the mash with a yeasty, damp odor, and a sound, too, of something that seemed to be alive.

"It won't be long," said Manfred. "We're almost ready. Let's hope no one dies drinking this stuff."

Felix shrugged. "I don't know," he said. "I don't think we have to worry."

Then he and Frieda went outside and found a place on a mound not too far from the kitchen, and from the top of it he was able to see a long ways. The sun came out, and Felix looked as though he might have been sleeping, but he was not. He just didn't want to seem obvious that he was looking out. Frieda sat next to him, staring into the distance, at the sky, the ragged buildings, absorbing the heat of the sun. She leaned against Felix: it could have been an accident, but she was delighted by the small, almost vernal heat that came up between them. He glanced over at her and thought that more than anything else he would have to wait. That was the first thing.

He sat there, drowsing in the sun, his eyes half open, his feet in mismatching shoes, one bigger than the other, and overall he appeared like a large, ill-dressed lizard, skinny, squinting, trying to obtain whatever he could from the sunlight. In the distance Russian soldiers went along, their shapes rising and falling as they climbed over the beams and bits and pieces that had somehow survived, broken tile, plaster, wire and ceramic sockets, iron banisters, the gears and works of an elevator, all collapsed now into junk. A couple of them came close to Felix, and as they did, they sniffed the air. Was that what they thought it was?

"You," one of them said. "Liquor."

"Not yet," said Felix.

"When?" said the Russian.

"Soon."

rmina woke from a dream where the orchids hung against the jungle wall like enormous red, pink, and blue butterflies that had suddenly stopped flying but still had their wings open, as though pinned against the green velvet of a case. In the jungle the water dripped and made a tapping sound in the leaves and then she woke to someone knocking on the door of her room in that same cadence as the falling drops.

"All right," she said. "All right."

The man in the hall wore an armband, which is what the police had these days for a uniform, and his hatchet of a face looked like it had been used on something it could never cut, like iron.

"I was sent to get you," he said. "We've found something."

He waited outside while she dressed. The box of the powder she used instead of bathing sat on the bureau, a heavy piece of furniture that had survived the last few years. She put some of it on her shoulders and underarms although she avoided the triangle of mirror she had propped up in the corner. She had become thin and her skin was as white as the powder. It disappeared on her like someone dropping a pebble into the rubble of a rocky shingle. She missed Rainer, and to try to make herself feel a little better, she put on her one pair of nylon stockings, which gave her the slight memory of those times when she had dressed to meet him. It was a small thing, but that is what she had.

In the street she walked next to the policeman, although they didn't speak. Armina kept trying to navigate by the old map she had learned by growing up here, and while she kept looking over the mounds of rubble she realized that the piles of brick were replacing her old sense of geography. Still, she wanted to resist this, as though her old ideas, even of landscape, had some essential quality.

They came to a semicircle of men with armbands who stood around something on the ground between two piles of bricks, and when Armina climbed over the rubble, it clicked and rolled around her feet. The young woman lay on her stomach, her sad, worn dressed pulled up to show the usual marks on her legs and hips. She lay against the dust and rubble with that same appearance, as though gravity had her in the strongest grip possible. In the dust there was a mark, about a half inch deep and shaped like a new moon.

Armina looked at the woman's bare feet, which were next to her mismatched shoes. The scent of the powder the woman used was the same as Armina's. The clouds dragged along, the shadows slipping over the landscape with an absolute silence. Armina lifted one of the shoes, looked at the heel, worn down to nothing, the nails inside sticking up an eighth of an inch. The young woman's heel had the pattern of the nails, as though it had been molded to wear the shoes. Armina sat down and thought of the miles it had taken to make those indentations. Maybe, after a while, the indentations made the shoes feel as though they really fit. Then she stared at the sky, where the clouds hung with such indifference. When Armina looked around, the landscape appeared somehow claustrophobic, as though the dust were so thick that she couldn't get away from it, or maybe this was just the fact that she had difficulty breathing. More than anything else, she had the desire to close her eyes, to put her head down, as though she could get through the next minute by being absolutely still. Maybe she could count, but what came after one? Two? She swallowed and stared at the sky, but then she closed her eyes again, as though the scale of it was too much.

Ritter walked up, too, took a glance, and turned away. A man with an armband brought Armina the woman's underwear and gave them to her.

"Here," he said.

Ritter stood in front of Armina and said, "Same old shit."

Armina shook her head, not knowing precisely what it was she objected to, the difficulty in breathing, the smell of dust, the nail holes in the woman's heels, the pedestrian remark, the horrible sense of becoming smaller, as though she were shrinking right here. For an instant she thought this is what the fatigue of the last years did: it made her smaller, as though indifference were going to have a physical quality. It left her straining, as though she could resist it by strength, by effort that was as much physical as moral.

"Come on. There's no need to be like this."

"What?" she said.

"Don't act like this," Ritter said.

Armina held the underwear in her hand. It had been worn so often as to be almost transparent.

"And what way is that?" asked Armina.

"Look," said Ritter. He gestured to the landscape, the piles of bricks that looked like a rolling and gray sea, marked by the shoals of buildings that stuck up from the swells.

"I can see," she said.

"Can you?" he said. "Well, then what is there to say?"

He gestured at the woman in the dust.

In the light of the rising sun the dust on the young woman's hair was like a film of gold, speckled with the gypsum from the mortar. In the distance the wind picked up and the dust blew in ghostlike shapes, each defined with the golden speckle. This field and the years that had produced it left the natural result of horror, which was just that: did one murder more or less matter? The notion that one more didn't matter was the indifference of fatigue, the result of having been ground down. Armina looked at the shoes and the worn cloth in her hands.

She stared at the gray dust next to the girl where that mark had been left by someone who had a stiff leg and who had trouble standing up. He had moved the tip of his toe as he struggled, scoring the dust with the curved shape. He had left ten or so cigarette ends, each smoked down to the end, just a half an inch, and each one of them was yellow after having been made wet by the dew.

So, she thought, Felix is still here. He hadn't been imitating other crimes when he had killed Gaelle. It had been him all along.

"Pull yourself together," Ritter said.

"It makes a difference," she said.

"What does?" he said.

"Another body," she said.

He shrugged.

"Look around," he said.

She glanced at the open field, the enormous sky, the shapes of clouds like mastodons.

"Think what you want," he said. "For me, well, I'm tired. We'll do what we can. Round up the creeps. Maybe we'll get lucky."

SHE WENT TO the black market behind the Reichstag where the first sellers had arrived with the last of their possessions: a mirror, a collection of books, some shoes, a French saucepan. One man had a clock covered with gilt leaf that was only partially chipped. Another had a fur coat, although it looked like it had green mange growing on it. Armina asked each one about Felix and where he was doing his business, but each one looked at her with a weary dismissal, as though she were asking about something a long way away that they didn't want to remember. It was as though she spoke to them through a curtain of fatigue.

"Don't know," they said. "Can't help you. You want a mirror? We can work something out. OK?"

"No, thanks," she said.

The interior of the Friedrichstrasse train station was the same, although many of the benches had been carted off for firewood. The floor was still shiny, like an ice rink, but people had brought their things to set up housekeeping, bags and suitcases, blankets, a folding chair, newspapers that were used to stuff arms and legs of coats and trousers. The overall atmosphere was one of uneasiness that came from hungry waiting. A few young men, in clothes that were only marginally better than those of the squatters, stood along the walls and in the places where the light didn't show so much. Women walked from side to side, some of them in old high-heeled shoes, their lips bright with homemade lipstick.

The Moth sat on the same bench. He was thinner, but his reddish hair was the same color and his face still had a crimson rash. His green eyes, rimmed with red, looked around as he sat in an oversize coat, the pockets of it filled with lumpy objects, a piece of cheese, a heel of bread, an onion, a dirty handkerchief, and a knife. He had lost an arm, and one sleeve was pinned up with a woman's hat pin.

"Well, well," he said to Armina. "To think, after all these years. Inspectorate E, wasn't it?"

"Inspectorate A," she said.

He shrugged. What's the difference, he seemed to say, between old friends.

"I've changed," he said. "Look, just look at my sleeve. No arm. How do you like that?"

She shrugged.

"I'm sorry," she said.

"Are you?" he said. He looked right at her now, his eyes lined with crimson lids. "Tell me. Say it."

"I'm sorry about your arm," she said.

"You know what I have trouble with? Counting money. See? I do it like this."

He reached into his pocket and took out some bills, put them on one thigh, crossed his other leg over them so just the edges stuck out. Then he used one hand to go through them, one, two, three, four. . . . He looked around the room with a dare: let someone try to touch his money. No one even looked in his direction.

"You see," he said. "I've got friends."

"I'm sure you do," she said.

"Have you noticed, that at the worst of times, when people are most confused, they are filled with desire? Why, don't you see, it is a variety of hope. And then, let me tell you, it is a buyer's market. There's nothing you can't get." He gestured to a woman at the entrance, who stared at the Moth. She looked thin, obviously hungry, and she took a step forward, but then the Moth stopped her.

"Unless you want her," said the Moth.

"No," said Armina.

"Well, remember she's here," said the Moth. "Not, of course, that I have anything to do with it. Not really. I just keep my eyes open."

He looked up at Armina.

"So," he said. "What can I do for you? Or is this just a social call? To see if I made it."

"I'd like to talk to you," she said.

"Oh, a social matter. I'm touched. Sit down," he said.

Armina put her hands in her pockets and sat down next to the Moth. Somehow, if she had her hands hidden away it wouldn't be so bad.

"So," he said. "Now that we're cozy like, what do you want?"

"Felix," she said. "A boy with a limp. He worked with a *gravelstone,* a woman with a scar before the war. He's grown up now, of course, but he's still around."

"How do you know?" he said.

"I've seen his work," she said.

"Yes, yes," he said. "And people like that are always less than truthful. Have you noticed how devious they can be? Why, you'd think after doing what they do, they'd want to tell the truth. Because after all, they know it, don't they?"

A young man went along the floor, looking for cigarette butts, which lay here and there like squashed insects. He picked them up and put them in a paper bag. Armina wanted to say that yes, that was one truth, the kind of thing that Felix knew, but maybe there were others.

"Don't you agree?" said the Moth. "Who can compete with what they know? You?"

"Have you seen him?" said Armina.

The Moth looked her up and down, leaned a little closer, and the things in his pockets pressed against her thigh.

"If you're my friend, you'll help me," he said. "My sleeve is coming undone. Put it back up, will you?"

Armina stood up and stepped to his other side. He kept his reddish eyes on her as she hesitated. The sleeve of his coat was heavy with grease and smelled of woodsmoke and the sour scent of the city, the stink of decay and carrion. She pulled out the stick pin and the sleeve fell down in what seemed to be a despairing gesture. She folded it again, high and tight, and she pinned it snugly against the stub of his arm, which he pushed against her hands.

"At the edge of the park. Near the Reichstag. He's got a still," said the Moth. "Do you feel better now, my friend? After all, I'm one of the few people you can really depend on, heh? Are you reassured?"

"You could say that," she said.

"Well," he said. "That's good. Everything is as it should be. Don't be a stranger, my dear, now that I've helped you."

Frieda leaned against the wall of the burned-out kitchen. Felix had no pressure gauge, but Manfred had taught Felix to put his ear close to the copper pot and to listen to the sounds. If the mash made a roiling noise and a quick bubbling, not to mention a hissing from the screw, it meant the still was getting ready to blow. Felix put more wood under the fire, watched the flames splay out on the bottom of the cooker, listened to see how it was going, and then sat down next to Frieda. She leaned against him now and then, trying to get comfortable, and once she turned to look right at him. She rarely looked at anyone straight on, but now she did so, her pale and beautiful blue eyes set on him.

"Sometime you and I should take a walk," said Felix.

"Where would we go?" said Frieda.

"Oh, we could go into the park," said Felix.

"What would we do?" she said.

She looked at him again, her glance piercing and frank.

"Oh, we'd walk around," he said.

"What would be the point of that?" she said.

"Getting away," he said. "You know, out of here, away from things."

She leaned against him.

"I'd like that," she said.

"Sure, you would. Sure," he said. "Why we'd pretend it was like before the war. Just walking along."

"Would you like that?" she said.

"Oh," he said. "It would be all right."

"That would be nice," she said.

"Maybe soon," he said. "This week. After we sell this lot."

"We could save a little for ourselves," she said.

"I won't need anything like that," he said.

The light from the window became more dim and a little blue. The fire under the cooker burned all the brighter as the light failed, and when Felix stood up to look out the window, his shadow fell across the wall. He stood still, hands on the sill, and looked out the window.

At first he thought that there was something wrong with his eyes. From time to time he saw little speckles of light, which, if they hadn't made him uncertain as to what was happening, would have been almost beautiful: little flecks like the glowing bits that came off a sparkler. But, this was different: the entire northern sky, beyond the broken-tooth horizon, seemed to be moving, and not only in motion, but it advanced with a silver and blue throbbing, like a silver curtain that was blowing in the wind. Felix closed his eyes. A slight, distant buzz came across the rubble.

The wall approached. The silver part of it looked like someone was tossing bits of a broken mirror into the air. Felix realized, when the first of the insects landed near him, that the blue came from the mass of dragon-flies that made the wall, the conglomeration of them forming one swarming mass. The insects were blue with silver wings.

Felix squinted. Then he stood and put a hand to his eyes, like a man saluting the distance. Yes, he thought, bugs.

"My uncle said he'd seen a swarm like that," said Frieda. "Before the war."

The light dimmed and the wall came across the park. Frieda and Felix went outside while a chattering sound, which was a rush of transparent wings, like cellophane, swept up to the building. The insects were oddly delicate in Frieda's hair, almost caressing. Just a bunch of bugs, he thought.

The insects moved south, and as the wall thinned out over the park, a woman with red hair and freckles, dressed in a gray coat, emerged from the mass of them. She was only visible as an outline, like a figure in the fog, but then the sun returned and she became visible as she came toward Felix and Frieda, although occasionally she looked back, over her shoulder, as though pursued.

What's her trouble? thought Felix. As though I didn't have enough to worry about.

Her reddish hair was a bright spot against the otherwise dull landscape and the glittering wings. Here and there some dragonflies launched them-selves again and darted one way and another. The woman walked with an upright, square-shouldered gait: she seemed to be straining, as though she had something heavy in her pocket. Even from a distance she seemed famil-iar. Her steady gait, so definite and yet suggesting something else, not anxi-ety, not worry, but desperation, left Felix thinking, Sure, sure. She needs a drink. A rummy. Why, what wouldn't she do for a slug of something to keep the DTs away. That's what makes her look that way. A good cus-tomer.

Armina walked the last distance through the glittering street, where a few of the dragonflies flitted around.

"What do you want?"

"Why," said Armina, "I thought you'd know."

"This batch isn't ready," said Frieda.

"Yeah," said Felix. "You'll have to wait. We're cooking now. Isn't that what you want? A little hair of the hound?"

"No," she said.

"No?" he said. "Then why do you look sort of sick? I guess you're one of those who's ashamed."

"You could say that," said Armina.

"Well, you'll have to wait. It's going to be a good batch. Get a bottle and come back tomorrow."

The mash had a breadlike, yeasty scent, which seeped into the air from the kitchen at the back of the building. Felix squinted at Armina, as though recalling the detail of a dream, then licked his lip, and reached for his lower leg, where he kept the ice pick, but then he stopped and stood up again.

"Well, well," he said. "Look who's here. Didn't recognize you at first. It's been a while."

Armina nodded. Yes, it had been a while.

"So," he said. "Where have you been?"

"America," she said.

"No kidding," he said. "America. So why come back?"

"You might be able to help me with that," she said.

"A poor man like me?" he said. "What can I do? Look at my coat. Why, I'm lucky to be alive."

About forty or fifty meters away, beyond a pile of rubble, men spoke to one another although the language was unclear. Not German, not English. Probably Russian. Still, even from here, the words were slurred and the men spoke in short argumentative exclamations. They sounded like hungry dogs barking at one another through a fence.

"Did you see those insects?" said Frieda.

"Yes," said Armina. "I saw them."

"Sort of sudden," said Frieda.

"Yes," she said. "They just arrive, out of the blue. And there they are."

"Just a bunch of bugs," said Felix. "Who cares?"

Three Russians emerged about thirty meters away, one pushing another, although even this was done with a fumbling ineptness. They couldn't just shove one another out of a boozy anger, but instead they had to think about it, weaving back and forth like figures in a mirage. Then they started walking toward Felix, Frieda, and Armina. One pretended to take a long draft out of a bottle. What we need, he seemed to say, is another drink. He stumbled then kicked the brick that tripped him. Why even the stones in this godforsaken place were worthless.

"You've grown up," said Armina to Felix. "Or at least you've gotten older."

"See," said Frieda. "She's an old friend."

He went on staring at Armina. She put her hand in her coat pocket and touched the pistol.

"Do you remember Gaelle? And working in the park?" said Armina.

"What's she talking about?" said Frieda. "What's that about the park. Aren't we going to take a walk there?"

"Maybe," said Felix.

"So," said Armina. "You're going for a walk?"

"Sure," said Frieda. "Why not?"

"Why not?" said Armina.

Felix took a step to the side, moving from one foot to the other, and when he did he made a quarter moon–shaped mark in the dust. Armina looked down, and then at Felix.

"I don't know what you're talking about," said Felix. "All of that was a long time ago. What difference does it make?"

"I want to go on a walk," said Frieda.

"And there were others, too," said Armina. "Weren't there? We never talked about them, did we?"

"Go be a snob to someone else," said Felix. "You're just a snob."

The Russians veered in one direction, as though bound by a rope, but then they corrected themselves, squinted at Armina, Felix, and Frieda, and took a more direct path. Two of them had a rifle slung over a shoulder.

"Russians," said Frieda.

"Customers," said Felix.

Frieda turned to Armina. "I think we should go."

The cooker in the kitchen of the bombed-out row house made a steady hissing. At first, it was like gas escaping, a mild *sssss,* but it seemed to get more intense.

"I don't like the sound of that," said Felix.

The hissing got louder.

"Go check it," he said to Frieda.

"Why me?" she said. "Why don't you go?"

An intense, watery hissing came from the still, and then a Bang! Coppery shrapnel flew in arcs out of the window, the edges of the metal as bright as a new penny. Armina turned, tripped over a stone, and dropped the pistol into the rubble. The smoke appeared like a gray pennant that curdled into a ball and rose along the side of the building.

Felix reached down and took the pistol and put it into the pocket of his coat.

"You were supposed to watch," said Felix to Frieda. "What did I tell you? Watch. Listen."

"I came out to look at the bugs," said Frieda.

Felix turned back to Armina.

"I haven't got time for you," said Felix. "I've got things on my mind."

Felix and Frieda went to the side of the building. The kitchen was covered with the mash, and the still was gone: just bits and pieces of copper, none bigger than a hand. In the middle of the fire sat one jagged piece of copper that had been the base of the entire thing.

The Russians stopped, as though the sound were a wall they had run into, and then they gesticulated to one another, throwing up their hands to suggest the explosions, the copper shrapnel, as though retelling it could make sense of the fact that they weren't going to get anything to drink here.

Frieda stepped backward, keeping her eyes on the Russians, and then as she turned she said to Armina, "You should go."

"I've got something to do," said Armina.

"No you don't," she said. "Believe me."

"It won't take long," said Armina.

The Russians came along in the circuitous path of drunkeness, heading one way and then another, bumping into one another and then shoving the one who had done the bumping.

"There's where you're wrong," said Frieda. "It can take a long time. A long time. You're going to need help."

"I've got something to do," said Armina.

"You should listen," Frieda said. "You won't ever forget. That's the worst part. At three in the morning you go through it again. I'm not waiting for that, and you shouldn't either."

Frieda's thinness, her delicate way of walking, her long fingers and slender legs made her seem vulnerable as she went as quickly as she could, not running, but obviously wanting to. Her dusty hair and her worn, gray dress, and her odd sense of disorder helped her disappear into the rubble. It was as though she had been erased.

The skin around Felix's nostrils was white, his breathing shallow and wet. His coat hung on his shoulders and made him look like a jacket hung on a frame made of sticks. He went into the building to look at his cooker.

The oldest of the Russians, a man of thirty or so, swayed back and forth. His eyes moved from Armina's hair to her breasts, to her stomach, her legs, down to her shoes. One of the younger Russians sang a song, humming the words he didn't know, but he looked Armina over, too, from her legs to her face. The oldest Russian took some potatoes out of his pocket, six altogether.

See, he seemed to say to Armina, these are for you. There are six potatoes. There are three of us. That's two for each. See? He dropped one, and when one of the younger Russians tried to pick it up, he bumped heads with the oldest. The oldest Russian pushed the younger one out of the way and picked up the potato. The other Russian, a young blond man, swayed back and forth as he stared at Armina.

"He has something," said Armina to the oldest Russian. "I want to show you."

The young blond man looked at Armina's face. The oldest man offered the potatoes again, swaying as he did so. Then he reached into his pocket and took out another potato. Seven potatoes. He said something in Russian, and one of the younger men pulled his pockets inside out to show that that was all he had. That was his last, best offer. Three of them. Seven potatoes. He shoved the potatoes in Armina's direction. See? You better take it. There are other ways of doing business. The older one swayed again.

"A pistol," she said.

She made a gun out of one hand, pulled back her thumb like a hammer, and shot it. She said, Bang! Then she did it again.

"Where?" said the man with the potatoes. He put them into his pocket, dropping one and picking it up, almost falling. Then he stood up and blinked.

Armina pointed to the apartment where the smoke rose from the window. She made the pistol out of her hand again. Felix came out from the building.

"Him," she said.

The youngest Russian, the blond boy with white skin, made a quick movement and grabbed Felix by the arm. Then he reached into Felix's pocket and took out the pistol: it had some nicks on the wooden grip and some of the bluing had gone from the barrel, although Armina had kept it oiled, and the metal underneath had a silver glint.

"You," the oldest Russian said to Felix. "Come."

"Don't you want to buy some booze?" said Felix.

"No," said the older. "Later. We'll find someone else. Come."

They dragged him through the rubble to an open place in front of a brick wall.

"Hey," Felix said. "Hey."

The two younger Russians stood back a couple of feet. The older one held Felix by the arm.

"Hey," said Felix. "It's not mine. It's hers. It's not mine."

"You had it," said the old Russian, who stood next to him. "That's it. Kaput. Bang."

"Yes," Felix said. "But there's more to it—"

"No there isn't," said the older Russian.

"Put him over there," said the older Russian. He gestured to the wall. "Make him stand."

"They don't always want to," said the younger one.

"It doesn't matter. He can stand or not," said the older one. "I don't give a shit."

"Wait, wait," said Felix.

"You had the pistol," said the older Russian.

The older Russian pulled Felix against the wolf-colored brick. Armina stepped forward, her hand out, palm up. Felix's skin was as gray as the lines of mortar that held the bricks together.

"Get out of the way," said the older Russian to Armina. "We'll take care of him now." He swallowed and looked around. A bird flew across the sky. "Reminds me of home," he said.

"Wait," said Armina. "I need to ask something."

"What?" said the older Russian. "I don't understand. *Nicht verstehen.*"

He spoke to the younger, boyish Russians, one with dark hair, the other blond. The blond hair was filled with highlights from the sun. One of the boys shrugged, then the other. What the hell, they seemed to say. We've got other things to do. They unslung their rifles, swinging them around from their left shoulder to their right, but they had trouble mounting the butt and had to try a couple of times. They swayed as they held their rifles up, and the muzzles described figure eights.

The charcoal-colored birds that had come to eat the insects now circled overhead, their shapes like glistening Vs against the sky, and as they turned in a widening pattern to find the place where most of the insects remained they cawed and squawked and fluttered against one another when they landed. The Russians glanced up at them and then back at Felix. The two younger ones worked the bolts on their rifles, flipping them up, pulling them back, letting the cartridge rise from the magazine, pushing the bolt forward, slapping it shut against the wooden stock. The actions of the rifles made a sort of subdued cackle.

The older Russian pushed Felix against the wall.

"Stay there," he said. "Right here. See. No moving."

"Wait," said Armina.

"Ask her about the potatoes," said the blond one in Russian. "I always feel horny afterward."

Felix put one hand to his thin hair, pulled his leg back so that it looked more normal.

"Wait until this is over," said Felix to Armina. He gestured to the Russians. "You're going to have some fun."

She held up her hand. The older Russian stared at her and then spoke to the others. What was she up to anyway? What's going on? They were getting hungry, too. Where were they going to get some bread? Some cheese?

"Look at you," Armina said to Felix. "Look at your leg."

He put his head up, chin out.

"You insult me when I'm facing this."

He pointed at the Russians.

"You limp," she said.

"That won't get you anyplace," he said.

"A minute," said Armina to the Russians. *"Ein Minuten."*

The older one shrugged. The barrels of the rifles waved around.

"One," said the older Russian.

"Wait," said Armina.

"Some fun," said Felix. "They like you."

"None of them wanted you," said Armina. "Those women in the park. Isn't that right?"

"You think you can make me angry?" said Felix.

The older Russian blinked, glanced at Felix, then at the younger soldiers and tried to remember what he was doing. He swallowed and put his hand to the back of his mouth.

"Did Gaelle push you away? I bet she wouldn't even take your money," said Armina. "I bet she wouldn't touch you. Not that way. Why, she wouldn't have anything to do with you. So, when Hauptmann asked you, you saw your chance. You'd do what you wanted and get paid for it."

The look of the fawning street urchin seemed, for a moment, to be suspended on Felix's gray face, like a mask worn at carnival. Then his face seemed slack, numb, without any expression at all, and it was this slackness, this emptiness that Armina realized had been the last thing the women in the park had seen. He reached down to his ankle, lifted the pant leg, and reached for the ice pick, but the older Russian grabbed him, pulled him up, shook him, and then took the taped handle with the long spike and the sharpened tip. Then the Russian threw it into the rubble, the thing making a small circle, like a propeller, as it flew away and landed among the black, squawking birds.

"So," said Armina. "She wouldn't take the money. Too disgusted for that."

"The women in the park learned something from me. Oh, yeah. They did."

Felix looked at her with that same slack expression, as though the nerves that controlled the muscles had been cut.

"Aim," said the older Russian.

Armina held up her hands. The Russians hesitated.

"Marie," said Felix. "There was Marie. In the gully. Some young-looking ones. Too dumb to come in out of the rain. They fought a little. But not much."

"And Gaelle?" said Armina.

"She could have saved me, see?" said Felix. "She could have brought me in from the dark. I washed her stockings."

He took a dirty, stained silk cord from his pocket and let it hang from his hand.

"Isn't this what you wanted to see?"

"What did he say?" said one of the younger Russians.

"Screw it," said the older one. "How would I know? Ah, shit, I'm not feeling so good."

He put his hands on his knees and vomited in slow, watery eruptions into the rubble. The younger ones waited, as though they had seen this before and knew he would get over it.

"That's all?" said Armina to Felix.

"One here the other night," said Felix.

His face seemed even more slack, gray, and inscrutable.

"Why?" said Armina.

Felix shrugged.

"They didn't like me," he said. "I could tell."

The older Russian tried to lean against the wall but fell down and dropped the pistol. The blue metal clattered on the stones and rolled into the dust at the bottom. The younger Russians leaned forward, their rifles mounted, but they still tried to help up the older one. Felix starting running.

He didn't go fast, but he limped quickly, up and down, as he went around the first mound of bricks. His coat flapped back, like gray wings, and his shoes made puffs of smoke like dust. Armina picked up the pistol, put the bead between the rear sights, just like in those endless hours on the range, and aimed for the heaviest mass, the middle of Felix's back. He looked over his shoulder as the pistol went off, Bang, bang. He kept on running, then slipped down on one knee, tried to get up, took another couple of steps and sat down on a pile of rubble.

"I'm shot. I'm shot," he said. "Can you believe it? Shot."

He tried to get up, limped another step, and then sat down. Some black birds that were feeding on the insects rose into the air at the shots. They squawked and whirled, like a collection of black flags, and then, with a swoop, settled down again.

The young Russians turned to Armina, but now they seemed more sober than before. They swung their rifles around, neatly shouldering them, one arm through the sling. The safeties clicked off. Armina held out the pistol, flat in her hand, offering it. Then she put it down. She stepped back and held up both empty hands. The older Russian swayed back and forth.

Felix slobbered and gasped as he lay in the dust and gray bricks, his bad leg twitching now and then so that diminutive clouds, like dust devils, rose from his shoe and then drifted away. He said, "I'm thirsty."

"That always makes me horny," said one of the boyish Russians. He nodded at Felix.

"Yes," said the other young one.

"She put down the pistol," said the first young one.

"Yeah," said the other. "She did." He turned to the older Russian. "We aren't going to need the potatoes."

"No," said the older Russian. He swayed like a wheat stalk in the wind. "I guess not."

"You aren't interested in her?" said the first young one.

"No," said the older one. "I didn't say that."

The pistol sat in the dust like something that had been buried and was now just emerging, the diamonds of the grip already filled with gray dirt. Armina stepped toward it, but the first young Russian, with a speed that was like a trap being sprung, picked it up.

"You," he said. "Woman. Over here."

Armina stepped backward, keeping her eyes on the Russian with the pistol. It seemed to her that as long as she could keep her eyes on his they wouldn't begin. She stepped backward into the rubble. Felix made that harsh, guttural breathing, like he was trying to cough up something he had been choking on for hours and the effort of it had left him exhausted and at the point where he was going to give up. His heels worked in the ashy dust, the puffs of it like doll-size ghosts.

The second young Russian took Armina by the arm.

"You have white skin," he said.

"Redheads are like that," said the older Russian.

"Yeah," said the first young Russian.

"You think it's red, too," said the second young Russian.

He lighted a cigarette, the scratch of the match on the abrasive strip of the box making small stars. She thought of those nicotine-stained butts in the park before the war, and of those nights in New York when she had considered them, the memory somewhere, at 3 A.M., between accusation and terror. Now, the little sparks from the lighted match left the smell of sulfur. The first young Russian said, "Over here."

He slowly lifted the hem of her skirt until her white skin, a garter, and the top of her stockings showed. The cool breeze washed over her skin.

"No," she said. "I'm a police officer. You don't want to touch me."

"What did she say?" said the young Russian. "What's that? Police?"

"Yes," said the second young Russian.

"Have you ever heard that one?" said the first young Russian.

"No," said the older one. "I've heard a lot of other ones."

The first young one put his finger under the stocking top and pulled it down with a yank, and the fabric ran in a ladder down her leg. He ripped the other one. Behind her Felix said, "Some fun," and then gurgled and made one last shape of dust before he lay perfectly still. In the squeak of the Russians' leather belts, in the clink of their equipment, the light breeze blew across the landscape in a slow, feathery hush.

"Leave me alone," said Armina.

"Let me finish my cigarette," said the second young Russian.

"I guess that one's gone," said the older Russian, as he pointed with his elbow to Felix.

"Yeah," said the first young Russian. "I guess."

"Let's forget this," said Armina to the older Russian. "Nothing happened. We can just go home."

"No," said the first young Russian.

"What's the rush?" said the older Russian.

"We're just getting started. Don't you like Russians?"

"Sure," said Armina. "They're fine."

"Russians are the best," said the first young one. "We'll show you."

"I believe you," said Armina.

"Seeing is believing," said the second young Russian.

"Show her," said the first young Russian.

The three Russians had their eyes on the distance, as though looking at the horizon beyond the chop of the ocean. Armina thought of those nights in New York, when she went through the things she had tried to make sense of. The torn stockings. The cigarette butts. The marks. Then she went back to looking at the older Russian, trying to catch his eye, to stare at him. That would slow things down. And as she went on looking into his blue eyes, the first young Russian dropped her skirt. She thought, that was my only pair of stockings.

"What's that?" said the older Russian.

"Let's not wait," said the first young Russian. "Come on. She's here. What are we waiting around for?"

"Someone's coming," said the older Russian.

"So what?" said the first young Russian. "They can join in."

The trail of dust, like smoke, appeared on the avenue that ran through the piles of bricks.

Felix was still and yet appeared ancient, like a figure from the ruins of Pompeii, the gray skin seeming to have been preserved for thousands of years: it made him anonymous and yet eternal, too.

Armina stepped back.

"She's going to get away," said the first young Russian. "What did we wait for? Now look what's going to happen."

"The British," said the older Russian. "That's who they are."

The older Russian took Armina's arm, touched her blouse, and said, "There are other fish in the sea."

An army jeep came along the mounds, its slow, constant passage marked by the green paint of it, which looked like a leaf in a desert. Two men sat in front, one hanging onto the dashboard, one at the wheel. The one at the wheel had a little mustache and wore glasses. Frieda sat in the back, her dress rustling in the breeze of the Jeep's locomotion, her arm seeming even more pipelike and thin as she pointed, with a sort of desperate attempt to make herself understood, at Armina and the Russians.

"All right," said the older Russian. "We'll look for someone else."

"Nothing works out," said the first young Russian.

"Oh," said the older Russian. "I don't know."

The Russians stepped back, the younger ones shouldering their rifles, the sheen of the bluing and the polish of the slings showing as streaks of silver. They walked with a slow, constant march, not tired, not enthusiastic, just a frank attempt to get through the brick and the dust. Only once did one of the young ones look back at Armina, as though she were something seen from the window of a train, momentarily appearing and then vanishing forever, reduced now to something less than a memory. Just a woman standing in the dust and then not worth looking at anymore.

The jeep stopped in a cloud. The man with the little mustache and glasses said, "Are you all right?"

"Yes. No," said Armina.

"Did anything happen here?" he said.

"No," said Armina.

"Well," said the man. "You were lucky. You can thank your friend here."

He gestured to Frieda.

"Made quite a scene," he said. "Threw rocks at us."

"Near brained me," said the other man in the front. "To get our attention. Why, I'm going to be all-over lumps for a week." He rubbed his head.

"Well," said the man with the mustache, "get in. We'll give you a lift."

Felix lay behind a low mound and his dusty shape disappeared into the rubble, like a stone thrown into the cobbles of a stony beach. No one in the jeep noticed he was there. The sky, which was a whitish blue, the color of gin in a bottle, was streaked with black where the birds flew in a widening circle. They flew around and around, as though the sky were an enormous glass bowl from which they couldn't escape. Armina put her fingers together, each one trembling, as though she had been standing next to a train track where an enormous engine had gone by at eighty miles an hour: the trembling ran from her fingers into her arms, torso, and stomach, down into her legs and knees. She tried to make it stop, but instead she got into the jeep with a shaky, trembling stumble, and when she sat down, she knew that Frieda felt it when they touched, a constant, vibrant twitching that wouldn't go away. Frieda felt it and closed her eyes and shook her head, as though she didn't want to be reminded of it, or of anything associated with that shaking. She shook her head and bit her lip, and when Armina tried to thank her, she shook her head even harder. They sat side by side as the jeep went around the piles of brick, over the holes in the road, and every time they touched, Frieda pulled away and shook her head.

"I'll get out here," she said.

Then she climbed over the side of the jeep and got down, glancing at Armina only once and then turning away, dismissing this moment with a sad acceptance and an obvious hope that this was another thing that could be forgotten. The jeep left Armina off, too, about a few blocks from the house where she had her room.

"Mind yourself," said the man with the mustache.

On the street women worked with an unstoppable insistence as they picked up the bricks as though solving an enormous puzzle, which, if just assembled correctly, would allow them to live again. Armina went by them, toward a wider, more cleared avenue, and when she turned into it, she hesitated and stood on the corner with her eyes closed: she could see those black birds, quivering in the air, swooping around in an enormous circle, and then settling down again to feed on the last glittering insects.

The trembling in her legs was more noticeable when she climbed the stairs to her room. It was not only constant but also left her with a sense of weakness, too, as though she had been sick and in bed for a month and was now standing for the first time. She found a place in the middle of the room, as far from the walls as possible, since there, at least, she had no possibility of being touched. Her fingers, against her lips, felt like the flutter of a moth's wings.

She took off her clothes and put them on her single bed. The stockings were run in long ladders, from the tops to the knees. She balled them up and put them in the trash and then piled some waste paper on top and pushed it down. She wet a washcloth from the jug of drinking water and tried to wash herself, but the dampness only made her feel cold in the room. Then she toweled, powdered herself, and put on some clothes so she could go downstairs and empty her waste basket, with the stockings included, into a bin where old and useless things were discarded. She dropped the stockings in as though she could get rid of the memory this way and then went back upstairs, angry now at the trembling weakness but not able to do anything about it.

She waited for the light to fade in her room. Maybe as it became dim, as the sun set, as that time came in the evening when the first bulbs filled the buildings with a golden light of the domestic, the trembling would stop. It lingered, though, like a note played in a church that left all of the wood—the timbers and beams and pews—vibrating with that last emotional intent: the touch of the young Russian's fingers as he tore her stockings, the smell of the cigarette, the sparks at the head of the match on the abrasive surface of the matchbox, contained in memory, even more than at the moment, the frank, ill-meaning atmosphere of the men in the rubble. It was the realization of the essence, in the most personal way, of those actions she had tried to resist those years before the war in Berlin and that haunted the city as though nothing had happened at all, as though some things are eternal.

She hoped the electric lamp in the corner would make the room warmer, not in temperature but in mood, and as she pulled the small chain on the light fixture, a man knocked at the door.

He gave her an envelope. It had obviously been carried in a pocket and had gotten wet in tropical rain, soaked enough so the ink of her name had run, just as it had probably been held in a hand so covered with dirt as to look like skin with a speckled and gray birthmark.

Dear Armina,

Of course I have been thinking of you. This thinking of you is a part of me, and I don't even notice anymore that I try to imagine what you are thinking and how you are feeling, to remember the scent of your skin and hair, to remember your eyes when you make a joke. It is like breathing, and how often during the day do you stop to say, I'm breathing.

How can I describe what it is like to miss you? When we were together it was as though an invisible film covered the two of us so perfectly that we didn't notice it, but now your part, the part that went over you, is empty, and I can feel it dragging on the ground behind me, its tug and its airy weight. It is a delicate thing, but it carries an enormous impact. And what could a small sound convey? Imagine, for an instant, the tick of the trap beneath the condemned man. It is like that. When I concentrate on this empty thing I drag around it is both a sound and a sensation, like leaves in the wind. But now, of course, this hush, this rustle, this susurrus is a reminder of how, without you, I am incomplete. And when I am aware of this, when I put it into words, I have the terror of almost dissolving, of being on the edge of vanishing.

This has been the most difficult part. I am one way when I am with you, but a different man when we are apart, and this sense of losing myself, combined with your absence, makes that rustling, dragging sensation a validation of how alone I am. Well, this is hopelessly romantic, but if I can't feel that after what happened on Truk and Palau and other places, if I can't admit how diminished I am without you, then I am less of a man than I would like to be. My job is not to be reduced by horror, but made more knowledgeable of what is precious.

But the subject I want to discuss with you is what do I have to offer you after what we have been through? I am convinced that you had moments in which you were left with an animal existence, just eating, enduring, living in the moment of the endless or dreary present. Or maybe not so dreary. Maybe terrifying.

So, I come to you on this basis: what can I do in the face of the life we have lived over the last years? Perhaps the answer is so deep that I can't articulate it, but that doesn't mean it isn't there. So I want to invoke a memory from a long time ago when we exchanged presents and when these gifts revealed an attachment and understanding so deep that we were in the midst of it without being able to say what it was. How can I convey that understanding when, in the touch of your lips, in that warm, full pressure, the certainty of attachment runs into me like a shock of recognition. Like something already known and just noticed when we are together? And whatever this quality is, it binds us together and makes us better people than when we are apart. I am much less of a man when I am separated from you. So it is this mysterious presence I am offering you, this quality I can't name but which is there and which makes itself known by its pleasures, its gifts, its potential. It is what we have, and, you know, it isn't small. It is everything.

I think of the perfume of your hair, of the trembling in our fingers when the fireflies in the woods glowed with that warm, greenish light. Can you remember that color, that yellow verdant glow, which in its delicacy suggested the unseen, the only felt and suspected, but which in our case is quite real? And this unseen quality is the most keen sense of not being alone. We have had enough of that, of existing in that interior discomfort, that turmoil in the darkness when we close our eyes.

Here a new sheet had been added.

Does this give you any idea of how I feel and what it means that I have now crossed the Pacific and am mailing this letter from San Francisco? It is as though I am approaching the shore of myself. Or of us.

And I want to say this is not only theoretical. We are practical people, and I want to take some action that is more than words on paper. And what I have done shows the power of beauty, although that may be overstating the case. I went into the jungle on some of the islands in the Pacific with a general, a man who was interested in or-chids, and I showed him some he had never seen before (chains of purple blossoms, cascades of petals that look like butterflies with an icy sheen on their wings). This botany, this searching for hidden beauty, was a small thing that helped us both after some of the worst moments.

When we returned to San Francisco, the general asked if he could do me a favor. Should we go out to dinner, to the top of a hotel with a view of the Pacific (which would have reminded me of you), but I said no. I only wanted one thing. And what was that? he said. I asked if he could arrange air transportation for you to meet me in New York. And, after some maneuvering and a bribe or more than one bribe, and some promises of one sort or another, it is arranged. You will receive a letter in a day or two with a ticket and the neces-sary paperwork, which of course is sent with what you must know is love, if that word can possibly sum up the feelings that attend this note, Rainer. P.S. I also want to say that no matter what we have seen, or how dreary we feel, no matter how appalled we may be, our sense of beauty returns, like a surprise hidden in the depths. This is what makes us human and gives us hope, and that is what I want to leave with you.

The light in the room was now golden from the electric lamp, and Armina hoped the power might last a little longer than usual and that the sense of the domestic would linger. She put the letter on her bed, one sheet of paper stained and running with ink, the other crisp and neat. Her fingers seemed odd, somehow more precise, her gestures untroubled. She realized that the trembling had stopped. The suitcase was under the bed, and she dragged it out with a jerk, opened it, and started to put in her clothes, her few skirts and blouses, an extra pair of shoes, a few books, the package of letters that she had tied together with a piece of string. Outside, when the dark came, the lights pierced it with a steady, warm glow.

Author's Note

The author wishes to express his gratitude for information obtained from Hsi-Huey Liang's *The Berlin Police Force in the Weimar Republic* (Berkeley: University of California Press, 1970).

About the Author

Craig Nova is the award-winning author of twelve novels. His writing has appeared in *Esquire, The Paris Review, The New York Times Magazine, Men's Journal,* and on Craignova.com. He is the Class of 1949 Distinguished Professor of the Humanities, University of North Carolina, Greensboro.

A Note About the Type

T his book was set in Adobe Garamond, a typeface designed by Robert Slimbach in 1989. It is based on Claude Garamond's sixteenth-century type samples found at the Plantin-Moretus Museum in Antwerp, Belgium.

Composition by Creative Graphics
Allentown, Pennsylvania

Printing and binding by Berryville Graphics
Berryville, Virginia